TINDERBOX

SOLDIER OF INDIRA

LOU DIAMOND PHILLIPS

ILLUSTRATIONS BY YVONNE PHILLIPS

Artwork provided by Yvonne Phillips
Cover design by Steve Beaulieu
Print and eBook formatting by Kevin G. Summers

Published by Aethon Books LLC. 2020.

Lou Diamond Phillips is currently starring in the FOX series "Prodigal Son," having recently starred on the acclaimed Netflix series, "Longmire," based on the Walt Longmire mystery novels by Craig Johnson. Other recent credits include Amazon's "Goliath," SyFy's "Stargate Universe," CBS' "Blue Bloods," and recurring roles on Fox's "Brooklyn Nine-Nine" and Netflix's "The Ranch." He received an Emmy nomination for "Outstanding Actor in a Short Form Drama or Comedy" for his roles in both Amazon's "Conversations in LA" and History Channel's "Crossroads of History." Recent film credits include Warner Brothers' "The 33," "Created Equal" directed by Bill Duke, and Sundance Festival favorite "Filly Brown," for which he was named Best Actor at the Imagen Awards.

As a director, Phillips recently helmed episodes of AMC's hit series "Fear the Walking Dead," "Longmire," and ABC's Marvel's Agents of S.H.I.E.L.D. As a writer, Phillips has co-written the screenplays for 'Trespasses,' and HBO's 'Dangerous Touch.' He wrote the Miramax feature 'Ambition.' He recently produced his play 'Burning Desire,' a romantic comedy in two acts, which received it's world premiere at The Seven Angels Theatre in Waterbury, Connecticut. Phillips was also asked by his good friend, novelist Craig Johnson, to write the forward to his collection of short stories 'Wait For Signs.'

Originally born in the Philippines, Phillips was raised in Texas and is a graduate of University of Texas at Arlington with a BFA in Drama.

Drawing from a lifetime of work in the film industry, Lou used his screenwriting experience in order to write an original science fiction novel called The Tinderbox: Soldier of Indira. It is his first novel, inspired by a reading of the famed fairy tale of the same title by Hans Christian Andersen.

**INSPIRED BY THE FAIRY TALE
BY HANS CHRISTIAN ANDERSEN**

PROLOGUE

IT WAS WRITTEN by the Predeciders that the planets of Indira and Mano were once a single planet. After centuries of mining the giant planet's core for thermal power, the millions of thermal chimneys drilled into the planet's shell caused it to split in a cataclysmic event that became known as the Great Schism.

The Predeciders, discovering their folly too late, evacuated millions into space aboard Astral Repatriation Communities (ARCs), where the survivors orbited the twin remains of their decimated planet even as the ragged halves remained locked in their own gravitational dance. After many generations, the planets were deemed once again inhabitable, and the pilgrims returned. Some to Indira. Others to Mano.

After many centuries of rebuilding, the wars began...

ONE

THE CRACKED QUILT of the desert floor stretched before the soldier like a puzzle with no end, reminding him of the mosaic-patterned tiles in a palace from his childhood. Everson couldn't help but note, with more than a little self-pity, that his childhood was now a world away, both physically and metaphorically. His own planet, Indira, was lush and green, yet another luxury he would never take for granted again.

He trudged forward on the barren rock that was the planet Mano, home of the enemy he had come to kill.

The twin suns of Femera and Amali beat down on him unmercifully, without the considerate benefit of a single cloud. The heat intensified the throbbing pain in his head, as if his temples were pumping boiling blood through the veins in his cranium. He hadn't seen it coming, but he suspected that the errant hoof of a fly-by birdun had struck him solidly in the head, sending him into blackness. As a silver lining, and in spite of the monstrous headache he now endured, he was sure that being rendered unconscious had probably saved his life. At the moment of impact, he had, after all, been involved in mortal hand-to-hand combat.

Everson turned and looked back toward the Grand Schism, where the Indirans, his people, had landed to begin—in his mind—their unwarranted invasion. There was only the singular line of his footsteps, a reminder of the many missteps he had taken in his young life to bring him here, the middle of nowhere.

He had no idea where he was going, and perhaps it was high time to formulate a plan. He half hoped to be discovered and saved from the brutal heat. However, the other half dreaded the treatment he would receive. He would certainly be recognized as an enemy soldier, with his swarthy skin and full battle gear. That is, if he wasn't simply killed on sight.

This thought irritated him more than frightened him, especially since he hadn't willingly chosen this path for himself—the path of a soldier. No, that was someone else's idea. And so, resentment fueled Everson's feet methodically toward a dubious future where even death would be a vindication. Not that it would change anything about his current predicament, but it gave Everson a smidgen of satisfaction to think that he had been right that the battle should never have happened.

With the plodding detail of placing one foot in front of the other, Everson recalled the pre-battle preparations, until he suddenly remembered the life-giving hydreeds he was carrying. Feverishly, his fingers fumbled with the clasp of the pouch attached to his utility belt. He finally wrestled it open and plucked a small, wrinkled, egg-shaped pod from the dozen or so packed inside. The plant from which the hydreed came grew in terrain much like this near the Asunder Chasm, Indira's equivalent of the Grand Schism, where volcanic activity and ground-splitting tremors were the norm.

Everson brought the pod to his face, his hand trembling with anticipation. His jaw worked as if he were praying under his breath, but he was actually trying to produce a mouthful of spit.

Nothing came. All he felt in his mouth was his parched lump of a tongue. He sighed in frustration, thought for a brief moment, and glanced all around him at the featureless desert. There was no sign of a living thing anywhere. Without further hesitation, he set the hydreed on the ground and unbuttoned his fly.

As he waited for a reticent bladder, Everson remembered his childhood and how his mother would bring out hydreeds just to delight him and his friends. There had been squeals of laughter at the transformation, at the percussive whump of expansion when the hydreeds had been dribbled with liquid. Presently, his anticipation was perhaps even greater than it was when he had been five. He danced a little in place as if to move things along.

A few errant drops of urine hit the dusty ground and were absorbed immediately. Everson adjusted his aim until a feeble stream hit the pod. He jumped back a bit when the hydreed expanded violently with a sudden wet, cracking thump that split the silent air. It wobbled before him on the cracked desert floor, a little larger now than the size of his head.

Everson quickly secured his pants and drew the heavy broadsword that he had reclaimed from a fallen comrade. He brought the blade down hard, and the hydreed split with a juicy crack. Then he buried his face in it.

The spongy pulp disintegrated in his mouth as he practically inhaled the contents, stopping only when his nose hit the solid rind. Dropping the drained husk, he stood for a moment breathing heavily. He consumed the second half with far less urgency, savoring the green coolness of each swallow as it flowed down his throat.

Everson squeezed the remaining pulp over his head and let it run down the nape of his neck and trickle down the crease of his spine.

Temporarily quenched, Everson took a moment to close his eyes. He couldn't shut out the alien world, its suns glowing orange through his closed lids. That glare was truth. It was reality. Once again, his mind drifted back to the pre-battle preparations, to the strategic checklist that seemed so simple to achieve. Though Everson had never so much as lifted a finger in battle, he knew in his heart that wars were not so easily won...

* * *

"We will deploy at the precipice of Mano's Grand Schism," Commander Giza had intoned shortly before the battle, in his flat, matter-of-fact military-speak. He was a scar-faced veteran of the wars, and his close-cropped hair did nothing to soften his features. "This will allow us to engage the enemy on one front only."

Unlike his gung-ho companions aboard the troop transport, Everson listened half-heartedly to the battle plan. He had been painted with the military's homogenizing brush, and now he was just another face in the crush of copper-faced young men in uniform, anonymous and interchangeable. At least he was lucky enough to get a window seat.

"We can expect to be met by Manolithic forces from the garrison at Front Tier," Giza went on. "Obviously, we will encounter infantry, but they will be buttressed by cavalry astride birduns."

The large screen behind Commander Giza switched its image from an aerial view of Mano's Grand Schism, a sheer-cliffed abyss with seemingly no bottom, to a picture of a birdun, the war steed of Mano's warmen.

"For those uninitiated, it is a flying creature indigenous to Mano. They are a mount, nothing more, and they are as stupid as they look."

Stupid was an understatement, Everson thought. More like an aerodynamic impossibility. The birdun was a winged creature, true enough, but its long neck and legs and fuzzy, bulky body were certainly inefficient applications of evolution. Not only that, it was a beast that had obviously stopped at a crossroads without picking a direction, with feathers quite sensibly on its wings but also adorning its haunches and the tip of its tail. The birdun was such an unlikely proposition that Everson hoped to see one in person.

"They are certainly no match for our Javelins," Giza said.

Everson glanced over his shoulder to where the wickedly efficient flying machines were docked, double-high, at the rear of the transport. From the shovel-shaped nose cone and its flattened fuselage to the dagger-thin wings at the aft, the Javelins reeked of sleek. The cocky Javelin pilots stood at parade rest before them, almost smirking in their superiority.

The commander now paced before the screen. "The birdun cavalry is classically armed with HEXes," he said. "Handheld explosives that are delivered by hand from above. Primitive but surprisingly effective if utilized correctly. We will also face TRAUMAs, troop augmentation machines."

The image shifted to a combat vehicle so malevolent it appeared to be a living thing.

"They are lethal. They are impenetrable. But they can be stopped. This is the extent of the Manolithic arsenal. Our military dominance has not allowed their technology to advance further. It is now time for the Indirans to occupy Mano in order to maintain peace between the planets. Make no mistake, it is a noble mission."

A battle was already brewing inside Everson. He didn't want to be here, but he knew that he would have to focus if he was going to survive.

"Nucruits," Giza said to Everson's unit of soldiers conscripted for less than a year, "magnetize your broadswords to full. The Manoliths have no such application and it might give you an advantage. But, for the love of Light, wait until you're clear of the transport lest you find yourself pinned and powerless..."

How Giza's laser eyesight found him even among the camouflage of his comrades, Everson didn't know, but find him he did. The commander's gaze bored straight through him.

"I would also caution you to keep your weapons away from the heads and metal helmets of your comrades," Giza added.

Everson's cheeks tingled, but he did not want to give Giza the satisfaction of looking away. He stared straight ahead as several snickers tickled his ears. He had gained instant notoriety within days of putting on the uniform when his magnetized broadsword had become ignominiously stuck to the helmet of another nucruit during a mock duel.

"I think I'd rather you die than engage in such an embarrassing display," Giza deadpanned before mercifully shifting his gaze. "Post conflict, we will march to Front Tier and secure it. Infantry, double-check that you have a full supply of hydreeds. It is a desert planet and you will dehydrate without them."

Everson gave the pouch secured at his waist a cursory grope. Through the fabric, he could feel the jumble of odd pods. They seemed unimportant to him at the moment. Just something else he had to carry.

Commander Giza stopped in the center of the screen, his baleful eyes burning with purpose.

"Raza has armed you. Raza has defined you. Now prepare your minds to fight." The screen filled with the image of King Raza the Forty-Seventh. Regal. Dignified. Intelligent eyes that also conveyed wisdom and humanity. Most of the soldiers had never actually seen him in person, but the projected image alone was enough to inspire absolute loyalty and sacrifice.

"Indira in Dignity. Indira in Death."

A single, massive clap resounded through the transport as the troops brought their hands together and bowed their heads to touch their clasped fists. The standard Indiran salute.

Everson followed suit simply because not doing so would have drawn more unwanted attention to himself. As he did, he glanced out the window at the passing stars, at Femera and Amali floating brightly in the void. He recalled his childhood astronomy lessons and his studious readings of the Pr12e, wondering if he would be on Mano long enough to see the fabled Aurora Constellation.

Or if he'd die before he got the chance.

Perhaps it was due to the hypnotic drift of the stars, but Everson lost track of time. He was shaken from his reverie by the sudden dimming of the transport lights, a signal that landing was imminent.

Everson felt the surge in his stomach that came with rapid descent, followed by the tooth-rattling jolt that marked touchdown. Within seconds, the soldiers all around him rose to their feet and moved like sleepwalkers through the darkened transport. Wordlessly, they shuffled to their respective posts and prepared to disembark.

Finally, Everson left his seat and drifted to the back of the transport, nearer to the stack of Javelins, where Commander Giza had personally told him to go. He could only assume that it was a judgment by Giza of his combat skills and that Giza did not want him cut down in the first wave. Everson was not offended. In fact, he was somewhat grateful for Giza's unintended kindness. He could feel an electric energy in the air that literally made his skin tingle. His senses were heightened, his body attuned to every sensation as the knowledge of the inevitable violence overtook him.

He heard the metallic *snick* and *clank* of hundreds of broadswords being removed from their racks, and he dutifully attached his own to the magnetic scabbard on his back. Now, he could hear the oily clicks of automatic weapons being checked. The shadowy transport echoed with the sound of accelerated breathing and the quickened cadence of hundreds of hearts beating like battle drums. Everson's nose was assaulted by the coppery smell of adrenaline. A vein ticked in his temple as if counting down the moments.

And then the iris door of the vessel began to open, allowing a blistering ray of light to fill the transport. Everson sensed the mass of troops leaning forward as one, as if collectively pulled by the gravity of inescapable Fate. The circular door continued to open, flooding the interior with light, and Everson couldn't tell if he was instantly flushed by the wave of heat blasting into the transport or by the blood rushing to his face. After a few blinks, his eyes adjusted and he could see the future.

Thousands of Manolith warmen were amassed in the near distance, awaiting their arrival. Everson was horrified. With a thunderous roar, the foremost Indiran soldiers charged, spilling out of the transport and onto the foreign soil. Contrary to his every rational instinct, Everson rushed forward with them. The Indirans and Manoliths came together like the turbulent waves of opposing oceans, determined only to obliterate each other and lay claim to the sand between them. The clash of swords and the repetitive reports of handguns were shortly joined by the seemingly ceaseless screams of the wounded.

In the midst of the melee, Everson flailed madly about, defending more than attacking, his frantic maneuvers more a reflex of desperation than expertise. Though his training had been intense and immersive, it could not have possibly prepared him for the blood orgy that was close-quarters combat. Men much more capable than he died all around him.

Everson had never met a Manolith. At the moment, he wished he never had. He was surrounded by them. They seemed innumerable, like a swarm. Their pale complexions were shocking to him, their expressions of hatred made all the more frightening by the fury with which they fought, as if the very fires of creation burned within them.

Somewhere in his terrified brain, Everson recognized that his anonymous enemies seemed to be no older than he was, young men barely beyond the threshold of manhood. An earsplitting battle cry turned him in time to see a warman rushing at him, his sword held high above his head and ready to strike. Everson crouched instinctively and thrust his sword toward the attacking Manolith. He was sickened at how easily the blade impaled the young man's body.

The fair-skinned Manolith looked right at him. The ferocity drained out of his face. He was the first enemy combatant to make eye contact with him. The moment seemed to expand, and they stared at each other with an almost identical degree of surprise. The warman fell away from Everson's sword, stricken and dying.

There was no time to mark the kill, either with relief or grief. There was another assailant close behind with another to follow that. And then another. Everson fought on because he had no other choice.

* * *

Shortly after the flood of troops poured from the transport, Commander Giza rumbled out of the convoy atop a massive fighting machine called a Marauder. His second-in-command, Colonel Canaan, grimly surveyed the brawl before them while Giza scanned the near distance through his field glasses. Neither was pleased with what they saw. Much to their mutual chagrin, they were outnumbered.

A thought occurred to Commander Giza and he instantly hoped that he would never be forced to share it. *I made a mistake.* He had prepared no other strategy than to overwhelm his enemy with superior numbers, and now he realized that he had seriously miscalculated. To add to his consternation, the Manolith forces were not behaving as expected.

"Why haven't the TRAUMAs engaged?" Giza wondered aloud. A phalanx of TRAUMAs sat as if dormant well beyond the fray.

Colonel Canaan's eyes flitted skyward. "And why are there no birduns?"

Suddenly, a squadron of birduns erupted upward like cinders spewing from a volcano. They had been hovering far down in the chasm, hidden by the hazy heat of distance, and now they emerged from behind the transports, the element of surprise fully realized. Commander Giza turned as the birdun warmen began throwing their HEXes, and the chaos and decibel of battle escalated.

"Javelins, now!" he barked.

Swarms of Javelin missiles jetted from the transports and dispersed to engage the birdun cavalry. With greater speed, agility and advanced firepower, the Javelins quickly turned the tide of attack. Giza allowed himself a brief smile of satisfaction. It might have lasted longer—except the world started blowing up around him again.

* * *

The Manolith leader General Bahn was seated at the controls of his TRAUMA, unmoving, unblinking, stoically waiting for the orange blossoms of bombs that would signal the attack on his enemy's rear. Though the battle was about to commence in earnest, Bahn was calm, almost content. This was where he wanted to be. This was the reason for his very existence.

The general's unflappable demeanor was as renowned and obvious as his towering height, but his patience had been sorely tried as of late. He was only here, at the edge of the Grand Schism and the edge of conflict, because he was following an order from the only person he couldn't defy—his sovereign, King Xander the Firm.

The king believed in an ancient prophecy, a dire warning that put Xander in fear for his future and dictated his every decision. Only recently, King Xander had removed every soldier from the capital city of Mist Tier and dispersed them to the outlying tiers, in spite of General Bahn's vehement protests. The pragmatic general put no faith in fairy tales and was infuriated that his king's childish beliefs could subvert his ability to competently carry out his sworn duty, to protect the kingdom.

Now General Bahn had to concede that sometimes a wrong turn could still lead to the right place. Because of King Xander's unfounded and unprecedented decree, the general was in the exact place that he needed to be, sitting in his TRAUMA, facing down an invading force. His only regret was that he wasn't close enough to see Commander Giza's dumbfounded expression when he unleashed his next surprise.

As his birduns dotted the sky and the first sparkle of HEXes preceded the percussive explosions, he forced himself to wait even longer, mentally maximizing the destruction he was about to deliver. Bahn calmly keyed his communicator.

"TRAUMAs, volley incendiary grenades now."

* * *

Commander Giza instantly registered the rattling blast of cannon fire followed shortly by the buzzing whistle of incoming incendiary grenades. As this latest barrage rocked his Marauder, he spun around with the most shock that had ever graced his face. The smoke still swirling before the immobile TRAUMAs left little doubt as to the origin of the projectiles, and Giza knew immediately that they had exceeded their expected range.

"Commander, I dare say that our intel was incomplete," Colonel Canaan said.

"Obviously. The TRAUMAs have been retrofitted with greater firepower." As if to punctuate the point, the TRAUMAs launched a second volley. The devastation was indiscriminate, obliterating Indirans and Manolith warmen alike.

Several of the transports took direct hits, suffering massive damage. The TRAUMAs finally advanced, moving forward at an alarming rate made more frightening by the array of weaponry that suddenly sprang from their metallic hulls: blades, buzz saws, drills.

"Javelins, detach and deter the TRAUMAs," Giza ordered.

Several Javelins traced ellipticals in the sky and descended upon the approaching TRAUMAs. Their weapons were as ineffectual as rain on stone. The war machines continued to barrel toward the battle, their hardware glinting and gnashing like the teeth of ravenous beasts. In desperation, an Indiran rider leapt from his Javelin and onto a speeding TRAUMA, quickly stuffing an explosive into a gun turret. He was rewarded for his bravery by being blown up along with the vehicle.

"Commander—" Colonel Canaan began to say before being cut off by Giza.

"I know! Javelins, provide cover. Marauder commanders, fall back."

The Javelins efficiently fell into formation, streaming into a staggered line before the oncoming TRAUMAs. They traced a screaming arc, and suddenly a massive wall of fire rose from the desert floor, its uppermost tendrils seeming to reach the planet's dual suns. Undeterred and unscathed, the TRAUMAs burst through the flames.

Commander Giza suddenly felt as if he were speaking a foreign language, the words as distasteful as they were unfamiliar.

"Convoys, prepare to evacuate while we still can," he muttered. "Infantry, retreat."

* * *

It was the sound that would haunt him. The sights were horrific, to be sure, but Everson would only ever recall them as a frenetic blur punctuated by staccato tableaus of savagery. No, it was the sound that penetrated his psyche deep enough to leave scars.

The concussions of explosions that he felt as much as heard.

The primal screams.

The *swish* and *chunk* of broadswords making contact with flesh and bone.

The sharp slap of pistols and bullets that sizzled through the air terrifyingly near to him.

Twice, he flinched at the metallic ping of slugs intended for his head but deflected instead into the magnetic gravity of his sword. Everson heard another sound cutting through the cacophony that he could not immediately place. It was the grinding of gears as the Marauders reversed into the transports.

Everson turned and saw many of his countrymen scrambling for the convoys. He needed no additional invitation, especially since the Manolith warmen seemed not content to accept retreat but continued to claim lives. Intent on the nearest entrance,

Everson saw Javelins buzz into the opening. Then, to his horror, the iris door began to close.

Desperate to reach the transport, Everson could see another nucruit in front of him stumbling toward safety, a rabid warman close behind and closing for the kill. The nucruit whirled around with wild eyes, brandishing his broadsword. Everson was close enough to hear the sword ramping rapidly to full magnetic power.

In his panic, the nucruit had disregarded his proximity to the transport. He was jerked from his feet and propelled backward through the air by the attraction of metal hull to blade. Pinned instantly, he dangled by the hand that now could not release the weapon.

There was no time to save him. As the transport's entry continued to close, Everson struggled forward, intent on his own salvation. Another enemy warman, blinded by bloodlust, clambered into the shrinking opening, firing his sidearm into the interior as he climbed.

The iris door sealed with finality, cutting off escape—and cutting the warman in half. Almost immediately, the transport's propulsion engines ignited.

Everson recoiled from the thermal blast of the engines, but not before he saw the magnetically pinned nucruit blister and burn in agony. The convoy wobbled into the air, buffeted by an unabated barrage of enemy incendiary grenades. The transport accelerated skyward while a less fortunate one was pummeled over the precipice before taking off. It hurtled into the abyss, ablaze in a roiling ball of fire.

Before complete panic could take him, Everson heard the last sound he would remember from this barbaric battle. Something struck him hard in the head, but, instead of registering pain, he reeled with the crack of a massive thunderclap that seemed to emanate from within his very skull. He was pitched headlong into blackness.

* * *

Consciousness came back in flickering frames of shadow and light and, for a moment, Everson thought he was home on Indira, prone on his back on the warm ground, his eyes closed as the bright light of the suns filtered through the fluttering fronds of a tree.

And then he realized he was moving. Being dragged, actually, by his feet. Everson's eyes fluttered open and fought to focus. Indeed, the bright suns' light beat down on his face, but it was being intermittently blocked by the hulking silhouette of whatever was dragging him.

Too confused to be frightened just yet, Everson struggled to raise his head, blinking until his eyes could filter the glare and see detail. The figure before him walked erect, making it, hopefully, a sentient being and not a beast. A dark hood hid what appeared to be a massive head atop sloped shoulders that led to long powerful arms. The creature was a good torso and head higher than Everson, making the possibility of attacking it ludicrous.

He craned his neck, and fear quickly unseated confusion. Countless corpses of his comrades were strewn in the near distance. Many were being dragged like him by the mysterious behemoths, bent and lumbering in the same direction, their ghoulish cargos in tow. To where? Everson turned his head and squinted into the still-blinding light. He instantly wished he really were blind.

Bodies were heaped haphazardly at the brink of the Grand Schism like rotting produce. More giants were silently, stoically, but steadily plucking them up and tossing them like trash over the precipice and into the abyss. Everson watched in horror as lifeless limbs flailed in the still air before falling into oblivion.

His countrymen. His friends.

This would also be his fate. An involuntary scream erupted from his throat. His ankles hit the dust. The massive creature carting him had spun, startled, to stare at his definitely-not-dead load. The face was like nothing Everson had ever encountered, and he cringed in revulsion.

It was certainly human, only more so. As in, more of everything. Albino features were swollen to bursting around a shapeless nose and a mouth that looked more like a crevice in stone. Impossibly black eyes that showed no white bubbled out from folds of flesh. Suddenly, its slash of a mouth began to scream.

If Everson hadn't been staring straight at it and scared senseless, he might have scanned his surroundings to find the little girl who must certainly be responsible for this silly squeal. But, no, this high-pitched, childish shriek was most definitely emanating from the mouth of the behemoth.

Repulsed, Everson rolled away, scrambling over the hard-scrabble ground to the still form of his nearest fallen comrade. He snatched up the dead soldier's broadsword, sprang to his feet, and spun to face the monsters. He slashed the air with the sword, bellowing a battle cry at the top of his lungs. It seemed it was all for show. The behemoths were not advancing. They stood, staring and swaying in place as if unable to process how a corpse could become so highly reanimated.

Everson didn't pause to ponder providence. He turned and fled in the only direction he could. Into the desert, with only a pouch full of hydreeds for water, toward whatever fresh horrors this pitiless planet had to offer.

TWO

THE SURFACE OF the Ocean of Manorain was calm and unruffled, giving no clue to the turbulent undercurrents found in its
depths.

Much like the azure eyes that gazed upon the water now.

Princess Allegra stood at the rail of her lofty balcony overlooking the ocean, staring without really seeing. Those chosen
few allowed to encounter the princess were always unsettled by
the unflinching faraway focus of her eyes. It was as if she were
looking through them to a better place beyond.

Allegra had been a prisoner in her own palace for the entirety of her seventeen years.

The person most disturbed by her countenance was her captor, her very own father, King Xander the Firm. Sadly, it was not
guilt that caused his disquiet, Allegra knew. It was not knowing.
Not knowing his own daughter's mind. Not being able to read
her thoughts.

It must be a characteristic of kings, Allegra decided, *the need
to know all.*

The proof of his paranoia was obvious and unavoidable, what
with the constant presence of guards and the many surveillance
cameras in every room. Upon puberty, Allegra had been forced
to beg for a pittance of privacy, pleading with her parents to remove the cameras from her bedchamber. It was the only battle
Allegra ever remembered winning, and even then only with the
intervention of her mother, Queen Nor.

No, her father had not been christened King Xander the Firm
by happenstance. And so Princess Allegra took not-so-secret
satisfaction in her father's discomfort whenever he was in her
presence. She knew, with bitter clarity, that the only privilege

she possessed was the privacy of her thoughts and, hence, the power to project herself beyond these palace walls.

So lost was Allegra in her ocean of discontent that she failed to sense the presence behind her until she heard an urgent whisper in her ear.

"Princess Allegra, King Xander has summoned the Four Tellers."

The princess calmly turned toward Geneva, her handmaid and also her best friend.

Allegra's eyebrow arched upward with insouciant disinterest. "Why should I care?"

"They might change their minds. There might be something new."

Her parents had given Geneva to her when Allegra had become a teenager, to ease the solitude of her confinement. They had chosen her carefully, an orphan who would view life in the palace not as imprisonment but providence. It was a wise decision, born of kindness and, once again, Queen Nor's idea. Geneva was a balm to Allegra's melancholy.

Even so, Allegra knew that her friend saw the world within the palace as a place of bounty and boundless luxury only because she had seen the worst of the real world. Gratitude could only come from comparison, and that was a luxury Allegra herself had been denied. Still, she remembered with tenderness and more than a little guilt of privilege that it had been several days before Allegra had realized that Geneva had assumed she could eat only what Allegra had left behind.

"Geneva, I adore your optimism," Allegra said. "But I'm afraid I'm destined to remain a prisoner until the day my father or I become Inflamed."

Geneva seemed near tears at the thought. "Don't speak so, Allegra."

The princess softened. "Come then. Let's see if we can take a listen anyway."

The pair swept silently down a deserted hall with the pretense of secrecy, even though Allegra knew it was little more than a game of make-believe. The ubiquitous eye of the camera in the corridor meant that anyone could easily be monitoring their movements.

They approached a pair of double doors. Arched and as high as the hall, they were presently ajar. Allegra held her breath and felt her heart quicken slightly. She had to admit that she still found a bit of intrigue invigorating. She peered through the gap between the doors.

The throne room was immense, with two ornate chairs sitting atop a dais, a crescent-shaped console encircling them in the front and a grand staircase leading to the royal bedchamber behind. Allegra saw her mother, Queen Nor, seated in her throne, upright in every sense of the word. Her father, King Xander, sat next to her, slightly slouched, his head resting upon his hand. Hovering behind her parents, as usual, was Chancellor Olaf. He was as long, straight and polished as the stick Allegra imagined was shoved up his backside.

Even at this distance, Allegra could see the ruddiness of her father's cheeks. She knew that the rosy blush was not a result of exposure to the suns but, rather, could be attributed to an ever-increasing exposure to terrazka, the liquor distilled from terranuts.

Xander rarely, if ever, ventured outside. Lately, he worried away his hours with little more than the counsel of Olaf and a bottle to stem the tide of time and circumstance. Unsurprisingly, Allegra found satisfaction in the fact that her father seemed to be as much a prisoner as she.

"The Four Tellers of the Tiered Cities!"

Allegra took an involuntary step backward, startled by Chancellor Olaf's proclamation. So snug was Geneva behind her that Allegra bumped into her and stepped on her foot, causing Geneva to stifle a gasp and a giggle. Allegra glared over her shoulder and gave her a not-so-gentle elbow in the midsection. As the guards opened the doors opposite her, Allegra turned her full attention to the room.

The Four Tellers flowed into the throne room in a swirl of fabric and mystery.

The man in front, The Why of Mist Tier, was most familiar to Allegra, but only because he resided in the palace and was a sometime shadow of Olaf and her father as they paced the palace corridors. She had never directly encountered the other three magi seers—The Where of Middle Tier, The When of Back Tier and The Which of Front Tier—and had only viewed them from a distance whenever they were summoned from their outlying tiers.

There were four major urban centers on Mano, named for their relative proximity to the capital city of Mist Tier. They were referred to as tiers because they all featured the tiered construction of the traditional Manolithic ziggurats. In truth, Allegra had precious little knowledge of her own city, gleaned mostly from books and the view from her balcony. Having never even seen the palace itself in its entirety from the outside, she had to content herself with the view of the massive ziggurats that capped the cliffs along the coastline, their levels like giant steps ascending toward the heavens.

As impressive as the buildings were, it was the natural beauty outside her windows that captivated Allegra's imagination most. The capital city had been christened Mist Tier for the constant spray that rose from the pounding surf that assaulted the base of the cliffs encircling the Ocean of Manorain. It could just as easily have been named Side Tier or Throne Tier, and in her more sardonic moments, Allegra fancied that she resided permanently in Salty Tier or Bitter Tier.

Suddenly, the skin on Allegra's cheeks tingled as if singed. She was certain that The Which of Front Tier had looked right at her. The last in line and the only female magi seer, she had taken the widest path to her position before the monarchs, and her arc had swept her closest to the now trembling Allegra.

So regal was the bearing of The Which that Allegra wondered if the average citizen would choose her as the true queen, had Allegra's own mother not been seated on the throne. In addition to her exceedingly exotic aura, The Which was adorned with a luminous amber stone embedded in her forehead like a third eye. It served as both tiara and testament to her position and had been painfully placed there when The Which was very young, shortly after she had exhibited an ability to divine events.

The Which didn't acknowledge Allegra as she passed, and now stood silently before the king and queen, seemingly uninterested in exposing her hiding place. That good fortune would not last long.

Geneva crept back up to Allegra like a winter's chill and draped over her shoulder like a cloak.

"I can't see," Geneva proclaimed peevishly.

In a blink, Olaf's eyes were on them. His movements were so subtle as to be almost imperceptible. He lightly touched Queen Nor's shoulder with a waft of his wrist and, when her eyes met his, lifted his chin slightly and without expression toward the open chamber door. Allegra saw her mother see them. The queen's brow twitched into a slight furrow, and her lips compressed into a thin line of wry disapproval. Wordlessly, she rose from her throne and approached.

"Nicely done, Geneva," Allegra purred, perturbed but not angry.

Allegra kept her eyes defiantly forward, but she could feel Geneva wilting behind her.

Queen Nor stepped up to them with an unwavering gaze of her own. "Darling, you know better."

Allegra thought she caught the smallest of smiles at the corners of Nor's mouth. "Why can't I be a party to this?" Allegra asked. "I doubt it will change my fate."

The Tellers turned as much as decorum would allow. Xander the Firm rubbed his forehead firmly.

"Don't be petulant, Allegra," the queen cautioned. "You have everything else you could possibly wish for."

"Except freedom."

Allegra saw a flash in her mother's eyes that reminded her of why Nor was equal in power to Xander. That glint of steel was the reason the chambermaids liked to refer to the crowned couple as King and Queen Neither and Nor. The queen's tone remained measured.

"You should be honored," the queen said. "It is your sacrifice that keeps this kingdom safe."

"Then, obviously, I am well pleased." Allegra's verbal curtsy was more ironic and effective than if she had done it physically.

Nor considered her daughter for a moment. She gave in to a fleeting smile that was thin but not without pride. Still, she closed the door in Allegra's face without comment.

As they departed the throne room, Geneva trailed Allegra like an inconsequential wisp of smoke after a processional torch.

"Allegra, I am so sorry," she said.

"Don't be," Allegra replied. "What more could they do? Confine me to my room?"

Allegra strode down the corridor with renewed determination. This meeting of the magi seers might not be so mundane after all. Allegra knew of the Prophecy. Everyone did. It was the primary domain of the Four Tellers and certainly the reason they had been convened now. Her father lived in fear of the future, and that future was arriving much more quickly than anyone desired. Anyone except Allegra, of course.

* * *

"That's your stubbornness," Queen Nor murmured as she executed an elegant pivot past Olaf and Xander and settled back onto her throne. The Which watched her closely until the king spoke and broke her concentration.

"And your subterfuge," he said. The king didn't bother to look at her, focused instead on the Four Tellers as if trying to read the readers. The Which noticed the king's blurry and bloodshot eyes and doubted that he could read much of anything.

"What news?" the king asked. "The Prophecy. Is everything as it was?"

"The Why of Mist Tier, report," Chancellor Olaf declared. He never missed an opportunity to impose protocol. A fact about him The Which greatly appreciated.

The Why's tone was dry and somewhat defeated. "The Prophecy remains as always, my lord. If Princess Allegra weds a common soldier, the reign of Xander the Firm will come to an end."

At the mention of Princess Allegra, The Which risked a glance at Queen Nor. The queen registered no reaction. Nothing from Xander as well, but this portion of the report was rote and oft repeated.

The Which had indeed looked at the young woman lurking at the door, had marked her piercing expression when their eyes met. As one blessed with foresight, it always seemed an over-

sight to The Which that the Four Tellers always spoke about the princess without ever speaking to her.

There could be value in that conversation, The Which opined, *if that intimacy were even remotely permissible.*

Olaf's voice, so unpleasant to others but not her, brought her back to the moment. "The Where of Middle Tier," he addressed.

A hiss of strained patience seeped through Nor's lips as The Where struggled to respond. "Isn't it ironic, Xander," the queen observed, "that The Where always seems to be somewhere else other than where he is?"

The queen's barb seemed to focus the nervous advisor.

"Still...still here, my lord," The Where stammered.

"I can see that," Xander stated flatly.

"No, my lord...I mean, yes, my lord. Still here. I meant 'still here' as in still here in the capital city." His mouth hung open as if waiting for the words to emerge. "If the actions come to pass, then they will transpire here, in the capital city of Mist Tier. Although, I couldn't tell you exactly where in the kingdom..."

"We understand," Queen Nor interjected quickly. "The Which of Front Tier, have you been able to become any more specific than simply 'a common soldier'?"

The Which met the queen's eye with confidence, knowing that her male counterparts would never do the same given the circumstances.

"I'm afraid not, Queen Nor," she said. "However, the Prededers were not random in their writing. It is a specific soldier who can access the Tree and harness the Dogs. Who that might be is still yet to be revealed. In all deference, I should certainly be the first to know since the Tree still stands on the outskirts of Front Tier. I anticipate an answer soon."

The Why stepped cautiously forward. "With that in mind, Your Majesties, the only thing that has changed...Well, I must defer to The When of Back Tier."

The When stood stock-still, his hands clasped serenely before him, his head bowed slightly, in deference or with introspection it was unclear. What was clear was that he was much older than the other magi seers and, fittingly, exuded an aura that was unrushed and measured like time itself. His deep voice resonated with tones more evocative of academia than alchemy.

"The only thing that has changed, Your Majesties, is time," The When said. "It has elapsed since we last spoke. The time is nigh for the Prophecy to be realized."

King Xander's hand flexed as if groping for a bottle. "Have we discovered any way to stop it?"

The Why sighed. "King Xander, the Prophecy is hypothetical. Like any prediction, be it storm or seismic activity, any number of elements must align for it to come true."

"Piss in a volcano! You're saying nothing!" Xander exploded. "You're supposed to divine, yet your counsel is providing no such intervention!"

The When raised his voice slightly but decisively. "The time is specific, Your Majesty. The Prediciders wrote that the time of the Prophecy will coincide with the appearance of the Aurora Constellation. As you may remember, Aurora is only complete every two thousand years..."

The When approached the dais and pressed an almost imperceptible button on the console. Twelve points of light erupted from the polished surface like a geyser and hovered in mid-air with no discernible pattern. The When pressed yet another discreet button, and the jagged shapes of the planets Indira and Mano materialized on either side of the floating cluster of lights. The When tapped a final button, and two larger glowing orbs representing the stars Femera and Amali floated upward from the console and took their places in the three-dimensional diagram.

"The constellation's configuration is dependent upon the rotation of our planets, Mano and Indira, in respect to one another and to our twin suns, Femera and Amali," The When explained.

With a wave of his hand, the holographic representation rotated. The random points of light began to slowly coalesce into a constellation.

"However," he continued, "it is the placement of the three moons of Indira that complete the crown of the Aurora Constellation and make her appear in the night sky of Mano." The When indicated the final three points of light as they drifted desultorily into place, crowning, literally, the now identifiable figure of a reclining queen. "That celestial event is less than a cycle away."

The When used three fingers to press the previous buttons, and the display dropped to the console and disintegrated. King

Xander continued to stare into the empty space as if he had seen a ghost. Nor recognized the look but said nothing. The Which watched them both carefully.

"However, I hasten to remind you," said The When, sensing the grimness, "if the Prophecy is to be fulfilled, it has only one night in which to do so."

The Why and The Where looked up hopefully. Surely, this could be interpreted as good news? But before the king could concede any optimism, the gathering was startled by a disturbance at the door. General Bahn muscled his way through the guards at the entrance.

"I will be allowed passage!" the general boomed, his size and stature dwarfing everyone else in the room.

Instantly territorial, Chancellor Olaf stepped forward. "What is the meaning of this disturbance?"

Bahn strode to the dais, still clad in his battle garb and trailing the dust of the battlefield behind him. The Four Tellers hastily made way. "I must make a report to the king."

"This is an egregious breach of protocol!" Olaf blustered.

King Xander raised his hand, silencing Olaf before he could become completely apoplectic. "Chancellor Olaf, I will allow it. General Bahn."

Olaf seethed but took a respectful step backward. Bahn regarded him with baleful eyes before turning his attention to the king. "Thank you, Your Majesty...I am happy to report that the warmen of Mano have repelled an Indiran invasion that attempted to land troops at the Grand Schism."

There was an audible gasp from those gathered. Xander leaned forward, suddenly invigorated. "I am pleased and mortified at the same time. When?"

"I have come directly from the conflict."

Queen Nor leaned forward as well, visibly reflecting on all the many possibilities. "Interesting timing, Xander," she murmured.

Xander, however, had turned his attention to The Which. In contrast to Nor's analytical thinking, Xander's reflex had always been to lay blame. "The Which of Front Tier, were you not aware of this? It's your domain."

The Which blanched slightly. "Forgive me, Your Majesty. I was here preparing for our conference."

Before Xander could pursue this punitive thread, Olaf interjected, "Your Majesties, I cannot help but be struck by the proximity of the attack to the impending arrival of the Prophecy. I find no comfort in coincidence."

"I just said the exact same thing, Olaf, only with fewer words," Queen Nor snipped.

The Which glanced gratefully at Olaf, wondering if he had distracted the king to illustrate his own brilliance, or if he had interceded on her behalf. Olaf avoided her eyes and she had to conclude that both could be true.

At the mention of the Prophecy, Xander deflated to his previous impotent state. He leaned back in his throne and only mumbled, "Yes."

"I'm glad that Chancellor Olaf has broached the subject," Bahn said, clearly sensing an opening. Olaf's eyes narrowed at the unexpected bit of diplomacy, but Bahn continued as if it were not out of character. "It was only by the Light of Femera and Amali that we had additional troops at the garrison of Front Tier. Only that and our increased firepower assured our victory."

The Which watched the general carefully. She knew that, as a mere soldier, his counsel had been discounted far too often in this throne room. As an outsider herself, she appreciated Bahn's tenacity and confidence. His strategy now was obvious but potentially effective. *The fight often goes to the aggressor*, The Which thought as Bahn cut to the chase.

"Now, I implore you, reinstate troops to the capital city of Mist Tier," the general summarized in no uncertain terms.

King Xander seemed stymied, but Nor was quick to rise to the defense. "Your words belie themselves, General," she said. "It was Xander's decision to redeploy soldiers to the outlying tiers. Why question it in success?"

"With all due respect, Your Majesty, it was a directive born of superstition and not military logic. To be blunt, we got lucky. Mark my words, the Indirans will attack again. And in greater numbers."

The king scratched his chin; then his attention drifted back to the magi seers and their less than linear way of thinking.

"Is it possible that the Indirans are aware of the Prophecy and believe they can use it to defeat us?" he asked the Four Tellers.

"As a matter of perspective, the Aurora Constellation is not visible from Indira. It only occurs in our sky." To The Which's surprise, The Where had responded first. She would not have expected him to have paid attention to the previous conversation, much less provide so cogent a point.

It prompted The Why to muse, "It is possible that the details of our culture would be unimportant to them."

"Unless they have studied the writings of the Predeciders as scrupulously as we have," The Which countered quickly.

Queen Nor turned to her, and The Which quickly deciphered that there was more than just curiosity in her gaze. The queen was sizing her up. Unlike King Xander and his chronic cluelessness, The Which knew that the queen was highly attuned to the presence of competing power within her sphere. Perhaps it was a particularly feminine trait. She also knew that the more she exerted her influence in these summits, the more she would be considered a force within the inner circle, a position that did not come without risk.

At the moment, Queen Nor's inscrutable expression made it difficult to tell if she thought The Which was a rival or a peer. It would therefore be prudent to let the queen have the last word.

"Our histories are as tied together as our futures," Queen Nor said. "Don't assume their ignorance."

General Bahn cleared his throat, reclaiming the floor before the discussion could continue down this dithering path.

"Your Majesties, I am simply a soldier," Bahn said. "The Prophecy is a matter for yourselves and the Four Tellers to decipher. But isn't it possible that the soldier in question is not one of ours? I know why you removed all our soldiers from the capital city. But if we cannot defend Mist Tier and the Indirans decide to attack the throne itself and overrun the city." Bahn drew a steadying breath. "Then isn't it possible that you are fulfilling the Prophecy with your own reckless decision?"

"General, you are being insolent!" Chancellor Olaf's voice cracked like a whip.

Though The Which often agreed with Olaf's decisiveness, the general raised an interesting point, one that she herself had not considered, and she was intrigued to hear more. But it was not to be.

Xander exploded like a HEX hurled from the hand of a warman. "Olaf!"

Olaf cringed while the others considered the floor. All except Queen Nor. She regarded her husband with flickering hope.

Xander turned a firm eye first to Olaf and then to the general. His voice was cold and controlled though crimson colored his already ruddy cheeks. "I am perfectly capable of disciplining my own subordinates. I am still king. For the moment, anyway. Mind your place, General. As you said, you are simply a soldier. And the Prophecy does not specify. So it could just as easily be you who betrays me. Knowing that, I would advise you not to question my decision. Or face exile yourself. Understood?"

Bahn feigned contriteness. He bowed his head and uttered a clipped, "Honor to Mano."

"Now," Xander rose, and all the dissonant energy that had clouded the room was quelled and came to focus. "We must harness the Dogs in the time that is left. Let the will of Femera and Amali choose a champion. The When of Back Tier, you will host the duel. Choose your two best to saddle the birduns. The Which of Front Tier..."

She looked up expectantly. The Which knew that she was destined to be the tip of the sword, the integral and irreplaceable player in Xander and Nor's defense against the Prophecy.

It is the myopia of those with only two eyes, The Which thought smugly, *that leads them to believe that only they are deserving of a destiny.*

"When the champion is chosen, you will prepare him to depart for TREE," the king concluded. "It shall be."

THREE

AS HE ASCENDED the seemingly endless steps of the Palatial Pyramid of Indira, Commander Giza grimaced. Once, he had viewed these very steps as a metaphor for his life and career. As a young officer he had attacked the steps with force and focus, rising quickly, mindful of his ascension, his sight set unerringly on the top in every sense of the word.

Now, even though he had achieved the pinnacle of his career, it was still his duty to climb these increasingly irritating steps. With each cycle of his life, Giza had become more and more aware of the creeping decrepitude of his mental fortitude and physical being.

He stopped now simply to catch his breath. He was far above the capital city of Agrilon, with its pyramids rising majestically out of the bosom of lush jungle. It was beautiful, but he couldn't remember when he had stopped taking joy from the stunning view. He sighed heavily, afflicted as he was with the woes and wounds of perpetual war. This was the worst climb yet, made all the more difficult by the gravity of the news he dreaded to deliver.

Giza entered the opulent counsel chamber that sat at the apex of the Palatial Pyramid. A solid mass of crystal, easily the size of a peasant's hovel, had been carved into a pyramid shape and topped the tip of the structure, sending shards of rainbow hue into the glowing interior. Six of the Wisened waited with the patience of the dead at their judicial bench, located above and behind the thrones of King Raza the Forty-Seventh and Queen Patra.

The Wiseneds' faces were as lined and leathery as dried hydreeds, and between them, they shared a whole head of shocking white hair. Small wonder, since the youngest of them was a few hundred years old. They never failed to remind Giza of the mummified remains of monarchs past who lay in temperature-controlled chambers in the catacombs far beneath his feet.

In addition to their intricate and traditional attire, King Raza and Queen Patra wore inquisitive expressions and an air of suspended judgment. Still, the commander knew better than to relax. His body ached from the torturous climb, but his heart ached even more.

"Commander Giza," King Raza commenced, "I expected you to be indoctrinating Manolith youth in Front Tier by now. I'm certain there is a good explanation for your presence here in Agrilon."

"I offer no excuses, Your Highness," Giza replied, bowing his head. "We failed."

Silence descended momentarily on the chamber, and Giza felt himself grow small and unsatisfactory. He was not just a warrior who had lost a battle. Those eventualities were to be expected. No, the dregs of his defeat went deeper to a confidence counterfeited, a trust betrayed. He and Raza were friends. In their carefree childhood, they had been almost inseparable, until they had been set upon their respective preordained paths. And Giza knew the worst was yet to come.

Raza remained compassionately quiet. The Wisened showed no signs of life. Instead, it was Queen Patra who called him to account.

"Perhaps you underestimated the fury of a people defending their homeland," she said.

Giza bristled, but he wasn't surprised. Patra was of the land, having been born and raised far from the cultured and cloistered environs of Agrilon and, therefore, had a deep-seated feudal streak when it came to the defense of one's domain. To say that her family farmed would be a gross understatement.

Aziz, Patra's father, was the guardian of vast lands that stretched as far as the eye could see. Likewise, their land was a legacy that stretched back generations, steeped in pride and tradition. But Aziz had not been content to rest on his laurels.

Under his stewardship, the family's reputation had grown as surely as they grew produce that was the envy of all of Indira, so much so that King Raza the Forty-Sixth had knighted him Aziz the Cultivator.

Aziz had taught young Patra that her dominion over nature meant that she was a protector of the world, not a superior being who lorded over it. So great was the humility of Patra the child that she remained unaware for years that she was the most beautiful flower her father had ever produced. But word of her fabled beauty had spread like the glorious light of morning until the day, shortly after she had blossomed into womanhood, a contingent from the capital came to harvest her. Giza respected her, not only as an insightful and seasoned sovereign, but as a farm girl who wasn't afraid to get her hands dirty.

Still, Giza himself was a much storied and decorated commander who had maintained Indira's military dominance over Mano and, as such, was unaccustomed to criticism or needling doubts about his ability or acumen.

"There were triple the number of warmen than we expected," he blurted. The sovereigns darkened, and Giza knew instantly that he had been rash to let his pride become provocative. He took a breath and backtracked. "Forgive me, King Raza, Queen Patra. I offer this not as explanation but simply as a report on what we now know to be true."

"Continue," Raza said patiently.

One step at a time, Giza told himself. *One foot in front of the other. Like marching into enemy fire.*

"As I said," he went on, "the garrison at Front Tier received a large influx of reinforcements."

King Raza leaned forward. "Could they have been aware of our invasion?"

"No, Your Highness. Not with enough notice to muster that large a force. Unfortunately, after the fact, our spies on Mano have informed us of the reason for the troop movement. King Xander has removed every soldier from the capital city of Mist Tier."

Raza pursed his lips and turned to the eldest of the Wisened, not for advice but for affirmation. The elder Wisened nodded slowly as if she could read Raza's thoughts.

"The Prophecy," she whispered.

"Yes," Giza agreed. "Perhaps more disturbing from a military point of view is the fact that the Manoliths have developed greater firepower. I can confirm improvements to their conventional defense systems. It is possible, therefore, that they are in possession of more long-range munitions."

Raza stared, but Giza knew it was not because he lacked opinion. Raza was a well-considered king, meaning that he considered everything for its own merit. Giza remembered that, as a young man, Raza had savored his meals in similar fashion, tasting each item and lingering over each distinct flavor.

"What say the Wisened?" Raza asked without turning.

Wordlessly, they huddled together like carrion eaters over a carcass. The commander and the monarchs waited. Giza cast his eyes downward, avoiding eye contact with the king. There was one more piece of news he had to share, and he simply wasn't ready. Finally, the elder Wisened raised her head from the clutch.

"It is as we have always feared." She spoke in a hissing whisper like a sword on a sharpening stone. "We Indirans have always been more advanced than the Manoliths. But we knew the day would come when they would become a threat to our peace. It is now more necessary than ever for us to neutralize them before they have the capability to attack us on our home planet."

Patra's response was unsurprising. "How can you be sure the Manoliths intend to attack us?"

"It is inevitable," the elder intoned undeterred. "The Manolithic civilization is rich in minerals and fossil fuels. But they have remained stagnant for one reason. They lack what we Indirans possess. An abundance of food. Water. A prosperous and productive populace. For their people to advance, they must take what we have. We cannot allow that."

"On the contrary," Queen Patra countered, "it seems to me that King Xander is more distracted by his own superstitious belief in the Prophecy."

"Perhaps," King Raza interjected. "But that hasn't stopped him from refining his military capabilities."

"I propose that is more of a response to our imperialism than a result of his own ambitions."

King Raza paused diplomatically. Knowing his friend well, Giza could tell that he was avoiding escalation with his wife, at least publicly. Still, it was clear that his opinion remained firm. "Patra, I'm afraid I must agree with the Wisened," Raza said at last. "I'm not willing to take that chance. The Prophecy is negligible. I don't believe in it."

"But King Xander does," the elder observed incisively. "And that is your opening."

It was what the Wisened always did. Distill the truth and administer the medicine. Patra was clearly not satisfied, but she acquiesced and did not pursue the point.

Commander Giza shifted uncomfortably. It was time. He swallowed hard, steeled his spine, and stared straight into the eyes of his king, his friend. "King Raza...I'm afraid that I must inform you of more unfortunate news. Everson was not among the soldiers who returned."

He had barely choked out the words when Patra's pained cry cut him to the core. Her hands flew to her mouth, too late to prevent the indignity of unfiltered emotion. Giza could not bear to look at her, remaining locked instead on the stunned face of Raza.

"I'm sorry," he said simply. He had never meant anything more in his life. Conscripting Everson had been a favor, and he had given his word. *Turn him into a soldier and then look out for him*. He had failed on both counts.

Though he appeared gutted, Raza continued as if there had been no diversion. Giza marveled at the king's composure. He himself felt on the verge of collapse.

"Commander Giza, prepare our full forces to attack Mist Tier on the night of the Aurora Constellation," Raza said. "Now leave us to mourn. All of you."

The Wisened receded like memory through a small door at the rear of the chamber. For only the second time in his life, Commander Giza retreated in defeat, leaving behind his pride and a past to which there was no returning. He had barely passed through the doorway when he heard Patra ferociously address her husband.

"Why must we persist in this violence?" she questioned. "Can you not consider the possibility that the Wisened are wrong?"

Giza could not help himself. He paused outside the open doors and looked back into the council chamber, empty now except for the king and queen. The emotional tension between them was palpable to him even at this distance.

"I cannot and will not question the wisdom of centuries," Raza fought back. "The Wisened are the oracle of the Predeciders."

Queen Patra rose, trembling, from her throne and approached Raza as near as her fury would allow. "And as such they advised your father and his father before him. Generation after generation of warring kings and their counsel has never changed. To what end? Now it has cost us our only son!"

Hearing it aloud finally forced a crack in Raza's imperiousness. A pained expression crossed Giza's face as he listened to his king's voice become thick with emotion.

"Patra, do not suppose that my heart is not broken as well. I loved Everson as much as you," he admonished her. "But I will not be alone in this responsibility. You agreed that the boy needed the discipline of the military."

"I never agreed!" Patra screamed. "I simply stayed silent. And that is my shame."

There it was, simply put. The shame. Commander Giza understood Queen Patra all too well. A knife turned in his heart as he was reminded again of his own complicity in this disastrous decision. He watched, helpless, as Patra hurried from the council chamber. Giza knew her as a queen, but now he saw her as a mother, perhaps for the first time, and, as such, he knew that she could never forgive him.

Giza looked at his oldest friend, King Raza, left alone in the spacious chamber. Stillness now reigned except for the shimmering shards of rainbow light that gently floated in the air as if set adrift by the stormy exit of the queen. After a moment, King Raza's shoulders slumped forward, the life seeming to drain from him. A moment more and he began to shake as rasping sobs consumed him.

Finally, Giza turned away, disgusted with himself for trespassing on another man's private pain. It was a hard truth to accept but, as Commander Giza walked away, his own eyes beginning to burn, he realized that there was nothing he could ever do to make this right.

* * *

Prince Everson dropped to the ground like a dead man, almost burying his chin in the soft sand of the rise that now concealed him. He had long ago lost track of time, and the blazing suns had nearly incinerated all his hope, but he still had enough sense not to run, arms waving, toward the first sign of salvation he encountered. The conflict between Indira and Mano was not renowned for taking prisoners.

With apprehension, he eyed the caravan of what seemed to be massive construction vehicles in the near distance as they rumbled across the desolate desert terrain. Whatever they were doing, wherever they were going, there was more than likely going to be food at their destination. His hydreeds provided relief from his thirst, but the fibrous meat was less than filling, and the effects passed quickly. If he waited much longer, the caravan would be gone, leaving nothing behind but tracks and one famished Indiran prince.

Moments later, Everson was sprinting for all he was worth, closing on the last vehicle in line. The gargantuan tires of the truck kicked up a wall of sand and rock into which Everson ran headlong. He threw up his arms to block the punishing, pelting spray, but they offered little protection. Sand seeped into his mouth despite his gritted teeth. He pumped his legs with determination, groping blindly before him until his hand finally fell on rough metal. With a mighty lunge, Everson pulled himself aboard the bed of the moving truck.

To his immense surprise, he landed in a tangle of Manolithic warmen. Jangling adrenaline surged through him like an electrical current, and his arms and legs flailed defensively. Just as he was about to throw himself from the moving truck, reason penetrated his panicked brain, and he realized that the enemy battalion surrounding him was, in fact, all dead. He was sprawled atop a pile of corpses, several bodies deep, in what was nothing less than an industrial-sized death cart.

Frozen faces stared blankly back at him while limbs—those that were still intact—were splayed at grotesque angles. Everson clamped his hands to his mouth to stifle the retching that now convulsed his empty stomach.

These were the young men he had recently encountered at the Grand Schism. But what seemed a faceless and ferocious horde before now struck him as only a pathetic and pitiful pile of wasted youth. They were obviously being transported to a mass burial somewhere. Everson had not counted the trucks before, but he was now nauseated by the size of the caravan he had witnessed, all the vehicles most certainly filled to the brim with the fallen.

Fighting his disgust, he burrowed into the ghastly camouflage of corpses to avoid detection. His wary eyes went to the front of the truck, where the driver sat in a cab that was really more of an open-air canopy.

Everson instantly recognized the sloped shoulders and massive hooded head of one of the creatures he had met earlier. The hulking figure seemed focused solely on the road in front of him, so Everson relaxed. He now had nothing else to do but go along for the ride. As fatigue and the steady rumble of the transport began to anaesthetize his nerves, Everson mused sleepily, but optimistically, that it probably couldn't get much worse.

FOUR

THE BACK TIER Arena was a bowl within the bowl of the surrounding mountains, and the heat sat in it like steaming soup. Back Tier was the most remote of the tiers and, consequently, the populace seemed to reside permanently at the back of the line when it came to receiving anything of consequence. It had been cycles since anything of note had occurred in the burg.

So today's championship bout had brought out every man, woman and child to witness the event in spite of the blazing temperature. As The Which watched, she found the good cheer and enthusiasm ghoulishly ironic considering that it was in anticipation of a blood sport that would result in the death of one of the combatants.

Warman Kohl was young, but not in relation to the mean age of most of his comrades in the cavalry. He was a survivor, with skill that was renowned among the ranks. The Which imagined he had to be surprised to find himself staring across the arena at a warrior even older than he. A man named Warman Ty, his scarred face impassive but resolute.

Ty was not only renowned, he was legendary. Kohl absent-mindedly stroked the matted mane of his birdun, a magnificent specimen with a discolored tuft of white fur. He would have to set aside his respect and admiration for a legend and focus on his expressed purpose: to kill the man. But The Which gave only passing thought to the mindset of her contestants. She was not nearly as enthusiastic for the coming battle as the boisterous commoners. She waited impatiently with The When and Chancellor Olaf, in a meticulously appointed royal box overlooking the arena. Her irritation was building apace with the raucous cacophony of the crowd. She was interested only in the result and cared little for the battle that would bring it.

At last, The Which watched the combatants climb aboard their birduns. The When rose from his seat and approached a massive ceremonial torch that stood unlit at the front of the loge. The spectators erupted in frenzied fervor. Both birduns and their riders circled high above the upturned heads, the waving arms and pumping fists, and came to a hover before the nobles. As if choreographed, the warmen raised a fist to their hearts and spoke in unison.

"Honor to Mano."

The When, The Which and Olaf offered perfunctory nods, and the warmen circled back to their starting positions. The When waited while squires handed swords and shields to the soldiers. No sooner were they armed than The When produced an igniter like a wand from the sleeve of his robe and held it aloft. The crowd grew respectfully quiet.

"As magi seer of Back Tier," his deep voice boomed, "I hereby proclaim One to Victory and One to Flame."

He touched the igniter to the torch, and an orb of orange flame blossomed from the massive receptacle. The warmen charged, their steeds galloping with surprising speed as they converged in the center of the arena. The crowd rose to its feet in anticipation of the collision. The powerful clash of their swords resounded throughout the arena, but the blow unseated neither.

The Which was not really watching. Instead, she cast side-long glances at Chancellor Olaf. Although he was faced toward the fight, she could tell that he, too, was not paying attention. The Which wished to engage him, but The When had reclaimed his seat between them, and his proximity made privacy impossible. The When was famously taciturn, but The Which was wary to give him reason to talk.

Still, the eyes of The Which were repeatedly pulled to the composed and patrician face of the chancellor. She felt certain that Olaf, and perhaps Olaf alone, was holding the throne together in his capable embrace. She'd witnessed firsthand the trembling hands of Xander, his rheumy eyes filled with doubt and fear.

Not every person was equipped to handle even a glimpse of Fate. Failure need only be suggested for Xander to crumble. He had never worked for anything in his life, and now, The Which surmised, Xander was nothing more than a petulant child in fear of having his favorite toy taken from him.

An especially boisterous roar from the crowd broke her from her reverie.

Kohl and Ty had stopped jousting and had moved to close-quarter combat, raining a storm of blows upon one another, steel sparking repeatedly on steel. The ferociousness of the exchange had the spectators screaming for blood.

The warmen were so well matched that each thrust was met by deflection from sword or protection from shield. As if seizing simultaneously upon the same strategy, Kohl and Ty urged their birduns to the air.

As ungainly as the birduns appeared, they maneuvered nimbly like windswept cinders. The swords of Kohl and Ty slashed in long, whistling arcs that failed to find purchase, due largely to the acrobatics of their mounts. The birduns dipped and dodged, keeping their masters a hair's breadth away from the lethal blades. So caught up in the fray were the beasts that they gnashed and champed at each other whenever they passed, froth flying from their bared teeth, their yodeling trills filling the air above the hubbub of the crowd.

Kohl's cheeks reddened as he grew increasingly frustrated by the agility of his older opponent. He quickly learned the cost of distraction. Ty's sword slipped past the shield of the younger warrior and sliced through the swell of Kohl's shoulder, drawing first blood.

The crowd crowed at the first successful strike, no matter how superficial it was. The battle was all to the throng, who knew that victory in the arena meant only certain death at the Tree. And so, entertainment and not empathy was the demand of the day. They watched with rapt anticipation as the younger warman gave ground, or rather, air.

Kohl urged his birdun downward to avoid the flurry of blows made freshly aggressive by the clamor of the crowd. Ty's blade swished just above his head, and Kohl crouched low over the neck of his mount to make himself a smaller target. He kicked his birdun even harder as they hurtled directly for the dusty floor of the arena.

The beast's hooves impacted the ground like a tremor while Kohl himself threw his entire body weight backward until he was prone along the beast's back. Together, they rebounded from the ground and shot skyward, ascending directly into the blazing suns.

Kohl arched his back and craned his head to look behind and see Ty barrel beneath him. His birdun did the same, its long neck curving elegantly as they executed a stunning somersault in midair. Not surprisingly, the crowd cheered, their allegiance seemingly dictated by showmanship.

The duel now demanded the undivided attention of The Which. She marveled at the ingenuity and grace of the young warman as he and his steed flipped, literally, from pursued to pursuer.

She felt a flutter of hope.

Perhaps this common soldier possessed the cunning to conquer the Tree and harness the Dogs. But then she remembered that success at the Tree was more a matter of suitability than capability, since the soldier in question must certainly have been preordained by the Prophecy. This blood sport was merely an exercise in will, Xander's frantic attempt to impose self-determination over destiny. And always at the cost of lives nobler than his.

Meanwhile, Kohl's acrobatic tactic proved to be nothing more than a momentary flourish. Warman Ty, with his vast experience, was neither surprised nor subverted by the move. When he and his birdun hit the ground, Ty pulled back mightily in the other direction, twisting impossibly to come hard about-face.

They jolted back into the air, Ty now at the ready and facing Kohl as he emerged from his revolution. Warman Kohl barely had time to duck beneath what surely would have been a decapitating blow. Their birduns banked hard.

Nearly clear of the passing opponent, Kohl's birdun stretched out its prehensile neck and sank its teeth hard into the haunch of the other birdun. Using the mouthful as a fulcrum, it executed a sharp right turn with one powerful flap of its wings.

Kohl found himself directly behind Warman Ty, and the young warman wasted no time. He lashed out with his sword and slashed a bloody furrow across the exposed back of his opponent.

Ty cried out in agony and surprise. He dropped his sword and groped madly behind him, his hands desperately slapping at his back as if to extinguish the searing pain he now felt. His birdun turned abruptly to face its attacker, its own safety now its only concern as its wounded haunch ran red. The erratic flight threw Ty further off balance, and he groped wildly for the mane of his mount. Gnarled fingers curled deep into the fur. But the wound was too deep. The blood flow too great.

Ty's strong hands and scarred but sculptured arms refused to comply. He slipped from his saddle and plummeted to the ground. The roar of the crowd clamored off the cliff walls like a landslide.

Warman Kohl hovered over his fallen foe. He stared into Warman Ty's eyes and appeared consumed with pride. But it was not pride in the victory. The Which was not greatly acquainted with the military mind, but she knew it was more complicated than that. Rather, it was a pride in understanding. Even in defeat, the more experienced Warman Ty served as inspiration.

Ty stared back at Kohl, unblinking and unashamed. The Which marveled at his magnanimity, especially considering that Warman Ty, perhaps even everyone in this arena, assumed he would win. But she recognized acceptance. Unflinching duty. Honor. The strength of character that could confront the consequence of a violent existence without fear.

Warman Ty almost smiled as he said in a surprisingly strong tenor, "Honor to Mano."

Warman Kohl nodded in return and whispered something to himself. Then he threw his sword with no pity, and it impaled Warman Ty straight through the heart.

The Which assessed the young soldier as he drifted slowly, almost contemplatively, to hover before the loge. She truly hoped that he was the one. His eyes spoke of bravery. But he was young. Although not as young as some of the warmen The Which had dispatched to the Tree, never to return.

If we continue to reap our best, there will be no one left but children and the incompetent to defend the kingdom, The Which thought ruefully.

There was a time when she might have given the young champion a nod of approval. But after so many sacrifices, she had come to think of such encouragement as misleading. Perhaps even condescending. It trivialized the challenge that still lay ahead of him. So she remained impassive, as if matters of life and death weighed little upon her heart.

The When waved his arm, dispersing cool blue crystals that extinguished the flame in the ceremonial torch.

"Congratulations, Warman Kohl," The When said with as much warmth as the smoldering torch. "You are our champion. Prepare yourself to depart for TREE."

* * *

It is a sad and sobering day when you realize your parents aren't perfect. Precocious child that she was, Allegra had come to that conclusion years before. Who better to have dominion and determination over the world than those who brought you into it? Yet her parents seemed to have control over nothing. Nothing except Allegra's world, of course, which seemed to grow smaller and more managed by the day.

Strangely, when she was being truly truthful with herself, it was not her father, King Xander, whom she resented most for her predicament. She knew what to expect from him: very little. She saw him for what he was, a sullen and solitary man who

rarely addressed her directly. No, it was her mother, Queen Nor, who caused Allegra consternation and confusion.

She had once believed Nor to be her only ally.

In her childhood, Allegra could remember her mother lavishing her with love and kindness, endeavoring daily to fill her world with every desire Allegra could devise. Only now did it occur to Allegra that the abundance of Nor's affections might have been motivated by guilt, knowing that Allegra's world was destined to be finite. However, Allegra never imagined that her mother's love might be finite as well.

To make matters worse, with the impending appearance of this accursed constellation, Nor's attentions were increasingly diverted to Xander's needs and concerns, as if he had become her child and Allegra had been demoted to a mere palace pet.

Her introspection was interrupted when Geneva gently touched her shoulder. Allegra seemed to notice her surroundings for the first time, surprised to find herself on her balcony without a clue as to how she had arrived there.

A sumptuous supper had been set on a portable table while an assemblage of musicians played a melancholy melody, undoubtedly at Allegra's request, though she couldn't remember giving them instruction. Pastel ribbons streaked the horizon nearest her as an indigo sky encroached from above. Apropos of Allegra's ability to find a dark cloud in almost everything, she couldn't help but notice thunderheads gathering in the distance above the Ocean of Manorain, lightning emanating intermittently from their blackened bottoms.

"Princess, your dinner grows cold," Geneva said.

"As does my heart."

Geneva nimbly replied, "Shall I run a hot bath, then?"

Allegra bubbled up in laughter in spite of herself. "No, thank you." She smiled as she pulled her friend into a warm embrace. Together, they turned and watched the ever-changing weather. A rising wind ruffled their hair. The rapidly approaching storm front pushed the warm air before it and whipped the water of the ocean's surface into wispy whitecaps.

"This prophecy defies reasonable thinking," Allegra said. "I'm only seventeen. How could anyone in their right mind assume that I would want to marry when I've seen so little of the world? This expectation that I would not only undo myself but the entire monarchy with a frivolous marriage is infuriating. Not only that, it's insulting."

Geneva remained quiet and listened.

"I've never even seen a soldier," Allegra continued after a moment. "How could my parents suppose that I would fall in love at first glance? Is that how love works, Geneva?"

The towering blue clouds now dominated the sky. Lightning flashed more frequently, accompanied by the requisite rumble of thunder.

"I don't know, Allegra. I've never been in love, either," Geneva answered after a time, taking a cue from the crackling sky. "But I've heard that it can strike as quickly and as violently as a storm over the Ocean of Manorain."

Allegra felt the first chill of a change in the atmosphere and held Geneva closer.

"That's fitting," she said. "I'd say I stand a much better chance of being struck by lightning."

FIVE

THE SKELETAL REMAINS of architecture, now archaic, stood as silent sentinels on the outermost fringe of Front Tier. Warman Kohl, the chancellor and The Which marched purposefully down the desolate valley between the jagged towers, robes billowing in the mournful wind, dust dancing in tiny tornadoes that appeared like apparitions and vanished just as quickly. Kohl quickly surmised that the buildings were pre-Schism. Unlike the ziggurats that characterized modern Manolithic tiers, these structures were tall and square with many floors, and Kohl could easily picture the bustling district this once was.

The three birduns belonging to the trio stood at the edge of the devastation but came no further. It was not because some sixth sense compelled them to avoid the ruins, it was simply because it was the border where the meager grass ceased to grow. Only Kohl's trusted birdun, Cap, kept a watchful eye on his master.

Kohl had raised him from a birdling. The immeasurable time spent in instruction and intimacy insured that the pair would move and almost think as a single being; every shift of his body weight, every nudge of his knees sure to bring instantaneous response. So strong was their bond that Kohl had risked the derision of his mates and had given in to the childish practice of naming his birdun. He called him Cap, not only for the discolored tuft of white fur atop his brow, but also because he thought it might defuse some of the mockery from his military friends if he claimed it was short for "Captain."

The Which's eyes narrowed resentfully as the last building in the row of decrepit structures loomed ever larger before them.

Kohl didn't understand why. He wasn't even sure what he was supposed to be looking for.

He had been expecting a literal tree and now peered up at the towering building in understandable confusion. But then all was made as clear as the letters on the façade: DEPART FOR TREE. The phrase was clearly legible although the words and some of the letters were oddly spaced.

It used to say something else, Kohl realized. As if reading his mind, which would not have surprised Kohl given her calling, The Which turned and educated him.

"The Tree has stood here since before the time of the Great Schism," she said. "It holds the secrets of our history and the key to our future. Warman Kohl, it is up to you to harness the Dogs and retrieve the Tinderbox."

Kohl straightened up as if at military attention. "Femera and Amali have chosen the right champion this time."

Olaf and The Which remained impassive, and Warman Kohl realized that his victory had earned him no rank with these two. In fact, they had said nothing more than "this way" or "follow me" to him since leaving the stadium.

Now The Which simply said, "I hope so." Without further preamble, she reached into a jeweled satchel slung over her shoulder and extracted a single item. "Take this. You will need it when facing the Dogs."

Warman Kohl stared at the object, incredulous. He was an exemplary soldier, used to taking orders and then executing those orders without question or delay. But that was only because those orders invariably made sense. This thing in the hand of The Which made no sense at all. It was a joke. It had to be. Had he really killed a good man, a legend, for this mockery?

"An apron?" he asked. "You're not serious?"

One glance at their faces and he could see that they were. Very. The bundle of cloth offered by The Which was unmistakably a blue checked apron, and neither of the nobles seemed to find any irony or amusement in it.

"Surely you do not question the wisdom of a magi seer?" Chancellor Olaf said. He was not a physically imposing man, slight of build though tall, but when he spoke, he brought the power and imperiousness of the throne to bear.

Kohl was quickly contrite. "No, Chancellor Olaf," he said, promptly taking the apron from The Which's outstretched hand. He examined it carefully, hoping desperately to glean some hidden use for the thing other than the obvious.

I'm supposed to harness the Dogs, not cook them, he thought.

"I only interpret what was written by the Predeciders," The Which said. Again, she spoke with such prescience that it reminded him to mind his thoughts. "In the bottommost level of the Tree, you will find three chambers presided over by three Dogs," she went on. "They guard the Tinderbox. Place the apron on the ground in the first chamber before the smallest of the Dogs. I cannot explain the reason why except to assure you that if you are truly the chosen soldier, you will be granted access to the other chambers and more will be revealed to you."

Warman Kohl glanced back at Cap. He seemed nervous, flitting his wings and shifting. A whisper of doubt passed through Kohl's mind. He had learned to trust Cap's animal instinct, giving him his head in battle and taking his lead. His anxiety now made Kohl wonder what danger his birdun sensed that he could not. Still, Kohl concluded, at least now his mission was clear. He turned back to The Which and could not resist one last parting jibe.

"As you command. But, if it's all the same to you, I'll be taking my sword as well."

He did just that and then pressed onward without waiting for a response. A massive pile of rubble blocked the main entrance to the Tree, and Kohl realized that he had to scale the exterior of the structure to get inside. He spied a ragged hole in the building far above him, and it occurred to him that Cap could convey him to that height with just a few flaps of his mighty wings. It also occurred to him that he was in no position to ask for favors, especially after his flippant farewell to The Which. And so, climb he must, although, in truth, the task was less than challenging for the capable warman.

From his earliest recollections, the young Kohl had been driven to rise above the confines of the drab brown ground of Back Tier. He had clambered up and down the rocky cliffs that circled the tier with agility and fearlessness, reveling in the freedom and unimpeded views. He would sit, dangling his legs over perilous precipices, dreaming of the day when he would be one with the sky. The cavalry, with its high-flying birduns, became his obvious ambition.

Kohl had barely broken a sweat before he hoisted himself through the opening and nimbly sprang to his feet. After allowing his eyes to adjust to the dusty dimness, he saw that he was in a utilitarian office where the furniture and cabinets had been cast haphazardly about as if in the wake of a great upheaval. He made his way through the clutter without giving it a second glance.

The dim room opened onto an even dimmer metal corridor that seemed to stretch the width of the building. Kohl drew his sword from the scabbard on his back and held it at his side, brushing against the annoying apron that he had tucked into his waistband like a sash. He scanned the featureless metal corridor, first for danger and then for clues. Kohl's keen eye caught the subtle shape of an electrical conduit snaking its way along the crease between the wall and ceiling. He followed it, his soft footfalls marking his progress like a metronome, until he came to a gaping hole in the interior wall.

Kohl peered down and down into darkness. It was an elevator shaft, and it seemed to descend completely down to the bottom level, Kohl's appointed goal. He sheathed his sword and swung into the void, moving down the elevator shaft without thought or concern. His hands found grip without searching. His feet fell confidently upon the slimmest of ledges. So casual was the climb that it never occurred to Kohl to be grateful for the gymnastic experiences of his youth. Anyone with less of a rocky start in life would surely have grown nervous as the darkness deepened the further he went, and his eyesight grew almost useless.

Finally, Kohl leapt the final few feet to the ground. His boots raised dusty rings into the air. His sword was drawn even before the dust settled, and he held it at the ready. The warman edged his head through the opening of the shaft and discovered a short hallway leading away in only one direction. He also discovered footprints. Many sets of them, some imprinted clearly on the dusty floor, others faded with time, all leading to a heavy metal door that stood slightly ajar at the end of the short hall.

Boots go in, but they don't come out, he observed.

It was a sobering reminder of the failure of others, but, strangely, something else disturbed Kohl more. He could survey the empty hall quite clearly when it should have been blacker than the elevator shaft this far down. An amber light spilled feebly into the corridor from behind the cracked door.

It was an emergency light that seemed ignorant of the fact that the emergency had long passed and it had no business being operable. After all, the rest of the building was an empty shell devoid of any indication of life. Obviously, there was a perpetual power source that fed whatever it was that operated down here in the bowels of the building. Kohl could guess what fed the Dogs.

He crept forward cautiously, adding his footprints to those of the warriors who had come before him. He stilled his breath and strained to hear, but no sound escaped the unseen space beyond the door. He raised his sword into position while he reached out with his other hand and carefully nudged the metal door open.

The warman was instantly overwhelmed by the stench of death. So much so that instinct nearly compelled him to backpedal in disgust. His stunned eyes surveyed the gruesome scene before him.

The bodies of countless champions carpeted the room. Some still reeked of recent decomposition while others had achieved a near fossilized state. Bare bones and smiling, naked skulls basked in the amber glow. The otherwise unremarkable walls of the square chamber were painted with the impressionistic patterns of splattered blood. Kohl swallowed the lump in his throat as he noticed that each corpse was accompanied by the cheery presence of a blue checked apron. They lay crumpled and impotent near the bodies of their bearers like the fallen flags of defeated armies.

The chamber contained nothing else except a pedestal at the far end of the room. A simple silver orb sat upon it, an odd piece of art in a garden of the dead. Beyond the mysterious sculpture, another door was embedded in the back wall, and Kohl supposed that it led to the second chamber.

But where in blazes was this infernal first Dog? The room offered no concealment, and Kohl was fairly certain that he was the only living thing in attendance.

He advanced on high alert, his sword held at the ready, eyes flitting about nervously. "The smallest of the Dogs," The Which had said. Kohl surmised wryly that "smallest" could be a deceptively relative term, especially considering the extent of the mayhem at his feet.

When he was halfway to the pedestal, he stopped and tried to whistle. A hesitant hiss was all that emerged from his mouth. He licked his lips and tried again. A lilting whistle fluttered through the air followed quickly by a nervous laugh, so ridiculous was the "here-doggy-doggy" sound in the somber silence of the morgue.

His chuckle choked short when an electronic eye whirred open on the orb. *In the name of Femera and Amali, what kind of Dog is this?* he wondered.

The orb and Kohl curiously considered each other. After a frozen moment, he remembered the apron draped at his waist. The apparel had clearly not done any of his predecessors much good, but following directions might prove to be the best policy for the time being.

He quickly and clumsily spread the apron on the ground without relinquishing his grip on his sword. Then he straightened and waited. The orb remained enigmatic. Kohl raised his free hand slowly to his sword and double clutched the hilt hard. He took a tentative step.

Suddenly, a laser sprayed from the orb in a flattened fan of iridescent blue light. Before he could react, the laser's light scanned him blindingly fast from head to toe before disappearing back into the orb.

Kohl gasped, as if sprayed with cold water, but he didn't seem to be harmed. He stood fast, clenching his weapon, waiting for some other overture.

To Kohl's amazement, the orb slowly rose from its perch and floated in midair above the pedestal. *Now comes the duel,* Kohl thought. *Now comes the test.*

He heard a seemingly inconsequential click. He barely had time to register the blades that sprang from the sides of the orb like lethal wings. The orb hurtled forward, its glistening blades nothing more than a whirling blur.

Noble Warman Kohl was summarily decapitated.

SIX

THE LIGHT OF dusk dimmed to a melancholy umber, both building and background growing monotone. Olaf and The Which
were dark shadows as they stood at the Tree, unsatisfied.

They had not spoken for a long time, trivial conversation
of little interest to either of them. The Tree had achieved per-
sonification in both their minds. It was a living, breathing being
with malevolent intent. It sat implacably at its outpost, patiently
awaiting the proper password and devouring all others it found
wanting. Finally, The Which released a frustrated sigh.

"We're done here," she said flatly, without turning to Olaf.

"How can you be sure?" he replied.

"I've sacrificed enough champions to the Tree to know."

Olaf sighed and nodded as well. He stepped to her, placing
as comforting a hand as he was capable of upon her shoulder.
"I must return to Mist Tier and inform the king. He prefers bad
news served fresh."

The Which finally turned to him, and the chancellor was
struck anew by her beauty and bearing.

"And I must prepare to Inflame the rest of our fallen," she
said quietly, seemingly unable to meet his eyes.

Olaf sensed something else behind her dutiful demeanor.
Something intensely personal. There was disappointment, to be
sure, but this time it seemed that she suffered the dashed hopes
for both of them. After all, they had most certainly made plans
together, quietly conspiring in hushed whispers behind the
closed doors of his chamber, ever mindful of the cameras that
could give them away. He had never dared touch her within the
confines of the palace lest their intimacy give truth to their treason. But that did not mean that he did not constantly desire to.

Olaf's father, Handel, had been a mere page in the court of Xander's father and predecessor, King Vaughn the Vigilant. Handel had been decorous and courtly, meticulous in his service and exceedingly proud of the legacy he would leave for his only son. Olaf, in turn, was a scrupulous and perceptive apprentice, shadowing his father constantly in the daily dispensation of his duties. So astute a student was young Olaf that he believed he had completely mastered the intricacies of the post even before he could fully grow facial hair.

Upon Handel's passing, the title of page was Olaf's by right. But that designation would never bring satisfaction to Olaf as it had to his father. No, his birthright, as he perceived it, was to advance far beyond a simple page and write a complete chapter that would change the course of his family history. His aspiration was firmly in mind when he poured his first goblet of terrazka for the callow young Xander. With the malleable and highly manageable whim of the next king at his disposal, Olaf quickly paved his way to the highest position his lineage would allow, that of chancellor, confidant and curator of the Crown.

Still, Olaf knew it was not enough.

Standing at the right hand of Xander's moral and mental decay, the chancellor's ambition grew into bitterness and covetousness. The monarchy was not built on merit, and the kingdom was left to suffer the incompetence. Olaf exerted what influence he could, but he was often left unfulfilled as Xander's paranoia grew with the approaching Prophecy. Many nights after Xander succumbed to drunken stupor, Olaf would convene the Four Tellers in a desperate attempt to divine a more reasonable direction for the Crown. It was during one of these strategic summits that epiphany flowered in Olaf's fertile imagination.

Perhaps the Prophecy was not a curse to be controverted, but a blessing to be embraced. If Princess Allegra were to wed a common soldier, the Prophecy foretold, the reign of Xander the Firm would come to an end.

And what would be so bad about that? Olaf had opined at long last.

The chancellor remembered that flash of inspiration well. He had been staring at The Which across a candlelit table, and a flush had come upon him as if he had suddenly been taken by illness. He would never forget the random thought that precipitated his sudden paroxysm of clarity: *What a fitting queen she would make.*

It all became so clear to him. With no male heir readily apparent, the power of Mano could fall to the next in the line of succession—the chancellor. And the Prophecy, not a bloody coup, would be to blame.

Certainly, Queen Nor and Princess Allegra were details to be dealt with eventually, but first things first. The Prophecy had to be realized somehow, and Xander had to fall.

The Which had been more than willing when he told her his plan, and had quickly become his consort and co-conspirator. Now, here they were. Standing again before this monolithic obstacle, their future held at bay by the inability of a single soldier to defeat the mystery of the Tree.

"Tomorrow is not a historic day for Mano," she said, and Olaf felt the full weight of her regret. Of another failure.

The chancellor moved his hand from her shoulder and gently caressed her face. "That day will come, my dear."

The Which warmly took his hand and kissed it. Olaf pulled her into a passionate embrace, and their lips came together. He held her there, feeling the soft cambers of her back. He wished he could linger, but the luxury of her embrace quickly turned his desire into resentment. *Why must we steal affection?* he thought. Why were they denied this most basic of necessities? It was not fair.

He pulled away abruptly and The Which looked at him askance. "But not yet, my queen," he murmured in explanation. "Sadly, not yet."

"I am holding on to hope with all my might, Olaf," she replied, looking longingly into his eyes. "Because of you."

He nodded slowly, grateful for her faith in him but unable to offer any other assurance. One more kiss, and then they boarded their birduns and departed. Kohl's masterless birdun watched but didn't follow. He huffed worriedly, stamped his hooves impatiently, and turned to stare at the ancient building where he last saw his master.

* * *

Everson jerked upright from a dead sleep in the bed of the Manolithic truck. He had been dreaming fitfully of battle and suspected that the pervasive smell of dried blood must have prompted his subconscious. He was still surrounded by a clutter of corpses, none made the fresher from a night in the open. He also realized, with more than a little trepidation, that his bed was no longer moving.

A furtive glance to the front of the truck confirmed that the driver was no longer present. Everson slowly extricated himself from the tangle of dead warmen, no easy task given the stiffness of his bunkmates. He crawled quickly, but gingerly, over the bodies and hazarded a peek over the side of the transport.

Everson's vehicle was still last in the line of the now parked trucks. Two of the large laborers stood at the open tailgate of the truck in front of him and were nearly finished off-loading the bodies there. The warmen's corpses were being loaded in handcarts and wheeled toward a large gathering of people who stood in stark silhouette to the rising suns.

Between Everson and the crowd rose a long line of forged metal frames. Everson felt a twinge of sadness and compassion as he realized that the crowd of Manoliths waiting somberly were mourners here to honor their dead. Atop each metal scaffold lay the body of a warman awaiting, Everson could only assume, immolation. At least they were receiving a warrior's send-off, though it must be little consolation to the widows and children in attendance. At any rate, Everson's escape definitely did not lie in that direction.

He scurried to the other side of the truck to see what lay behind him. Here he found a meager orchard, vast in area but populated by spindly trees that stretched in long uniform rows away from him for some distance. Lumbersome bodies cast long shadows beneath the skeletal branches, and Everson observed that the laborers were carting barrows of ash from the recently cremated, transporting their loads from the pyres to the orchard, where they spread them on the ground around the trees, ostensibly as fertilizer.

Everson tried to recall if he had ever seen his grandfather Aziz the Cultivator engaging in such a practice. Then again, the soil of Indira was replete with life and did not need to have life imposed upon it, as the barren land of Mano obviously required.

A loud mechanized rattle from the back of the truck caused his heart to leap into his throat. Someone was opening the tailgate. The stiff corpses at the rear of the truck jolted into a sickening downward shift, and Everson knew it would only be moments before he was caught up in the slide.

He slithered over the side of the vehicle, hung from the lip for a moment, then dropped twice his body length to the ground. He landed flatfooted and was immediately deposited on his rear with a forced and audible grunt. With no time to think about how much it hurt, Everson scrambled into the scant cover of the trees. He flattened himself in the ashes of his enemy and peered wide-eyed behind him.

It appeared that he had avoided detection, mostly because all eyes were now trained on the ceremony beginning around the pyres. The twin suns, Femera and Amali, sat higher in the sky, and their unforgiving light gave stark clarity to the sorrowful faces of the mourners.

They were suddenly people to Everson, no longer just the enemy, and his heart went out to them: the wives, the children, the parents.

Two figures stood out from the rest, not only because they waited on a raised platform, but because they possessed the unmistakable air of authority. The woman, especially, was adorned in such an ornate and regal manner Everson wondered if Queen Nor herself was deigning to reign over such a lugubrious affair.

Everson had learned many of the Manolithic beliefs and practices in his studies, but their funereal rituals remained foreign to him. He watched now, feeling more than just a little guilt.

* * *

The Which waited on the raised dais beside the intimidating presence of the Grand Incinerator, highest priest of their order. He wore flowing black robes that only heightened the ashen features of his face. He stood, unmoving, a sword held in one hand, as if he were a statue erected in the name of inscrutable judgment.

Extending far to the side of the dais stood a long line of similarly clad, but lesser priests, each waiting patiently before their respective scaffolds. The number of mourners huddled behind them made it clear that no denizen of Front Tier was untouched by loss. The Which could sense the oppressive aura of sorrow held barely at bay. It would break soon, she knew, like a cloud swollen with rain. A lesser priest led an obedient birdun to the foot of the dais, and she knew the time had come.

"Grand Incinerator, commit the souls of our fallen to the Light," The Which ordered.

The Grand Incinerator stepped from the platform and approached the trusting birdun. He raised his sword and pointed it ceremoniously at the twin suns.

"Warmen of Mano, we honor your sacrifice," he said, his voice strong but raspy, as if it had rusted with disuse.

With surprising strength and violence, the Grand Incinerator plunged his sword into the heart of the birdun. Accustomed to the primitive practice, The Which remained impassive as the creature screamed in agony, its head whipping wildly atop its long neck. It staggered, still bleating, and then slumped heavily to the ground, eyes rolling madly, its sides heaving in death throes. One of the large laborers, more muscled than most, stepped forward and, with one mighty heave, rolled the quivering beast beneath the first scaffold.

"May this birdun carry you to the Light and Beyond," proclaimed the Grand Incinerator, his bloody sword held aloft. "May the offering of your flesh and blood bring life to our barren soil. Ashes to dust. And may Femera and Amali grant you your Harmonious Equal that you may find Harmony and Balance in the

Afterlife. From Flame we have risen and to Flame we must return."

The Grand Incinerator raised his other hand high to the heavens. The long line of acolytes did the same, almost simultaneously as if in ritualized salute. Each held a small HEX in their hands, more diminutive than the combat version, but still potent.

The Grand Incinerator dropped his arm like an executioner's blade and hurled his HEX decisively into a mound of ebony-colored rock, as luminous as dark crystal, which was piled beneath the scaffold. Upon impact, both HEX and stone exploded in a massive fireball that engulfed the dead warman above it.

In rapid succession the ignition was repeated down the line of scaffolds with their similar mounds of crystal, and the ground fairly rumbled with the rippling explosions. The grief-stricken wails of the mourners filled the air, along with black smoke and flickering tendrils of flame. The Which watched silently, as she had so many times before.

Will it ever end? she thought.

* * *

Everson recoiled reflexively, entirely unprepared for the thunderous pyrotechnics during a funeral ceremony. He stumbled backward, his ears ringing and his nose stinging from the smell of sulfur and charred flesh.

He bumped into something large. Instinctively, he knew it was not a tree. He cringed and turned in dreaded anticipation. There, as certain as suns rise, stood one of the large laborers, his eyes bulging, an expression of equal astonishment on his boulder face. Everson winced as the behemoth's mouth yawned open, then the high-pitched shriek coalesced into a single, intelligible word.

"Help!"

The sound was almost instantly muffled as the brute wrapped Everson up in his arms. Everson struggled with all the success of a newborn against its swaddling. He could still hear the giant's squealing cries for help, and he knew he did not have long before the crowd of Manoliths came to investigate.

His arms pinned, Everson couldn't reach for the sword sheathed on his back. He clawed at the creature's sides, to no avail. He tried stomping on its feet, but the thick work boots of the laborer offered him little impact. Finally, in feral desperation, Everson opened his jaws and bit down hard on a mouthful of hairy chest.

Everson would not have thought it possible, but his captor's cry of pain reached a volume and pitch more strident than before. The thing's huge arms ripped him from his suckling grip. Everson was flung to the ground, and then the laborer retreated, whimpering pathetically.

Springing to his feet, Everson spun around. The mourners had drifted toward the orchard thanks to the commotion. An older woman nearest the dais stepped forward beyond the others. Her blue eyes were blazing and still wet with tears. Angry red scratches were clawed into her cheeks, made by her own fingernails in demonstration of her grief.

Everson saw rage and disgust ripple across her face and knew exactly what she was thinking. Here, in the flesh, was the cause of a lifetime of pain and suffering, of poverty and loss. She raised a trembling finger in his direction and screamed, "Indiran!"

Everson turned and fled. The blood-chilling bedlam of enraged voices approached fast behind him. The wounded laborer reached feebly to detain him, but Everson blew past the tepid attempt. For a fleeting moment, he entertained the notion that he could outrun the mob. Then the first rock struck him squarely in the back, causing him to stumble and almost fall.

Two teenage boys, virile and full of vitriol, ran ahead of the pack, scooping up stones and hurling them in a steady barrage at Everson's back. The bloodthirsty rabble soon followed their example.

Everson redoubled his efforts as the torrent of projectiles rained down around him, some whizzing by dangerously close to his head, others painfully finding their mark. The Manolith boys were closing the gap.

Everson realized that flight was futile. He would have to fight. He groped frantically for the sword on his back and had just unsheathed it when a rock bashed the back of his head and sent him starry-eyed to the ground. The sword slipped from his grip.

Before Everson had time to recover, the first boy was on him like a beast of prey. The mob converged, and Everson's only solace was that there was simply not enough room for all their flailing fists to find him. He curled into a tight ball, his arms positioned protectively around his head, blindly enduring the cascade of kicks and blows that pummeled his every exposed part.

The elder mourner found his abandoned sword. She plucked it from the ground and held it high above her head, her scratched face a warlike mask of retribution. Her countrymen made way for her to approach the prostrate enemy. They screamed their approval as she stood over Everson and gripped the sword with both hands, ready to bring it down on his hapless head. Only the voice of complete and commanding authority stayed the stroke.

"Cease!" bellowed the regal woman from the ceremonial platform. She strode through the mob, her presence alone enough to quell the violence. "Make way!"

The mob reluctantly but respectfully parted. Everson saw her in snatches and glimpses as she approached, his assailants slowly clearing a path to where he lay. The suns shone behind her, flaring in his eyes as he looked up from his prone position, and she appeared as a shadow, confidently closing in on him. When at last she stood above him, he could see her face clearly for the first time. She was stunning.

He now noticed an amber stone set in her forehead. That idiosyncrasy sparked a distant memory, a footnote from his studies, but he was too overwhelmed at the moment to contemplate it for long.

The noblewoman snatched the sword from the older woman's hands. The elder mourner snarled in cheated outrage, but one look from the noble and she shrank into sullen submission.

"Lift him." The noble nodded to the two breathless boys who had led the charge.

The two teenage boys roughly pulled the soldier from the ground and held him upright. Everson's brown face was bloodied, and he could barely stand of his own accord. He viewed the strange woman through a haze of pain as she stepped exceedingly close to him, as if observing him from a normal distance was not assessment enough. He very nearly expected her to sniff him.

"An Indiran soldier..." she murmured lightly. A small smile played about her lips. The peculiar stone embedded in her forehead seemed to pulse with a faint light. "Perhaps this is an historic day for Mano after all."

SEVEN

EVERSON WAS AS wary and nervous as a small creature huddled in the wild, ready to bolt at the first sign of attention. He had been deposited in a relatively comfortable chair at an immaculately hand-carved table sitting in the middle of an austere but elegant dining hall. He had seen better.

The two Manolith guards who'd seated him now stood rigidly at the entrance, only recently having grown bored with staring at him as if he were a pile of excrement. One guard appeared to be as young as Everson, so the prince expected a certain amount of posturing. The other was older, well-worn and haggard with the hatred that had been festering for years.

Everson tried to ignore them. Instead, he eyed yet another large laborer, this time female, as she methodically fulfilled her tasks. She was slightly smaller than the males Everson had encountered, but her features could hardly be called feminine. She was setting the table, her ungainly hands carefully placing napkins, utensils and plates, her black marble eyes never straying from the space directly in front of her. Nothing about her was threatening except for her size and the fact that a shriek from her would probably outclass all the others that Everson had heard so far. Still, he had encountered nothing but conflict and a fair amount of physical abuse since arriving on this planet, so he remained understandably on edge.

Everson also noted an oppressed nature about the laborer. There was care and meticulousness in her glacial movements, to be sure, but there also seemed to be a distinct fear of making a mistake, as if the consequences could be dire. But when she started placing food in the center of the table, all Everson's concerns fell away. Before he could fully assess the menu, the regal woman, his presumptive savior, breezed into the room lightly, as if Everson had been formally invited to dine and she was merely a tardy hostess.

"Sorry to keep you waiting," she said warmly as she settled into a seat at the head of the table. "Are you comfortable?"

The woman possessed an ethereal air that seemed to affect the very ambiance of the room. Everson knew that he was in the settlement nearest the Grand Schism, so he quickly concluded he must be in Front Tier. That would make the noblewoman sitting so pleasantly with him The Which. The stone embedded in her forehead only punctuated that fact.

He knew a bit about the Four Tellers of Mano, but he had always assumed that they were charlatans putting on a show of otherworldly omnipotence to placate and manipulate the populace. Now, sitting in the very presence of an actual magi seer, he wasn't so sure.

"All things considered," Everson replied after a considerable pause.

"You're still alive," The Which continued without a hint of threat. "Have you considered that?"

"Extensively. And I keep reaching the same conclusion. Why?"

Instead of answering, The Which sat back in her chair and narrowed her eyes. Everson felt properly scrutinized, and he silently hoped that the quickened pulse in his neck was not obvious.

"I must say, you don't speak like a soldier," The Which said.

Everson mentally kicked himself. He was proving to be green at every turn. It had never occurred to him that he would have to adopt a clandestine persona. The Indiran military certainly provided comprehensive preparation, but espionage was not, as of yet, a necessity for a nucruit. Then again, Everson had much more to hide than the average infantryman.

"We educate our soldiers on Indira," he sidestepped nimbly. "Is that not the case here on Mano?"

The Which raised her eyebrows toward the stone in her forehead until they underlined its oddity. She cast a quick glance to the guards on either side of the entrance, who pretended not to listen.

"I am not of the military and I am not familiar with their methods," she said. "As a magi seer, I oversee Front Tier and foresee our future."

Everson forced his face to remain blank, as if the confirmation were meaningless to him. "I'm honored," he said as blandly as possible.

The female laborer had measured her movements even more when The Which had entered, almost as if to avoid notice, and now placed the final dish on the table. Her eyes still unengaged, she turned to The Which and curtsied, a gesture Everson found to be near ludicrous given her size. The Which nodded and the server's decisive exit was the most rapid exhibition of movement she had displayed thus far. Everson waited until she was out of earshot.

"Your servants," he began tentatively. "They appear very...different. I've run into a few of them. Literally."

"Of course." The Which smiled. "How could you not notice? Those are the Leftists. Their ancestors were left behind on the planet before the Great Schism. To escape the toxic environment, they took shelter below ground and evolved there, it seems. The subterranean environment led to their poor eyesight, and their size can be explained by the sudden decrease in gravity. Unfortunately, they also have decreased

mental capacity, so they labor. Is there not a subspecies on your planet?"

Subspecies? Everson had never heard the word, and even if he had, he certainly would not have thought it applicable to a living being who could be considered a person. To be fair, there was indeed a hierarchy on Indira, but from serf to sovereign, each person took pride in their position and was respected and valued for it. *Subspecies*. The offensive term made Everson regret that he himself had judged the Leftists based solely upon their appearance. After all, he believed that the enmity between Indiran and Manolith could partially be blamed on the distinct difference in their skin color.

"No," he replied simply, remembering to appear noncommittal. "Although I've not been to every part of Indira, so I couldn't say for sure."

"What part of Indira are you from?" the Which asked. "And what should I call you?"

"You can call me soldier," Everson answered quickly. "Where I'm from doesn't matter."

The Which smiled even more deeply. "There, you see. Now you sound like a soldier." She gracefully and graciously gestured to the waiting food. "Please, eat something."

Everson didn't need to be told twice. He hadn't eaten in days and his stomach growled to remind him. He spooned portions onto his plate and dug into the food with fervor, shoveling in mouthful after mouthful before the previous one had even been swallowed.

"I'm sure it's not like the bounty you're used to on Indira," The Which continued, "but it's the best we have to offer."

"I'm grateful," said Everson through distended cheeks.

The magi seer let him eat for a moment, watching him carefully all the while, and then ventured forward, with an air of casual conversation. "I'm aware of the battle that took place at the Grand Schism," she said. "How is it that you remain here on Mano?"

"I was left for dead," Everson replied without thinking. His chewing slowed to a more reasonable rate, and he was pleasantly surprised at how palatable this food was now that he allowed it to rest on his tongue long enough to taste it.

"So no one on your home planet is aware that you're alive?"

Everson abruptly stopped eating. Looking up from his plate for the first time since serving himself, he noticed that not a morsel had been placed on the plate of The Which. Obviously, she had not eaten a bite. How could he have been so stupid? Had this Which saved him from the mob so that she could have a private audience to his slow, agonizing death by poison? Or perhaps he had ingested something that would make him helpless against her questioning? He threw down his spoon in self-disgust.

"If you intend to kill me, you needn't have been so gracious about it," he said.

The Which sat back in her chair, eyebrows askance. After a moment of silence, she picked up her own spoon and scooped up a healthy mouthful of food from the Indiran's plate. She popped it into her mouth, chewed and swallowed.

As she delicately dabbed the corners of her mouth with her napkin, she said, "On the contrary, I need you alive. You may be able to do something for me. Think of it as a favor in payment for your life."

Everson felt foolish, but he picked up his spoon, took another bite of the admittedly delicious food, and turned to the Which. "I'm listening."

The Which looked to her guards, and her features seemed to darken. Though their eyes remained mostly focused on nothing, Everson could see right through their amateurish attempts to appear unengaged. He imagined their ears were so burning with interest that melted earwax should be dripping from their lobes.

"Leave us," The Which commanded firmly.

The guards looked surprised and more than a little disappointed. They hesitated, glancing nervously between The Which and her prisoner.

"Do you forget that I am a magi seer?" She grew firmer still. "I do not foresee my death at the hand of this Indiran. Do as I command."

The guards reluctantly complied, retreating into the hall, where they would not have the opportunity to eavesdrop. The Which took a slow measured breath.

"Many young Manolith warmen have undertaken a challenge," she began, suddenly intimate. "All of them have failed. I think, perhaps, you might not. You might even enjoy it. It will appeal to your soldier's sense of mission."

My "soldier's sense of mission"? The irony nearly made Everson laugh aloud. He hoped that the smirk he could not control would be construed as cavalier.

"What kind of challenge?" he asked.

"Now where is the fun in spoiling the surprise?" The Which smiled thinly, but there was no mirth in her eyes. "Besides, it's either that or languish in one of our prisons until you rot."

"As a soldier and now a prisoner of war," Everson countered quickly, "is it not my duty to accept the consequences rather than give you a strategic upper hand?"

The Which looked at him without responding for a moment. Suddenly, and for no reason that Everson could discern, her features softened to the point that he was reminded how pleasant her face could be.

"Do you want this war to end?" she asked with a sincerity that seemed entirely genuine.

The question so caught Everson off guard that he could only think to respond with a question of his own. "Why would I not?"

"This conflict began before you were born. What is the one thing our warring worlds have never tried?"

Everson shrugged, at a loss.

"Diplomacy," The Which answered for him. "Cooperation. I repeat your question to you. If you could help to put an end to the death and suffering, why would you not?"

Everson put down his spoon and said, "You have my full attention."

* * *

The universe certainly has a twisted sense of humor, The Which thought.

The Prophecy did not specify that the champion of the Tree and the common soldier destined to wed Allegra would be one and the same, but suddenly The Which saw a connection that had previously eluded her. With the fateful night of the Prophecy so near, why should it not be so?

But a union between an Indiran and a Manolith? It was a consummation devoutly to be wished but doubtfully achieved. The very proposition seemed unthinkable. Yet there was an unlikely logic to the idea.

The Which tingled with anticipation, even though the Indiran's laborious climb up the side of the Tree was far less inspiring than Kohl's agile ascent. She knew she had no real reason to be this optimistic, but she also knew that there were those times when she must heed the quiet but empirical voice of the universe without question. So she remained steadfast in her hope, even though she could hear the snickers of her two guards every time the Indiran slipped and nearly fell to his death.

They stood behind The Which with a huge and humorless Leftist. *They're simply ignorant*, The Which thought, shaking her head as yet another sophomoric snort insulted her ears. *They are a product of their breeding. Little is expected of them, so little is what their unimaginative minds offer.*

Unlike the Indiran, The Which reflected, who was a most uncommon "common soldier." Something he had said continued to resonate with her. "We educate our soldiers on Indira." She made a mental note to add that to her list of reforms should she and Olaf come into power.

Yes, the Indiran remained an enigma. He had shown neither excitement nor fear when she had described the Dogs in their chambers and the elusive prize of the Tinderbox that lay at the odyssey's end. He had accepted the apron wordlessly, without question or the obvious scorn that Kohl had not been able to suppress. The Which had expected some sort of reaction or opinion from him, but he had left her unsatisfied and alone in her enthusiasm for the mission at hand.

He seemed too smart to bribe, and too brave to threaten, so she had tried neither, appealing instead to his compassion. It was not a quality one expected in a soldier, but her instinct about the young man proved correct, and her sincerity became the key to unlocking his obstinance. Whatever his motivation, there he was, clumsily climbing the Tree just as she had asked, with only her word and his sword to sustain him.

She felt the stone in her forehead glow with inner energy and she shuddered. The stone was always portentous. Whether it was a good thing or a bad thing, The Which wished she knew.

EIGHT

EVERSON STRUGGLED INTO the opening of what The Which called the Tree and promptly collapsed. He was not fond of heights. The climb had been arduous, and he remained sprawled where he was for a few moments to catch his breath and get his bearings.

In her optimism, The Which had given him a satchel to hold whatever prize he was supposed to retrieve from this misnomer of a Manolithic monument, and presently it lay strapped across his heaving chest.

Dutifully, Everson leaned forward with a groan, reached behind him, and clicked his broadsword from its magnetic scabbard. He noticed immediately its diminished connectivity. Either its power pack was low, or The Which had drained the energy to the minimum magnetism. It was still a formidable weapon even without all the bells and whistles. He *snicked* the sword back onto its scabbard and glanced about.

The cluttered interior instantly piqued Everson's interest. Here was history and, therefore, an education.

His worlds history advisor in Agrilon, Master Vici, had certainly been worldly and well-versed, but the massive tomes from which he taught had been ancient, and Everson had long suspected that the pompous Master Vici had filled in the blanks about Mano with conjecture and opinion.

Now, the young prince thought, *perhaps I can figure out a thing or two for myself*. Like why the Manoliths both feared and revered this so-called Tree, and why they doggedly adhered to dogma decreed centuries before.

It occurred to Everson that this stringent religiosity was something that their two civilizations had in common. In which case, the Indiran could rest assured that his skepticism was universal and not colored by race. After all, he held little regard for the Wisened of his own culture. He had witnessed his mother scoff at their immutable philosophy more than once in the privacy of their palatial gardens. As Patra had once told him, "Even the oldest tree knows how to create new blossoms every season."

Everson carefully picked his way through the wreckage, examining the overturned furniture. There were boxy, utilitarian chairs, tables, desks and cabinets all made from some lightweight metal, and Everson concluded that this must have been a pretty boring place to spend one's time. He reached out and flipped over what he deemed to be the lightest cabinet and instantly found himself screaming in shock and surprise. A faceful of flying fur, fangs and leathery wings greeted him, whirling in frenzied motion. He pinwheeled away, frantically swatting the air in desperate defense.

The ferocious flurry subsided as quickly as it had erupted, leaving Everson panting and scanning the room in panic. He spotted the nasty culprits almost instantly. There were three of the creatures, two of which flapped away in ragged and erratic flight through the jagged opening. The third landed in the gap and turned as if to dissuade pursuit.

The thing was large enough to be intimidating, with a plump body covered in nappy, matted fur and a bullet-like head that tapered to a sharp snout. Red eyes like pustules glared at Everson as the creature puffed itself up and spread its translucent wings wide in an effort to appear more menacing. It worked. Everson edged back slowly, arms held protectively in front of him should the thing launch another aerial attack.

He had studied zoology with Madame Irina, and there had been a meager section on the indigenous creatures of Mano, scant because of a lack of eyewitness accounts. He remembered seeing a rudimentary sketch of this particular pest, probably drawn from the memory of a returning soldier, but the rendering fell far short of the real thing. The creature was called a verm, and it was the scourge of waste dumps and other places where cleanliness had fallen into inattention.

The verm's hideous face grimaced into a hiss, revealing multiple rows of tiny needle-sharp teeth. If Madame Irina's textbooks were correct, its bite could be quite painful, but it was the infection from the verm's polluted mouth that caused the real long-term damage. Everson had no intention of finding out and was greatly relieved when the verm turned quickly and flew off in pursuit of its cohorts.

The soldier passed a shaking hand over his face and neck, feeling for blood. His fingers came away with only sweat, and he breathed a shuddering sigh. He glanced about the room with much less enthusiasm than before. His eyes fell upon the cabinet that he had moved. A small plaque was inset near its top. He moved toward it, kneeling to inspect it more closely.

The small metal plate was copper, but it had oxidized with age, its edges framed in an antique patina of green. Upon it were four words stamped into the metal in simple block letters.

DEPARTMENT FOR MILITARY RESEARCH.

His fingertip traced the letters in the final two words, and he remembered the oddly spaced signage on the front of the building. He ticked off letters in the plaque—the *t* and the *r* in *military* and the two *e*'s in *research*. He spoke the word aloud.

"Tree."

Everson shook his head wryly. This culture had devised an entire mythology based upon what it could read, yet the truth lay in the spaces between.

He rose to his feet, gathered his resolve, then crept cautiously into the corridor outside the room, sword cocked at his shoulder. The encounter with the verms had left him more than a little skittish.

For no other reason than it felt right, he turned left and followed the corridor into the interior of the building. He soon came upon the gaping entrance to an elevator shaft. He peered down into the endless blackness.

"The bottom level?" he groaned. "Oh, for the love of Light..."

* * *

Birdun and rider detached themselves from the glow of the suns' halos and descended into the Tree ruins near Front Tier. Before his beast had fully stopped, Chancellor Olaf dismounted and quickly strode to The Which. Her two guards were slouched in boredom, but quickly jerked upright at the sight of the nobleman. The Leftist stood nearby as well, staring blankly.

Olaf paid them no mind. His attention was firmly focused on The Which.

"I came as quickly as I could," he said.

"Is the palace aware of your absence?" asked The Which, mindful that her message could have made its way to unintended ears.

"I told the king that I had to officially confirm the death count from the Inflammation. He won't ponder it much. The only death Xander gives any consideration is his own."

Olaf glanced cautiously at the two guards. He moved closer and lowered his voice. "What is the reason for such secrecy?"

"I have another champion in the Tree," The Which replied.

The chancellor's brow furrowed. "How? We've not had another selection challenge."

The Which savored the news for a moment, basking in Olaf's intense anticipation.

"He is an Indiran soldier," she said finally.

The look of unadulterated shock on Olaf's face eclipsed every other emotion that had come before. "You've harbored an Indiran! Do you not think that places us in peril?"

"On the contrary, I believe that Fate has led him to us. Do you remember what General Bahn said? Perhaps the prophesied soldier is not a Manolith at all."

Olaf seemed to forget the entourage and countered at an indiscreet volume, "But an Indiran? How could the Prophecy ever come to pass? How could we possibly arrange such a marriage? It's impossible!"

The Which smiled and resisted the urge to caress the concern from his face.

"You are assuming romance, my love," she said. "The Prophecy has never specified that the participants have to be willing. They must simply wed. And after..."

Olaf picked up the thread and his consort's intimate tone. "After, we insure that Xander has no heir to take the throne."

"And that there are no survivors of the royal family. Control of the Crown will finally be in the hands of those most fit to lead."

"Yes, my queen." Olaf's grin matched her own, and The Which struggled not to take his hands. Twice he leaned forward as if to give in to his enthusiasm, and twice The Which tilted her head to receive his lips. Finally, Olaf half-glanced at the nearby guards, and his ardor visibly cooled.

"I have faith in your vision," the chancellor said succinctly. "Let's hope that your Indiran is the one." He looked to the enigmatic Tree. His lips parted as if to say something else, but nothing came out. Olaf raised a hand and pressed it against his mouth thoughtfully as if to further silence himself.

The Which could not interpret the vulnerability of his expression, but she could not help but think that her pragmatic and imperious lover appeared to be...*praying.* She waited for something more, but Olaf turned quickly and walked away. The way he held his shoulders, the rigidity of his spine, and the stiffness of his gait—all indicators that he was struggling mightily to maintain his composure. But against what emotion, she could not be sure. Then he leapt nimbly aboard his birdun and took flight without looking back.

Olaf's abrupt departure left The Which slightly unsettled. Doubt crept into the space in her heart that had previously been filled with conviction. Never before had she desired. Now, she desired intensely, for so much and with so much longing.

Had the mere act of wanting clouded her clarity? Had she deluded herself into thinking that her will and the will of the universe were one and the same?

If the Indiran failed, what then? More of the same. A future for her planet harshly dictated by a merciless war and an incompetent king. And what of her? Would she be destined to persevere in the lonely life of a magi seer, consigned to bitterly administer the lives and destinies of others?

That was all well and good for the three remaining Four Tellers. They were men and, more so, they were recluses. They would be perfectly satisfied to dither away their time in chaste and isolated contemplation.

The Which was a woman, the inferences of which were rarely acknowledged by her peers. Only Olaf saw her beating heart, the vibrant blood that ignited more than cerebral imaginings. What would become of the two of them?

The Which knew that they could not continue their affair indefinitely. In the censored, insidious culture of Xander, they were bound to be caught and accused of collusion. They had not even consummated their love.

No, she reasoned resentfully. *Xander the Firm would never allow so influential a coupling.*

She sighed heavily, seeing an alternate and all too tragic turn of events. The Aurora Constellation would come and pass, leaving providence as distant and unreachable as the stars themselves. In this moment, with the Tree poised to bear fruit so sweet that it would make the wanting worthwhile, The Which could only wait and hope.

This common Indiran soldier had to be the one.

NINE

EVERSON FELL.

He landed flat on his back, the air forcefully expelled from his lungs, yet he was grateful. It could have been far worse. Impact had come much more quickly than his frightened brain had expected.

Given his displeasure with heights, Everson had inched down the elevator shaft slowly and carefully, clinging to each handhold with tenacious anxiety, not daring to look below at the precipitous drop. His nervousness had not allowed him to remove a hand from the wall even to wipe away the sweat stinging his eyes.

To clear his vision, he had shaken his head vigorously from time to time as if in vehement denial. Not that vision was all that helpful in the near darkness into which he had descended. It was during this reaching and peering and shaking for the hundredth time that he had lost his balance and tipped backward into the void.

Looking up now, Everson realized he could have jumped, so near had he been to the bottom. Here it was again, yet another example of his inability to judge his place in the world. He shifted slightly on the dusty floor of the elevator shaft, wincing as he felt the new spots where bruises were sure to blossom. He expected he would have a lovely blue sash across his back where he had landed on his sword.

It will match my new blue apron, he thought. He continued to lie on the floor, gathering his breath, when the thought of more of those verms finding him—and finding him delectable—forced him stiffly to his feet.

Everson peeked out the opening of the shaft and studied the short hallway that led to the open door. He saw the unidirectional footprints and immediately understood the implications.

No one ever leaves this place.

He pulled his sword from its sheath with a sibilant *snick* and then became immobile. He couldn't force his feet to move forward. Cold fear crept in like a freeze that chilled his very marrow.

No one is forcing me to do this, he thought. *If I never emerge from this building, no one will come looking for me.* It was an option. He could just stay here, hiding, surviving on verms and whatever other disgusting delicacies he could rustle up. He could let the war wage on without him. At least then he would be alive.

Four words materialized in his conflicted conscience. "*Department for Military Research.*" The antidote that could cure this plague of war could very well reside in that room. The prince heaved a resigned sigh and walked down the hallway.

Everson pushed open the door to the chamber and instantly wished he hadn't. The stench was overpowering, and the sight that accompanied it was worse. The prince swallowed hard, wishing for the first time that he possessed more of his father's conviction and less of his mother's compassion. An orb glowing dimly at the far side of the room gave him something to focus on, and he started toward it.

His very first step met with resistance when his boot encountered something round and not without substance. The object rolled away from him and wobbled to a stop. Everson was shocked to suddenly find someone staring back at him.

The severed head of a warman was so fresh that, for a stunned moment, Everson thought it still alive. The blank stare seemed a bland judgment, and the prince suddenly felt self-conscious. He stared back, studying the fixed features until he was finally satisfied that the disembodied head held no life, much less an opinion.

The warman had been handsome in life. His headless body lay nearby, and Everson could see that he had been strong and stout. The very embodiment of a champion. Yet he had failed. Self-consciousness easily segued to self-doubt.

Everson's next thought was of imminent concern. What in the worlds had wreaked such havoc? There was nothing else in the room save for the orb that sat on a pedestal before the door to the second chamber. He recalled The Which's simple but obviously insufficient instructions. He was supposed to engage a small Dog, and once that trial was tamed, pass through to the second chamber where another challenge awaited. Simple. But the decaying remains of his predecessors gave ample evidence otherwise. He moved toward the orb because there was no place else to go. Everson quickly reasoned that if the Manoliths called this building the Tree, then maybe the Dogs were not quite so literal as well.

The electronic eye on the orb whirred open, and Everson nearly turned and ran. Instead, he froze. He had the immediate sense that he had awakened something best left slumbering, and was afraid that the slightest movement would result in his joining the casualties on the floor.

After a long pause, he willed himself to advance, only to freeze again as an electric blue laser fanned out from the eye of the orb. It swept over him as quickly and completely as a gust of wind and then disappeared back from whence it came.

Everson knew that he had been scanned. They had similar technology on Indira, but it was used to detect illness within the body. In this case, he concluded that the orb might have been examining him for weaknesses that it could exploit. If this thing was the Dog that The Which had predicted, he wondered if it could also sense fear.

As if in answer, the orb floated upward from its pedestal, and with it rose the hair on the back of Everson's neck. The orb hovered in midair, as if waiting. Everson assumed it was his move.

He suddenly had an epiphany and remembered the blue-checked apron stuffed carelessly in his satchel. He quickly retrieved it and presented it to the orb like he was peddling kitchen wares. It elicited no response. Everson shook it slightly as if to say, *"I have the flaming apron, now what?"*

He remembered that he was supposed to spread it on the floor. Apron in one hand, sword in the other, Everson searched beneath him. He'd have a difficult time finding enough space amidst the corpses to suitably spread the apron.

Everson raised both hands and shrugged as if in apology. As counterintuitive as it might seem, he then slowly sheathed his sword. The orb remained motionless as Everson knelt, gingerly moved a few sprawled body parts, and spread the apron on the floor as neatly as his trembling hands would allow.

The young prince stood, his breath shallow, unable to even remotely imagine what might transpire next. Aside, of course, from the very real possibility of his death.

In that moment, it occurred to Everson that he had never said goodbye to his father. His mother, of course, had found a way to send him off with her blessings and prayers. She had reluctantly acquiesced to the wisdom of Commander Giza, who had advised her not to be present at the transport lest Everson's covert identity be revealed to the rest of the troops. Instead, she had exercised her sovereign privilege and had insisted that Giza grant Everson a day's furlough to visit the palace. The young prince had welcomed the opportunity to see the queen, though it had often grown uncomfortable with her sudden outbursts of tears contrasted by equally awkward silences.

He had not encountered his father during his stay. Not that he had wanted to. He was sure that Raza had been aware of his presence, but he had stayed absent because of his pride and a desire not to cast doubt on his decision to conscript his own son into the military. Now, Everson regretted the anger that might forever remain the tenor of their parting.

The prince came out of his reverie with a start when he realized that the orb was slowly drifting toward him. He watched in dreaded fascination as the thing floated within an arm's length of his face. They silently studied each other. Everson had already endowed the silver ball with intelligence, and now he searched the cold electronic eye for any indication of intent. Was it presenting itself to him much as he had presented the apron to it? Everson reached up ever so slowly to grab it.

The orb flitted away from the soldier's approaching hand as if suddenly coy. It stopped and hovered again, just out of reach.

Everson cautiously persisted in his pursuit. This time, the orb zipped laterally, deftly avoiding his hand.

So, this is a game, he thought and grabbed at it more quickly. *Like playing with a pet.* Up went the orb as if teasing him. Everson frowned at the little silver ball. At least it was showing no signs of retaliation.

Another quick grab garnered the same results. The orb hovered unperturbed, tauntingly near but far enough away to execute an easy escape. The soldier swatted at it with increased aggression, his frustration mounting. The orb zipped around him, forcing Everson to spin in a near comical pirouette. Now more angry than anxious, the prince lunged wantonly at the elusive orb, but it dipped, danced and dodged like one of the little buzzers that pollinated his grandfather's orchard.

Everson stopped, panting, his forehead glistening with a sheen of sweat. The orb stopped as well, considerably less taxed by the game of chase. The thought of his idyllic childhood spent collecting insects on his grandfather's farm gave the soldier sudden inspiration.

The orb seemed to watch curiously as the soldier bent slowly over and picked up the apron. He gripped two corners in both hands and held the apron out in front of him as if preparing to set a table. The orb remained immobile. With a leap and a swoop of cloth, Everson brought the apron down upon the orb and quickly gathered the edges in both hands.

He yelped loudly in surprise when he was jerked off his feet. Everson was suddenly airborne and being dragged around the room by the trapped and inconceivably powerful little ball. He clung to the cloth tenaciously, unwilling to let the orb go now that he had caught it. It didn't occur to him that it might be *he* who was actually caught.

The orb zipped around the room with Everson in tow, making sure that he slammed against every wall and even the ceiling. He bounced off the hard surfaces, grunting and gritting his teeth, but he refused to be shaken. Finally, the orb executed an elegant little flip and dumped him decisively onto the hard floor, freeing itself from the apron and Everson's stubborn hands.

The now incensed prince sprang to his feet and vengefully drew his sword. He chased the orb around the small chamber, slashing indiscriminately and stumbling over dead bodies. His anger and frustration were only exacerbated by the insistent thought that a fully magnetized broadsword would have been the perfect weapon with which to snare a cheeky little metal ball right about now.

The orb remained maddeningly elusive, sometimes appearing as nothing more than a silver streak in the amber light. It circled the room as if in a centrifuge and came up fast behind Everson. It did not slow in the least as it rammed itself into the back of his head.

The sword flew from Everson's grip and he collapsed onto his hands and knees. Pulsating spots danced before his eyes, like myriad little orbs. His mouth hung slack, breath neither coming nor going. He thought he was going to pass out. He was completely unaware of the orb as it returned to hover over the small of his back.

Everson shook his head, his breath coming back and the blackness receding from the edges of his vision. He was just about to reach for the painful lump on the back of his head when the orb jabbed a long, sharp needle hard into his back.

The scream that erupted from Everson's mouth made the high-pitched shrieks of the Leftists sound like music. The white-hot, excruciating pain tensed every fiber in his already beleaguered body as the orb extracted fluid from his spine. The procedure was mercifully quick, and then the orb removed the needle effortlessly from his back. Everson's trembling arms could hold him no longer, and he collapsed face-first against the dingy floor.

Even so, Everson was now painfully aware of the orb's violent capabilities, and he didn't want to let it out of his sight. His cheek scraped against the gritty floor as he strained to move his head. His eyes rolled as if they were loose in their sockets, but finally he glimpsed the orb moving purposefully back to the abandoned and disheveled apron.

A long needle still protruded from the orb's base, obviously the cause of the searing pain in his back, and Everson watched as the orb used it to tidy the apron back into a flat mat. The silver sphere then hovered above the now neat checkerboard pattern as if waiting for something. When Everson made no move to join it, the orb zipped over to his prostrate form and tapped him hard on the head with the needle.

Everson blinked. That tapping reminded him of his childhood elocution classes administered by Master Abel, a slight but stern Indiran with delicate hands that all too often wielded a thin and highly lacquered black baton. That baton was deployed frequently, tapping Everson soundly on the head when his mind wandered or when he found the windows more interesting than table settings. Master Abel would place it under his chin, pressing upward until Everson's head had achieved the proper haughty angle befitting a prince. It had poked him almost daily between the shoulder blades to remind him of his posture.

Despite all of that, Everson had been very fond of the fastidious instructor, who always had a twinkle in his eye and who had lavished loving praise upon him when he performed well. The prince had heard it rumored that Abel preferred the intimacy of men, but such innuendos were meaningless to his affections.

Everson blinked again, some semblance of rational thought coming back to him. He had heard that people on the verge of death often conjured images of their life. Was that what he was experiencing now? Master Abel would be flattered, and his delicate hand would fly demurely to his mouth if he only knew. Everson felt the tapping again, and he realized that the orb was trying to get his attention. He raised his head with much effort and looked at the insistent silver ball floating too near his face.

The orb promptly returned to its airspace above the apron. Everson watched in confused fascination as a thin stream of fluid dripped from the needle and onto the apron. He suspected that that same fluid had recently been in his back. He didn't have long to ponder it. A bright neon-blue grid rose in a three-dimensional shaft from the humble apron. The needle retracted with a click.

The orb rose within the framework and, as it did, seemed to pull hundreds of smaller orbs out of the checked pattern. They floated in a schematic pillar for a moment, and then they began to swirl as if caught in a vortex. Everson began to wonder if he was experiencing a pain-induced hallucination. One by one, the smaller orbs locked into place until they formed a shape floating within the glowing grid.

The educated Indiran instantly recognized the double helix configuration of a DNA strand. For what purpose it was being shown to him, he had no idea. The orb, seemingly satisfied that Everson had acknowledged its first presentation, began to spin and rise even higher. As if caught in its draft, the double helix spun as well, its components flying apart from the centrifugal force, the recognizable shape deconstructing into a whirl of spinning orbs. More miniature orbs shot up from the checkerboard pattern on the apron and swooped into the grid in long elliptical spirals.

Everson closed his eyes briefly, the maelstrom before him making his head spin. When he opened them, the storm of orbs once again coalesced into a pattern. The movement abated, and Everson could see two distinct DNA strands slowly revolving within the grid.

If I can't make sense of one of them, he thought tiredly, *two certainly won't help.*

Everson flinched as the orb zipped toward his face, stopping short at an uncomfortably close distance. Behind it, the entire three-dimensional display dropped into the apron and disappeared as if it were never there.

The orb hovered. Everson stared at it, swearing he saw the electronic eye blink as if its patience was being tried. He suddenly felt as if he were ten again, called before one of his many masters to deliver a lesson for which he had not studied.

"I...I don't know what you're trying to tell me," he said.

Everson not only flinched again, he barked a short, startled yelp when the needle once again clicked out from the bottom of the orb. He expected searing pain, probably in one of his eyes, but like Master Abel from his past, the orb only used the needle to persuade him to rise.

It calmly tucked it under his chin and gently applied upward pressure until Everson got the idea. He reached his feet with all the ease and grace of a man three times his age. Once erect, he sighed, reluctantly resigned to his new role as puppet.

Everson was convinced that the orb possessed intelligence when it dipped forward in a nod and then zipped to his fallen sword. He watched in amazement as his blade leapt through the air, obviously pulled aloft by some strong magnetic force. It pinged onto the underside of the silver ball with a metallic ring of metal on metal, and then the orb flew it dutifully back to Everson. He held out a hand to the approaching orb, but it circled behind him and courteously slid the sword back into its sheath. He then felt an encouraging bump on his shoulder.

Everson walked warily forward, his mind still in a slight state of confusion. When he passed the pedestal, the door before him slid open, a percussive *crack* and a grating scrape the only indication that it had been centuries closed. He could now see clearly into the second chamber, devoid not only of character but, thankfully, corpses. He was about to cross the threshold when the orb flitted in front of him.

"What now?" asked the rightfully paranoid prince.

The orb quickly retrieved Everson's apron from the floor with an appendage and returned it to him. Everson took it with a small nod of thanks. The orb nodded in return and moved to the side, indicating that Everson was now free to proceed. The prince, still not without reservation, passed through the portal and into the second chamber.

He jumped as the door loudly scraped shut behind him, blocking any exit. Everson frowned in resignation and then waited for a moment for his heart to return to regular rhythm. There was no way to go now but forward.

There was nothing to see in the chamber save a lone table sitting in its center, simple and without adornment. Everson looked around and noticed there wasn't a chair.

He approached the table, perused it quickly and deduced only one use for it. He spread the apron on it, making sure to smooth it neatly as the orb had done. He stepped back, waiting to see if the blue grid would appear. Everson tensed, a rippling of pimpled skin descending his neck as if cold water had been dribbled on the crown of his head. Something or someone had moved up directly behind him.

He turned quickly to his right, but the figure was quicker. Everson surveilled the blank corner of the chamber behind his right shoulder. Positive that he was not alone, he spun to the left, but again, the stranger was nowhere to be found.

Instead of turning back around, Everson warily circled in the same direction, scanning the back of the chamber for the threat he was certain was there. It proved to be an unfortunate maneuver, since whatever it was smoothly slid the soldier's sword from its scabbard from behind him.

Everson spun around, shocked to be facing a person of equal stature and terrified to see that she brandished his sword above her head. *Not a person,* he realized. She was obviously made of some metallic alloy. Her face and body were silver in color and elaborately constructed with intricate detail. The serene, almost kind, features of its face were undoubtedly feminine, framed by flowing metal locks so finely wrought as to seem almost fluid.

Instead of cleaving Everson's head in two, the android inexplicably turned the tip of the sword toward her own face. Everson watched in confused amazement as she pushed the sword into her own mouth. The blade disappeared slowly in a glow of molten metal and spitting sparks until there was nothing left but the hilt. The android then casually tossed the useless hilt aside, turned to face Everson, and held her hand to her mouth. Everson half-expected her to burp.

Something did emerge from the android's mouth, but it was less predictable. She began spitting gleaming coins, freshly minted from Everson's blade. They tinkled brightly into the android's hand until there were twelve in all. She then approached the apron-topped table and, with a tilt of her silver head, indicated that she wanted Everson to follow.

The android woman settled into position on the far side of the table, and Everson stopped on the side opposite, facing her. With a slight of hand almost too quick to follow, she laid out the coins on the apron in alternating squares as if starting a board

game. She looked up to Everson expectantly. The prince eyed both the board and the strange android dubiously.

"You must think I'm dim," Everson said. "What are we playing for, my life?"

The android simply tapped the table.

Everson sighed with as little petulance as possible and simply muttered, "Blazes."

He scanned the board for a moment and made a hesitant move, unfamiliar as he was with the rules of this particular game. The android moved without hesitation. Everson moved again, more confidently this time, a strategy materializing on the checkerboard pattern before him. Again, the android moved immediately after. And so it progressed, quickly and with growing aggression until Everson gleefully jumped every one of the droid's pieces with one of his own.

"Ha!" the prince exclaimed triumphantly.

His victory was short lived. The blue neon grid exploded from the checkerboard with a metallic growl, and Everson cringed. The coins in their blue squares began to glow with an intense silvery light. The points of light quickly detached from the metal and floated upward, stopping at varying heights above the tabletop. Everson studied the configuration and, for the first time in this disingenuous dungeon, understanding came quickly. The android moved around the table to join him, assessing Everson like a mentor awaiting proof of a postulate. Everson nodded slightly at his silver hostess.

"I know what that is," he said simply.

It was the Aurora Constellation, the harbinger of Mano's dreaded Prophecy.

The android scooped up all twelve coins from the apron with one sweep of her silver hand. As before, the blue grid and would-be stars tumbled to the tabletop and disappeared. With an almost stately air, the android proffered the coins now neatly stacked in her outstretched hand.

Everson considered the coins with a mixture of surprise and unexpected gratitude. Having been born into royalty, it was not the money that impressed him, but the act of unsolicited generosity. It was a virtue he often associated with his mother.

"Thank you," he murmured as he took the money, slipping it into his satchel. Before the tinkling of coins stopped, the door to a third chamber scraped upward with an ominous groan. The android gestured politely in that direction. Everson nodded and moved toward the opening—only to be stopped by a double tap on the tabletop. He turned to find his silver hostess gathering the apron and presenting it to him with a courteous bow.

"Of course. How could I forget?" Everson smiled. Apron in hand, he passed into the third chamber.

Once in the room, the door slid shut. This time, Everson wasn't surprised. This chamber was even smaller than the previous two and was devoid of any additional accoutrement, neither pedestal nor table. Its only feature was a large inscrutable black box the size of an armoire that sat against the far wall. Its façade was covered with many tiny lights that blinked drowsily. Various luminous displays undulated with indecipherable meaning. Everson was immediately reminded of the command centers he had toured upon entering the military. This most certainly was the brain behind the old Department for Military Research.

He approached the blinking box, positive that the apron would prompt some sort of response. He spread it neatly before the device and stepped back to wait. There was nothing at first, but Everson had learned that nothing in this perplexing place was an indication of things to come. His patience was rewarded, quite literally.

A slot opened in the black box, and the machine began to rapidly spit out gold coins in great number. They piled up in a gleaming heap at the base of the box. Even though he was not entirely conversant with the currency of Mano, Everson knew that this was a small fortune. He moved forward to collect the prize and stepped directly onto the apron.

The moment his boot made contact with the cloth, the neon blue grid shot upward. It collapsed onto him like a net, instantly encasing him. Everson's eyes widened and his heart began to pound as the lights on the machine began to blink excitedly and the displays flashed an incomprehensible, dizzying array of data. The machine began to shudder and hum like a troop transport preparing for takeoff.

Two openings, like eyes, awakened on the surface of the box. Everson would have screamed if it were not for the blue grid mask that clamped his mouth shut. Before he could blink, twin red lasers shot from the openings in the machine and penetrated his mesmerized eyes.

Everything went white…

Then Everson's vision cleared like steam dissipating quickly from a winter window. The sight that greeted him was both stunning and deeply confusing.

He had somehow been transported into an opulent throne room, albeit one in the throes of violent battle. Indiran soldiers and Manolith warmen clashed in close-quarter combat all around him. There were even large Leftists engaged in the fray, though Everson could not easily ascertain for whom they fought. Yet no one seemed to take notice of him.

He raised his hand against the onslaught and was immediately transfixed. His flesh shimmered with an ethereal blue glow that made him question if it were corporeal at all. The elaborate cuff adorning his wrist prompted him to inspect the rest of his body. He was clad in Manolithic couture of such finery that he suspected someone of taste and substance had lent him this livery. Of course, this could all be some laser-induced hallucination.

Everson moved through the melee like the apparition he apparently was. He viewed the violence with real despair. Hallucination or not, it was all too real and reminiscent of the carnage he had encountered at the Grand Schism. The prince mourned the falling Manolith warmen as much as he grieved the dying Indirans.

He gazed helplessly at the stricken faces, their features contorting as the life left their eyes. Death was death, and its cruelty was democratic. Unable to watch any longer, Everson cast his gaze upward. Though he did not find mercy there, he at least discovered beauty.

She stood atop a curved staircase that ascended in a sweeping arc from behind two ornate thrones. She stood quite still and stared directly at him. The sight of her took his breath away, her gaze like a hand compressing his heart. Everson was certain that he could detect recognition in her countenance. They had met somewhere before, somewhere between the Tree and this vision of a possible future.

She was incandescent and the prince knew it was not just his imagination. This girl glowed, much as he himself was glowing. Everson surmised that they might just be spectral spectators, immersed but apart from this turmoil, as if the battle at hand was nothing more than a backdrop to their meeting.

The prince knew. He simply knew down to the core of his being. This was the Manolithic princess, Allegra.

As if the gravitational pull between Indira and Mano had finally grown strong enough to reunite the long-estranged planets, Everson was drawn to her, moving without conscious thought and almost without will. He felt as if he were floating and that the world around them with its hatred and violence no longer mattered.

Everson began to climb the stairs, his unwavering gaze embracing every detail of the waiting princess. He could see the gentle rise and fall of her bosom. The blush beneath her luminous eyes. He was now almost close enough to touch her. Instead, she reached for him.

Her alabaster hand floated in the air like an invitation to dance. Everson took it, and the touch was like a pure and perfect chord of music, harmony melding with melody in a vibration felt as much as heard. He ascended the final step and they were face-to-face. Their heads inclined together to kiss.

The magic of the moment was shattered by a strident scream. Everson looked over Allegra's shoulder at a maniacal man hurtling toward them. Murderous eyes blazed in their hollowed, darkened sockets. A spray of wild hair jutted out at lunatic angles beneath a golden crown. Judging by his crown, this rampaging man could be none other than King Xander the Firm.

"Never!" bellowed Xander, nearly upon them. The king raised a blood-coated sword high above his head, his face twisted by rage. Everson instinctively pushed Allegra out of harm's way as the blade came down.

* * *

Allegra gasped. She was shocked and chilled as if a monstrous wave had swept her into the icy depths of the Ocean of Manorain. She stood in the center of her room, her chest heaving to regain the breath that had so abruptly abandoned her. Her eyes were wide, the pupils mere specks as she stared intently at nothing.

Geneva flew to her side. "Allegra, is something wrong?" she asked. "You look flushed."

Allegra groped blindly for Geneva's hand with both of hers, desperately in need of an anchor to keep her from slipping further a-sea. After a moment, she regained enough composure to speak.

"What happens when Femera and Amali align?" Allegra asked. "When they eclipse one another?"

Geneva stared at her, dumbfounded. Allegra realized that she probably appeared unhinged, her tone frazzled and insistent for no apparent reason. All that she had ever reaped from the stars was cruelty, yet here she was, randomly contemplating the heavens.

"Geneva," Allegra said, undeterred.

"They become star-crossed," Geneva replied quickly. "There is intense light and darkness at the same time. I've only seen it once. Why?"

Allegra nodded. Star-crossed. That was it exactly. Two celestial bodies destined not to collide but to simply pass at a point in their opposite trajectories, so aligned that they might appear as one.

"That is the only way I can describe what I just felt inside," Allegra said.

"Did you have a vision?"

"No. I saw nothing. Just a feeling. A very intense feeling."

Allegra continued to stare straight ahead, as if searching for something she had glimpsed and then lost, as one might peripherally sense a comet or the ground shadow of something in flight. Geneva watched her with concern.

Allegra could feel Geneva staring at her, but she did not want to break the spell. The princess could discern a new focus, a pinpoint of light in the blackness of infinite space, like the sparkle of an approaching star. It was far away, dancing at the edge of her awareness, but, still, Allegra had the surreal sense that something was now searching for her. The emotion that now coalesced within her was not fear.

It was hope.

* * *

Everson dropped to his hands and knees, crying out against a phantom pain. His face glistened with sweat as if he had indeed engaged in some physical confrontation, but a frantic assessment assured him that his head was still attached.

Gone was the princess and the mad king and his bloody blade. Gone was the entire throne room and all its inhabitants. Gone even was the grid that had snared him into being an unwilling witness and participant. Everson was once again in the third chamber with its sepulchral silence, facing the now docile machine and kneeling upon the slightly rumpled apron.

He flipped around and sat heavily on his rump, wiping the sweat from his face and trying to process the dream or vision or time travel that he had just experienced. It had been so real, so palpable, and Everson guessed that it was of paramount importance that he remember every detail. These three strange machines The Which called Dogs had been waiting lifetimes to deliver their directives only to him, and it irritated Everson that their clues did not come complete with further instructions.

Was this last revelation a warning of what would be if he didn't piece together the puzzle of the Prophecy just so? In which case, the promise of his own demise was not just a possibility but a probability. *Not a very good motivational tool to take up the cause*, Everson thought wryly.

Still, he was certain of one thing. He would never forget the vision that was Allegra.

Everson looked to the inscrutable black box, hoping to receive some sort of prompt. But the machine had returned to its somnambulistic state, lights blinking drowsily, graphs undulating with little urgency. He missed the much more interactive android. Still, Everson suspected that this state of nothing was once again simply a prelude to a very serious something. In the interim, he decided to collect the clutter of gold coins still piled at the base of the box. He figured that everything presented to him during this cryptic initiation was worth retaining for future purposes.

The task brought him closer to the machine, and as he busied himself with plucking up coins and placing them in his satchel, he grew unmindful of the dormant machine. That is, until a slot in its face slid open at Everson's eye level.

His gaze clicked to the opening, a coin in his hand now forgotten. He watched, staying as still as sorrow as a small shelf emerged from the blackness of the box. Upon the shelf sat an object as innocuous and seemingly inconsequential as the apron. Everson identified it easily but had long thought such objects archaic and prone to pretension.

It was a Tinderbox.

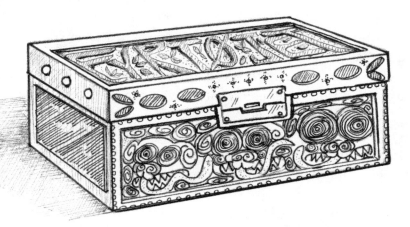

TEN

THE WHICH HAD never before felt as if she had left her own body. Until now. It was like she was soaring in uncontrolled flight. The edges of reality had become blurred, her peripheral vision forced out of focus by rapid forward motion.

The future, previously indistinct but much anticipated, walked toward her in the guise of an Indiran soldier.

"You're alive!" The Which exclaimed, breathless.

The young soldier was dirty and disheveled, bruised and bearing the scratches and scrapes of obvious struggle. His sword was gone, but, The Which saw with unbridled excitement, the satchel was strapped securely over his shoulder. She also discovered quickly that his insolence was still intact.

"After what I've just been through, I'm not surprised that you're surprised," he groused.

The Which was undeterred. All that mattered now was what might be in that satchel. "What did you see?"

"I didn't see any Dogs."

An impatient sigh slipped her lips before she pursed them. It would be so much more pleasant and efficient if this pawn would simply acquiesce and acknowledge his place in her grand plan.

"Obviously you did," she corrected him curtly. "You just didn't recognize them. They were the destiny omniscient guides."

"Destiny omniscient guides. DOGs." The soldier shook his head and exhaled an ironic little laugh. "Well, that certainly explains a lot. Maybe something you should have told me before."

"What form did they take?" The Which continued as if the interview was going perfectly as planned.

The soldier glanced over The Which's shoulder. Not only were her two guards and the massive Leftist still there, they were edging closer and straining to listen in. It was a not-so-subtle reminder to Everson that he was still a prisoner and that he should tread carefully.

"They were a form of weaponry," he said. "That's all I can say. I've never seen anything like them."

"And so?" The Which leaned forward, her pupils dilated, her lips parted slightly like a lustful young maiden. Her features, normally so serene and inscrutable, took on an edge of near feral desire. "You have what they gave you?"

"I have something, yes."

"I want to see it," said The Which, her eyes darting greedily to the satchel, where she assumed the soldier had stowed the prize.

"It's a rather plain item to have cost so many lives," he replied calmly.

"True. So it should not pain you to give it up," The Which countered, equally as calm. In contrast to the steely insistence of her eyes, The Which smiled and expectantly extended her hand. She would not be denied.

"I know of your Prophecy," the soldier said.

The Which recoiled as if he had slapped her. "The Prophecy? How could you know of our Prophecy?"

The young Indiran gave her such a condescending smirk that she had to press her fingernails into her palms for restraint.

"As I said before, Indirans are educated," he stated. "Apparently, our leaders want us to get to know you before we try to kill you. The question is, why would you want King Xander's reign to end? Isn't that what's supposed to happen if your Prophecy comes true? Do you have designs on the throne?"

The eyes of The Which grew as glassy and reflective as windows closed to the midday light. Her shoulders drew back proudly. Her neck seemed to lengthen, and she stood pillar straight.

"You are not just a common soldier. Who are you?" she whispered, as if raising her voice would release a torrent of uncontrolled fury.

"I'm not the one who's going to marry a princess, I can tell you that," the soldier retorted. "But at least now I know why you've kept me alive."

"Give me the Tinderbox!" hissed The Which.

"So you can enslave me and lead me like a lamb to the altar? I think not."

Her nostrils flared and she inhaled slowly through them. The Which remembered that the soldier was indispensable to the larger aspirations of her plan. She relaxed into a more reasonable posture, her head tilted to the side.

"You talk as if it's a sacrifice," she said. "It's actually quite a promotion, don't you think? Marry a princess? Become a prince?"

The soldier clenched his jaw and his face became strained. It occurred to her that he was stifling a laugh, but she herself could find no humor in her proposal.

Not to be distracted, The Which continued, "And Princess Allegra is quite beautiful, I can assure you."

Much to her satisfaction, the soldier's face paled at the mention of Allegra's name. At least for a moment, he appeared far less smug.

"I'm not tempted by beauty," he said after a brief pause. "And, like many of us on Indira, I don't believe in your Prophecy. I think it's a fable. But this..."

Everson reached into the satchel and retrieved the Tinderbox.

Femera and Amali had drifted down to the horizon. Their ruddy glow was pervasive and painterly, making the air thick and lending luster to every detail. The moment became imbued with historic importance, like an antique painting depicting an armistice or the coronation of a king.

The Which could feel the weight of the moment pressing down on her. She stood self-consciously still, as if pointedly aware that she was the focus of the tableau. She clenched her fists into tight little rocks to keep her hands from trembling. The soldier displayed the Tinderbox with a forced casualness as if it were nothing more than a mere souvenir.

The Which heard a derisive snort, and she threw a glance at her guards, annoyed that her magical moment was being sullied. The guards and the Leftist looked downright let down by the sight of the common object in the Indiran's hands. They had not known what to expect from this clandestine vigil and likely hoped for something more impressive to justify them standing here all day waiting for this prisoner whom The Which insisted on treating like some esteemed ambassador.

What were they expecting? The Which groused to herself. *Something with the subtlety of a bomb, probably.*

"This obviously has power," the soldier continued. "It's connected to the DOGs in some fashion. I think that you think it controls the outcome of the war. Some secret weapon to defeat my people. I wouldn't be a very good soldier if I surrendered that to you, now would I? I'll hold on to it, if you don't mind."

The Which exploded. The verbal dance was over, and it was time to pay the piper. "I do mind! You are not in control here."

"Am I not? I know that you won't kill me. It doesn't serve your purpose. And I will not become a puppet in your fairy-tale aspirations."

"Then what do you want, soldier?"

The soldier fidgeted and cast a nervous glance to the guards and the Leftist. Killing him would go a long way toward comforting their offended sensibilities.

"I don't know," he admitted. "Time, I suppose. Time to figure out what I need to do."

"Time is something that I do not have the luxury to give," The Which said. "I'm afraid you've become confused by my politeness. I cannot kill you. But I can make you hurt."

The Which turned to her guards and they straightened expectantly. "Take the box," she ordered.

The two guards stepped forward, smiles curling into sneers as they finally had something to do. The Leftist moved his massive bulk behind them but without the same apparent glee. Instinctively, the soldier's knees bent slightly, his center of gravity lowered, and his muscles went taut in preparation to fight or flee. The guards were just slipping their swords from their scabbards when The Which added, "Without killing him."

The guards stopped, their hands still gripping their half-drawn swords, but their enthusiasm considerably dampened. The henchmen glanced blankly at each other and then back to The Which, who offered no addendum. Finally, the elder guard cautioned a suggestion in a tone both hopeful and helpful, "Can we cut him just a little?"

"With my blessing."

The guards drew their swords. The soldier bolted. He stuttered first left, darted right and then waffled into a feeble backpedal. The Tree was at his back, and before him, beyond the advancing henchmen, there was nowhere to run. The predatory trio fanned out, blocking any possible avenue of escape. Within moments they closed the gap and moved to within grasping distance of the Indiran.

Clutching the Tinderbox protectively to his chest, the soldier suddenly found himself in a spastic game of keep-away. He dodged and ducked, changing directions in a jerky jig that kept him just out of reach of his pursuers. It wasn't long before he was narrowly evading the aggravated swipes of their swords.

The circle of evasion grew smaller and tighter, and The Which could barely follow the frenzy of flying limbs and weapons. An angry thrust of the younger guard's blade hummed past the prince and nearly impaled the guard's elder partner. In the apologetic pause that followed, the Indiran scrambled away, only to run face-first into the chest of the Leftist.

After a grunt and an unsuccessful grab from the unarmed brute, the soldier skittered backward. The elder guard was poised to strike, and he brought the hilt of his sword decisively down onto the crown of the soldier's head. The Tinderbox flew from his hand.

The eyes of The Which locked onto it like a drowning person intent on the shore. The box soared some distance in a tumbling arc and descended into a jumble of jagged rubble near the Tree.

The front of the box scraped a rock upon landing, yellow sparks flashing briefly.

The soldier struggled to raise himself on wobbly arms, writhing weakly at the feet of the panting guards. They looked eager to deliver a few more vindictive blows, but their prisoner gave up the fight and flopped feebly into the dirt.

Inelegant for perhaps the first time in her life, The Which scrambled madly after the liberated box, her robes flapping loosely about her, arms extended with fingers splayed and grasping. She plucked up the Tinderbox triumphantly. Her vindication turned quickly to confusion and concern.

A single red light above the striker panel on the box blinked ominously. Trepidation trickled through her just before she heard a sound—a vibrating buzz, low and threatening like the warning of a carnivore—and it came from the direction of the fallen soldier.

She turned in time to see her entourage backing slowly away from the fallen soldier. They stared not at the prisoner, but at a space in the air just above him. It took The Which a moment to pinpoint their focus.

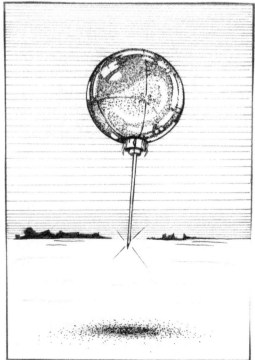

The source of the disquieting growl was a small orb floating inexplicably and protectively over the inert Indiran. Two razor-thin blades erupted suddenly from its sides. The Which fled in panic, the Tinderbox clutched to her bosom.

She glanced over her shoulder as she ran and then stopped some distance away, helplessly transfixed. Seemingly without reason, her henchman gyrated in a bizarre pantomime;

their arms and swords flailed against the air; their feet raised ribbons of dust as they jerked and jigged. Then, like a silver thread woven into an ornate tapestry, unnoticed and then unmistakable, she identified the orb as it zipped around her men. Beneath the incessant buzz, she could suddenly discern their strident cries of pain. Geysers of red mist billowed about them.

Their clumsy counterattacks, their pitiful attempts at protection, all were futile before the fury of the orb. The elder guard lost an arm; the younger one, his head. The towering mass of the Leftist was felled, his hamstrings severed. Within moments, the surgical onslaught was complete, and the victimizers, now victims, had collapsed into quivering heaps, soon to be still. The Which knew that she was next.

Before hysteria could root her to the spot, she dashed away. She ran aimlessly, turning down avenues at random, her eyes frantically searching for a door, an alcove, any place that might provide sanctuary. But the abandoned buildings were pitiless and without providence. Her terror intensified as her options dwindled.

The low, menacing growl had escalated to a roar, and it reverberated off the archaic walls, making it impossible to locate the whereabouts of the murderous orb that was no doubt hunting her. The Which's desperate whimpers punctuated her gasping attempts to find breath, but she dared not pause to recuperate.

A silver streak appeared in her periphery and she knew that the orb had found her. An involuntary shriek escaped her, and she stopped, cowering, her head swiveling from side to side. She caught a glimpse here, a glimmer there—reflections cast fleetingly on buildings slashed with hard shadows.

The orb was circling her. She turned and turned until she was disoriented and dizzy. White spots flashed before her eyes, confusing her further and exacerbating her sense that the orb was all around her. The maddening sound was fraying her nerves and flaying her rationality.

"Get away from me!" she cried. Even through her terror, The Which was livid with a sense of injustice. She was in possession of the Tinderbox now, why was she not the master of the orb?

Still it stalked her, and it was clear that its intent was not benevolent.

The Which stumbled over rubble and tumbled down hard in the center of the deserted street. She writhed in her tangle of robes, her lustrous, long hair falling into her face. Still she clung tenaciously to the Tinderbox with both hands, refusing to let it go. She managed to raise herself on one elbow, her ragged breath sawing at the dust-filled air.

She became aware of her raspy panting and bit down on her panic. She then realized something else; it was the only sound she could hear. The diabolical buzz had blissfully abated. The Which looked up, hopeful.

She screamed.

True to form, the orb had appeared out of nowhere and hovered just before her face. The Which cringed but couldn't help but notice with a blink of optimism that the razor-sharp wings had disappeared and that the orb had reverted to its spherical silhouette, like a benign bauble. She heard a subtle *click* and she cringed again.

A long needle popped out of the bottom of the orb and rotated slowly toward her like the small arm on a timepiece. It stopped when it was pointing directly at her face, and The Which knew that her time had come. She only had a moment to hope that there would be no pain.

The orb lunged forward, sending the needle into the polished amber stone embedded in The Which's forehead. It penetrated the gem easily, little more than a puff of shrapnel and a spark to mark its passing. Her skull and brain provided even less resistance.

ELEVEN

A COMET CREASED the blackness of space, streaking past the jagged bulk of the planet Indira. King Xander the Firm, watching through a telescope, barely registered the celestial phenomenon, seeing it as little more than an irritating distraction, searching instead for less brilliant but more foreboding heavenly bodies. His straining eyes caught sight of them, the three moons of Indira just emerging from beyond the half-curve of the broken planet. Though he knew that they were inevitable, the sight of them filled him with fresh terror. He stared so intensely that he could see the slow rotation of the planet that held them tethered and turned them toward their predestined places in the Aurora Constellation.

An immense scraping sound filled his head. It was as if the very planetary plates were shifting beneath him, groaning in cataclysmic complaint. He knew it was only his imagination, but he imagined that it was the sound that had preceded the Great Schism and heralded a world torn asunder. King Xander, ashen and shaken, reluctantly tore his eye away from the massive telescope.

"I can feel the heavens moving," he muttered to himself, turning to the audience of three gathered in the observatory.

Queen Nor, Chancellor Olaf and The Why of Mist Tier all looked up expectantly. They had stood quietly while Xander had peered pensively through the high-powered lens of the telescope. Now, they almost looked bored.

Actually, it's worse, Xander realized. They were humoring him; looking at him as if he were a child. They were hovering in that neutral place, waiting to see if he would do something worthy of their presence or if he would throw a tantrum that would send them all scurrying. It was all there in their bland expectation, and he hated them for it. He might have to entertain a bit of patronizing from his wife, but, blast it all, the other two were supposed to be his lackeys.

How dare they judge me! he thought, anger supplanting his desperation.

How can they not understand? The Prophecy named him, not them. He was the target. He was the inevitable victim if they could not forfend fate.

To make matters worse, their disregard...no, their *disrespect* was putting the kingdom at risk. It was treasonous. How obvious did it have to be? He was the kingdom and the kingdom was he. He was the Chosen One. The end of Xander the Firm was the end of their way of life. Their culture. Maybe even their very existence.

Xander turned away from his advisors in disgust. He felt very much alone. He thought of the young warman from Back Tier, the last would-be savior to have failed, like all those before him who had been dispatched to the Tree. But the king was not thinking of the tragic loss of a young and noble life; he had never even met the warman or known his name. Rather, he was confounded by the unfairness that kept this accursed anticipation hanging over his head.

Should he simply order up another champion? And another? He could fill up time and space with Manolithic bodies and still not prevent the arrival of Aurora. Why not just overrun the Tree with his army? Hammer it with HEXes until it was disemboweled and its secrets revealed? But he couldn't because the Prophecy had prescribed otherwise.

The Prophecy had set a course as unerring as an orbital path, and to deviate from it would be to invite disaster. Still, disaster was already on its merry way to his doorstep. A night wind blew into the opening through which the massive telescope protruded, and it ruffled Xander's hair and his concentration.

"The alignment is near," he said. "Is there nothing more that we can do?"

The Why stood with his head bowed. "We cannot stop time, m'lord."

Olaf took a confident step forward.

"There are many turns in the road to destiny, sire." Olaf spoke smugly. "Have faith. Perhaps an unseen hand is at work."

"Easy for you to say," Xander replied, forlorn. It seemed that every social interaction of late was terribly taxing, and it left him feeling weary to his core.

The king raised his hand to his haunted and haggard face. He absently stroked his bedraggled beard and discovered it still damp from dribbled terrazka. He lurched suddenly and purposefully out of the observatory, remembering that he still had a half-empty bottle.

* * *

No one was surprised by the monarch's sudden departure. They all knew the reason. The chancellor watched him slouch away with the smooth, blank expression that comes from constant friction, but the queen watched Olaf.

She sensed an unusual serenity about him that struck her as odd given the circumstances. She had long viewed him as the very embodiment of a busybody: incessantly busy with his plans and strategies, busy with the constant custodial care of the king, busy with everyone else's business. So much so that Nor often judged that his reach exceeded his grasp. But now, Olaf had no business being calm. His empty-handed optimism hinted at something else afoot.

"This Prophecy has consumed him. He can think of nothing else," the queen said, as much to herself as to the room.

She turned to the two men, noticing immediately that Olaf looked away. The Why still had not looked up, but the queen cared little for his complicity.

"Your thoughts, Chancellor Olaf?" Queen Nor asked suddenly.

It had the desired effect. Olaf's head snapped toward her, a look of surprise and guilt on his face. It was obvious that his mind had been elsewhere, and the last thing he expected was for the queen to solicit his input. He stared at her blankly for a moment too long.

"Am I interrupting something?" the queen continued pointedly.

"Of course not, Your Highness." Olaf chuckled. He recovered his composure with an obsequious smile. "I was simply lost in thought. Concerned for the well-being of our king. I merely wish to remain a calming presence for him."

The queen raised a doubting eyebrow and stepped closer to him. "Believe me when I say, Chancellor, that your concern is beginning to concern me. And *calm* is not a word that anyone I know would ever attribute to you."

"You're very rarely calm," The Why offered helpfully.

After a poisonous sideways glance at The Why, Olaf tilted his head toward Nor in seeming sincerity and deference. "My Queen, you misunderstand me," he said. "I am not complacent. I have come to believe that this will pass, so I optimistically plan for the day after the accursed constellation."

Queen Nor studied the chancellor's face, but he was once again unreadable. There was honesty in Olaf's eyes, but even that left the queen feeling uncertain. She could not find reason to refute his statement, so she had to take him at his word, as glib as his position seemed to be. She had caught him out once. She doubted he would allow her to do that again. At the very least, she could make sure he knew his place.

"Well, then, in the meantime, Olaf, perhaps you should concern yourself with calmly clearing the king's liquor cabinet," Queen Nor sniped. "If Xander drives himself to madness, then he will fulfill the Prophecy all by himself."

The queen did not wait for a response. She left the observatory and turned in the opposite direction from that of Xander.

TWELVE

EVERSON SMELLED TOBACCO. Not the acrid assault of smoke, but the warm, rich aroma of well-cured leaves. It was the first sensation to pierce the heavy cowl of his unconsciousness, even before he became aware of the insistent yellow glow that permeated his closed eyelids.

His eyes fluttered open only to find his field of vision almost entirely blocked by the Tinderbox. Then, like a hanged man jerking to a stop beneath the gallows, the orb dropped into the scant space between him and the Tinderbox. He was not yet beyond flinching at such antics, and the little surge of adrenaline he felt cut through the lingering effects of sleep. The orb hovered a hair's breadth from his face, in a fashion now familiar to Everson, with little consideration for his personal space. It seemed to stare at him in concern, and he had the undeniable impression that it was assessing his health.

Then it winked out of sight, leaving Everson to stare at the Tinderbox. Obviously, the orb had returned it to him, emphasizing, it would seem, his ownership of it. The last thing he remembered before passing out from pain was an annoying buzz filling his head, matching the fuzziness of his eyesight. At the time, he recalled, he had thought it was a by-product of the blow to his head delivered by the elder guard. Now he realized, it must have been the orb, but how it had been summoned, he didn't know. How long had it then hovered over him, guarding him? And what else had it done?

After a moment of hazy recollection, Everson realized that something was not quite right. It wasn't just the quality of the light, it was its direction. It was low, as it had been when he passed out, but now it came from behind him with the unmistakable starkness of morning. Everson had been unconscious for the entire night.

He roused himself gingerly, acutely aware of his injuries and grudgingly thankful for the military conditioning that had honed his resilience. Rising stiffly to his feet, Everson glanced at the enigmatic Tinderbox and, once again, mused wryly that instructions would have been helpful.

"Destiny omniscient guides," he snorted. "Omniscient, maybe. Guidance, no." He scooped up his dubious prize and returned it securely to his satchel.

Now that he was standing, the orb's industry was painfully evident.

Everson eyed the carcasses of his captors from a grateful distance. He took no satisfaction in their deaths, even though it meant his freedom. Only recently they were men, and now they were nothing more than anomalies to the landscape, grotesque mounds.

Despite his better judgment, he approached them. As he neared the dead men, he wondered if his eyesight was still affected by the blow to his head. It appeared as if the fallen forms were rippling with movement.

Standing before the bodies, Everson was reminded of the Indiran military mantra: Indira in Dignity, Indira in Death. Everson doubted that any Indiran, even King Raza the Forty-Seventh himself, could bring dignity to these deaths. Overnight, the men had been reduced to moldering meat. Their flesh, what was left of it, was oozing and chewed. An uncountable number of insects had found the bodies and currently engaged in a feast.

Everson thought of a sunlit classroom where he had been the only pupil. The room had been warm, making it easy for his mind to wander, and he remembered thinking it was a waste of his time to learn about creatures that he would probably never see. Fortunately, because of Madame Irina's enthusiasm and insistence, Everson, the reluctant student, now knew what he was looking at.

Manoliths called the insects decaydas. Like the verms Everson had encountered at the Tree, the description of these insects had come from Indiran battlefield survivors. Carrion eaters, it was reported that a swarm of them could clean a man-sized carcass in little more than a day. Everson was a believer. The decaydas before him were voracious.

No wonder the Leftists cleared the battlefield at the Grand Schism so quickly, he thought. *There would have been nothing left to honor.*

The decaydas were twice the size of one of Everson's newly acquired gold coins and, similarly, their metallic shells glowed golden in the morning light. The shells were split down the middle and would intermittently flex open to reveal translucent and heavily veined wings underneath. Wicked pincers twitched around their mandibles.

Fortunately for Everson, the majority of the gore caused by them was masked by the mass of insects, their bodies forming a raised and writhing mosaic that was almost beautiful in a way.

Nevertheless, Everson turned away.

He scanned the desolate space between the ruined buildings for any sign of The Which, but she was nowhere to be seen. The fact that he was once again in possession of the Tinderbox seemed evidence enough of her fate. The orb knew no quarter.

Still, The Which had represented his only real human interaction on this planet, and her treatment of him had been civil if not at times kind. And, though it might have been a ploy, she had spoken of peace, which was a concept that was sorely unconsidered in this conflict. No, he didn't wish death upon her.

Searching for her would certainly be the moral thing to do, but Everson knew that if he found her alive, as improbable as that was, it might only result in him becoming a prisoner again. It was probably a thread better left not pulled.

With no place else to go, and a murmur of hunger in his mid-section, he set out for the nearby settlement of Front Tier.

Climbing a rocky rise halfway between the Tree and the outskirts of Front Tier, Everson clutched the satchel tightly to his chest to silence the telltale tinkle of coins ag-ainst the Tinderbox. He had initially sought out the higher ground to scan the terrain when the sharp sound of voices and the rhythmic rustling of organized movement had made him curious but instantly cautious. What he saw as he topped the ridge made him flatten himself against a nearby boulder to avoid detection.

An entire battalion of Manolithic warmen stood in formation beneath the blazing suns. Their swords flashed like the sparkling ripples on a lake as they moved with crisp precision, snapping from stance to stance in a choreographed kata of martial exer-cise. Their attention was focused on a rigid officer who paced before them, barking commands, his military bearing unbend-ing even in the heat. The aggressive preparation was a powerful reminder to Everson that there were still battles left to wage.

If Everson knew his father and Commander Giza at all, he knew that they would not long abide the defeat handed to them at the Grand Schism. They would retaliate, swiftly and decisive-ly, and with nothing less than the overwhelming vehemence of a full-scale invasion. Regardless of the Prophecy, King Xander would soon find his very existence in jeopardy, and it would have nothing to do with the stars.

Everson cared little for Xander's welfare. Rather, his heart was with the infantry, who he knew would certainly be the first line of defense. Looking at the young men below him with their fierce expressions and their mock-battle posturing, he knew the cost to both sides would be staggering.

Here again was a crossroads. Self-preservation screamed at him to simply slink away and take his chances in the desert as a deserter and fugitive. But Everson would like to think that cowardice was not in his character. He could certainly be accused of apathy, but, then again, he had never in his young life been burdened with responsibility for anyone other than himself.

Now he was beginning to embrace the idea that he could possibly avert massive devastation with one master stroke, and that the answer might be contained in a little box of tobacco. He simply had to figure it out. If not, ironically, everything could go up in smoke.

A large temporary barracks had been erected along with other outlying buildings in a makeshift bivouac. From behind the barracks, out of his sight, he could hear the odd warbling of livestock. He assumed that it must be the restless cries of their cavalry mounts. Their birduns.

A breeze brought a whiff of gaminess to his nose, confirming what he suspected. A corral was concealed behind the boxy structure. Aside from the fact that he was mildly curious to see one up close—after all, one had knocked him senseless in the battle—Everson concluded that a birdun would be a welcome alternative to walking in this oppressive heat. He had to have a plan, he knew that. But it was difficult to impossible to formulate a strategy with little practical knowledge of his surroundings and even fewer tools at his disposal. The one thing that he did have, the Tinderbox, was obviously much more complicated than meets the eye, and Everson didn't feel at ease enough, exposed as he was, to pause and figure it out.

Contemplating the immensity of it all—the war, a prophecy, whether he would ever get home—was overwhelming, so the soldier decided it was best to get back to basics. How would he survive? Evasion in enemy territory was one of the first lessons a nucruit learned. Finding sustenance, food and water, was a close second. Continuing toward Front Tier, all things considered, seemed to be the best idea, and providence had just provided him the means to get there, a corral full of birdun.

Besides, how hard could one be to ride?

THIRTEEN

TWO SWEATING WARMEN carried buckets of grain to the long feeding troughs that lined one side of the corral. Everson had watched them make a number of trips already, their dispositions souring each time. Hearing snippets of their conversation, he gathered that this was their punishment for sloppily made beds at this morning's inspection. To add insult to injury, the two warmen often looked jealously to the front of the barracks, where the sounds of their comrades engaging in battle drills could still be plainly heard.

"We're not flaming scullery maids!" Everson heard one snap to the other. "How's this supposed to teach us to kill Indirans?"

The other one grunted in agreement. They were so mired in their misery that they didn't notice Everson lying flat on the ground on the other side of the corral. The warmen emptied their buckets into the last trough and tossed them down carelessly where they stood, clearly not having learned a lesson about discipline. They sauntered off, scrubbing the sweat from their faces with grubby hands, in no hurry to receive their next bit of busywork.

After they had disappeared around the corner of the barracks, Everson slithered under the lowest rail of the pen and proceeded through the milling birdun in a stealthy crouch. Those lucky beasts who had eaten first now gravitated toward the back of the pack, trying to muscle their way past the rest of the herd who hungrily pushed forward.

Pummeled by a flapping wing, Everson couldn't help but wonder how a simple wooden pen, open to the air, was supposed to detain a creature that could fly. Then again, he didn't know much about birdun. They quickly gave him a glimpse into their personality.

The beasts nearest Everson were skittish and shied away. Their long necks undulated, nostrils flaring. The bulbous eyes on the sides of their heads bulged indignantly at the intrusion. Worse, they began to bray and bleat in a high-pitched warble that was sure to attract attention.

Everson discovered fast that waving his arms to silence them only scared them more. Sure enough, it was only moments before Everson heard an angry bellow coming from around the barracks. He barely had time to drop to the ground before one of the beleaguered warmen reappeared.

"Shut your flamin' snouts! You been fed!" shouted the warman, seemingly as eager as Everson not to invite inspection. The warman's presence only seemed to raise the volume of the birduns' braying, as if they were trying to alert their keeper to the stranger in their midst. The warman didn't take the hint. He threw his hands up in disgust and left.

Everson was on his hands and knees, peering beneath the belly of a beast until he lost sight of the warman through a tangle of shifting legs. He was just about to rise when a nearby hissing sound froze him in place. It was followed by a slight but sudden impact that made him flinch. He felt something warm and steady drilling away at the top of his head. The smell was instantly recognizable. His camouflage was pissing on him.

Everson recoiled and stood quickly, shaking his head violently and swatting at his hair as if it were on fire instead of dripping with birdun urine. He looked up angrily as the guilty birdun lowered its long neck to see what the fuss was all about. Everson noticed right away that this particular birdun had an odd patch of white fur atop its brow, like a crown. It also wore an expression of such curious innocence that Everson's anger dissipated, and he almost laughed.

"Thanks," he muttered and began to elbow his way once again through the throng.

After an exceedingly close communion with the herd, Everson finally reached the gate. He slipped open the simple rope latch and sidled out of the pen, keeping a wary watch for war-men. Turning to close the gate, he discovered the white-capped birdun standing expectantly behind him. Everson shook his head.

"You piss on me and now I'm marked as property?" he asked.

Even so, he held the gate open. The birdun obediently walked out. Cheekiness aside, this one would work as well as the next.

"Come on, friend," he said. "Let's go for a ride."

There was nothing left to do but commit. Everson grabbed the scruff on the birdun's neck and launched himself onto its back. The response was immediate and explosive.

Warbling loudly in protest, the birdun bucked in a circle before blasting into the sky. Everson's fear of heights gripped him in his gonads as the birdun commenced a vertiginous vertical climb with no sign of levelling off. He couldn't help himself. He glanced down and watched as his distance from the ground grew from "painfully injured" to "no doubt dead."

Finally, the birdun curtailed its climb, and Everson relaxed slightly, thinking that the mad ascent was over. Then the beast banked hard to the left, and Everson squawked in surprise and renewed terror. He panicked, wrapped his arms around its serpentine neck, and held on for dear life.

That only seemed to irritate the beast more. The birdun banked just as maniacally in the opposite direction, and Everson very nearly threw up. He tried squeezing his eyelids tightly shut, but it didn't really help. He could hear himself screaming like a child and once again questioned the good sense of any universe that would choose him as a champion.

He opened his eyes just in time to see the birdun dip its head and twist its neck into an impossible diving corkscrew. Everson felt his rump overtaking his shoulders, and suddenly the reassuring bulk of the beast beneath him was gone, leaving him dangling from its neck.

Everson was losing his grip, fast.

To make matters worse, his weight was forcing the creature into an unnatural and untenable flight posture, and Everson realized that his frantic struggles might only succeed in pulling

them both down. He swallowed his panic and forced himself to focus. With an effort that made his midsection cramp, he kicked his legs upward and regained his seat.

Breathing hard, he clung to the beast in a full-body hug. Everson was more grateful for the coarse and smelly fur against his cheek than he ever had been for the fine linens of his royal bedroom.

Even so, Everson cuffed the creature hard on the back of its white-capped head. "Cut it out!" he shouted. A bit of discipline went a long way, as he'd learned from Master Abel.

The violent gesture seemed to shock the birdun, and it coughed out an annoyed bleat. Everson flinched himself when the creature's head twisted around unnaturally to look him in the eye with an offended glare. Still, his reprimand had the intended effect of jarring the beast back into a sense of obedience and duty. With a shake of his head and one last petulant huff, the birdun straightened out, both figuratively and literally, and proceeded to fly straight and level.

"There you go," Everson said, tentatively stroking its white tuft. "Now we understand each other."

Finally, with the birdun's powerful wings flapping in a constant but controlled rhythm, Everson relaxed as much as could be expected and looked forward to the uncertain distance.

Everson soon came upon the jagged ziggurats of Front Tier, and his birdun circled as if to descend. The prince wiggled vigorously in his seat, knowing no other way to let his mount know that he didn't want to land. He had intuited while they flew that left and right could be achieved easily enough with a tug on the neck and a nudge of the knees, but up and down required a different direction altogether.

Given the close proximity of the Manolithic bivouac, Everson feared that Front Tier would be swarming with warmen and would not make for a suitable or safe haven. Better to proceed to Middle Tier, thereby putting distance between himself and the battalion. The birdun struggled a bit more, but Everson convinced it to fly on.

Now, after soaring over the fractured spine of a small mountain range, the vista opened up to them. Everson could see the settlement of Middle Tier sitting like a blemish in the middle of a great expanse of flat and untouched desert. So isolated was the tier that it was clear that no military installations had cropped up, and the soldier grew optimistic at his chances of remaining undetected.

Approaching the remote settlement, Everson began to wonder why it was here in the first place. Not only was the terrain unforgiving and unaccommodating, there was no apparent evidence to justify the genesis of a township. There was no water that would have given birth to a port. There was no indication of mining or, for that matter, any other obvious natural resource that would have drawn a community to this location.

Everson surmised that Middle Tier must certainly refer to the Middle of Nowhere, since the place seemed to have been randomly dropped from the sky.

No matter. The buildings meant people, and people meant food and water. He would scurry like a verm and scavenge what he desperately needed to survive. And, by the Light of Femera and Amali, he might even stumble across some inspiration that would give him a clue as to his next step in this crackpot crusade.

Everson was just about to lean forward to urge his mount downward, but the birdun was already inclined toward their destination. He noticed with more than a little concern that the birdun was picking up speed.

As eager as he was to be back on solid ground, the velocity of this descent seemed to fly in the face of safety. It was rapidly resembling a fall.

His eyes on the fast-approaching desert floor, Everson started to lean slowly backward as if the creature came equipped with a reverse gear or, better yet, brakes. He alternately repeated "no" and "whoa" with rising urgency and volume, but the birdun was nonresponsive.

Everson was now fully supine along the back of the birdun, his boots up around its ears. He pulled back for all he was worth, but he feared his only reward would be two fistfuls of birdun mane. His mount would not be deterred from its precipitous downward dive.

Everson braced himself. A crash landing was imminent.

Within spitting distance of the ground, the headstrong birdun flexed his massive wings until they billowed like wind-filled sails. His forward momentum came to a head-snapping stop. Another flap of his powerful wings raised a dust cloud and sent the creature careening back skyward.

Everson did not go along for the ride. He was jettisoned from the back of the beast and flew, arms and legs flailing uselessly. He hit the ground hard and skipped like a stone upon a pond. He flopped to a dusty stop on his back just in time to see the white-tufted birdun pass overhead, unencumbered but trilling and warbling as if in effort to have the last word.

Everson lay on his back for a moment, catching his breath and considering the now empty sky. Miraculously, nothing seemed broken.

"For the love of Light..." he grumbled. "It's barely worth trying to stay alive."

FOURTEEN

THE REPETITIVE RAUCOUS caws of echrow birds kept Everson skulking by the wooden fence, fearful that their clamor would call the farmer to the field. Like him, the flock was there for the crops and would not be inclined to go away any time soon. After another grumble from his belly, the soldier decided that the insistent din was consistent enough to be dismissed and that no alarm had been raised. He slipped between the wooden rails.

Keeping a watchful eye on the adjacent farmhouse, Everson scurried into the field, his battered body protesting each hunched step. The manicured and uniform rows of plants grew only thigh high, and the soldier dared not stand erect in direct view of the farmhouse windows. Even the casual eye would be drawn to him as to a scaffold against the sky. Accordingly, Everson did not venture far into the field and knelt quickly, giving relief to his aching body.

He inspected one of the peculiar plants nearest to him. The royal purple leaves were large, gleaming with a waxy sheen in the late afternoon glow. Thick yellow veins radiated out across their broad surfaces like fingers splayed on a skeletal hand. Touching one of the leaves, Everson noted that they were coarse and fibrous, almost as if they were cloth instead of vegetation.

He gazed out across the field, and the carpet of purple put him in mind of his mother's salon in Agrilon, where he used to play as a child. He quelled a momentary twinge of nostalgia.

Everson tore off a portion of leaf and popped it into his mouth. He had only chewed once when his face twisted into a grimace of disgust. The taste was not only bitter, it was exceedingly salty, as if the plant had pulled nothing but minerals from the inhospitable ground. The crops seemed more fit for fabric than food. He spit out the barely chewed mouthful and was just about to scrub his tongue on his sleeve when he felt the unmistakable burn of a very sharp blade being pressed against his neck.

"The food is under the dirt. But you'll never taste it," a gruff voice grumbled from behind him.

Everson raised his hands slowly. "I can pay for it," he hurriedly assured the unseen assailant. He considered the small fortune stored casually in his satchel, and he finally acknowledged that the DOGs might indeed be omniscient. Everson then decided to brashly press his lack of advantage.

"Unless you're the type of person who would rather kill an unarmed man," he said.

"A thief, you mean," came the retort, and then nothing more but the persistent pressing of the blade.

"Please, sir, I'm starving. I got left behind on Mano after the battle of the Schism..."

"A battle? I haven't heard of any battle," the voice growled.

Everson took a slow breath, mindful of the edge of the blade and the edginess of the man who held it. "It's how I came to be here. Believe me, it certainly wasn't my choice. Just as it wouldn't be my choice to take something that isn't mine. As I said, I would very much like to pay for some food. I have coins."

Everson waited for what seemed like forever after that. The pulse in his neck twitched rhythmically against the weapon as if annoyed by it. Finally, mercifully, the blade was removed. Everson let out a long sigh of relief and turned slowly to face his captor.

The farmer had taken a few steps back to put prudent distance between himself and Everson, who was obviously not Manolithic and was dressed like an enemy soldier. He was short but stout, dressed simply in well-worn clothes, a suspicious scowl peering out from between his unkempt ginger hair and untrimmed beard. The peasant might have been anonymous and unremarkable if not for the tumorous hump residing on his right shoulder. A gnarled and withered arm dangled uselessly below it, resembling more the limb of a tree than the limb of a man.

In contrast, his left arm was sturdy and well-muscled, no doubt from years spent performing solo duty in this very field. In his good hand, the farmer held a reaping tool, its curved and wicked blade still poised in threatening readiness.

"I mean you no harm." Palms up in submission, Everson slowly stood.

The farmer growled at him, "I don't have blood on my conscience, soldier. Can you say the same?"

Everson answered honestly, "I wish I could."

The farmer fixed his eyes on Everson, likely noticing how his gaze kept flitting to the man's worthless arm.

"Never mind my arm," the farmer said. "I'm still more than capable."

The farmer jerked his weapon curtly at the house, indicating that Everson lead the way. He did so obediently. At the threshold, the farmer pushed open the rough-hewn door and ushered him inside.

Everson glanced back as he entered, and he barely kept his jaw from dropping. The white-tufted birdun landed in the field behind the unsuspecting farmer and stared after Everson almost wistfully. It didn't take long, though, for the crops to demand his attention, and he dropped his head and snatched up a healthy mouthful of purple leaves. It clearly found the plants far more delectable than Everson had. Only then did it occur to Everson that he had interrupted the birdun back at the corral before the beast had had a chance to eat. That certainly would have earned him the right to be cranky.

Well, maybe both of us will get to eat now, Everson thought just as the latch on the farmhouse door clicked closed.

* * *

"Jonas?!"

Everson found himself staring at four Manolithic females: three teenaged girls and the stalwart woman who'd shouted the farmer's name, who was most likely their mother. It was immediately evident that the girls had gotten the best of both of their parents.

Everson was wounded by the instant mistrust and fear on the pretty girls' faces. He was used to a far more receptive reaction from the fairer sex. Then again, he had to remind himself, he was quite obviously the enemy. His uniform didn't come with an explanation or apology.

The single room was sparse but comfortable, imbued with a dignified hominess illuminated by numerous oil lamps. Beds occupied the corners while a large handmade table dominated the center of the room. A cluttered kitchen counter ran along the wall where the women stood, paralyzed in the process of preparing a meal.

The smell of cooking food made Everson's mouth water. He also noticed, with chagrin, the vegetables growing at the roots of the purple plants he'd tried, sitting on a sideboard, awaiting cleaning. Jonas, the farmer, pushed past him and approached the table, still brandishing his farm implement.

"I couldn't very well leave him outside for all of Middle Tier to see, now could I, Mare?" Jonas said.

Mare had no response for the rhetorical question. Their daughters dutifully looked down but continued to steal glances at the dark-skinned oddity.

Jonas turned toward Everson, exasperation deepening the lines on his ruddy and care-worn face. Everson, for his part, stood politely and completely at a loss, uncertain about the protocol, since he was certainly not a guest but not quite a prisoner either. For a protracted moment, there was nothing but the sound of a bubbling pot.

The farmer began to pace in the limited space, his long and unwieldy weapon threatening to overturn lamps and displace pottery. He grumbled under his breath. Something about misfortune being his birthright, if Everson heard correctly.

Jonas stopped pacing, looked hard at Everson, and appeared to make a decision. He tapped the table decisively with his weapon and said, "Sit down. You said something about payment for food?"

Everson cautioned a glance to Mare. This was obviously news to her, but, once again, Mare declined comment. Everson moved slowly to the table and held up his hands to illustrate his passivity.

"I have to reach into my satchel," he said.

Jonas wagged his weapon at Everson as if he could have possibly forgotten about it. "Slowly. I'll have no guilt if you take away my choice."

Everson delicately lifted the leather flap and slipped his hand into the satchel. Almost instantly, his fingers encountered the Tinderbox, and he paused. He still didn't know how to use the device, but he felt certain that any application would be far too potent, especially considering the restraint of his host. There were two dead guards and a Leftist back at the Tree as reminder that, left to its own devices, the Tinderbox could prove lethal if engaged. A shadow of distrust flickered across the farmer's face as Everson hesitated, so he bypassed the Tinderbox and grabbed a handful of coins.

He extracted his fist from the satchel and deposited four gold coins onto the table. He regarded the women and couldn't help a surge of satisfaction. Their anxiety had been replaced with unabashed awe. Everson felt himself nodding as if to confirm that the riches were real. It had been a long time since he had seen a purely joyful face. Jonas, on the other hand, looked deflated.

"Fair?" Everson asked in confusion, ready to retrieve more coins if necessary.

"I can't accept that," Jonas said, unable to take his eyes off the money.

There were audible gasps from his wife and daughters. They looked at Jonas, bewildered as if they had been rudely awakened from a brief but beautiful dream. Everson thought he understood. Jonas was overwhelmed by an amount that Everson merely considered adequate payment.

"I'm not looking for a bargain," Everson offered encouragingly.

"And I'm not looking for trouble," Jonas snapped, glaring defensively at Everson and then his family. "If Jonas the terranut

farmer suddenly shows up at market with such riches, the war-men will take notice. They'll ransack my home to know the rea-son why. I've given enough to the military."

Everson saw Mare nod out of the corner of his eye. He reluc-tantly but respectfully pulled back a single coin. The girls looked to their father. Jonas finally rested his weapon against the near wall and took the chair opposite Everson like he was ready to negotiate.

Everson waited while Jonas worried his beard with his good hand. After much consideration and with considerable effort, Jonas waved backhanded at the coins as if disgusted. His daughters' shoulders slumped a little further.

Removing another coin, Everson was prepared to stop and return it to the others and call it a deal. Though Jonas watched the receding coin with longing and regret, he didn't act.

Everson covered the pair of coins closest to him with his hand but didn't take them off the table.

Jonas eyed the remaining pair in the center of the table and slowly nodded. "I'll find a way to make that work. Mare."

The girls squealed. Mare dashed to the table and snatched up the coins before Jonas could change his mind. She huddled together with the girls, passing around the gold coins so that each could touch them, barely able to contain their excitement. Everson smiled and saw that Jonas allowed himself a thin one in return. Before the moment could get too cozy, the farmer rapped the table twice for attention.

"As good a cook as my wife is, you've still overpaid," he said. "Girls, set the man a place."

His daughters enthusiastically went to work, their initial fear forgotten. Everson returned the rejected coins to his satchel. The soft clink of metal on a mound of metal was unheard by the others, lost in the clatter of crockery and utensils.

Perhaps, Everson thought, *if this poor farmer had known the extent of my fortune, he might have accepted the initial offer.*

He knew that that wasn't the point. It wasn't what he could afford to spare, it was what they could afford to risk. He studied Jonas, who quietly watched his family. There was a curious expression on the farmer's face: relief, certainly, along with satisfaction at having provided for his family. But there was also the hint of something deeper that could not be righted with a sudden windfall of wealth.

As he considered this, one of the daughters brought him a small cup of water and he realized how parched he was. He downed it in a single gulp before it occurred to him that they probably didn't have much to spare. The understanding of their poor condition prompted him to ask, "What do you mean, 'You've given enough to the military'?"

The bustle at the counter subsided and Everson wondered if he had crossed a line. Jonas turned his gaze toward him, and the question hung between them like stale air. Everson could tell that he had not offended the farmer. No, he had done something much worse. He had summoned the man's sadness to the surface.

"Obviously, I was never fit to serve," Jonas said, his already deep voice taking on a darker timber. "Instead, they took my sons. I lost them both. One to the war and the other to the Tree. I still don't know why. It's left me to run this farm with nothing but my wife and daughters."

The eldest daughter was bringing Everson's plate to the table as her father spoke. Everson saw the almost imperceptible tightening of her jaw and the prideful elevation of her head at the mention of her and her sisters. But she said nothing. She placed the steaming plate in front of him, and Everson looked up to give his thanks, but she was already returning to the security of her mother's side.

"But I have to say," Jonas continued, clearly having seen his daughter's injured expression as well. "This family would've been ash without them. The girls work harder than the boys ever did."

A grateful smile grew upon the elder girl's face, and her cheeks flushed self-consciously. Mare gave her daughter's hand a loving squeeze.

"You have a fine family," Everson said, a little more at ease. "Thank you for allowing me in your home."

The aroma had been tantalizing him from the moment he had walked in the door, and he eagerly took his first bite. Jonas was wrong about Mare's cooking. The food was delicious, and Everson would have happily given his entire cache of coins for the meal.

"Why does your planet attack ours?" Jonas asked.

Mare gasped. She stepped toward Jonas, wringing her hands. "Jonas! Don't anger him."

"I can ask any question I want. It's my house."

The farmer's wife looked to Everson with tremulous concern, but she had no reason to be. It was an honest question that deserved an honest answer. Everson owed the man at least that in lieu of more money. He savored the bite in his mouth, chewing and swallowing it slowly. The meal might be taken back depending on his answer.

"My people believe that you are a threat to us," he said.

Jonas grunted. "You haven't spent much time on Mano, have you?" he said. "Take a look around. How is it possible that we are a threat?"

"I'm beginning to wonder that myself." He shrugged. "Sometimes you have to face the truth to know it."

Jonas looked evenly at Everson, then nodded in apparent agreement. Everson wondered if he could do the same. If anyone had a right to be bitter and disagreeable, it was Jonas. Everson could remember all too well the Manolithic mob that had wanted to kill him. He couldn't say that he held it against them, but it made the kindness of this simple farmer that much more impressive.

For the third time today, Everson's mind returned to Indira. There was a rolling meadow near the Palatial Pyramid that had once been beautiful and pristine. Unlike the Manoliths, the Indirans buried their dead, and the meadow had become a veterans' cemetery overrun with gleaming white headstones. When barely in his teens, Everson would sit on a hillside overlooking the meadow, trying to fathom the meaning behind the rows and rows of anonymous markers. In the end, it was the meadow itself that became a living, breathing entity to him. It was a ravenous monster with cruel white teeth that fed on bravery.

Jonas interrupted his thoughts and gestured to Everson's mostly untouched meal.

"We made a deal," he said. "You should eat now and leave before you bring any more peril to this home."

Everson nodded. He didn't really want to leave the warmth and relative calm after all he'd been through, but he couldn't refute the farmer's concerns. True, he had paid for his meal and a moment's peace, but it didn't seem quite enough to the prince.

"Let me offer you something else. May I?" Everson asked.

Jonas didn't answer and appeared a little put-upon, as if he had climbed a hill only to find another one. He looked to his family, clearly his compass in all matters. Mare seemed equally conflicted.

"I know that you're stalling, and I understand it. I do," Jonas began slowly. "There is nothing but death for you out there, and if I were you, I'd put it off as long as possible, too. I bear no malice toward you, soldier. It's just the wage of war. But that's not on my head or on this house. We've done right by you. Maybe it's best we leave it at that."

Everson smiled and looked the farmer in the eye. "I am very grateful, Jonas. For everything. You have shown me a great kindness. But if, as you say, my time is limited, then I would very much like to return the favor."

Everson looked at Mare and the girls to include them. "I would like for that to be your memory of me."

A silent discussion seemed to pass between Jonas and his wife while Everson waited politely. Finally, Mare's eyebrows went up and she shrugged as if to say, "What could it hurt?" Jonas wasted not a moment more and decisively extended his good hand as a signal for Everson to continue.

Everson loosened the pouch secured at his waist and dug inside with his fingers. He pulled out a couple of brown and wrinkled hydreeds and set them on the table, precisely where he had placed his last payment.

"You're a good farmer," Everson said. "You could farm these."

"What are they?" Jonas asked.

"May I have some water?" Everson knew it was easier illustrated than explained.

Intrigued, Jonas once again nodded to Mare. She wordlessly crossed to a homemade water still. There, she filled a small cup from the spigot and brought it to the table, returning to wait and watch alongside her daughters.

Everson was surprised to find himself excited, as if he had suddenly become the entertainment at a dinner party. He nodded his thanks to Mare and smiled openly at the girls, anticipating their stunned reactions to the hydreed. He finally got the blush to which he was accustomed.

Without further ado, he dipped his fingers into the cup of water, bringing immediate protest from Jonas.

"Don't waste it," he said. "It's all we have for drinking."

"Exactly."

Everson grinned and sprinkled the water on the hydreed. It literally leapt off the tabletop and expanded in midair with its signature percussive whump. Utensils and plates were sent clattering to the floor as the entire family jumped back in surprise. Everson almost laughed at their shocked expressions.

Jonas stood abruptly, tipping his chair to the floor. He stared at the bloated object still wobbling on his table with suspicion and awe.

"What in blazes?!" he exclaimed.

Everson reached out and hefted it to show that it was harmless. "It's called a hydreed. Just a few drops and it provides you with a hundred times the water you had." Everson gestured to the reaping tool left leaning against the wall. "Cut it in half."

Jonas retrieved the weapon and swiftly brought it down upon the hydreed. It sliced through the thing with frightening ease, and Everson was reminded that this very blade had recently been pressed against his neck.

He picked up a dripping half and handed it to Jonas. He gave the other half to Mare.

Jonas sniffed warily at his portion and took a tentative bite. His face registered instant astonishment. He took another, larger bite. Seeing his reaction, Mare quickly bit into hers and passed it to her daughters. Their expressions of delight were nothing less than effervescent, and Everson beamed with satisfaction.

"The plant grows in an area of Indira called the Asunder Chasm that is very like your Grand Schism, which is why I think the plants might flourish here. The hydreeds, when in this state." Everson raised one of the dried and wrinkled hydreeds. "Can be kept indefinitely. You can hydrate and use them, or you can plant them and grow more."

He put it back on the table. This time, he would not have his offer refused. The farmer regarded him with burgeoning under-standing and said, "A plant like this could be a real blessing to this planet."

"And make the person who grows them very rich in a very short time."

"Yes, but how would that person explain the introduction of a plant never seen on this planet before?"

Everson smiled. Jonas smiled back.

"You seem to be a very clever man, Jonas," Everson said. "I'm sure you'll think of something by the time the crop comes in."

Jonas looked to his family. Hope glimmered in their eyes. Then Jonas surprised Everson when he looked back to him, blinking rapidly against the rising moistness in his eyes.

"Generosity is a luxury here on Mano. Thank you." Jonas paused and then exhaled heavily. "I cannot harbor you here. It's not safe for you or for my family."

He lowered his eyes and his gaze fell upon the terranuts on Everson's plate. For a moment he looked dejected, and then his features brightened.

"But there is one place that can provide you refuge here in Middle Tier," Jonas said. "It might even be the safest place for someone like you on the entire planet of Mano."

FIFTEEN

THOUGH THE SHADOWS were long and the vendors' time short, the open-air market in Middle Tier still bustled with activity. Those Manoliths industrious enough to have stalls hawked their wares for all they were worth, determined to protect their place at the top of this economic food chain by squeezing out every drop of value from the day. Those less well-heeled walked the aisles with handfuls of trinkets or candies and were so bothersome that Jonas often wondered how they ever made a sale at all.

Meanwhile, the beggars, who were literally on the fringes, sat on the dusty ground with their hands and their cups extended, though their haggard faces showed little hope of getting them filled. Not for the first time, Jonas wondered how those poor unfortunates expected to receive anything from people who had little to nothing to give. Through the hubbub, Manoliths of every stripe were happy to give a wide berth to the massive bodine as it lumbered through the center of the square, pulling a cart driven by Jonas.

The bodine was a beast of burden, as large as the cart, and its thick brown hide with overlapping plates made it look like it was chiseled from stone. Jonas not only used his to pull his cart to market, he also found it useful in moving boulders and providing shade at lunchtime. Yet it was not the creature's size that sent people scurrying out of its way.

They were known to be docile and peaceful beasts, but they were also widely renowned for the rich, resonant emissions that erupted periodically from both ends. Anyone who had ever experienced this toxic fog firsthand never forgot it.

Jonas was in a foul mood, and it could not wholly be attributed to the tainted air he was forced to breathe. Earlier, Jonas had emerged from his home, preoccupied with the preparations for his perilous undertaking, only to find a lone birdun chewing a swath through his field. He had angrily chased the pest away, but the fact that it was there in the first place was vexing.

Birdun were herd animals and rarely traveled alone. Not only that, but wild birdun had long abandoned even the perimeters of urban areas. No, this particular creature had to be a deserter from the cavalry, maybe even from as far away as Front Tier, where the bulk of the birdun warmen were ensconced. Jonas added it to the long list of grievances he had with the Manolithic military.

Feeling on display atop his cart, Jonas had new cause to be ill-tempered. He was used to hard work. Quite literally, he single-handedly attended to the duties that his daughters did not yet have the experience or know-how to handle. He did all of this with stoic resolve. What he was not used to was the feeling of fear, and it made him angry.

He had valid reason to be so, for he was not just transporting terranuts in his cart.

Looking out over the horned head of his bodine, Jonas grimaced. It figured. The crowd before him parted to reveal two warmen walking down the center of the thoroughfare. They did not step aside. Rather, they looked directly at him and approached apace. Jonas was not one to lie, but he inwardly prayed that he had it in him to do so convincingly.

He reined his bodine to a stop.

Without discussion, the ranking warman approached the cart while the other stepped inexplicably to an adjacent market stand. He stole a basket and rudely dumped its contents. The hapless vendor standing there didn't protest. The warman then casually strolled to the cart as if shopping.

"Allowances," said the ranking warman, jerking Jonas's attention away from the back of his cart, where the other browsed the terranuts. Jonas looked down and read the name stitched on the breast of the warman's uniform. Rommel. The warman looked up expectantly, but Jonas could think of nothing to say. Instead, he mutely reached into his tunic with his good hand to retrieve his allowances.

"We need to requisition your produce for the garrison," Rommel explained, though it was already self-evident. The other warman busily grabbed the largest terranuts and placed them in his stolen basket.

"All of it?" Jonas croaked, sweat collecting under his ginger fringe of hair.

"Just give me your allowances, please."

Jonas produced a small metal card from an inside pocket of his tunic and handed it to Rommel. He glanced nervously over his shoulder. The bastard at the back was still happily collecting terranuts, and it was a big basket. Rommel swiped the card in an electronic device hanging from his utility belt. He quickly scanned the information displayed on a small screen.

"This isn't your day to deliver," Rommel said.

Jonas forced a chuckle, but Rommel didn't share his amusement. The warman's blank stare did nothing to reassure Jonas that this exchange would go well. If he was sent to rot in a military prison, his farm most certainly would be lost, and his family left destitute. This was the cost of a conscience.

"What can I say? My terranuts are the best." Jonas leaned forward and raised his eyebrows as if imparting privileged information. "The baron's ordered more."

To Jonas's immense dismay, Rommel seemed unimpressed at the mention of his patron. In fact, the explanation prompted the warman to examine Jonas's information more closely. Jonas grew more paranoid. He had nothing to hide, other than what was in his cart, but he didn't know what was contained on his account.

Given the current environment on Mano, Jonas didn't know what constituted treason or what would be just cause for detainment. He racked his brain, hoping desperately that his secret enmity for King Xander and his military had not caused him to commit some unconscious but recordable act of civil disobedience.

Meanwhile, there was always the very real chance that the warman at the back would dig deeper, convinced that the better terranuts lay at the bottom of the cart, and find Everson buried beneath them.

The plan to smuggle the Indiran had seemed quite sound sitting at Jonas's table. Unfortunately, they hadn't anticipated such a debilitating delay. If Jonas could not talk his way out of this situation and quickly, Everson could end up suffocated by vegetables.

"It says here you're the father of two warmen," Rommel said.

The statement took Jonas by surprise, and for an instant he was at a loss. He stammered and was forced to resort to the truth.

"Yes," he said softly. "Yes, I am, but my boys are gone…"

What else did they have on him? On Mare and his daughters? Jonas was a breath away from exploding and raging against an oppressive monarchy that had cost him his sons and kept him impoverished, when he noticed the look in Rommel's eyes. The warman's expression had softened ever so slightly. Jonas also thought he could detect a modicum of respect.

Jonas took a breath and spit out the greatest lie he would ever utter. "I'm honored to have sacrificed for Mano."

Rommel nodded once. He turned to the other warman, who had very nearly filled his basket.

"That's plenty," he said, handing Jonas back his card. "You're free to continue."

"Thank you. Enjoy the terranuts," Jonas replied, trying not to look overly relieved. He gathered the bodine reins in his good hand and flicked them once across the beast's broad back. The creature strained forward with a healthy blast from its backside, as if it were an engine starting. To Jonas, it was the sweet smell of success.

* * *

Tobias loved his clothes. He loved the way the fabric felt and how it made him feel. He reveled in the fact that he had multiple shirts, trousers and waistcoats and that he could combine them in different ways depending on his mood. He was proud that his garments were expertly tailored and that they fit his decidedly challenging physique to perfection.

Not everyone like him could possess such luxuries, and each day he felt fortunate. Tobias was a Leftist and a front-of-the-house Leftist at that, though he had only ever heard other Leftists use that term, usually because there was a certain amount of jealousy involved.

Considering all of that, Tobias was understandably annoyed when he opened the heavy wooden gates to Baron Ayers' estate and a farm cart rumbled through, trailing a powdery cloud of dust. Customarily, all deliveries were received at the kitchen entrance around back and the courtly Leftist would be spared such indignities. As he approached the cart, scowling and brushing the brown dust off his white sleeves, he recognized the harried deliveryman. It was Jonas, the terranut farmer, and he was a favorite of the baron who employed Tobias in this grand manor. Still, Tobias thought primly, just because one had the baron's affections didn't make it permissible to upend a well-established routine.

The gracious and spacious courtyard was sequestered by high stone walls, and there was ample room for the farmer to have parked his cart and his monstrous bodine out of the way, but, no, he had driven it nearly to the stately front entrance. Yet another reason for Tobias to be affronted. The Leftist was about to direct him anywhere but where he was when Jonas threw down the reins, swung his legs over the bench, and scrambled into the bed of his cart. Then, inexplicably, he started tossing terranuts aside as fast as his good arm would allow.

"I need to see the baron!" shouted Jonas without slowing his madcap clearing of produce.

Tobias quickly concluded that the man was unhinged. As terranuts bounced and rolled about his feet, the manservant tried to make sense of this unscheduled and unorthodox visit. The crazy farmer was creating havoc virtually on the front steps of the dignified mansion, a mess that Tobias himself was going to have to clean up.

"I can help," Tobias offered in a high-pitched but gentle voice as he tentatively approached the cart.

Jonas looked up, sweaty and obviously exasperated. He glared for only a moment before returning to his task, snapping at Tobias between his grunts of effort, "I said I need to see the baron, you marble-eyed moron! Now!"

Tobias was unused to being addressed in this manner, but his lifetime of privilege had not blinded him to the inherent differences between Manolith and Leftist. In his most self-congratulatory moments, he wondered if his elevated status might not put him on a level with someone like this lowly farmer, but he didn't like to get too full of himself. Regardless, he wasn't overly offended, at least not to a degree he would ever reveal. Besides, Jonas had always seemed benign, if not polite, and he must have some reason to abuse his produce so.

Tobias was about to comply with the farmer's demand when a mellifluous tenor kept him in his place.

"I admit, Jonas, that your terranuts are the best I've ever had," the baron said as he stepped from the house and into the courtyard, his long arms held wide in mock indignation, "But I can't have 'em for every flamin' meal!"

Though Baron Ayers was rich and titled, Tobias was always amazed that he seemed to care little for his appearance. His clothes were opulent, of the finest fabrics, but they hung on the tall man's lanky frame like rumpled bedsheets. The noble's narrow but pleasant face, still mirthful from his own joke, suddenly grew confused and concerned.

Jonas was not responding even though the man he had requested, a man whose very presence usually demanded immediate respect and deference, was now cautiously approaching the cart. If anything, the farmer was digging in his produce more manically than before. He was wild-eyed and sweating profusely, wantonly tossing terranuts hither and yon, audibly cursing his useless arm.

"Jonas? Have you gone mad?" the baron asked.

Despite his intimidating size, Tobias took a startled step backward as a dark young man exploded from under the terranuts where Jonas was digging. He popped up suddenly into a seated position as if he had been sprung by a lever, and he sucked in braying gulps of air. His hands groped at his back and scratched wildly; Tobias could only assume because the pressure from the load of vegetables had been immense and painful. All in all, it was quite the entrance.

Jonas flopped back against the side of his cart, spent. "Forgive me, Baron, I was preoccupied."

Baron Ayers stepped up to the cart, his mouth agape, staring in shocked disbelief at the young man who, Tobias could now plainly see, was wearing the uniform of an enemy soldier. Even though the courtyard was enclosed and highly private, the baron nervously glanced about for prying eyes. He lowered his normally boisterous voice to a near whisper.

"You're Indiran," he whispered.

"Barely," Everson replied, his breath only now slowing to normalcy. The Indiran turned to Jonas with a slight frown. "Jonas, do you transport manure in this cart?"

"Of course," Jonas replied, seemingly surprised by the question.

"Well, not to seem ungrateful," the soldier continued, "but you might have told me that before I chose to lie face-first on the planks."

Before the conversation could drift further afield, the baron turned decisively to his equally gob smacked manservant. "Tobias, get him to a room. Quickly."

SIXTEEN

THE THIRD-FLOOR GUEST room, with its quaint and inviting balcony, afforded a magnificent view of Middle Tier, and Everson was fascinated by his first real exposure to a Manolithic city. The geometric rigidity of the majestic ziggurats stood out defiantly against the fading light. The thatched and tiled roofs of lesser dwellings filled in the gaps. Everywhere, warm yellow windows dotted the blackness as evening gave way to night.

Everson imagined the activity behind those windows, the lives of people he would never meet. Meals were being set on tables. Soon, people would put up their feet, perhaps having a drink or a smoke, gratefully putting aside the demands of the day and recuperating for another. Children would be playing, or studying their lessons, or washing up for bed. Babies would already be asleep, milk from their mother's breasts crusting around their little mouths. It was not hard for the prince to imagine this exact scene occurring in countless homes on Indira, separated by the vast distance of space and ideology, but indistinguishable from the business of living as it was conducted here.

All people wanted the same thing. To live. To find love. To raise their children in peace. To fully realize and revel in the Divine Spark that had created them. Everson stood in the balmy blue evening of Middle Tier and wondered: *If kings knew the names of each of their subjects, would it make a difference?*

His eyes were drawn to movement. He tried to track the path of something in flight, almost indistinct against the rapidly darkening sky. After a moment, he recognized the shape of a lonely birdun. Everson wondered if it was his flighty, white-crowned friend. He presumed the beast would have returned to the pen and his brethren, but that particular birdun seemed to be a rebel.

Takes one to know one, thought Everson.

The creature appeared to be approaching, sailing lazily over the rooftops and quiet streets. Briefly, the soldier made a mental note of the lack of foot traffic after dark, and he wondered if there were some sort of curfew imposed because of the war. He strained to see if this birdun had a white crown of fur atop his head, but a knock at his door diverted his attention.

The baron's giant Leftist butler timidly pushed open the door and peeked inside. After a nod from the Indiran, he entered with a basin of water and a lush hand towel. Everson glanced at the bed between him and the Leftist. His satchel rested there, his money and the Tinderbox hidden inside, and he resisted the temptation to snatch it up. Instead, he crossed to the small table where the Leftist deposited the basin and towel.

"For washing," explained the Leftist in a soft, almost feminine voice.

Everson dipped his fingers into the water. It was warm. He knew that Jonas's family, and perhaps many on Mano, could never afford the luxury of using the precious commodity in such a fashion.

"Thank you," he said, and the Leftist turned to leave. "I'm sorry," the prince continued quickly. "What was your name again?"

The oversized man stopped, surprised. "My name?" he said. "Tobias."

"Thank you, Tobias."

The Leftist stood flummoxed for a moment. His big eyes blinked twice, the large black pupils disappearing briefly beneath the plump lids. Finally, he managed a feeble, "You're welcome."

Everson began to wash and Tobias stayed. He watched curiously as the dark-skinned young man meticulously cleaned his hands and then delicately addressed his face, taking care not to splash the table with water.

Reaching for the towel, Everson was amused by Tobias, who seemed to be scrutinizing him with intense fascination. "Am I doing this wrong or something?"

The Leftist blurted out, "Your skin. It's very dark."

Everson smiled. "Yes. You expected it to wash off?"

His smile faded a little when he realized he had been inadvertently correct. He patted his face dry and playfully raised the towel for inspection.

No reaction came from the manservant, except to ask, "Do all your people look this way?"

Everson recalled that The Which said the Leftists had "decreased mental capacity." *Maybe so*, he mused, *or maybe she had just never had an extended conversation with one.* To his thinking, it was a fair question and evidence of an inquisitive mind.

"Yes, lighter or darker, depending," Everson said.

"It looks strange," Tobias replied simply.

Coming from an albino giant with perpetually dilated eyes, Everson found it very difficult not to chuckle. "If you've never seen it, I suppose it does."

"I think I like it," Tobias said unexpectedly.

Everson reached up, way up, to place a comradely hand on the manservant's massive shoulder. "I'm glad, Tobias, because there's nothing I can do about it."

Finally, Tobias grinned in return and the prince was struck by how pleasantly it transformed his face. After all the anxiety he had endured to reach this place, Everson was pleased to have common ground with this peculiar host, even if it was just solidarity in their oddity.

Then Tobias said, "The baron will be expecting you for a meal."

* * *

After leading him on a serpentine tour that took them past innumerable guest rooms, sitting rooms, an impressive library and even a much-used art studio, Tobias ushered Everson into the extravagant dining hall. Baron Ayers was already present, waiting expectantly with his wife and a striking young woman Everson could only assume was their daughter.

"Young man, welcome." The baron beamed from his seat at the head of the table. "This is my wife, Baroness Carlotta, and our daughter, Miranda. Please sit."

"Thank you for your kindness," Everson replied.

He had brought his satchel with him, and he hung it on the chair nearest the baron opposite the pleasantly smiling women. Carlotta, like her husband, had an ease about her. Her long silver-streaked hair flowed luxuriously to her shoulders, and she twirled a lock in her fingers. Everson noticed paint under her unpolished fingernails.

Miranda, seated next to her, also seemed comfortable in her own skin—and beautiful skin it was. Her dark hair only accentuated the creaminess of her complexion and her arresting green eyes. She looked slightly younger than Everson. The blatant directness of her gaze prompted the prince to avert his attention to the walls instead.

Numerous works of art were on display in the great dining hall, many of them no doubt created by Carlotta's hand, but it was a dominating tapestry that hung behind the baron that drew Everson's interest. It was an artistic depiction of the Great Schism, the once joined planets of Indira and Mano separating in a starburst of fiery color, the escaping Astral Repatriation Communities ringing the bisected super planet in a stylized halo.

Everson was pondering the prominence and significance of the tapestry when his host gently interrupted his thoughts.

"You needn't have brought your satchel," the baron said. "I assure you, your belongings will be quite safe in your room."

"I didn't mean to imply mistrust," Everson replied quickly and then paused. This was the first interaction with his benefactor, and it would set the tone for whatever might follow. "I know that you've put yourself and your family at risk by taking me in. It's just that I have a few...personal items that I like to keep near me."

"Understood." The baron smiled, not pressing the point.

"I didn't get your name," Miranda chimed in, and Everson got the impression that she was unused to waiting long for anything.

"It's Everson," he said, happy to accommodate her. In all honesty, he was self-aware enough to know he was not without vanity, and he found Miranda's attention flattering.

"Everson," the baron repeated and glanced at his wife, a look not lost on Everson.

"It's a very nice name." Carlotta nodded and picked at a speck of paint under a nail. "Not common."

"A little more common on Indira, perhaps," Everson replied, though he had never actually met anyone with the same name.

It occurred to the prince, perhaps a little too late, that his name might actually have meaning to a family as erudite as this.

"Well, fortune has delivered you to us, Everson," the baron said, holding his arms out magnanimously.

Carlotta was still picking thoughtfully at her nails. She spoke without looking up. "May I ask what you would have done if Jonas had not brought you here? Obviously, you cannot feel safe here on Mano."

"I'm forced to admit, Baroness, that I'm not a very good soldier," Everson said. "I have no plan. I've just been stumbling blindly along, trying to survive."

"Fate works that way sometimes," Miranda contributed. She stared sweetly at him, her green eyes glittering.

"Miranda, don't be forward. If our guest had lighter skin, I'm sure he would be blushing," Carlotta quipped, finally looking up and offering an apologetic expression.

She need not have defended Everson's virtue. More than once as a teenager, he had succumbed to his pubescent impulses and had taken advantage of the more carnal offerings that his royalty had afforded him. In fact, he had become quite adept at identifying those dark-eyed girls who were willing as opposed to those who were merely flirtatious.

Everson could tell that Miranda hadn't yet, but that she certainly wanted to. As liberal as his host seemed, the prince did not doubt that nothing would turn him conservative more quickly than the deflowering of his daughter. Not surprisingly, Everson thought of Allegra. "Forgive my daughter." The baron chuckled. "She's always had a taste for the exotic. Gets it from me, I'd wager. Where is your home on Indira?"

"I come from the capital city of Agrilon," Everson said.

The baron nodded thoughtfully, as Everson had expected he might. Again came the meaningful glance between the baron and baroness. Everson wondered why he was edging toward transparency. Perhaps it was because the truth was simply less complicated, and he already had all the mystery he could handle hidden in his satchel.

"And what did you do there? Prior to becoming a soldier?" the baron asked.

Everson stared at the baron for a moment. The truth, a lie, neither would suffice, and neither would make him feel any better about himself.

"Nothing much, I'm afraid," he finally muttered.

Everson was suddenly awash with regret as his mind returned to Agrilon. *Nothing much* was an egregious understatement...

Another birthday, yet nothing had changed for young Prince Everson except for the suffocating expectations that grew along with his age. He felt like a hydreed in reverse. Instead of expanding into usefulness, he was contracting into a withered shell of himself to be kept in a state of perpetual readiness.

Most of the revelers had departed, leaving Everson with his closest cousins and friends in the Agrilon palace. The young men lounged on luxurious cushions, passing a water pipe and smiling appreciatively at the bevy of scantily clad girls who were gyrating for their entertainment as a combo of musicians played a stirring and seductive number. The prince sat among his mates, staring blankly into space, unaware of the suggestive smiles on the faces of the dark-skinned dancers.

The music came to a stuttering stop. The girls faltered and halted their dance, the smiles leaving their lips in sudden self-consciousness. Everson's entourage looked over their shoulders in irritated confusion, but the prince already knew what was coming.

King Raza and Queen Patra stood in the doorway.

"Leave us," King Raza commanded, splintering the guilty silence.

The exodus was instant. The young men scurried past the royal couple, telltale smoke trailing from their nostrils. The dancing girls bowed their heads in supplication and executed near comical curtsies as they fled.

The musicians noisily tried to gather their instruments, only to decide them best abandoned. Only Prince Everson remained motionless, sprawled on his cushions.

The king strode stiffly to confront him. Patra followed, looking more disappointed than angry.

"Still celebrating your birthday, I see," murmured the king.

"One only turns eighteen once," Everson quipped, not moving his eyes to his parents, much less anything else.

"It's been over a week, Everson." Patra sighed. "We have harvest festivals that don't go on as long."

Everson offered only a sullen twitch of his shoulders.

"Well..." Raza nodded. "If one is unencumbered by accountability or expectation, I suppose the party could go on forever."

Everson's unrepentant eyes met his father's, and he saw instantly that Raza was equally intractable. A glance at Patra's face, however, revealed an unexpected glimmer of remorse. Everson could tell that his mother was conflicted, caught in the middle, and he could not tell which of her loyalties would prevail. Patra's equivocation brought a fresh wave of resentment. He had always considered his mother to be his best friend.

Surely, the young prince thought, *she can recognize her own imprint in my resistance?*

For as long as Everson could remember, he had witnessed Patra's rebellion—her subtle but incessant mockery of the Wisened and their dogma, her disdain for pageantry, and her preference for the simple pleasures of the populace—all of the defiant little idiosyncrasies that were really nothing more than the unconscious efforts of a simple farm girl to retain her identity and individuality in the face of antiquated tradition. He had been her confidant and sounding board, and her opinions had taken root in a deep and resonant way. Queen Patra had supplied the framework upon which

the tendrils of Everson's discontent had found purchase and support. Now, the prince felt even more sullen and alone, recognizing that his mother was reluctant to reap the bitter fruit after she herself had planted
the seeds of his rebellion.

"This is how you prepare to be king?" Raza queried
loudly, likely thinking that Everson's darkening mood
was directed at him. "You waste your hours with your
layabout friends? You entertain your mind with nothing more than the gyrations of dancing girls?"

Everson sprang from his cushions, his face finally
defiant and spoiling for a fight.

"If I were looking forward to becoming Raza the
Forty-Eighth, I might agree with you," he snapped. "But
it's not a fate I welcome, Father."

"You have no choice!" Raza exploded. "You have only
responsibility."

"So you expect enthusiasm as well?"

"I expect you to know your place and act accordingly."

The queen gently put her hand on her husband's
arm. Everson and his father had been engaged in this
contentious dance for some time now, exchanging petty comments and recriminations almost daily, and it
was clear that Patra wanted to impose peace without
really choosing a side.

"Raza..." Patra intoned softly. "He doesn't have to
become king tomorrow. He's still a young man."

"But a man nonetheless. Not a boy. It's time he started acting like a man," the king countered, showing no
sign of softening.

Everson stepped forward assertively.

"And how do I do that?" Everson sneered. "Learn to
wage war? Continue to blindly enforce the will of the
four-hundred-year-old Wisened, who haven't changed
their clothes much less their minds in centuries? The

way the Razas do it, there isn't much to being king, as I see it."

"Everson, do not make it impossible for me to defend you," Patra cautioned.

But King Raza no longer seemed angry. Instead, his face had taken on the cold calmness of resolve, and that was infinitely more intimidating.

"There's no need to defend him," Raza said calmly. "There's no need for further discussion. Everson, you leave me no choice. You have no self-discipline, so you force me to impose discipline upon you. I have already spoken with Commander Giza. You're going into the military immediately. As you have so indulgently pointed out, you're eighteen now. Conscription age."

There was an audible intake of breath from Queen Patra, and Everson saw her midsection contract as if she had been punched in the gut. She quickly set her jaw, biting down on her emotion and the torrent of protest that Everson hoped would come. But, still, his mother refused to defy the king completely.

She regained her voice, but not, in Everson's estimation, her backbone. "Perhaps there is some interim step we can take."

"Baby steps are for babies, Patra," Raza said. "Our son has to grow up one way or the other."

Raza's and Everson's eyes were locked in an unblinking battle of wills. The prince, though stunned, refused to show remorse.

"You will be going into a unit with other nucruits so no one will know who you are," he said. "Commander Giza has been ordered to treat you like a common soldier. Maybe then you will appreciate the position that you so resent now..."

The food arriving drew Everson back to the present. Tobias was fastidiously overseeing the presentation. Not surprisingly, Jonas's terranuts were the centerpiece of the meal, since the baron now had a surplus of them. There were a variety of meats that Everson could not identify, but that didn't matter; they smelled delicious and looked roasted to perfection.

There was also a bowl of deep red manoberries, the fruit used to make the potent manoberry wine that accompanied the meal. Though the baron did not boast, he poured the wine with such care and pride that Everson assumed that both the orchard and the winery were housed on the baron's estate. Baron Ayers finished filling his own glass and raised it to Everson.

"Well...we'll see what we can do to get you back home safely," he said.

Everson sighed. "I'm not so sure that's what I want to do, Baron."

"You would choose to stay here on Mano?" Miranda chirped, her eyes suddenly aglow as she peered coquettishly over the rim of her wineglass. Everson made a mental note to track her consumption.

"There's nothing pulling me back to Indira. At least here, I might find purpose."

Miranda purposefully sipped her wine. Carlotta fixed Everson with a contemplative gaze and then nodded her thanks and dismissal to Tobias. The Leftist shooed the kitchen staff from the room, departing close behind them. Carlotta returned her attention to their guest.

"A noble thought, Everson, but you are not inconspicuous," Carlotta said. "I'm afraid your only mission for the time being will be to stay alive by staying out of sight."

The baron nodded as he served Everson a generous portion of everything. "The baroness is right. As usual," the baron added. "You're welcome to stay here indefinitely. Until the war is over if need be. Although, given the conditions here, I must say I'm surprised anyone would choose to remain."

Everson looked at his heaping plate, at his goblet full of wine, at the walls laden with art, and the easy elegance of the Family Ayers. It was not unlike his own existence, though now he was acutely aware of his privilege.

"Forgive me for saying so, Baron, but it looks to me like you live rather well," he said.

"Thank you, but I wasn't referring to my own home," the baron answered. "I was referring to the conditions for the people of Mano."

Miranda let out a long-suffering sigh. "Father, must we get political?"

"Why not? Everson wishes to stay here; he should know the truth," the baron continued, undeterred. "And, finally, I have someone other than my own family to talk to without fear of being turned in for treason."

"I've seen how some of your people have to live," Everson said and took his first bite of meat. The savory richness of the meat sent shivers of appreciation throughout his body. The prince gave a passing nod to his guilt of privilege, but it didn't stop him from taking a second bite.

"You've seen the boils but not the virus that causes them," the baron countered, draining his glass and refilling it. "We are cursed with a king who lives only for power. The power of the throne and the power that he can leech from this planet."

"Xander the Firm?" Everson asked as if it rang a distant bell. "I've heard of him."

In actuality, the reign of Xander the Firm was a much-studied subject in the Palatial Pyramid.

"Xander the Infirm, if you ask me," snorted the baron.

"He didn't," Miranda huffed. Everson intuited that Miranda's preferred topic was herself.

"Miranda, let your father talk. It keeps his heart pumping," cajoled Carlotta, her attention now committed to a filet of that delectable meat.

"I'm just afraid he'll chase Everson all the way back to Indira," Miranda said, more to Everson than her mother, pursing her plump lips to remind him that there was ample reason to remain.

"It's quite alright. I'd like to know," Everson said.

He turned back to the baron and was reminded of his instant fondness for the man. Baron Ayers did not put on airs. Everson felt he could ask him anything and receive an honest answer.

"The people seem to live in fear of the military," Everson observed. "Why is that?"

"We've been living in a state of martial law for some time now," the baron said. "Xander blames the war, but it's really a way to keep the populace under control. He builds up the military, but there is no allocation for civic improvement. Roads, hospitals, schools. There is no education and no mass communication, because ignorant people have to trust and obey the word of the throne. Something must change or my people will never thrive."

"If only the Prophecy were true. That would solve a host of ills," Carlotta mused.

Everson's eyes snapped toward her. The baroness was looking at him with an expression of quiet expectation, and Everson knew that he had been baited. He was on the verge of divulging everything he knew about the Prophecy and the Tinderbox, when the baron mercifully relieved him of the need to respond.

"While I don't discount the Prophecy completely, dear wife, I have always believed the future of Mano relies more on action than impotent hope. At any rate, Everson, that is the world that you think you want to stay in."

Everson reflected on everything the baron had told him. In his short time on Mano, he had seen enough to grudgingly accept that the Prophecy might be true, both the hope that it inspired and his potential part in it.

As tempting as it was to luxuriate over this magnificent meal, the soldier very much wanted to return to the privacy of his room to finally have a chance at deciphering the mysteries of the Tinderbox. At the very least, if he could figure out how to operate the thing, then maybe a direction would become clear and he could finally take charge instead of drifting about at the whim of an indecipherable destiny.

SEVENTEEN

EVERSON REMOVED THE Tinderbox from his satchel and sat at the end of his bed. He turned it over and over in his hands, examined the top and the bottom, pressed on the sides, opened it, closed it, and it was still only what it appeared to be. He did notice one anomaly. There were three raised but miniscule bumps above the striker panel, and Everson suspected they might light up, but he had no idea how to engage them or what they might signify. He sighed in defeat and figured he might as well get some use from the confounding contraption.

Opening the box, he extracted a single rolling paper. He then took a pinch of tobacco, fleetingly wondering how long it had sat in its container. No matter. He intended to use the Tinderbox somehow, and maybe its obvious application was the answer.

He expertly rolled a cigarette, a skill he had acquired from the farm boy nucruits with whom he had shared his barracks. He placed the cigarette between his lips, pulled out a wooden match, closed the Tinderbox and scraped the match once on the striker panel. He set the Tinderbox aside on the bed where he sat.

Everson raised the lit match, but before he could touch it to the tip of the cigarette, a slight puff of wind blew it out. Irritated, he glanced over his shoulder, blaming the open doors of his balcony. He reached for the Tinderbox to retrieve another match when he stopped in surprise.

The unlit cigarette tumbled from his lips. The orb was floating expectantly before him.

Everson excitedly snatched up the Tinderbox and discovered that one of the three bumps on its face had lit up and was blinking red. The other two remained unilluminated. His mind ramped into overdrive. Three lights, three chambers, three DOGs. First light, first DOG. With trembling fingers, he opened the Tinderbox and fumbled for another match.

He struck the match and, although it was already aflame, he struck it again. To his immense delight, two of the lights flickered to life just as something blew out his match. Before he could look up, his forgotten cigarette appeared in front of his face, its tip glowing and giving forth a delicate tendril of smoke.

It was held in a silver hand. Everson raised his eyes to the waiting android from the Tree and found himself surprised at how happy he was to see her.

He took the proffered smoke and leaned back on the bed, reclining casually on one elbow. He took a deep drag, the tobacco surprisingly smooth and aromatic.

"Pour me a drink," he addressed the waiting android, wanting to bask in the glow of his unexpected success but also to confirm that he was, in fact, the one in control here.

She nodded politely and scanned the room. She quickly spied a corner table where a pair of dusty bottles and a cluster of goblets sat. The android held up a hand as she crossed, and Everson interpreted the gesture as a signal to wait.

A little mollified, he realized he had commanded her like, well, she was a dog. He was about to apologize for his brusqueness when a sheath on her forefinger retracted, revealing a corkscrew underneath.

Everson almost laughed in amazement. The android opened the wine, the corkscrew mechanically whirring like the hand tool it literally was. She delicately poured a tasting portion into one of the goblets. *Whether or not there are grander aspirations in store for my helpmate*, Everson thought, giddy for the first time in ages, *she would be an absolute hit at the baron's next dinner party.*

She brought the goblet to Everson and handed it to him. He made a show of smelling the bouquet, taking a sip and swishing it in his mouth. In keeping with the standard upheld by the baron and baroness, the wine was an artistic achievement.

"Excellent choice," he exclaimed, with a courtly tilt of the head. The android seemed not to share in the joke. She dutifully returned to the corner table and poured a proper portion. When she came back, Everson accepted the goblet but also took a moment to appreciate her exquisitely sculpted face, the angelic but immutable expression, the lifelike flow of her locks.

"You need a name," Everson decided and drank to it. True to character, she cocked her head at an inquisitive angle and waited. Everson swallowed his wine and blurted out a name without thinking.

"Rex."

The android, now Rex, didn't seem to take issue. Everson said the name aloud a second time and liked the sound of it even more. After all, she was a DOG designed to topple a king. Rex it was.

Having dispensed with that detail, the prince moved on to his next order of business. As much as he would have liked to while away the evening getting to know Rex, there was something else to be done.

The vision shown to him by the third DOG had stayed with him; it resonated with the wonder of a dream whose meaning is unclear but also with the visceral longing of a memory. Everson now believed that he had been shown this specific sequence of events because it was meant to be a rendezvous, both in time and place. He knew where he was supposed to go, but he wasn't yet sure about how to get there and what he was supposed to learn along the way that might help him once he arrived. Obviously, Everson concluded, a little reconnaissance was in order.

He set his goblet aside and once again picked up the Tinderbox. He quickly extracted a match and swiped it three times along the striker panel, confidently blowing it out when he was done.

As he expected, Rex was now absent from the room, and in her place stood the hulking black box, its numerous graphs and lights lazily awaiting instruction. The prince stood decisively and crossed to the third DOG.

He drew a deep breath, then addressed it. "I want to see Princess Allegra."

He braced himself for the lasers he was sure would come, comically widening his eyes to allow them in. The DOG had previously shown him a vision, and that was what he expected now. Instead, the highly polished black façade, with its lights and graphs and indicators, also proved to be equipped with double doors, like a cabinet, and they opened now, extending outward like an invitation to an embrace.

It became suddenly clear to Everson that the DOG would not just show him Allegra, it would take him to her. Without a second thought, he stepped in.

* * *

Silence had descended upon the Mist Tier palace like a pall. The halls became even more shrouded in secrecy, gossip curtailed as if Xander's fear and fatalism had become a contagion. Allegra was used to isolation, but even the meager trickle of information that had sustained her had dried up, leaving her in a desert of uncertainty.

Her mother had not visited her in some time, no doubt attending to the infantile demands of the needy king. Only Geneva, with her undimming devotion, had tried to penetrate the malaise. She had even brought a toy soldier to Allegra's room and had tried to stage a mock wedding, though Allegra had not played along. Geneva had remained silent, but dejection darkened her face like a funeral veil. The princess felt badly for her but not enough to put aside her own concerns and console her. Allegra, for her part, had retreated into quiet hope, a hope so delicate that it could be extinguished if revealed. Still, Allegra had to ask herself what it was exactly that she was hoping for. Other than her freedom, her wants were undefined, the consequences completely unpredictable.

Her other servants avoided interaction with her, but she could not discern whether it was out of sympathy for her plight or, worse, because they actually blamed her for this sad state of affairs thanks to the Prophecy. If the latter were true, the princess couldn't blame them.

What would the end of Xander's reign really mean? Would he die? Would they all die? Or would they simply become enslaved by the invading Indirans?

This paranoid propaganda, the princess knew, was being spread by the loyalists when they dared to discuss the Prophecy aloud. Even though derision for Xander was fairly universal, the denizens of Mist Tier lived in privilege compared to the rest of Mano, and change would not be welcome, especially if it came at the hands of foreigners.

Such were the thoughts that plagued Allegra's restless mind as she lay in bed, her eyes closed, but sleep remained elusive. Suddenly, a wave of warmth washed over her as if a fire had been ignited in her hearth. So soothing and reassuring was the sensation that she was unafraid when she felt the weight of something settling on her bed. Allegra opened her eyes.

A young man sat very near to her. His face was new to her, but his presence was not. Allegra was immediately reminded of that "star-crossed" sensation that had sent shivers to her very heart, as if it were possible to be pierced by a ray of starlight. Here was that feeling made flesh. She was not surprised that he wore the uniform of an enemy soldier or that his skin was a pleasing brown.

Xander feared two things, the Indirans and the prophesied soldier who would end his reign; this young man, quite possibly, was the aggregate of her father's most reviled imagining. He looked at her with an expression that Allegra had never experienced but had long tried to picture.

Behind him sat a massive black box that had not been there before, its doors open wide. She did not question the fantastical visitation. As magical as the moment was, Allegra knew it was not a dream. She felt the subtle shift of weight on her bed as he leaned forward. She could feel the warmth of his breath.

She reached up to touch his beautiful face...

* * *

Everson fell back on the bed, tingling and breathless from the encounter. This had been very different from their first meeting, which had been nothing more than a tantalizing tryst between phantoms.

This had been real. He had been there. In her room. Sitting very near to her on her bed. She had almost touched him.

Accordingly, Everson had fled. In more ways than one, this had been a maiden voyage; a test run to determine the capabilities and, perhaps, the boundaries of this newfound power. He had been mindful that impetuous contact might result in unintended and irreversible consequences. And so, he had receded back into the black box before he could do or say anything that he'd have to pay for later.

Allegra was everything Everson remembered from the vision in the Tree and more. Her blonde hair, luminous in the moonlight, had been loose and flowing, encircling her face like the golden frame of an ornate cameo. He had been able to watch her sleeping for a moment. The privilege had left him feeling guilty, as if it were too intimate, as if he had trespassed on her dreams. And then she had opened her azure eyes and looked right into him.

It was abundantly clear by her gaze that she somehow recognized him. But how was that possible? Their first encounter had been a vision of the future, a possible projection of events yet to transpire. As far as Everson knew, it was a premonition shown only to him by the third DOG.

Was it possible that the princess was privy to the vision as well? That would explain their familiarity the second time, in her bedroom. But which time, in actuality, was the first time? Everson's mind reeled with the timelessness of it all.

He sat up and surveyed the room to which he had been so abruptly returned. Everson no longer felt isolated and alone. Allegra had almost touched him. All other things aside, he now knew that he could see Allegra whenever he so desired. He had the third DOG, the black box, at his disposal. He had begun to think of the device as a...space cabinet, for lack of a better term. It was simple but accurate because when the double doors on the cabinet opened wide, they revealed what appeared to be a view of endless space. Or maybe it was simply the space that existed between Indira and Mano. Regardless, stepping through that space was like stepping through a portal. In the universe of the Tinderbox, it seemed that time and distance were relative, nearness existing concurrently with the infinite. It was all connected. And, now, so was Everson.

EIGHTEEN

MIRANDA AYERS WAS returning from a walk in the family orchard. Normally, she would have been in the streets of Middle Tier, but King Xander's curfew prohibited it. She was naturally a child of the night, drawn to the mysteries of moonlight and the seduction of darkness, but tonight she felt a special need for the clarifying effects of the night air. Miranda had found their guest much more intoxicating than the single glass of wine that she had not finished, and she needed to walk it off. She could think of other physical pastimes that would alleviate her restlessness, but that was a fire best left unfed for the moment.

As frivolous a front as she liked to present, nothing eluded Miranda but the wind. She engaged in playful and petulant banter with her father only because it entertained her. In actuality, she was quite proud of the baron's antiestablishment stance.

Her parents discussed politics daily, and though she often rolled her eyes, Miranda listened and learned. She knew that her family was somewhat insulated from the war and its subsequent restrictions, but it was abundantly clear that King Xander's preoccupation with the Prophecy was causing hardship and suffering among the common folk.

As a diversion, Miranda had often accompanied her mother into the marketplace to purchase food staples and basic art supplies, luxuries long a thing of the past, always shadowed by the reassuring presence of Tobias. His intimidating bulk was a sad necessity since robbery and crime were on the rise as desperate people became even more desperate. It was not surprising to Miranda since there seemed to be fewer and fewer stalls selling goods and more people with their hands out begging. She understood the basic economics. The poor were getting poorer, and those on the cusp were having a harder time holding on.

Taxes were higher to fuel the war machine, but that was only the most obvious diversion of funds. Craftspeople, metalworkers, carpenters, even seamstresses were underpaid to support the military, leaving little time and raw material for them to manufacture goods that might bring them a fair price in the free market. The work force itself had been gutted because all of the able-bodied young men had been conscripted into service, transformed into warriors rather than learning a trade or taking their places as the heads of households. All in service to the whim of the king.

This was the reason Miranda's father could never direct his scorn toward the warmen. The baron considered them victims of circumstance, as helpless as the lowliest of peasants, unable to determine their own destinies or improve their conditions.

Miranda herself was not convinced, even though she recognized that many of those intimidating soldiers were merely young men no older than she. In other circumstances, she might have been sympathetic, but they were the face of authority and they wielded the king's law like a cudgel. They were the ones who collected the taxes or randomly stopped citizens to check allowances or, worst of all, dragged people away to who knows where for the simple crime of being outside after dark.

This is how you protect the citizens from the enemy? Miranda had often thought, ironically.

No, all in all, Miranda did not just tolerate her father's fiery progressiveness, she admired it. If anyone was going to change the pitiful conditions for the populace, it was going to be someone like him.

And so, it was into this oppressive malaise that the soldier from Indira had appeared, and Miranda had become instantly invigorated. Xander's curfew had greatly curtailed social interaction, even among the elite, but, even so, the lady of Ayers had long ago realized that there were few people who could challenge or inspire her when she was invariably the best educated person in the room. Which was why Miranda hoped that her parents could see as well as she could that this uncharacteristically erudite and courtly soldier was her perfect match.

Miranda drifted thoughtfully down a darkened corridor, pausing when she heard her parents' muffled voices emanating from their room. The insistent tone of their conversation told her that they were not simply exchanging late night pleasantries. Miranda leaned into the sliver of light that slipped through the cracked door, and the hushed discussion became distinct.

"Don't you think he could be the one?" the baroness pressed, an edge of excitement to her voice.

There was a long pause. The anticipation was almost enough to force Miranda to scream aloud and demand her father's response. Patience was not one of her many attributes.

Instead, she held her tongue and her breath and listened intently. The soldier was the one for what? For her? She was of age and she certainly felt as if she deserved more. As much as she loved her parents, their interests were not hers; they had achievements while she had dreams. And when she tired of their conversation, her only other option was Tobias. While she was quite fond of him and was grateful for his service, the Leftist was often too timid to discuss much beyond the weather, which, since they lived in a desert, was a fairly limited topic.

Finally, Baron Ayers spoke. "It's possible. But I do know that he is much more than he wants us to suspect."

Miranda released her breath in a disappointed sigh. It wasn't about her. She heard her father's floppy footsteps approaching the door. Miranda dashed down the hall to her room, doing her best to tread as lightly as possible despite her haste. She slipped behind her darkened door just as light spilled into the hall.

Miranda held her door slightly ajar and put a surreptitious eye to the crack. The baron had turned in the opposite direction and was walking away from her. She watched as he disappeared slowly, descending the stairway at the far end of the hall. Miranda knew where he was going.

There was only one area in the entire mansion that had been off-limits to Miranda. In fact, The baron was so secretive about this place that he had forbade Carlotta and the servants from entering there as well. Not surprisingly, Miranda had harbored an almost uncontainable amount of curiosity about the room behind the door when she had been younger, but, eventually, she had concluded that her father was so transparent with his thoughts and feelings that his secret place must certainly be, in reality, fairly dull.

Now, however, her interest was piqued anew. She had never purposefully disobeyed her father, but the circumstances in the household had substantially changed, made ever so much more unstable and perilous by the introduction of their intriguing new houseguest. Miranda could easily rationalize her need to know.

As difficult as it was, she waited just a few more moments after her father had disappeared before she crept down the hall after him. That particular staircase led to only one place, so there was little chance of losing him. Of more concern was the fact that the stairwell was so narrow and devoid of hiding spots that she knew she couldn't follow too closely for danger of being discovered and turned away. She moved quickly but carefully down, passing landing after landing, switchback after switchback, the air growing so thick with dust and silence that any errant sound would be magnified. Mindful of the creaks, Miranda placed her feet so delicately on the endless and ancient stairs that it made her thighs hurt.

When at last she caught sight of him, Baron Ayers stood in the dim and dusty light at the foot of the final staircase, at the bottommost level beneath his mansion. She tucked in as tightly as grout to the bricks of the stairwell and watched as the baron punched a code into a keypad inset in the wall. No other such mechanism existed anywhere else in the baron's home. A heavy steel door slid open, and the baron stepped out of the archaic darkness and into bright artificial light.

Again, Miranda waited as long as she thought prudent. When she peeked around the corner of the door, blinking at the sudden brightness, she saw the baron some distance ahead of her; the space beyond the door was, in fact, not a room but rather a long and narrow corridor.

Her father moved determinedly down this new corridor, and the light preceded him, staying just ahead of him as if triggered by his presence. There were no obvious fixtures from which the glow emanated. As Ayers strode purposefully forward, the light gradually revealed a pristine but featureless passageway constructed of a material unfamiliar to Miranda and which she suspected to be otherworldly since she had never encountered anything like it in Middle Tier. Apparently, the baron's secrets were not as boring as she had thought.

She slipped into the hallway and tiptoed after him, knowing full well that, if he turned, she would be easily caught and soundly rebuked. Fortunately, whatever was on his mind, whatever his purpose, it kept him focused squarely forward, and Miranda was able to close the distance as much as she dared.

Ayers arrived at the end of the hall and faced another steel door accompanied by its own keypad. Miranda pressed herself against the wall behind him and held her breath as the baron entered yet another code. The door slid open and Miranda's eyes grew wide. Beyond her father, she could see a medium-sized chamber crowded with equipment. At first, with its twinkling lights and gleaming surfaces, the room could be construed as festive, but the somber air of secrecy and solitude suggested a much more covert purpose.

Baron Ayers moved immediately to a chair that sat before a centrally situated console, its surface studded with buttons and dials. A wide, concave screen was suspended above the console, its semicircular structure dominating the room as if it were a miniaturized amphitheater. With her father's back to her, Miranda was able to creep to the open door and hover there, one eye peeking around the jamb.

The baron initialized a sequence on the console and waited. After a brief moment, the black screen began to glow silver, and light filled the hollow within the concave curve. A moment more and the concerned face and uniformed torso of an Indiran officer appeared in three-dimensional but diaphanous form.

"Yes, Baron?" the severe-looking man asked. Though he was obviously high-ranking and stringently disciplined in his de-

meanor, Miranda sensed something haggard and somewhat sad about the man.

"Commander Giza, I have a new development," her father replied.

She saw the man's face brighten with interest, but Miranda was suddenly fearful that she could be seen lurking in the doorway over her father's shoulder. She had never experienced such technology, but it was clear that this Commander Giza could see her father and that it would only take a flick of his eyes to see her as well. She eased slowly away from the door, expecting at any moment to hear a cry of discovery. It never came and she turned and scurried away down the strange corridor as quietly and as quickly as she could.

One thought chased her all the way back to her room.

"As much as I want Everson for myself, there are those who might actually need him."

* * *

The day had started off more brightly, as if there were three suns in the sky instead of two. Princess Allegra had allowed Geneva to brush her hair, and now she noticed that they were engaged in a game of avoiding eye contact with each other. Whenever Allegra looked at her handmaiden in the mirror, Geneva looked down and vice versa. No doubt Geneva had noticed the change in her demeanor, the self-satisfied arch of her eyebrows or the mischievous tilt of her head. Likewise, Allegra knew that Geneva's downcast eyes masked her amusement. If they kept toying with each other much longer, Allegra knew they would burst into giggles.

"You seem curious, Geneva," Allegra finally observed.

Geneva suppressed a grin and countered, "Only because you are acting curiously, m'lady."

"You're itching to ask, aren't you?" the princess queried, turning fully to face her best friend.

Geneva shrugged her shoulders and returned to brushing the hair at the side of Allegra's face. "I didn't want to disturb your happiness by questioning it. You have a right to feel how you feel, and that's no one's business but your own. Besides..." Geneva finally looked into Allegra's eyes, and the princess was elated to see the old conspiratorial sparkle. "I knew you would tell me eventually."

Allegra chuckled and took the brush out of Geneva's hand. "Let's just say that I have found a reason for optimism. Or...rather...it's found me."

"That makes me very happy, Allegra," Geneva said, beaming.

"Now." Allegra clapped her hands as if getting down to business. "There is something that you can do for me right away."

"Anything."

"I need you to ask my mother if she will entertain me for breakfast. I'm very curious to see how my parents are faring."

The mirth left Geneva's face and she spoke in a suddenly serious tone. "I will do that for you on one condition."

Allegra leaned back, surprised. "Geneva, are you taking advantage of my good spirits to negotiate? I must say that I wouldn't have expected that of you."

Geneva couldn't hold a straight face any longer. She burst into giggles while exclaiming, "No, no! I just want you to promise to tell me everything!"

"Oh!" Allegra exclaimed, both of her hands flying to her mouth. She burst into laughter and the two young women embraced, their giddiness a welcome release from all of their pent-up frustration.

After they had composed themselves, Geneva accomplished her mission quickly, and Allegra suspected that her mother had given her consent without consulting Xander, and she harbored hope that Nor was equally inclined to see her after such a long absence. As Geneva hurriedly helped her to dress, she prepared herself mentally for whatever state of dysfunction her parents might be enduring. Now, sitting at a too-long table in the formal dining room, Allegra was quietly pleased to find her parents as miserable as she. The queen had fallen into silence after the requisite greetings and the trivial but untrue observations on their well-being. Xander had not spoken at all. Allegra noticed that he had not touched his meal, choosing instead to break the day with drink. The princess waited for her mother to condemn the debauchery, but the rebuke never came.

Allegra reasoned that the queen probably preferred Xander's anaesthetized silence over his irrational and inconsequential ramblings. The Aurora Constellation was inevitable, and no amount of frittering would dissuade it. But this forced normalcy was a farce, and Allegra could abide the charade no longer.

"I saw a soldier last night," she said.

King Xander's glass fell from his hand and shattered on the floor. He turned on his daughter, his eyes burning through the terrazka haze with a mixture of fear and accusation.

"Where?" he questioned.

"Only in a dream." The princess shrugged nonchalantly as if she were just making conversation. She felt the icy heat of her mother's offended glare. Allegra was familiar with her mother's many nuanced emotions, but she had never experienced her cold fury.

"That's not funny, Allegra," hissed the queen.

"It's a portent. A sign," Xander exclaimed, leaning desperately toward his daughter in a gesture that Allegra found both satisfying and disturbing. She could not remember the last time her father had engaged her in any sense. Now she had something he wanted.

"What did he look like?" the king continued, his eyes beseeching.

"Much more handsome than I expected," she said, ignoring her mother. She leaned forward herself, her eyes wide with seeming innocence. "It must be the uniform."

She had purposefully omitted the Indiran detail. Allegra wanted to raise her father's hackles but not an alarm. The princess did not doubt that her parents could make her life even worse, like banishing her to some dungeon in Back Tier, and she did not want to place further obstacles between herself and her newly found reason for hope.

"Do you wish for your father's reign to end?" the queen challenged Allegra, still staring. "Is that why you mock your father so cruelly?"

Allegra stood. She could reconcile her father's apathy, even his outright resentment, but her mother's antagonism in defense of this tyrant hurt.

"I only wish for an end to this punishment that I have done nothing to deserve," she argued.

"Allegra..." said Nor, her features softening. She did not make promises lightly and even ventured into compromise with caution. "Perhaps after the Aurora Alignment. Perhaps then things will be different. Xander?"

True to form, the king's response offered no incentive to his daughter's patience or understanding. "How can I be certain of anything right now?"

Allegra smiled grimly at the queen, victorious in her expected defeat.

"You see, Mother?" she said. "Don't tease me with false hope. My father has never compromised much less changed his mind."

The princess turned on her heel and marched out of the room. She would not say another word about her Indiran paramour, not even to Geneva. Rather, she would pray to see him again, consequences to the kingdom be damned.

* * *

Queen Nor stared after her departing daughter, the mother and the monarch within her at opposing ends of an unwinnable war. She could not be effective at both, and in the absence of a capable king and partner, she had made her choice. Save the kingdom. She was committed, but that did not mean she was happy with her decision.

Even though Allegra's upturned chin was haughty and provocative, Nor could not help but notice her daughter's beauty and determination. She was born to be regal. Queen Nor realized that she could be looking at her very own younger self, a proud young woman who'd had her future hijacked and harnessed to a fate not of her own choosing.

The marriage between her and Xander had been arranged, inbred from title and contrived to strengthen the monarchy. The young Nor had willfully resigned herself to her duty, but, then again, she'd received the substantial benefit of becoming queen. What did her daughter stand to gain from her sacrifice of being locked away, sequestered from the world and the normal social interactions of a girl her age?

"You realize that we wouldn't be in this predicament if we didn't have a daughter," Xander sniped, glancing about for a fresh glass.

The queen turned to her husband, aghast. Rarely, if ever, did Nor allow her emotions to run rampant over her reason, but now, twice since she had risen, she felt the constricting clench of rage overtake her. She took both of Xander's clammy hands in hers. It was not an act of affection. She needed to anchor her hands to prevent herself from slapping him.

"You may never say anything like that to me again," Queen Nor said in a tone electric with tension. She stared intensely into the king's eyes to make sure that he comprehended. "I have always stood by your judgment, Xander. But I must tell you as your equal, you are letting this fear make you irrational."

The queen rose, towering over her husband, the possibility of an explosion still palpable.

Xander appeared unmoved. He stared out the window toward the Ocean of Manorain. The surface was unruffled this morning. A layer of thick mist lay over it like a duvet. The low-slung twin suns would burn it off soon enough.

"I no longer recognize you, Xander," Queen Nor continued, not really caring whether she had his attention or not. "Perhaps that's what this Prophecy really means. You will simply allow yourself to disappear."

Xander continued to find the view out the window more deserving of his interest. Nor shook her head in disgust. She knew that nothing, neither coaxing nor condemnation, would register with her husband right now, so it was pointless to waste her breath. She turned and left the king with his drink and the placid ocean.

NINETEEN

EVERSON GAZED AT the brightening sky of Mano. The suns shone differently here. They were brighter, hotter, than on Indira. He was sure that had something to do with the foliage or moisture in the air, but climate or atmosphere or whatever the academic subject was didn't really stay with him much beyond the test he'd had to take for it. Still, he found himself contemplating the differences in the two planets, knowing full well that they once had been one.

More than likely, Everson mused, *the hemisphere that became Mano was arid already when it was a part of the larger planet.* The Great Schism would not have helped that and probably made the harsh conditions worse. But now that they were relatively the same size, locked in orbit with each other and equidistant from the suns, might not Indira and Mano eventually evolve to be more like one another?

That wouldn't be such a bad thing, Everson concluded, *in many different ways.*

He had slept late. Given the plush comfort of the baron's guest bed, he was surprised that he hadn't slept even later. An insistent thought had nudged him awake and then stayed with him like the residue of a dream.

When should he visit Princess Allegra again?

Everson's impulse had been to summon the space cabinet and climb through the portal, but he knew that such an impetuous liaison with a princess was far from advisable. Appearing magically at the palace of Xander in the clear light of day would only lead to disaster.

No, as much as he ached to see Allegra again, maybe even talk with her this time, he would have to force himself to remain patient. The only question now was how to fill the rest of his day.

Everson sat up shirtless in bed, arms draped languidly over his knees. The previous night had been the first time he had removed his uniform since departing Indira, and he was in no rush to put it back on. It stank. Moreover, the blood, sweat and dirt had permeated his clothes to the point that the grime was now an undergarment. A full body washing was not only desirable, it was necessary and should be his first order of business.

As if in answer to his thoughts, there came a soft knocking on his door. Tobias entered, holding a stack of neatly folded garments. The Leftist stopped just inside the door, arrested no doubt by the sight of Everson's exposed torso. Judging from his quizzical expression, the soldier was certain that Tobias remained fascinated by the dark pigment that covered the entirety of his body.

Looking down, Everson was embarrassed to discover that his dirty body had left numerous brown smudges on the crisp white sheets and pillow. The Leftist must certainly think him a liar now, since it indeed looked as if his color had rubbed off during the night.

He was just about to explain when Tobias offered his bundle politely and said, "I've brought you fresh clothes."

"Good. Because I'd like to go out, Tobias." The discussion of his skin, and perhaps another remonstration, could wait until later.

* * *

At the outskirts of the marketplace, Everson recognized a familiar face. He knew that friends in this foreign land were few and far between, so it would be wise to feed those relationships that had proven helpful to him. That was exactly what he intended to do as he approached one of the vendor stalls, regardless of the fact that the old acquaintance he'd spotted wasn't human.

The proprietor of the terranut stand eyed Everson suspiciously as he neared. In addition to the fine clothing supplied by Tobias, he wore a patterned scarf wrapped around his head that obscured everything except his eyes. Everson knew it made him look like a bandit, but it was preferable to his naked face, which would instantly advertise his alienage.

After he made his order and the terranut seller started counting his produce, Everson felt a tap on his shoulder that was more akin to a thump. He turned to Tobias, who was standing behind him like a bodyguard. The shifty vendor looked up curiously as he sacked the vegetables, and Tobias gave a slight tilt of his head and moved a few paces away. Everson followed, impressed again by the Leftist manservant's decorum and discretion.

"Why are you buying terranuts when you were delivered in a wagon full of terranuts that we don't need and that are now overflowing the pantry?" Tobias asked, his large face registering sincere concern and confusion.

Everson was about to grin at Tobias when he remembered that the scarf concealed his mouth, so he winked instead. "Because, as you said, those terranuts are back in the pantry, and I need terranuts right now."

Everson returned to the vendor, who held out his hand, palm up, but continued to clutch the sack of terranuts tight to his chest. *Ah, payment first*, Everson rightly observed. *Trusting soul.*

He reached into his satchel, retrieved a coin, and placed it into the vendor's hand. The vendor's eyes went wide, and he quickly handed over the sack of terranuts, as if he thought his buyer might rethink the transaction.

Looking at the sack of vegetables, Everson couldn't help but notice that these terranuts were puny in comparison to Jonas's produce, nor did they boast the same deep nutritious color. It confirmed his faith that he had done the right thing by placing his hydreeds in Jonas's capable hands. He would have to tell his grandfather Aziz the Cultivator that he had found a kindred spirit.

He also couldn't help but notice that the vendor did not attempt to give him change for his very valuable silver coin. Without comment, Everson nodded his thanks and took his leave but not before noting that the vendor exhaled rather audibly. Obviously, the greedy little man had been holding his breath.

Everson had noticed the white-capped birdun shortly after he and Tobias had entered the bustling marketplace. It had been impossible to miss. Its large wings had been flitting nervously, shooing away giggling children who seemed intent on collecting birdun feathers as souvenirs. The beast had brayed at them, annoyed, but its attention kept returning to a nearby terranut stand. From its flaring nostrils and the way its head shook impatiently atop its undulating neck, Everson could tell the beast was hungry.

So could the vendor. He had emerged from his stall with a stick and had chased away the creature, raising pitiful trills of protest as the beast had skittered away in fits and starts. Even so, the birdun had not ventured far, and Everson was sure it had been watching as he had made his purchase.

It occurred to him that the birdun might actually recognize him, but he wasn't sure how. He didn't know if the creatures imprinted by sight, and he wondered if it was able to see through his disguise. It was also possible that the beast had detected his scent, although Everson was certain he smelled better today than yesterday. Regardless, the birdun's sinewy neck had straightened and it had raised his white-capped head to optimum viewing height, only lowering it now as Everson approached, meal in hand.

The prince was quietly pleased that he was bringing the birdun terranuts from the very stall that had rejected it. He was also pleased that Tobias was following closely behind him, not just dutifully but with seeming curiosity. Everson knew this without having to turn around since the Leftist's massive shadow obliterated his own on the ground before him.

Everson reached into the sack as he stepped up to the waiting birdun, whose face was now on a level with his own. The creature was looking at him expectantly, and Everson now had no doubt; the birdun definitely recognized him. Before he could contemplate that further, he noticed a long, syrupy drip of drool dangling from its mouth. The poor thing was very hungry but had the restraint to wait for the food to be proffered. Everson didn't waste another moment and he held out a terranut.

"Here you go," Everson murmured gently. "Sorry to keep you waiting."

The birdun delicately wrapped its prehensile lips around the first offered terranut and took it gently. The creature chewed it slowly, as if savoring its good fortune. *Someone trained this beast*, Everson thought, *and they trained it well*. It had belonged to a very specific someone and was not just another mindless military mount. He gave the birdun another terranut, hoping that the shady vendor could see where his overpriced produce was going.

"Why are you doing this?" Everson heard Tobias ask. The courtly Leftist had stopped short, and it occurred to Everson that he might be afraid of the birdun. Curious, he mused, but it was quite possible that Tobias had never encountered one of the creatures before, at least not up close.

"To be honest, Tobias," Everson said, now stroking the birdun's tuft of white fur while he chewed, "I'm simply repaying a favor. I wouldn't be here if it weren't for this fine fellow."

Tobias didn't comment but continued to watch the eating birdun with bemused fascination. Everson held out a terranut to Tobias and indicated that he should give it to the creature. The Leftist tentatively complied and let out a peep of laughter when the beast took it in its genteel and deliberate manner. The smile stayed on his face, but he flinched slightly when the birdun lifted its head to more closely examine him.

"Why is it looking at me?" Tobias chuckled nervously.

"If I had to guess, I'd say he's remembering your face," Everson replied.

"Why?" Tobias frowned.

Everson handed another terranut to Tobias to give to the birdun. Not for the first time, he wondered if something beyond his reckoning was directing him, as if these seemingly random encounters were part of a bigger picture.

"In case he sees you again," Everson mused. "I've crossed paths with this particular birdun a few times now, and I doubt it will be my last."

"You, maybe," Tobias said doubtfully. "I don't get out much." He suddenly seemed self-conscious that the birdun was still staring at him.

Everson had an epiphany, much like the one he had with Rex, and he said suddenly, "We need to give him a name."

"Like what?" Tobias asked, and Everson could tell that he was dubious about the proposition. Even so, that didn't stop him from reaching for more terranuts. Everson put the whole sack into the manservant's massive hand and watched in amusement as Tobias continued to feed the beast. It became quite the dainty affair, with Tobias having to pluck terranuts from the sack with a finger and his thumb because his fist was too large and the birdun's prehensile, grasping lips lifting them from his hand with equal delicacy.

"I don't know," Everson continued. "Something that suits him."

Relieved of the feeding duties, he returned to stroking the birdun's discolored patch of fur atop its head. "For instance, Tobias. Look at this cap that our friend has."

The birdun's attention suddenly shifted to Everson, as if he had said something that had drawn the creature's interest.

"See there? He knows that I'm talking about him. Maybe he knows that his cap makes him special. I've not seen this coloring on any other birdun. Although, granted, I've not seen that many."

Inexplicably, the birdun leaned forward and nuzzled Everson's face, nearly displacing his disguise. Everson laughed and adjusted the scarf but not before wiping a nice smear of saliva from his cheek.

"Well, he certainly seems to be in agreement," he said, studying the creature, who continued to gaze at him, its eyes blinking slowly. The birdun swallowed the masticated vegetables in its mouth, lifting its head and shaking it as if to hasten the mouthful down its long neck. The action gave Everson a clear view of the shaggy white fur that completely capped the birdun's head and suddenly, it came to him. "Tobias, do you know what a 'Taj' is?"

"No," Tobias replied, regaining the birdun's attention with a terranut.

"On my planet, it can be another word for 'crown,'" Everson informed him. "It can also refer to the rings of light that you sometimes see around the suns and we call that 'Femera Taj' or 'Amali Taj.'"

"I've seen that," Tobias said brightly, as if happy to finally contribute to the discussion.

"I can tell you, my friend," Everson continued, noticing that the Leftist was nearing the bottom of the sack. "This birdun once took me for a ride, and he flew so high that I was convinced he was going to circle the suns and drop me off on the other side. What do you think of the name Taj?"

Tobias did indeed think for a moment, as if dutifully following instructions, until finally he nodded in conclusion. "Since I've never heard it before, I won't confuse him with someone else."

Everson chuckled. He couldn't refute Tobias's odd logic, but, then again, it was an odd and eclectic collection of allies he was acquiring.

"Taj, then," Everson decided as Tobias fed the newly christened Taj the last terranut.

Their sack now empty, Everson and Tobias took their leave from the satiated birdun but not without objection. The curious beast took a few steps after them as if it suddenly considered himself to be a part of their party. Though Everson was pleased that they had bonded, he was trying to keep a low profile in the bustling market, and a large winged creature was not conducive to that end. He held his hand up to the birdun, palm out in a decisive gesture.

"No, Taj," he said firmly. He repeated it, hoping that the beast would not only understand the command but become familiar with its new name. "No, Taj."

The birdun stopped but gave him a markedly befuddled look. Everson realized he was giving the poor beast mixed messages by feeding it and then abandoning it, but it would have to do for now. He backed away, maintaining eye contact, and Taj watched him go, snuffling, trilling and tossing its head in grudging compliance.

Everson and his large shadow, Tobias, meandered through the market, taking in the various sights, sounds and smells. Aside from the occasional double take at his eye-catching headgear, the market goers were far too intent on their own personal errands to pay him much mind. It also occurred to the prince that, given his elegant new attire and his accompanying Leftist in gentleman's clothes, he might be taken for an obscure royal, and as such the peasantry would naturally avoid eye contact. Whatever the reason, Everson was grateful for the unimpeded passage, and he browsed the bazaar as if he were in a museum.

In the center of the square, one plaintive voice rose above the clamor of the other vendors hawking their wares. Everson turned toward the sound. In a space too small to be considered a stall stood a haggard young woman holding a baby on her hip.

"Tunics. Handmade tunics for sale!" she shouted in a reedy voice. She held out her free hand to the inattentive passersby. "Will no one help a widow of the war? Good tunics, fair price."

The soldier saw two older children sitting on crates behind a rickety table that held her meager offerings. The young boy and girl appeared to be guarding the tunics, but Everson doubted there was much danger of theft. He studied their mother for a moment, sensing the young widow's growing frustration as she watched every imagined sale walk past with nary a glance.

Everson started toward her.

"You're going to buy tunics now?" Everson heard Tobias ask from behind him. He didn't answer and he felt the Leftist close the distance until he was looming over Everson's shoulder.

"You don't like the clothes you're wearing?" the manservant asked more insistently. "They're very nice. Very elegant. I thought I picked the best ones," Tobias explained plaintively, his high voice growing higher. Again, the prince did not answer but held up a silencing hand. He heard a heavy sigh before Tobias concluded, "You're very strange."

Everson couldn't disagree. He turned and cast a warm glance at Tobias. The large Leftist had stopped in the middle of the lane and was allowing him to go about his nonsensical business unencumbered.

The beleaguered young widow took an involuntary step back as Everson approached. She eyed him uneasily. The baby on her hip, however, gazed openly at the well-dressed stranger with innocent curiosity.

The soldier doubted that the woman had ever encountered an Indiran, but he was painfully aware that he was tacitly responsible for the loss of her husband. He lowered his head to further obscure his dark skin and eyes. The gesture did nothing to put the young woman at ease.

The prince examined the neatly folded stack of sturdy but unimpressive tunics. It was obvious that the young widow possessed skill in fabrication, but she lacked sufficient capital to purchase the raw materials that would make her wares desirable. Furthermore, Everson calculated, even if her product was made precious, expensive clothes were a luxury not likely afforded by the shoppers in this particular marketplace. It was a vicious cycle of economics that would never allow the desperate young widow to get ahead.

The soldier looked past the tunics to the two children. The boy and girl looked back at him noncommittally. Everson smiled behind his veil and then realized the children could not see his friendly overture. They were beautiful children with unkempt and uncut blonde hair and clear blue irises, but the hollows of their cheeks matched the sallow cavities of their eyes.

"I will buy," Everson said firmly.

"A quarter Xander, sir," the young widow said quickly, holding out a tunic to prevent the stranger from changing his mind. A tremor of defeat trickled through her when the man did not immediately take the garment. Instead, he reached into a satchel he had slung over his shoulder. His gloved hand quickly reappeared and placed a handful of gold coins on her tiny table.

"I'll take the lot, thank you," said the prince.

The young widow was thunderstruck. She clutched her baby closer to her as if in sudden fear of dropping it. Tears brimmed in her eyes. She finally spoke in a voice so soft and tremulous that her words might have been more thought than statement.

"Femera and Amali bless you, sir."

Everson turned to Tobias, who was still standing in the lane like a boulder in a river, forcing pedestrians to sidestep his girth, grumbling and glaring. Tobias paid them no mind, his large dark eyes still fixed curiously on his ward.

"Tobias..." Everson prompted.

Everson walked away as Tobias stepped forward and scooped up the armful of tunics. The manservant nodded respectfully to the stunned young woman and hustled to catch up to the Indiran.

"Why do you need so many tunics?" Tobias queried as he fell in step with the smaller man.

Everson stopped and, once again, his smile was masked by his scarf, but the crinkles showed at his eyes.

"Why do I need so much money?" Everson asked, and he placed a congenial hand on Tobias's arm. "The baron isn't charging me rent, and I doubt he'll make me pay for food. So why not give it to someone who can actually use it? Now, if you would do me a favor. Distribute those to the poor. Use your best judgment."

Everson gave Tobias a pat and started to walk away.

"You're not strange," the Leftist said suddenly. "You're just unpredictable."

Everson nodded courteously at Tobias. "I'll take that as a compliment, Tobias."

He watched as Tobias departed to carry out his directive. Everson turned and walked through the market with a buoyancy not attributable to his now lighter satchel. The prince happily concluded that this must be the reason money was sometimes referred to as tender.

* * *

Manfred, the elder Leftist and chef in the baron's mansion, was more harried than usual as he bustled about the kitchen, overseeing the preparation of the midday meal. Baron Ayers himself had come down to the kitchen early this morning, before suns rise in fact, to inspect the stock and personally tailor the upcoming menus from Manfred's best recipes. With the arrival of their mysterious guest, his patron had become even more discerning and had taken it upon himself to elevate the standard of the already exquisite service.

The baron also made it a point to expressly caution the staff against speaking of their guest outside the confines of the manor upon pain of immediate expulsion. Manfred was happy to comply, but he did have to admit to a degree of peevishness since it was his understanding that their boarder was nothing more than a common soldier, interplanetary ambassador or not.

The rear door to the kitchen opened and the hunched bulk of Tobias filled the frame. It still irked Manfred that the door, indeed the entire mansion, had been constructed before the presence of the Leftists and that no accommodation had been made for their size. The majority of his staff had to stoop to enter, and new hires invariably sported purple bruises on their foreheads during their indoctrination. It was a constant reminder to the proud chef that his kind were forced daily to bow their heads.

Tobias cleared the entry, revealing the Indiran directly behind him. All activity in the kitchen ceased, and every massive head in attendance turned toward the alien soldier as he removed his gloves and the scarf that was wrapped around his head. The young man's dark skin was now clearly visible. There were audible gasps from those Leftists who had not yet encountered him. The soldier didn't react. Just extended his hand to Tobias.

"Thank you for going with me, Tobias," he said. "It was very educational."

Tobias shook the soldier's hand firmly, his large hand engulfing the smaller brown one. The manservant appeared proud of the soldier's acknowledgment, and Manfred knew it would make him even harder to deal with. Everson nodded politely to the curious kitchen staff and took his leave, exiting through an interior doorway. No sooner was he out of sight than Manfred sidled up to Tobias.

"Interesting day, Tobias?" Manfred asked lightly.

"Yes, Manfred. As Everson said. Very educational."

"What is he like?" pressed Manfred.

Tobias's response came with no hesitation at all. "He's very kind."

"The baron is kind," Manfred countered almost defensively.

Tobias turned to him, and the elder Leftist could see that his younger comrade had given this a lot of thought.

"The baron is as kind as prudence allows," Tobias said. "This one is different. If it were up to Everson, I believe we Leftists would finally be treated as equals."

With that, Tobias left Manfred standing alone as the hubbub in the kitchen rose to its normally productive din. In that moment, Manfred decided to outdo himself and cook up a reputation that would resound even to Indira.

* * *

Everson felt a little guilty for thinking it since this household had shown him nothing but generosity, but his first thought upon seeing the door to the guest room ajar was that he was glad he had taken his satchel with him. He pushed the door open cautiously and stopped short, a surprised flush rising to his cheeks.

Miranda was waiting for him. She stood in the open doorway to the balcony, the pervasive afternoon glow outlining her in gold. The warm light shone through the diaphanous gaps of Miranda's low-cut and clingy dress, giving Everson no doubt about the lithe figure beneath it. She was so striking, he had to wonder if she had purposefully composed herself in such an alluring tableau.

"Miranda, what are you doing here?" he asked.

"Waiting for you," she replied.

"Aside from the obvious."

"I just wanted to talk to you. Alone." Miranda drifted toward him, and Everson was tempted to retreat through the door. Instead, he casually deposited his satchel on the bed and moved to meet her.

"I don't have nearly as much time as I thought," she continued, the hint of a pout tugging at her lower lip.

"What do you mean?"

"The time of the Aurora Constellation is near. Does that mean anything to you?"

Everson sighed. The Prophecy had an annoying and persistent habit of reminding him that time was marching on even if he wasn't.

"I'm beginning to think it's supposed to," he confessed.

"I overheard my parents talking last night." Lady Miranda lowered her voice. "That and...well, I am now privileged of other information, but I'll leave that to my father to reveal."

The revelation that there were secrets in the house made Everson's scalp tingle. Or perhaps it was the fact that he could feel the warmth emanating from Miranda, a sensation his body had felt before his mind had comprehended it. She was very near to him now, and Everson still wasn't convinced that discretion was the motivation behind her intimacy.

"I think they believe you're the soldier the Prophecy predicted," she concluded.

"I have a hard time believing that I am the key to such a grand plan." The prince wasn't being coy for the sake of false modesty. Confirming Miranda's supposition would only make her complicit. He had no idea where all of this was going, and involving anyone else might only bring peril to their heads. Everson smiled self-consciously, but the lady of Ayers did not smile back.

"Sometimes your opinion is not what matters," Miranda quietly admonished him. "Sometimes you have to give yourself over to something greater than yourself and make peace with it. This could be the purpose you seek, Everson."

The prince was deeply touched by the selfless counsel of this beautiful young woman. He gazed into her green eyes and silently acknowledged the possibility of an alternate reality. In another time or in a different place, Everson might have chosen Miranda, if the universe had not already chosen for him. Or so it would seem.

Again, he wondered how much his free will might play a part in this celestial design. Was he still capable of making a choice, or was his path predetermined? And if he chose wrong, did the fate of two kingdoms hang in the balance? The fact that he was thinking of Allegra even as he was looking at Miranda gave him part of the answer. He remembered the way her hair had spilled about her pillow. The way his heart had leaped when she opened her eyes to look into his.

Miranda seemed to keep pace with his tumbling thoughts and, once again, Everson was impressed with her insight. She finally returned his smile and said, "I'm only sorry that I'm not the one you are destined to love."

Miranda leaned into him and gently kissed his mouth. Everson did not prevent her. Her lips were soft and sensuous, and, for a brief moment, he thought of nothing else.

They were forced apart abruptly by the sound of someone clearing his throat. Everson and Miranda turned to find Baron Ayers standing in the doorway, considerately considering the carpet.

"Sorry to interrupt, dearest daughter, but I require a moment of Everson's time as well," he said.

Everson watched wryly as Miranda reverted back to the coquettish and entitled ingénue. But he knew better. The young lady of Ayers possessed more depth and substance than she would ever care to admit.

"He's all yours, Father," she said, feigning disinterest. "I believe I've taken all that I'm allowed."

Her father indicated the open door. "Everson..."

Everson and Miranda exchanged parting glances and an unspoken affirmation that their kiss would never be forgotten.

* * *

Everson was astonished to discover the depth residing beneath the baron's mansion. If he had thought to do so, he would have counted the flights of stairs to get a better sense of the distance they had travelled to reach this bottommost level. Regardless, they had descended in silence, and Everson could only assume it was because he had been caught taking liberties with the daughter of his host.

"I just want you to know, Baron," the prince began contritely as they both came to a stop before a solid steel door, "nothing more would have happened with Miranda."

The baron turned to him, as if surprised that the subject had resurfaced. "I'm not a prude, Everson. Miranda is a young woman and she knows her own mind. My only fear is that she might have given you an incomplete picture of how things are."

Baron Ayers stepped back, revealing a keypad next to the door. Warning bells went off in Everson's head. Memories of the Tree flooded his mind, snippets of anomalous technology.

As soon as the baron entered a code, the door slid open, and Everson winced at the sudden bright light. When his eyes adjusted to the change in illumination, he found the baron appraising him with an indecipherable expression.

He nodded for him to follow through the opening.

"Where are we going?" Everson asked, his senses on high alert, almost to the point of combat-readiness. He didn't comment on the advancing and seemingly self-motivated light.

The baron's answer was measured, and his meticulous tone conveyed the importance of the historical context. "I don't know if you know, but Middle Tier used to be the capital of Mano. My mansion used to belong to the kings past. They eventually moved the capital to Mist Tier to be close to the planet's only constant supply of water. At any rate, my mansion was built atop the hull of an ancient ARC that landed here."

"An ARC?" Everson asked. He was faintly familiar with the term but couldn't recall the acronym.

"Yes, the Astral Repatriation Communities."

That answered the mystery of Middle Tier's random placement. The settlement had literally fallen out of the sky. Everson saw that they were approaching the end of the corridor and another enigmatic door.

The baron continued his tutorial. "After the Great Schism, your people survived aboard similar ones. The capital city of Agrilon is also built around an ARC."

They stopped before the door, but Everson noticed that the baron did not immediately engage the second keypad. His host sighed heavily and placed a steadying hand on Everson's shoulder.

"Which is how I'm able to communicate with Indira," he said.

The statement was so unexpected and outlandish that it froze Everson to the spot. He stared, unable to process, trying to restart the stuttering engine of his mind. He was dimly aware of the baron punching in a code and the door sliding open next to him. He unconsciously followed the baron into the control room, barely taking note of the complex gadgetry within the chamber.

"You've been in contact with Indira?" he finally asked, still stunned.

"A moment," the baron replied, holding up a finger in lieu of a real answer. He quickly moved a second chair before the console and gestured for the soldier to sit. He then slid into his own chair and initialized a sequence. The concave screen glowed with life.

Commander Giza appeared, a hologram so dimensional in form as to be sitting in the same room.

"Baron, we've been expecting you." The commander spoke to the baron but looked at Everson.

Everson felt suddenly insubordinate, facing his commanding officer out of uniform and, worse, draped in Manolithic finery as if he were on vacation. He burned with embarrassment.

"He can see us?" Everson blurted, not grasping the fact that he could be heard as well.

Before the baron could answer, Everson was further mortified to see Queen Patra and King Raza enter the frame. His mother reached out, like him, fooled by the clarity and intimacy of the projected image, believing for a moment that she could touch him.

"Everson!" she exclaimed with such wonder and relief that it brought a lump to Everson's throat. Likewise, his father stared at him with unabashed gratitude and emotion.

"By the Blessed Light of Femera and Amali, you're alive!" he exclaimed.

"Yes, Father," Everson muttered, overwhelmed.

Tears might have filled Everson's eyes if it were not for the irrational anger he felt welling up inside him. For reasons he could not comprehend, much less control, he once again felt like that resentful teenager called to account before his parents. Even in spite of the soul-searching he had undertaken as of late. Ambushed and betrayed, he turned on the baron with an accusatory tone.

"I trusted you, Baron," he said.

The baron met his eyes with unflinching calm. "I know. Forgive me, Everson. But what I'm doing is not only for your good but for the good of millions."

Everson snorted derisively. He hated himself for it, but still he did. "Everyone seems to know what's best for me without actually consulting me about it."

He waited for an eruption, but it didn't come. After a moment of awkward silence, his mother stepped forward.

"My son, do you not recognize that we've all taken far too many painful steps to find ourselves in the same obstinate place as before?" she asked. "You're alive, that's all that matters."

Everson studied his parents and saw a level of acceptance that he did not recognize. He had given his father ample reason to become confrontational, but the king had not risen to the bait. Clearly, the news of his apparent death had given his parents a different perspective.

Everson conceded that his mother was right. He had seen and learned many things. He had endured pain and had felt pain for others. He would be a fool not to evolve. Everson took a deep breath and nodded.

"Do not be angry with the baron," King Raza began. "He is an ally and his motives are pure."

Everson cast a remorseful glance at the baron. He extended a conciliatory hand, and Ayers did not hesitate to take it.

"I've always found it ironic that both our peoples wage war in the name of peace," Baron Ayers opined. "I am a traitor to my own planet for the same reason."

It all made instant sense: this chain of events, the baron's covert identity, even Everson's own presence among those who would set the tenor of the war. The baron's words resonated. Everson had grown slowly accepting of the mysterious machinations of an unseen hand, and now it was time he embraced his own destiny.

"Don't attempt to rescue me, Father," he said. "I have reason to be here."

The baron patted his leg in gratitude. "I'm glad to hear you say that."

"We've already planned to invade Mano," Raza said, reclaiming some of his royal temperament. "Getting you back is a very fortunate coincidence. But, mark my words, I'm coming personally to ensure your safety."

Commander Giza, who had faded back respectfully, moved forward in protest. "Your Highness, I cannot recommend that you travel to Mano. It is far too dangerous."

"Commander, I have been responsible for losing my son once," Raza snapped. "I will not allow it to happen again."

Everson was moved by his father's newfound devotion, but he found the imminent invasion a more immediate concern.

"Mother, what do you make of all this?" he asked.

"I agree with the king," she replied. "About the invasion. About everything. I would mobilize every last man on Indira to bring peace and to bring you home."

It was done. The monarchy had arrived at a mutual mandate, and Everson knew that meant there was no stopping it.

"What can we do here?" the baron eagerly inquired.

"Keep my son safe for the time being," the king ordered. "And then ensure that he is in Mist Tier the night of the Aurora Constellation. It may sound bold, but we will all convene in Xander's palace itself."

"It shall be done, King Raza."

Everson knew that this was the pivotal moment when hypothetical preparation became irrevocable action. This was the moment when he could reveal all and tell his parents about the Tinderbox and its attendant DOGs. But the soldier still feared what they could become in the hands of someone intent on complete victory, even if that someone was his own father. He'd seen what the orb and Rex could do firsthand, let alone the ability to teleport on a whim through the space cabinet. Perhaps there was yet another way.

If Everson had access to Allegra, was it possible that he could also convene with King Xander? He remembered the vision of a maniacal tyrant with a bloody sword in his hand. The prince would have to engage the man before that rampaging, unreasonable specter became reality. And it would have to be soon in light of the scheduled storming.

Would Xander willingly step down if he knew what destruction lay in store? Would not then the Prophecy be fulfilled? From what Everson understood, it only called for Xander's reign to end, not for him to die.

It seemed a reasonable course of action, all things considered. Untold lives would be saved. Surely, he could make Xander see the humanity of such a decision. The merciless alternative would be all-out war.

"Father, I know that I'm not qualified to advise you on military matters, but I have a request," Everson said.

"Yes."

"I've seen the suffering of the people of Mano, and the price they have paid for this war. Please make this battle as surgical as possible."

Oddly, Raza smiled. His expression threw Everson into a distant and almost forgotten memory.

When he had been a young boy, before the tumult of his teenage years, his grandfather Aziz the Cultivator had given him the sapling of a fruit tree to bring back to the palace. The excited young prince had found the perfect spot for it in the palatial garden. He had lovingly tended to it daily, watching in fascination as it had reached for the light and blossomed. When he had brought his father the first piece of fruit bestowed by the plant, Everson remembered seeing this same expression.

It was pride.

The resonant voice of his father, King Raza the Forty-Seventh, brought Everson back to the present.

"Spoken like a true king," he said.

TWENTY

OLAF SHOULD NOT have approached her body. Viewed at a distance, her regal vestments should have been enough to identify her, if confirmation was all that he sought. But, as if by some somnambulistic gravity, he had been drawn to her side, where he could clearly view the decimation. The vision of her beautiful face would now forever be usurped by the aftermath of the decaydas' industry.

When he had not heard from The Which, Chancellor Olaf grew concerned. After all, he had last seen her waiting expectantly outside the Tree, victory and vindication all but within her grasp. He had forced himself to be patient, but when news was not forthcoming, doubt and paranoia wormed their way in.

The Which had claimed to have an Indiran soldier at her behest, and that was a detail not likely to be kept secret for long, especially with an entire garrison of warmen ensconced in Front Tier. For all Olaf had known, his beloved could have been in the clutches of the cretinous General Bahn, his interrogation and torture wresting their subterfuge from her.

Olaf had fabricated an excuse to go find out for himself that would have been painfully transparent to anyone other than his distracted king. He had informed Xander that he needed to consult with The Which about which tier would be best to elect a new champion from, a suggestion he had hoped would illustrate his undying devotion to the monarch's welfare. Xander had simply waved his assent without a second thought.

Olaf had immediately boarded his birdun and had set out for the Tree. In retrospect, it was a trip he wished he had never taken. He screamed his grief violently into the silence of the ruins until he was empty and spent, a husk of what he once had been when The Which had loved him.

The return trip to Mist Tier had been a blur, made hazier by the tears that seemed ceaseless.

Upon arriving back at the palace, Olaf had fled to his chambers, fearful of any encounter that would require him to behave normally. He had collapsed onto his bed, numb and motionless, surrounded by the elegant accoutrements of his achievements.

This luxurious life meant nothing without her.

Now, at this late hour, the chancellor roused himself to deliver the calamitous news to Xander. He found the king in his royal bedchamber, in a state he quite expected. Xander was drunk. Queen Nor was nowhere to be found.

"Pray tell me you've found a way to suspend time. Otherwise, leave me be," Xander slurred, aware enough to recognize that someone else had entered the room.

Olaf swallowed hard, struggling to overcome his disgust and devastation.

"I...I have most disturbing news to report," he said. "The Which of Front Tier has been killed."

Xander's unfocused eyes found Olaf. He wobbled to his feet and swayed unsteadily. "What? By whom?"

"Your Highness..." Olaf trailed off, the effort of relaying even false facts bringing a wave of nausea. Her eyes had been eaten away. Most of her face had been gone. Olaf steeled himself and forced the image from his mind. He mechanically recited the words he had practiced with each painful step up the curving staircase to the royal bedchamber. "We don't know. It appears to have been a commoner driven to desperation. Robbery perhaps."

King Xander flopped back into his chair, the effort of remaining upright apparently too taxing. His watery eyes stared into space and a shaking hand went to his throat.

"It's like a noose tightening around my neck," he grated.

Of course, the king held no remorse for The Which—no mention of the monumental loss to the kingdom. Olaf felt his grief edging toward rage.

Xander continued morosely, "My own daughter dreams of soldiers."

A jolt of fear shot through Olaf. "Indiran soldiers?" he blurted. He already suspected that the Indiran was responsible for the death of The Which.

Xander's attention hinged toward the chancellor. "Why would you say that?" rasped the king, his reddened eyes now vengeful rather than vacant.

Thankfully, Olaf's adroit and devious mind did not fail him, the fog of his sorrow dissipating in the heat of Xander's stare.

"I only echo General Bahn's presumption," he said.

King Xander pushed himself forcefully from his seat. He stalked toward Olaf.

"Don't humor me, Olaf," he said. "You are as afraid as I am. I can see it in your eyes."

Olaf almost laughed. For the first time, he was grateful for the monarch's arrogance. How could this king be so clueless as to so misconstrue his bereavement and guilt?

Xander was very near to him now, too near, his eyes locked on Olaf's with a knowing leer. The sour stench of terrazka assaulted Olaf's nose, but he refused to give ground.

King Xander continued, his tone certain, "There is an unseen evil at work, and the only face you can put to it belongs to the wretched Indirans. It surrounds us. It mocks our futility."

Olaf needed this. Without knowing it, he had needed the galvanizing effects of Xander's incompetence to prevent him from slipping into his own self-pity. He felt the strength of his convictions returning, the drive of his ambition, the plans that he had fashioned with his intended. He owed it to his love to persevere.

"Don't be fatalistic, sire," Olaf said. "I assure you, my every thought is consumed by the timely need to arrive at a solution."

"Timely? Hardly." Xander sneered at him, then turned his back. "Notify General Bahn, the troops are now on high alert. They must be ready to move at a moment's notice. Tell him to conscript more soldiers if necessary."

"Sire, there are no more men of fighting age," Olaf said.

"Then lower the age, blast you! For the love of Light, Olaf, use some imagination! Enlist young women if you have to! Just tell him!" Xander roared. "And no one gets in or out of the royal palace upon pain of death. I will ride out this storm one way or the other."

Olaf was all but forgotten as Xander's attention returned to his bottle. These infrequent interludes of lucidity were enough to delude Xander into believing that he was still in charge, and Olaf was happy to cede to him his misconceptions.

His mind was once again rife with plot, and the king was commanding his way right into his hands. The son of a page would take the Crown.

In the wake of his loss, perhaps he would take Queen Nor as well.

* * *

Allegra's balcony doors were open, but it was not a restless breeze that awakened her. Her body was covered with bed-sheets, but she roused to find herself tingling with a sensation like stepping out of a steaming bath and into the cool night air.

Even before her eyes fluttered open, Allegra anticipated what she would see. She sat up, an expectant smile already gracing her face, only to be disappointed that her soldier wasn't standing at her bedside.

Maybe it really was a dream... she thought.

Then she spotted the large black box that had brought him before sitting in the center of her room. She studied it for a moment, her anticipation tinged with anxiety. It simply sat there with no sound or movement, like a specter of negative space, ominous in its nothingness.

Wearing only her nightgown, Allegra slid from her bed and tentatively approached the waiting shape.

As she neared the end of her bed, tiny lights and confusing displays hummed to life on the dark façade. She stopped, suddenly feeling vulnerable in her nightclothes. Before she could dive back under her covers, the box opened, its double doors swinging silently outward. Allegra held her ground and peered into the dark interior, hoping to see her soldier.

The box appeared to be empty. Rather, Allegra realized after a moment, the box appeared to be endless.

She seemed to be looking through a portal into space. The blackness was infinite, spotted with a drizzle of stars, their glittering light diminishing with the immeasurable distance. She was understandably apprehensive.

Am I simply supposed to trust and throw myself into the void?

The decision was made for her in the form of an intense blue light that shot out from the interior of the box.

The beam of light enveloped her, and Allegra went rigid. She was lifted slowly from the floor to hover in midair, her nightgown fluttering gently in the breeze from her balcony. Only her eyes seemed to retain their independence, and she watched with mounting concern, helpless as the blue beam pulled her toward the maw of the black box.

She fought to calm her racing heart. After all, she wanted this; to be transported far from the cruelty of her father's prison, to once again see her unlikely ally.

Far be it for her to be finicky about the vehicle of her conveyance. Princess Allegra surrendered to the mysterious power, and she floated into the blackness and the unknown. The doors closed behind her.

* * *

Everson had never known romantic love. He had known young women, certainly, but his casual acquaintance with love had only come from a distance and only as a concept. The prince had no doubt that his parents shared love, but theirs was not the stuff of giddy preoccupation so often associated with the emotion. The manner in which Raza and Patra meticulously maintained their respect and affection over the years had led Everson to believe that love was an eventuality, like wisdom, that was only acquired with time and experience.

Never did he conceive that love could be an occurrence both sudden and overwhelming. Until now.

Everson had not given thought to the late hour when he had summoned the space cabinet. He had only wanted the manor to be still and quiet and the chance of interruption to be lessened. When Princess Allegra emerged through the portal, slightly flustered at the abruptness of the trip, but flushed with anticipation, her alabaster features made even more fair by the virginal allure of her white attire, Everson understood why poets were compelled to muse eloquent upon the miraculous and inexplicable effects of love.

He had positioned himself near the open balcony doors since that had proven to be such an effective locale for Miranda. He stood, nervously shifting on the spot, not knowing what to expect. The last thing he expected was for Allegra to be wearing her nightgown.

"Good evening, Princess," Everson said, trying his best to seem composed and courtly.

Allegra's eyes darted around the room, taking everything in, obviously astounded to be anywhere other than back in her quarters in her father's palace. "Where am I?" she asked, breathless.

"I think it's best that you don't know for now. Do you know who I am?"

"We've not been formally introduced, but I have an idea."

"My name is Everson," he said without extending his hand, as if he dared not disturb the electric air between them lest there be sparks.

"I'm Allegra," she said, equally as forthright, and Everson was impressed with her lack of pretension.

"I know."

"You're Indiran."

"Yes."

"Fitting."

Princess Allegra drifted slowly toward the soldier, the room growing warmer with every step despite the open balcony doors. She was almost within touching distance when she stopped.

Everson blanched, caught, knowing that the princess had seen his eyes drifting involuntarily downward.

"Forgive me, I didn't have time to dress," she said.

Everson noticed pink blossoms flowering in the delicate territory beneath her clavicle before he self-consciously looked away.

"I'm not offended," he said, attempting lightness, but fearing he had only succeeded in sounding lascivious. He was prepared for her disdain, but, instead, her face became enraptured with delight.

Everson thought it was intended for him, but Allegra stepped past him, onto the balcony and into the panoramic view of Middle Tier.

A few random lights still burned warmly in the darkened structures in spite of the late hour. Though the tier was of a size that suggested an abundant population, the streets were quiet thanks to the curfew.

"I've never been outside the confines of my father's palace." She spoke to the night rather than turn to Everson. "I apologize if I seem dazzled by the newness of it all."

Everson joined her on the balcony, moving gently to her side as unobtrusively as possible, aware of what this moment must hold for her. The princess finally turned to him; the initial rush of passion subsided and was replaced by a gentle wonder.

"Are we really here, or is this just another dream?" she asked.

"I can assure you, Princess, it's quite real," he said.

She regarded Everson, who was no longer dressed in uniform but wearing clothes that would have made any suitor presentable.

"Let me touch you?" she said with innocent candor, a question rather than a request.

As Everson looked back at her, there was no doubt that he would desire nothing more. Allegra stepped nearer and they both stopped breathing. She reached up with exquisite slowness, and with a tenderness reserved only for mothers and lovers, she caressed his cheek.

"Quite real," Allegra murmured.

"Getting more real by the moment," Everson replied thickly.

Allegra released a girlish giggle. Everson smiled, but he was somewhat bemused. Technically, this was their first date, and even though he had managed his expectations, Everson still felt a certain amount of pressure to make a good impression. Allegra was nothing less than a relief. Her childish wonder, her enthusiasm that sought to neither flatter nor conceal, her entire presence was reassuring to Everson in spite of the fact that they had, for all intents and purposes, just met. He had never spent much time discovering his true self, but the prince now imagined that this invigorating young woman could inspire him to do just that.

"So..." Allegra said, beaming. "How does it feel to be in an arranged marriage?"

"I might have resented it until I saw you," Everson answered honestly.

"Yes," the princess said, and she tilted her head in a way that almost made Everson stop listening. "I didn't believe it until now. And now...everything seems to make perfect sense."

Everson held the steadiness of her gaze. A stillness embraced them both. He was so focused on her eyes that the details of the room grew soft around her, much as light diminishes with distance from a candle's flame. He knew what would usually happen next. But this time was different from any of the other times that had come before. This was something new, like a gift unopened and pristine.

Even at his relatively young age, Everson knew that moments like these were few and that they became the stuff of cherished memory. So even though Allegra's eyes had given him permission, Everson did perhaps the most princely thing he had ever done. He recognized the moment for what it was, and he simply let it be.

* * *

Geneva moved thoughtfully down the darkened hall, a single candle held before her to light her way. The general lighting for the entire palace was controlled from a central command center, much like the all-seeing surveillance cameras, and Chancellor Olaf had imposed a curfew on their use, literally flipping a few switches and throwing the palace into darkness. How forcing the staff to bump about blindly was keeping them safer was beyond Geneva's reasoning, but such decisions were not made with input from servants such as she. It was her opinion, which she uncharacteristically but wisely kept to herself, that the chancellor often did things simply because he could.

Sleep was an impossibility for the handmaiden, her mind overflowing with concern for her best friend and mistress. Geneva fancied herself similar to the single candle, lonely in her feeble attempt to illuminate these dark days. It was an occupation harder and harder to accomplish, since the princess seemed not only immune to her efforts, but consciously deflecting Geneva's consolation.

After breakfast, Allegra had returned to her quarters even more sullen and remote than before. To the consternation of Geneva's scandalous curiosity, Allegra had not divulged a single detail of what had obviously been a disastrous meeting with her parents.

At first, Geneva was merely disappointed, but her friend had grown increasingly uncommunicative as the day wore on, and Geneva had become hurt and concerned. She could deal with Allegra's anger and resentment, had even reveled in the camaraderie created by her rebellion, but being shut out by the young woman she worshipped wounded her deeply.

Geneva found herself outside the door to Allegra's room, and she could not resist the temptation to check on her. She gently pushed open the door, not intending to enter, only to peek in. She was seized with instant alarm. Allegra's bed was empty.

She gasped and hurried to the bedside, the delicate flame of her candle extinguished in the rush.

Dropping the now-useless candle, Geneva's hands groped wildly at the rumpled bedsheets. There was no warmth here; this bed had been vacant for some time.

"Allegra?" she cried aloud, but silence was her only answer. Her eyes fell upon the gently billowing curtains that framed the open doorway to the balcony.

Geneva's panic ramped to near hysteria and she scrambled onto the balcony. Tears already flowing from her eyes, she stopped herself at the stone railing in terror of what she might find over the edge. Praying to the mercy of Femera and Amali, vowing her eternal servitude and chastity, Geneva summoned every fiber of her courage and peeked over the rail.

Emotion gushed out of her in a wail of relief. No broken body lay pitifully on the cliffs. All Geneva saw were the black rocks jutting far below, sodden but stalwart in their ceaseless standoff against the ocean's pounding surf.

The sobbing handmaiden collapsed, trembling against the rough coolness of the stone railing. *Curse this king; curse this palace; curse this Prophecy that would even allow me to think such bleak and morbid thoughts.*

But the crisis still remained. Princess Allegra had somehow escaped.

Geneva struggled to slow the heaving bellows of her breath. She had to think. Her allegiance to Allegra's secrecy was in direct conflict with the overriding concern she had for her best friend's safety.

This was not something that she could, in all good conscience, keep to herself.

* * *

Queen Nor had been in the observatory when Chancellor Olaf delivered the disturbing news about The Which. She had gone there mostly because Xander would not be there, but also because the queen found herself compelled to view the heavens.

Unlike the paranoid king, Nor had not peered through the telescope set unerringly on the Aurora Constellation as if she could change the cosmos. She was content simply to consider the vast canvas of the night sky.

She knew that the stars were moving, just as she knew that the planets were rotating and that the suns were destined to rise. Though she was queen and sovereign of all that she surveyed, it made her feel small and insignificant.

Nor had always been a serious person, but she could remember a time when she might have considered herself happy. Her life had certainly been marked by moments of joy. Her marriage to Xander had been cause for planetary celebration. Their union was supposed to have heralded a new direction, a new era that would bring an end to war and usher in an age of peace and prosperity.

In her youthful altruism and optimism, the fresh new queen had believed it to be so. But with each successive dawning of the male and female suns that ruled the sky, Nor realized that the monarchy was, in reality, a promise unfulfilled, a vow eventually to be forgotten.

The birth of her daughter had rejuvenated her. For a time, Nor knew the joy that only comes when the care of a child supersedes all other concerns. The beatific smile and musical laughter of the baby Allegra had filled Nor's days, and she had been content. But once again, time had crept up on her, and Allegra had grown, maturing into an independent and inquisitive child who had wondered why the walls of the palace had become the boundaries of her world.

The Prophecy had been lore long before the intersection of Nor and Xander. When Allegra had emerged a girl, Nor had recognized the quiet salutation of Fate, but she had set aside the sign like an unwanted heirloom, knowing full well that it would one day reappear. Xander's response had been far less refined. Of course, there had been the requisite desire for a male heir, but the king's dark expression when presented with a daughter spoke to a much deeper disappointment and a far more personal foreboding.

The relationship between Nor and her husband was never the same.

Now, Nor perched stiffly in the elegant sitting area of the royal bedchamber and stared at her husband. Xander was sprawled prostrate upon their bed, mouth open and drooling, his ragged snores rending the otherwise regal air.

Queen Nor was beyond disgust. She was beyond feeling much of anything for Xander. He was not the reason she had remained steadfast in her defense of the realm. She was still queen of Mano, and that was a responsibility that the universe had bestowed upon her as certainly as it had dealt them this curse.

It occurred to her that no provision had been made by the Prediciders for what would come after the Prophecy was fulfilled, if indeed it came to pass. In Xander's potential absence, someone still had to rule if the Manoliths as a race were going to survive and not be swallowed by the invading Indirans.

The queen heard a timid rap at the chamber door and wondered who could possibly have business at this late hour. She shook her head tiredly. There was no sanctuary in this place. It was more than likely Chancellor Olaf, checking in on her as if he thought that was a reassurance to her. In truth, if she were forced to endure him much more than minimally required, she might have to join Xander in drink.

"Enter," commanded the queen. Unexpectedly, Geneva the handmaiden appeared, her words tumbling hurriedly and almost inaudibly from her mouth.

"Forgive me, Your Highness. I'm so sorry to disturb you." Geneva stopped just inside the door, not daring to enter further.

"No bother," the queen reassured her. "And you're certainly not disturbing the king."

As if contributing to the conversation, Xander snorted drunkenly in his sleep. Though the handmaiden's head remained bowed, Nor could see that her cheeks were wet with recent tears. Her hands wrestled worriedly with each other.

Some additional drama concerning Allegra, no doubt. What better way to bookend her day?

"What is it?" The queen sighed.

Geneva finally made eye contact. "Your Highness, there is something that I think you must know."

* * *

The queen swept imperiously into Allegra's bedchamber. Unlike Geneva, who trailed like flotsam in her wake, Nor was concerned, but not overly alarmed by her daughter's absence. One of the tangential benefits of Allegra's captivity in a secluded wing of the palace, overlooking the cliffs and with no other way out, was that Nor considered it an impossibility for harm to befall her daughter.

Whatever had occurred here, the queen quickly concluded, it had been of Allegra's own making.

"I only fear for her safety," Geneva whimpered.

It must be difficult to live one's life in a constant state of apology, Nor thought fleetingly; however she did not respond out loud.

Instead, she expertly assessed the deserted room but found no evidence of Allegra's escape.

Nor felt authoritarian anger tightening her jaw. Not only had her daughter defied her, she had outsmarted her. The queen wasn't sure which stung more. She now regretted removing the surveillance cameras from Allegra's room.

"Return to your chambers, Geneva," she ordered. "Tell no one. I'll handle this."

* * *

"I cannot bear the thought of returning to that prison," Allegra declared darkly, taking a sip of wine.

"For the time being, I'm afraid you must," Everson replied. "No one can suspect that we've met."

The pair were reclined comfortably on the guest bed, sharing a glass of the baron's exquisite wine. Allegra was tempted to tell him that this was her first glass of wine, but, for the time being, she decided to keep the list of her many firsts to herself. There had been that awkward, heart-pounding moment when she could tell that the soldier knew what she was thinking, desiring, but he had allowed the impulse to pass. Allegra still hadn't decided whether she was disappointed or relieved, but Everson's restraint had allowed them to move into more mundane but certainly safer territory.

They had talked into the middle of the night and had now circled back to a subject that Allegra was delighted to discover was a consternation to them both—the Prophecy.

Allegra set down the wine and popped onto her knees, her eyes aflame. When she had first learned of the Prophecy, from this busybody chambermaid or that, she had been a young girl not quite in her teens. At that age, the idea of love and marriage had been inconceivable, but the magical connotations of her supposed destiny had confounded her even more.

Young Allegra had stared into her looking glass on many occasions, examining her features, trying to reconcile how she could be the object of such a preposterous notion.

Allegra had found her face acceptable enough, but, in her sequestered existence, she'd had no inkling of how the opposite sex might see her. Was she pretty? Was she desirable? Was she lovable; not in the cute and platonic context of childhood but in the way of a woman whose charisma could inspire longing and devotion?

With the insecurity and uncertainty of untested sensuality, Princess Allegra had long wondered how any young man could possibly fall in love with her. Everson's enamored expression the entire time they talked had finally given her the answer.

"Why?" she said brightly. "Why can't we just run away together and let the cursed Prophecy play out as it will?"

Everson regarded her, and, at first, it appeared to Allegra that he was actually considering it. But then he grew serious and his eyes became distant.

"There was a time not so long ago when I would have agreed with you," he said. "In fact, I did run. I ran away from everything every chance I got. Strangely enough, I ran so hard that I ran into my own destiny."

"You mean with me?"

"Yes."

Allegra gazed at Everson with gratitude and wonder. No one else had ever spoken to her so plainly. It occurred to her that she was a blank slate to this young man. Everson's candor came from the fact that he seemed to harbor no preconception or judgment about her. The thought was exhilarating.

As close as she was to Geneva, they would always be princess and handmaiden and, accordingly, there would always be the veneer of privilege to their discourse. She was a responsibility to her mother and, even now, she couldn't tell where she stood in order of importance to her. She was a curse to her father, a grotesque tumorous growth too large to cover up and too entrenched to amputate.

But here before her was a real opportunity for a new beginning, a fresh start. As if she needed any other reason to find Everson exceedingly attractive.

"I never imagined a common soldier could be so noble," she said.

Everson smiled thinly and looked away. Allegra studied his thoughtful face, and she could sense the weight of things that he was not quite ready to share. The two had discussed many things as they had edged toward each other on the bed, first sitting and then easing into a familiarity that made them comfortable enough to recline together without assumption, a single glass of wine the excuse for their intimacy. They had passed the glass back and forth as easily as they had shared personal details and thoughts. Everson had told her about his childhood as the grandchild of a simple farmer, about the lush beauty of Indira. But he had not revealed many of his experiences as a soldier.

Allegra was well aware that there was a war. But she had never given it much thought, and until now, she had never considered how harshly it might affect the lives of those involved. She knew that Everson had seen things that she could not imagine, horrors that he would never forget. So she didn't press. There would be time, she hoped. She would make the time because, for the first time in her young life, Allegra realized that she could be strong enough to share in someone else's pain and help them to shoulder it. Just being with Everson had helped her to know this.

"The common soldier is very noble," Everson said. "More so than most nobles I've seen. The bravery. The honor. The duty. It's time I lived up to that. So we must be patient."

Allegra nodded but was still compelled to ask, "When can I see you again?"

"Soon. Very soon," he said. "As daring as you make me feel, we must be careful. There is far too much at stake. Not least of all, any life that we might make together."

It became very clear to Allegra just how much thought Everson must have given this. He had been strategizing even before he had taken the risk of contacting her. Without knowing her, he could not have predicted if she would be sympathetic to his cause or if she would raise an alarm because he was an enemy intent on overthrowing her father.

And, though the proposition had never been tested, Allegra had no doubt that her father would be ruthless enough to execute any soldier, Indiran or otherwise, who came in contact with her, just to circumvent the Prophecy. Knowing this, it was also clear that, if she were to simply disappear, Xander would be relentless in tracking her down, reaping a swath of suffering for anyone in his path.

No, if they were to achieve long-term resolution, it would require immaculate planning and impeccable timing. She needed to trust Everson and wait for his instruction. Although, one thing he had said kept rising above all the other heady concerns, and Allegra couldn't help but fixate on it.

"Have you really been thinking about a life together?" she asked, suddenly aware of her heart beating faster.

"Lately, yes. I have," Everson answered, his eyes downcast as if shy about the admission.

Princess Allegra reached out and gently caressed his face. Everson locked eyes with her and nothing else seemed to matter. Allegra leaned forward, closed her eyes, and kissed him. Kissed anyone, for the very first time.

* * *

Unseen in the shadows beyond the open door of her daughter's bedchamber, Queen Nor stood watching as Allegra emerged from a black box that appeared out of nowhere and stepped into the quiet darkness of her own bedchamber.

She glided to her bed, a contented smile upon her face. The queen noted with cool detachment that her daughter's step seemed lighter, her hands held at her sides, splayed and floating as if riding on a current of air. Allegra appeared to move to music that only she could hear.

The princess slipped between her sheets and rested her head on her pillow though she did not immediately close her eyes. Even at a distance, Nor could see the enchanted expression on Allegra's face and could easily hypothesize the cause. It wasn't an emotion that she had anticipated for her daughter. Ever. Shrouded in the darkness outside Allegra's room, Nor shook her head wryly. Even in the most normal of times, such a preoccupation for a young girl often led to nothing but turmoil. And these were far from normal times.

The queen also witnessed that the large black box, which had materialized and returned her daughter, had now disappeared. Leaving no trace.

Sorcery was at work here. Yet Nor was strangely inspired and invigorated.

This new development might actually be a mystery that she could solve. As Olaf had once observed, there was no comfort in coincidence, and Nor was convinced that Allegra's nocturnal delinquency was a product of the Prophecy handed down by the Prediciders. If so, then, ironically, her daughter was not only the cause, she was the potential cure.

Perhaps Queen Nor and her husband had been going about this all wrong. They had spent all their time and considerable effort defending against the Prophecy when they should have gone on the offensive and taken the fight to its source. After all, here was the proof that the Prophecy could be as insidious as a whisper through a locked keyhole.

Perhaps, instead of hiding Allegra from covetous eyes, they should have put her on display in all her beauty, tempting the destined suitor to come forth and into their waiting hands. Regardless, something new was now in motion, and the queen's nimble mind knew that it was not too late to change strategy.

TWENTY-ONE

COMMANDER GIZA STOOD on an observation deck high above a cavernous hangar as a sea of Indiran soldiers prepared to board a fleet of troop transports. On the last ill-fated mission, Giza had taken only the number of men he had deemed necessary to secure Front Tier. He would not make the same mistake twice. This time, he was mobilizing a force large enough to take the entire planet once and for all.

Giza was not ignorant of the fact that many of the battalions below him should not be making the trip. After the recent rout at the Grand Schism, it was too soon in their rotation for them to be returning to battle. But Commander Giza had no other choice. He needed to deploy every last fighting man available to insure a decisive victory. The one concession he could make to their battle fatigue was to place those overburdened battalions in the second and third wave of attack and hope that the conflict would be blunted before they would be called upon to enter the fray.

Standing beside Giza was King Raza himself. Despite Giza's repeated protests, Raza had abandoned the regal vestments of the throne and was dressed for battle. To the commander's knowledge, no ruler of Indira had ever personally waded into war. Though reticent, Giza was nonetheless impressed, and he could not deny that Raza's presence was an inspiration to his men.

Giza was also not surprised to see Queen Patra appear on the other side of the king. Commander and queen nodded formally to one another, and Giza felt a twinge of regret. Something was torn between them that would never be mended. Everson's survival had not been by his hand, and Giza knew that his spotless reputation would forever be marred in his monarch's eyes for allowing him to be lost on enemy soil.

Giza gazed down and soberly wondered which of these other brave young men would not be coming home. He truly hoped his king was right, and that this would be the last great planetary battle.

Queen Patra surveyed the throng of other mothers' sons, no doubt thinking the same thoughts as Commander Giza.

"Bring my son home," she said, taking Raza's hand firmly in hers.

Her husband turned to her. "If I return, so will he."

* * *

The Prophecy could not arrive soon enough as far as General Bahn was concerned. At least then there might be some change, and if that meant a change in regime, so be it. He was sworn to defend Mano, but the supreme warman had concluded long ago that the best interests of the planet were not always synonymous with the best interests of Xander the "Infirm."

Still, Bahn was a good soldier to his core and believed deeply that insubordination was tantamount to anarchy. He didn't have to be politically sympathetic with his leader, or even agree with his judgment, to follow orders.

The general's time in Front Tier had not been without incident. To Bahn's consternation, The Which had been assassinated, and Bahn could not fathom any motive for the murder. Her demise only confirmed his bias and lack of faith in the mystics.

After all, what good was the former magi seer's foresight if she had not been able to predict her own death? In the final analysis, Bahn rationalized that The Which's violent passing was fair recompense for the lives of his valiant warmen sacrificed to the Tree.

Now, the general knew that an Indiran invasion was imminent. He also knew that the incursion would not occur here, in Front Tier, the site of their last resounding defeat and the stronghold of most of the general's forces. No, Bahn surmised, if he were the aggressor, he would aim the tip of his spear right into the heart of his enemy—the capital city of Mist Tier. Of course, the seat of power was the one place that Bahn was not allowed to defend, his hands tied by no less than royal decree.

So when Chancellor Olaf unexpectedly entered his field office, General Bahn greeted the emissary with intrigue and cautious optimism, even though he despised the man.

"To what do I owe the honor, Chancellor Olaf?" said the general without rising from his seat.

"I have information regarding the murder of The Which," he said, apparently bringing news so urgent he couldn't be bothered to quibble over protocol per usual. "This information is very delicate, General. It is not to be repeated. To anyone."

Bahn had to admit to a grudging admiration for Olaf's political maneuvering. His own integrity would never allow him such license. It was truly an art to phrase directives in such a way as to never be held accountable, and the chancellor's administration of late had led the general to judge him a slippery character indeed.

There was a time when Bahn had dismissed Olaf as a mere sycophant, but now he felt sure there was purpose to his posturing. He just couldn't be sure which way the chancellor's insidious and abundant wind was blowing. Still, if Olaf's agenda allowed him leeway to pursue his own ends, then the warman was certainly interested.

"Go on," Bahn said, impatiently nodding him along.

"The Which had captured an Indiran soldier—"

"What?" the general interrupted, abruptly springing to his feet. "How is this possible?"

"I do not know the particulars," Olaf answered calmly. "I only know that she was holding him until I could take custody. He must have escaped."

The general realized that Olaf's last statement was a prompt and not a conclusion.

"The Which and the bodies of her entourage were found near the Tree," the general offered, although he suspected that the chancellor already knew.

A small contingent of his warmen on a routine patrol had discovered the scene of the crime. They had reported it to him immediately and had touched nothing until the general had arrived. The evidence had been inconclusive and confounding, providing few clues and little closure. The location near the Tree was obviously of great concern. The Which would have no reason to be there other than to deliver another champion and, to the general's knowledge, no such appointment had been made.

Not for the first time, the thought made Bahn bristle, since the champions were culled from the best his troops had to offer. And the sacrifice of his finest was only compounded by the deaths of those who had died in the challenges, never to even see the inside of the cursed Tree. No, the Prophecy and the childish superstition surrounding it continued to vex him, and he was more than ready to be shed of it.

Still, even if The Which had been delivering a champion, which was unlikely, it didn't explain why she would be accompanied by her own armed escort. Front Tier had been made safe when they repelled the Indiran invasion, and his diligent application of martial law ensured the settlement's security and compliance. The only conclusion that Bahn had reached was that The Which's armed guards were protecting something. Or guarding it with force. Like they might with a prisoner of war.

The Which's entourage had not simply been killed, they had been slaughtered. It seemed inconceivable that the damage could have been inflicted by one person and that the perpetrator could have escaped unscathed. Moreover, it was obvious that The Which had fled and that the murderer, or murderers, had run her down and had dispatched her just as viciously.

This revelation involving an Indiran now made sense, but the general found the implications far more unsettling than if the criminals had proven to be a desperate band of disenchanted commoners.

"Perhaps they were trying to prevent him from entering. I don't know. It's all speculation at this point," reasoned the chancellor. Bahn detected something brittle beneath Olaf's dismissiveness, but, before he could identify it, the chancellor proceeded quickly to his intended point. "But, obviously, we need to recapture him. As quickly and as quietly as possible."

General Bahn sat back down in his chair and eyed Olaf dubiously. He wondered why the chancellor was turning to him. Was it because Bahn himself had first raised the possibility of Indiran complicity in the Prophecy? Or perhaps Olaf was simply trying to tidy the incident before it became public knowledge.

Of course, that raised other questions: who else might be aware of a fugitive Indiran; who might be harboring him; and why was this information only now reaching his ears?

"I'm sure you already have a plan, Chancellor," Bahn said. "All due respect to the dead, but The Which might still be alive had the two of you come to me in the first place."

One of Chancellor Olaf's eyes twitched as if he'd been slapped, but he collected himself, stepped forward, and placed both his hands decisively on the general's desk. "We've had our differences in the past, General, but know that I now agree with you on many fronts. As you may suspect, Xander's judgment is clouded. If it were up to me, your troops would be returned to Mist Tier. He would never allow that. But he has ordered me to inform you that the military is now on high alert. Therefore, he would not question a large contingent decamping to Middle Tier. This is where I believe the Indiran has fled."

The general needed no further encouragement. "I can mobilize troops immediately."

"Scour the tier," Olaf continued, returning to his decorous posture and comportment. "And be prepared to advance to Mist Tier at a moment's notice if need be."

"I must say, you're quite comfortable being in charge, aren't you, Chancellor?"

The chancellor would not be goaded. "I only look to serve the Crown during our king's incapacity."

* * *

Cloudshine.

It was a term that the precocious princess had coined as a child. Long before Allegra had realized that it was actually a part of her prison, the young princess had loved her balcony and the ever-changing view it afforded. The tempestuous ocean had many moods, and Allegra had admired them all.

Her favorite atmospheric phenomenon was when towering blue clouds blocked the suns, yet light would still pierce through in long, sharply defined rays, as if the clouds themselves were bursting with a luminosity that they could not contain. She called it cloudshine.

Allegra had always invested the painterly phenomenon with optimism, as if the universe itself were sending her a sign. After her magical evening with Everson, it was cloudshine that had greeted her when she opened her eyes. The sight had filled her with joy. That buoyant feeling of faith had stayed with her all morning, long after the ephemeral rays of cloudshine had dissipated.

She was so exhilarated that she had barely registered Geneva's absence while she moved to her vanity and started brushing her own hair.

Allegra's demeanor cooled considerably when Queen Nor entered her bedchamber.

"Good morning, Allegra," said the queen, making herself comfortable on the vanity's padded bench, much too closely for Allegra's comfort. "How did you sleep?" she continued as if yesterday's belligerent breakfast had never happened.

"Pleasantly enough, Mother," Allegra replied.

"No more dreams?"

The princess returned to brushing her hair as if the task required all her concentration. "Not of that sort."

Allegra heard her mother sigh and only looked up when Nor gently removed the brush from her hand and placed it on the vanity. Still, she did not turn fully to Nor, instead choosing the indirect contact of their reflections in her looking glass.

"Those dreams are a product of a mind in turmoil," her mother said. "I don't believe I've shown you enough gratitude for your sacrifice. It hasn't gone unnoticed."

When Allegra didn't respond, Nor delicately turned her daughter's chin to face her.

"Allegra, I do look to your future. I know things cannot go on as they have. This Prophecy may prove to be empty and, if it is, I will do everything in my power to release you from this burden."

Allegra gazed into her mother's eyes, wanting desperately to believe her. "I hope so, Mother," she said.

The queen offered a slight smile, and Allegra tried to remember the last time she had seen such a giving expression on her mother's face. Nor then reached up and tenderly stroked Allegra's hair.

Allegra felt a little tickle at her ear and she reached up to scratch it. Her mother intercepted her hand and held it firmly.

"What is it?" Nor said, appearing concerned.

"It's nothing," Allegra replied, glancing askance at her mother's hand on hers. "It just felt like...It's nothing."

"Oh, forgive me, Allegra," the queen said as if in sudden understanding, releasing her daughter's hand. She looked at the jewelry adorning her own hand. "I must have scratched you with one of my rings." She pursed her lips and shook her head in apology. "My affection has grown clumsy, I'm afraid. Out of practice."

"Don't be silly, Mother," Allegra hastened to assure her, although she was more than a little pleased to hear Nor acknowledge their estrangement. "I barely felt it."

"Are you sure?" Nor insisted.

"No more bothersome than a breeze," Allegra said lightly. "Here and gone."

Queen Nor studied her daughter's face, her eyes. She even seemed to glance again at her ear. So intent was her mother's appraising gaze that Allegra wondered what she was looking for. "Be patient, my daughter," Nor said finally. "Misfortune comes from rashness."

Allegra nodded compliantly. Nor leaned forward and kissed her cheek. Then, with one last glance of reassurance at her daughter, the queen took her leave.

She had been gone barely a breath before Geneva scurried into the room.

"Allegra, I'm so sorry," Geneva began, even before arriving at Allegra's side. "Was she harsh? Is there some new punishment?"

"What are you talking about?" Allegra asked.

"She didn't chastise you? She knows you went missing last night."

Allegra's face grew dark. She rose from her vanity with a sinking feeling that she had been duped. The princess rapidly revisited the conversation with her mother in her head. She had said nothing incriminating.

"How could she know that, Geneva?" Allegra asked.

Geneva's hands were engaged in their familiar wringing, and she stepped back timidly.

"Geneva, how does she know?" Allegra pressed.

Geneva's chin fell to her chest. "Forgive me, I told her. I saw that you weren't in your room and I...I panicked."

Allegra looked upon the guilt-ridden face of her friend, her best and only friend, and shook her head in resignation. There was no way she could find fault with Geneva. She had only been concerned for her welfare.

"Geneva, you will be the undoing of me yet."

Geneva wiped a hand against the sniffles at her nose. "So she wasn't angry?"

"On the contrary. She was more loving than she has been in a long time...which worries me even more," said the princess, absently scratching at that annoying tickle in her ear.

* * *

Chancellor Olaf returned to find a flurry of pages fluttering around the palace in search of him. Apparently, Queen Nor had requested his presence, and promptness was not a suggestion. Given all the talk of instant death being bandied about the corridors, the pages were highly motivated to find him, and an entire ream of them descended on him almost immediately after he dismounted his birdun.

Olaf hastened to the throne room, wondering what new and distressing development could have possibly prompted the queen to bypass Xander and summon him directly. He found her pacing impatiently before the empty thrones.

"Where have you been?" she said. "I've been calling for you."

Olaf was prepared to answer, somewhat. Bahn had set his orders in motion even before he had left Front Tier, and the chancellor had no doubt that the road to Middle Tier was already trembling with the weight of the massive troop movement. Paranoid about the transparency of the palace and, worse, fearful that the queen had somehow divined his designs, Chancellor Olaf had no choice but to take refuge in the truth.

"I've been carrying out the king's orders," he said. "I had to meet with General Bahn because the king has put our troops at the ready. I took the liberty of interpreting his orders, and I have repositioned Bahn and a large force to Middle Tier so that they might be close at hand."

Queen Nor registered no reaction. Her expression grew thoughtful and she paced away from the nervous chancellor. Olaf knew that she had the right, by Law of the Harmonious Equal, to upend any unilateral decision made without her consultation. He feared that Nor would veto the troop movements just to put him in his place, castigating him for taking such ambitious initiative on his own. But when the queen turned back to him, Olaf saw with relief that she was nodding in apparent agreement.

"Good," she said decisively. "I need to be in constant contact with the general. I want to know the whereabouts of every last soldier in our army."

"I don't understand, Your Majesty." This was not the agreement Olaf had hoped for.

"I do not wish to worry the king with this information, but our daughter has managed to make her way outside the palace walls. There is only one reason a young woman sneaks out in the middle of the night, and that is to meet a young man. I've set the trap and I want him apprehended the second they meet again. Understood?"

"Completely, Your Highness," Olaf muttered.

The queen swept past him and out of the throne room. Olaf was eviscerated. Though she was not yet aware of the Indiran soldier, the chancellor knew it was only a matter of time. He was also convinced that the fugitive alien and the clandestine lover had to be one and the same.

Olaf had told General Bahn that he believed The Which had died preventing the soldier from entering the Tree. He knew exactly the opposite to be true. The Indiran had been emerging, and the chancellor felt more certain than ever that he had done so with the legendary Tinderbox in hand.

All of them in the royal court had long believed that the ancient artifact must hold some miraculous power, King Xander more than anyone. The more elusive the Tinderbox had become, the more they all became convinced that it was truly the key to defeating the Prophecy and, by extension, the weapon they needed to win the war. Now, if Olaf's suspicions were correct, the thing had been released and its ominous powers put to use.

His beloved and her entourage had not just been murdered, they had been slaughtered. The amber stone in her forehead had been destroyed, shattered as if to mock her gift of foresight. Princess Allegra, the very nexus of the Prophecy, had managed to escape her captivity and rendezvous with her prophetic intended without a soul seeing her. Violence and magic. In a tidy little box.

Olaf bitterly recognized that Bahn would now have to report directly to the queen. If the general did manage to apprehend the Indiran soldier, Olaf would be relegated to reactionary status. No longer in control of the game. With this disastrous turn of events, he didn't know whether to be hopeful that he might still find a way to be in possession of the Tinderbox or if he should be terrified that the blasted thing might yet fall into Xander's undeserving hands.

Chancellor Olaf stared covetously at the empty throne, so near to him yet so far away. He grieved The Which anew. His plans, his dreams, even the direction he might take, all of it was so much clearer when she had been by his side. He tried desperately to conjure the words of comfort and advice she might say to him in a moment such as this. Sadly, all he could think of was that he had failed to tell her that he loved her the last time they had been together.

* * *

Though considered nothing less than a pestilence by farmers, echrows were actually beautiful creatures. Their plumage of predawn gray was speckled with uniform flecks of white. In sharp contrast, their long beaks were bright orange, and when they took to the air en masse, as they always did, they reminded Jonas of bonfires that sent up swirling clouds of smoke dotted with insistent orange cinders.

One such flock erupted now on the far side of his field, and their echoing cries made Jonas look up from his work.

He, Mare, and their daughters were tilling a parcel of field nearest their house. They had harvested this section of terra-nuts and were turning the stubborn soil to aerate and soften it in preparation for planting. A noxious mound of bodine dung and a pile of mulched terranut plant compost were waiting close at hand. Jonas, in deference to his sons, could not bring himself to spread the readily available ashes of fallen Manoliths as fertiliz-er as so many other farmers did.

The one-armed cultivator was eager and excited to get his precious collection of hydreeds into the ground, and he had cho-sen this patch of land closest to the back of his house so that he could keep constant watch on the emerging plants.

Mare and the girls had lodged an initial complaint, since this plot's proximity would ensure an extended period of the odor of bodine excrement wafting inside through the rear windows, small as they were, but Jonas was finally able to convince them of the wisdom of his decision. Not only could he properly police the crop, the position would keep the alien plants from falling under the casual inspection of any passersby to their farm. The prom-ise of the wealth that the hydreeds would bring was enough to persuade his family to abide the malodorous assault for a while.

Now, sweat dripping from his ginger brow, Jonas scanned the distance in the direction of the echrows' clamor. The swirl-

ing gray eruption of creatures soared away, and he could see the cause of their indignant departure.

A roiling cloud of dust billowed beyond his field, and Jonas could now hear the intimidating rumble that accompanied it. A long column of Manolithic TRAUMAs and trucks laden with warmen emerged from the dusty haze, with unmistakable urgency and determination.

Middle Tier would shortly be occupied. Jonas cast a worried glance to Mare, and her face reflected his concern.

Everson's sanctuary was no longer safe.

TWENTY-TWO

HAVING A PET was a simple pleasure, but one that Tobias had never experienced. He was in the studio stretching fresh canvases for Baroness Carlotta when one of the front-of-the-house Leftists burst in and agitatedly told him about the creature that had landed in their courtyard. Tobias rushed to the front to discover the white-crowned birdun, Taj, waiting expectantly.

After the conversation with Everson in the market, the manservant gleefully assumed that Taj was specifically seeking him. After all, Everson had said that the beast was trying to remember his face. And the fact that Taj actually seemed to brighten upon seeing him was all the proof Tobias needed.

He fed him terranut after terranut, murmuring, "Taj," over and over to further imprint the name on the beast and to familiarize him with the sound of his voice. Tobias had little guilt about plundering the baron's produce since the pantry was virtually overflowing with the vegetables courtesy of Jonas' last delivery. The Leftist smiled in delight as the birdun nuzzled his hand, musical trills bubbling from the creature's snout. Their bonding was interrupted by an insistent pounding on the courtyard gate. A gruff male voice yelled for admittance.

Tobias muscled open the heavy gate to discover a near breathless Jonas standing on the other side. The manservant's first thought was that they certainly didn't need any more terranuts. A second, closer look at the man's harried face made the Leftist realize that vegetables were probably not the reason for the visit.

* * *

General Bahn strode through the marketplace in Middle Tier on his way back to his TRAUMA. When his phalanx of war machines roared into the marketplace, many of the commoners in the square fled, the appearance of the military making their errands seem suddenly unimportant. Many of the old vendors remained, apprehensive about the horde of warmen but afraid to leave their wares unattended.

Their goods are safer now that the military is here to instill order, he observed wryly. Though he would never admit it aloud, Bahn often took it personally when his uniform provoked enmity from civilians. He knew that he presented an intimidating authority figure, partially by design, but it was authority that protected them. It was authority that kept the peace. He supposed that only peace would remind them of that, so, during wartime, he saw no other choice than to remain warlike. If that made people ill at ease, then perhaps they were guilty of something.

The queen herself had contacted him while he was en route, and as soon as he ascertained that he wasn't being ordered into an about-face, he hadn't hesitated to be forthcoming about his mission. He owed Olaf no real allegiance, and he certainly would not expose himself to any accusation that he had misinterpreted the Crown's commands.

Queen Nor was highly intrigued to learn that the general's quarry was nothing less than an Indiran soldier and that said soldier had undoubtedly been responsible for the death of The Which. She had endorsed his intentions and then, much to the general's surprise, had given him an uplink to a tracking device that she had assured him would be activated sooner rather than later.

Bahn immediately dispatched several of his officers to question every vendor present and bang on the doors of those who weren't. As in every tier, this marketplace was the heart of the settlement, and the general knew that more than just goods and services were bartered here. The wiliest of the merchants also traded in information, their ability to remain in the know keeping them, literally, on top of the market.

After a lifetime of service, Bahn was reminded that he held little regard for those who only looked out for themselves, but those were exactly the people the general needed to exploit now. He knew it wouldn't take long. There would be plenty of informants who would mistakenly believe that the military would be indebted to them for a bit of intelligence. The others, Bahn would simply threaten. In his experience, the selfish had little spine.

A few choice nuggets of information quickly came to light when the shopkeepers were asked if they had seen anything out of the ordinary. A bothersome birdun had apparently been wandering aimlessly through the market, but the general dismissed the observation as merely an oddity.

A few envious vendors also offered the gossip that a young war widow had recently come into a great deal of wealth. The general ordered a search to find whatever hovel this woman was hiding in when one of his officers supplied him with a more immediate and tangible lead.

Bahn was dubious at first, since the greasy little vendor trembling before him appeared to be nothing more than an opportunist whose first question was whether or not he would be paid for his information. After being assured that imprisonment would be his compensation if he didn't talk, the unscrupulous salesman relayed a tale that quickened the general's heart.

The vendor had encountered a dark-skinned stranger who, stranger still, had purchased a bag of terranuts to waste on the wandering birdun. But the detail that had most captivated the general had been the description of the mysterious man's attire. He had been dressed like a nobleman.

The general was well aware of Middle Tier's penchant for pernicious progressiveness. He had long yearned to quash the liberal leanings of the elite in this entitled tier. Now he had his just cause.

As General Bahn climbed back into his TRAUMA, he knew exactly which door he was going to knock on first.

* * *

Everson thoughtfully studied the grand tapestry that was the focal piece of the baron's dining hall. Now, knowing the political proclivities of the Family Ayers, he thought he understood why Baroness Carlotta had been inspired to memorialize the Great Schism with such reverence. It signified unity and the dissolution of that unity, a time when their respective forefathers had lived in harmonious coexistence until their industrial folly had torn their world asunder. Reunification was a philosophy to which the Ayers' aspired, and that dominated their thinking as undeniably as this tapestry ruled this room.

Still, a subversive thought kept undermining Everson's attempts to fully embrace the Ayers' nostalgia for a time they had actually never known. There was a certain color-blindness implied by the world that the baroness had envisioned. Try as he might, Everson could not believe that equanimity to be true.

After all, it seemed clear that their predecessors had segregated themselves onto separate but equal ARCs according to their color, and that they had purposefully steered their celestial crafts away from one another. How else could the races have remained so pure, regardless of time or environment? It seemed obvious to Everson that those original pilgrims had imposed a cultural isolationism, each believing themselves to be superior and aided in their xenophobia by the vast but temporary gulf of space. Everson came to the sad conclusion that the enmity between Manolith and Indiran had not originated with the Great Schism; it had preceded it.

If this hatred has been passed down through the generations, Everson wondered, *how long will it take to undo it?* Even with a universal commitment, it might take as much time to extinguish the flame as it had taken to maintain it. Everson was beginning to believe that his union with Princess Allegra might be the first step in the rehabilitation of their shared origins.

Baron Ayers interrupted his thoughts and brought him back into the conversation they had been having.

"We must depart for Mist Tier first thing in the morning," he said. "I can get you there, but I have to admit, I don't have a flaming clue how to get you into the palace."

"We may have to wait for the invasion and try to look for an opening in all the confusion," Everson replied.

He wasn't sure why he was still withholding information. He knew how he was going to get into the palace. He had the Tinderbox. He still harbored some slim hope that the conflict could be resolved peacefully and with diplomacy. Even so, Everson conceded that he still had not hit upon a rationale that would bend the will of Xander.

Both Everson and the baron were startled as Tobias burst into the room, his naturally wide eyes even wider. The typically genteel Leftist caused the doors to slam loudly against the walls in his haste.

"Forgive me, I don't wish to interrupt, but I thought you should both know," he said, barely able to catch his breath. "The tier is overrun with warmen. Master Everson, I worry for your safety even here."

The baron remained calm and thought for the briefest of moments.

"We'll have to put you in the lower levels," the baron decided. "It's the most secure place in the mansion."

Everson was already rising from his chair. "I'll gather my things."

* * *

King Xander felt like he was already dead and that he had become a phantom. Most subjects who encountered him in the corridors didn't look at him, and those who did seemed to look through him with blank expressions and the stiffened postures of the ill at ease. There was a time when they would cower and bow at his passing, but the king had to admit that his once regal stride had become a less than awe-inspiring shuffle.

The Prophecy stated quite simply—the reign of Xander the Firm will come to an end. Repeat a supposition often enough and people will eventually believe it to be true. He was abandoned, his subjects distancing themselves from him as they might from the stench of a rotting corpse. Still, Xander had never considered it a condition of the Crown to be loved. There was always Olaf, but, these days, the king put little stock in the chancellor's counsel. He could see the tarnished patina of judgment in Chancellor Olaf's eyes, and he resented him for it.

His only true ally, by marriage and by the Imperial Law of the Harmonious Equal, was Queen Nor. She had stood by him through this entire debacle, seeking solutions to the infernal Prophecy and even going so far as to ratify, without question, his decision to sequester their daughter. So Xander had been more than surprised by the queen's vehement defense of Allegra at that latest irritating and unnecessary breakfast.

He had merely said that they wouldn't be in this predicament if they didn't have a daughter. An offhand comment. A random thought. And one that was irrefutably true. It certainly didn't warrant a vicious attack, especially since he was already set upon from all sides. After all, it wasn't as if his unfiltered thoughts, as insensitive as Nor deemed them to be, would have any real consequence.

Perhaps it was because Allegra had been born later in his life, when the weight and demands of the Crown had already been heavy on Xander's head. Or maybe it was just his inherent nature that made him as unyielding and unnurturing as the unforgiving rock of which he was king. Either way, Xander had never possessed a speck of paternal instinct for his daughter.

He hadn't asked to become a father, just as he hadn't asked to be burdened by this preposterous Prophecy. He was the victim here. He was blameless. In fact, the more he thought about his wife's sudden and nonsensical defense of Allegra, the more deeply wounded and indignant he became. Xander found it highly unreasonable for Nor to expect him to embrace the very vessel of his undoing.

As he often did, Xander found himself wandering into the observatory. Even though Mist Tier's sky was bright and featureless, he mechanically put his eye to the telescope's eyepiece, as he had thousands of times before.

The brightness of the day caused by the twin suns' glare gave him nothing but stabbing rays of pain in his hungover eye. He winced and pulled away from the lens, standing forlorn and without reason in the deserted observatory.

One night, and one pointless day—that was all he had left.

Why do fools take such comfort in the daylight? the king wondered morosely.

Dangerous things moved during the day as easily as they crept through the night, their insidious advance camouflaged by the warmth and brightness. The two suns in the sky, like the eyes of a benevolent universe, looked down on the ignorant and lulled them into complacency and a deluded sense of safety. King Xander the Firm knew better.

The Aurora Constellation was coming, and with her she brought the Prophecy. The stars and moons that defined her shape were approaching their destinations even now. Though he had never viewed her fully formed in real life, Xander had seen renderings of her: A regal queen, her patrician face in profile, reclining on her throne with her hand on her chin as if in judgment.

The king was struck by a thought that had never occurred to him before. It left him feeling freshly victimized and awash in self-pity. *Of course it's a woman who's come to judge me*, Xander thought resentfully. *A man might have been more merciful.*

* * *

Princess Allegra stepped from the glittering blackness of the space cabinet and into the warm glow of Everson's room. She was titillated at the brazenness of sneaking out during daylight. At least she was dressed properly this time.

Everson was waiting to receive her, standing almost formally by the bed. She ran into his arms and kissed him before he could even utter a word. After a heated moment, she broke free and gazed into his eyes, breathless.

"Everson," she said, "I didn't dare dream I would see you again so soon."

"It can't be for long," he replied, and she noted the urgency in his tone. "You can't be missing, or it will raise an alarm. I need you to find the most secure place in your father's palace, and I need you to stay there tomorrow night during the constellation. Don't come out, whatever you might hear. And I would urge you to take anyone dear to you there as well."

Allegra absorbed the gravity of Everson's words, the sobriety and sincerity of his expression. This was not a trivial tryst. This was a prelude to an event that could forever change the course of her life.

"My family," she said, surprising even herself. "I know they've been horrid to me, but they're still my parents. I don't wish them harm."

"I'll leave that to your judgment," Everson replied. "But it is imperative that you say nothing to them until after nightfall."

"As you wish," said Allegra, impressed beyond words at Everson's ready compassion. That he would show mercy to those who would see him dead astounded her. To her simple understanding of war and warmen, he had been trained to take lives, not save them. The more she learned about this young soldier, the more she felt fortunate that the universe had chosen him.

"I don't expect them to be willing participants. But no matter what happens, no matter what your parents might think, I believe we can end this war and stop the fighting."

"I wish that with all my heart."

Everson pulled the princess into him and kissed her deeply. Allegra felt a flutter in her ear and wondered briefly if it was a giddy by-product of passion. She was so inexperienced in such matters and she knew that she had much to learn. But when the feeling moved from her ear to her cheek, she knew that the blasted tickle had returned.

She broke away from Everson and she brushed her hand against her cheek as if trying to replace an errant wisp of hair.

She glanced shyly at Everson. He was looking at her curiously, obviously confused by her sudden disengagement.

"Allegra, what is it?" he asked, concerned. "Did I do something wrong?"

Allegra was about to apologize and explain when she saw something jump from her face to his. Had she blinked, she would have missed it. It landed on his cheek, no bigger than a freckle, and then scurried into one of his nostrils. Her mouth hung open in disbelief and she stared at Everson's nose, not completely sure that she hadn't imagined it. But then Everson grabbed his face, and Allegra knew that something truly strange and nefarious was happening.

"What in blazes..." Everson exclaimed, shaking his head and wrinkling his nose, stopping just short of sticking a finger up his nostril.

As she reached out to him helplessly, a thought, consisting of one word, struck her with the force and sting of a slap to her face. *Mother! Of course!*

Allegra's face flushed with sudden anger and betrayal. Her mother's affection, so unexpected yet so welcome, had been nothing more than a distraction while she planted her device in her ear, infecting her, as it were, with her treachery. Now there was no doubt. They had been caught.

Before Allegra had time to burrow into her fury, she saw the tiny device emerge from Everson's nostril. It scampered up the bridge of his nose and came to rest right between his eyes. She gasped and reached for it, her fingers poised like pincers, but the thing expanded suddenly and violently, bloating in the blink of an eye to nearly the size of Everson's head.

Allegra screamed and stumbled away, her hands pulled back protectively. The legs on the device, as fine as filament before, were now long arachnoid extensions that clamped viciously onto Everson's head, anchoring themselves solidly in place. Allegra could see his eyes rolling wildly between the thing's skeletal legs, but his cries of protest were muffled beneath the bulbous abdomen. He clawed frantically at the mechanism, but it was immovable.

Allegra had been unsure whether the insidious thing was creature or contraption until she saw a small red light begin to blink on its back. It was obvious it was some sort of weapon or tool and, unfortunately, because of that, it couldn't be killed. There was no guarantee that it could be stopped at all, whatever it was now doing to Everson.

Allegra realized just how naïve she'd been. How trusting. The queen was more devious than she could ever have imagined, and the princess was sick that she'd been the unwitting bait in her mother's trap. With a cry of rage and desperation, she flung herself at Everson and grabbed the device with both hands. She jerked at it but only succeeded in nearly pulling Everson off his feet. She twisted it, trying to wrench it free, but it seemed fused to his face.

"I can't get it off!" Allegra screamed in frustration.

As if in reaction to all the grappling, the abdomen on the device began to gyrate angrily. Allegra backed away in fear, uncertain of the mechanism's lethal capacity and worried that she would instigate more harm than help.

As Everson continued to wrestle against the tenacious legs wrapped around his head, a stringy, viscous substance began to spurt from the gyrating abdomen. The ropy material shot out in long looping lassos and began to encase the struggling soldier from the feet up. Ankles, then knees, were quickly secured.

Panicked, Allegra dove to Everson's legs and tried to remove the bizarre restraints, but they were tightening and hardening instantaneously.

His legs now immobilized, Everson fell to the floor with a thud, his hands joining Allegra's in their futile attempt to tear away the webbing. The thing's abdomen continued to spin, the mesh methodically advancing past Everson's waist.

The device then changed its trajectory, now targeting Everson's arms. He flailed wildly to avoid the ensnaring strings, but they persisted in a virtual flurry of coils. Allegra realized that he would be completely mummified in only a matter of moments.

Everson's eyes, so wild before, now seemed to focus intensely. He strained to see onto the bed, and Allegra tried to follow his unwavering gaze. An almost comic frown creased Allegra's brow. It seemed that every new bit of information only served to confuse her more. Everson was staring at a silly little box on the bed, and Allegra, for the life of her, couldn't figure out why.

* * *

Queen Nor's prediction proved to be right. A red light flashed to life on the electronic grid of Middle Tier inset on the console of General Bahn's TRAUMA. He recognized the location immediately. The supreme warman allowed himself a self-satisfied smirk. He had intuited the culprit correctly and was already speeding toward Baron Ayers' mansion.

Still, the general had to shake his head at the inefficiency of it all. Olaf with his secrets and hidden agendas. The queen, who had obviously developed clandestine technology without including the military. The king...well, the king and the Four Tellers of Mano, now three, existed on another plane entirely.

Once this Prophecy nonsense is done, a little old-fashioned communication might be in order, he thought wryly.

Not much later, the heavy wooden gate that secured the baron's courtyard exploded in splinters as an incendiary grenade launched from Bahn's TRAUMA blew wood and masonry into the air. His war machine emerged from the billowing smoke and entered the grounds even before the shrapnel and debris had settled.

A horde of warmen soon followed, scrambling through the haze, weapons drawn to engage any possible resistance.

The TRAUMA screeched to a halt just before the front door, and General Bahn exited the vehicle.

Before Bahn could enter the mansion, the ornate double doors were flung open and a defiant Baron Ayers filled their frame.

"You have no right to enter my home by force!" he exclaimed. "I am a noble!"

The general calmly drew his sword and held it at his side, not even deigning to threaten with it. "Move aside, Baron Ayers. For your own safety."

The two men stared coldly at one another, both resolute and righteous, but only one with a weapon and an army behind him. The baron stubbornly held firm for a loaded moment, for all that was worth, before his head drooped and he stepped aside.

* * *

One arm was pinned, but Everson endeavored valiantly to keep the other free. The sticky strands spewing from the strange device still whipped at him as he dragged his body across the floor with one arm. He inched painfully toward the bed, his eyes never leaving the Tinderbox. Allegra struggled to extricate him from his bonds, but it was pointless.

"Tell me what to do!" Allegra shouted. "Everson, tell me how to help!"

Everson tried to instruct her, but the sound of his unintelligible grunts, muzzled by the thing on his face, made him realize his efforts at speech were pointless. He stretched out his free arm, straining as the restraints tried to pull it back. He gripped the edge of the bed and, with a mighty effort, pulled himself closer to it. His groping fingers closed around the bedsheets and he tugged, gathering cloth and edging the Tinderbox toward him. Once it reached his fingertips, he made one last lunge and grabbed it.

Tobias burst through the door. "Everson..."

Allegra screamed involuntarily and leapt away from the massive brute. Tobias stood and stared, completely stymied. He was likely shocked to discover a strange young lady in the guest room, but probably even more so to see Everson on the floor, nearly mummified with a seemingly living metal thing clamped aggressively on his head.

Everson's forearm was his only appendage left liberated, and he held it out to Allegra, the Tinderbox in hand. He tried desperately to signal her, flicking his eyes repeatedly to Tobias standing in the doorway and shaking the Tinderbox insistently.

"I don't understand!" Allegra cried, eyes darting between him and Tobias. "What is that?"

Heavy booted footsteps pounded up the staircase.

"They're coming!" Tobias shouted, in a voice even higher than normal. "The warmen are coming." He turned and slammed the door, fumbling to lock it with his cumbersome hands.

Everson tried every possible way to communicate with only his eyes. Rolling them, widening them, flicking them madly as if in the throes of a seizure. Allegra continued to shake her head like a clueless partner in a parlor game.

The industrious device was near victory, strand upon strand of its sticky web landing on Everson's forearm. In a matter of moments, the Tinderbox would be enshrouded as well.

Mercifully, something clicked. Allegra snatched the Tinderbox from Everson's hand just as the webbing began to fall upon it. Not knowing what else to do with it, she tossed it to the Leftist. Tobias caught it clumsily just as the door beside him exploded inward.

A handful of warmen poured into the room, swords drawn. They immediately took tactical positions around the princess and the now fully incapacitated Indiran. For once, Everson was grateful for the fact that Leftists seemed to fall below the consideration of most Manoliths. While the warmen focused on him and Allegra, Tobias, ignored and unnoticed, surreptitiously slipped the Tinderbox into his tunic.

Allegra regained her composure in surprisingly quick fashion. She stomped protectively in front of Everson, glaring at the rigid warmen, who held their swords at the ready.

"I am Princess Allegra!" she proclaimed. "No harm shall come to this man!"

The warmen parted, though not for her. A uniformed man, taller than the rest and even more statuesque from Everson's perspective prostrate on the floor, strolled casually into the room. Allegra blanched, the imposing man's presence far more intimidating than the others even though he held no weapon.

"Princess Allegra, I'm General Bahn," he announced politely. "We've never had the pleasure although I bring regards from your mother, the queen."

From his lowly position, Everson was impressed anew as the diminutive princess stepped bravely to the Manolithic general.

"Well, then. Since we are now well met," Allegra said confidently, "as a member of the royal family, I command you to release this man."

The general coolly considered the fiery young princess before his eyes moved pragmatically to Everson's packaged and useless body.

"Forgive me, Princess," he said, "but I'm afraid that's for your father to decide."

TWENTY-THREE

UNDER ANY OTHER circumstance, Allegra would have enjoyed the ride back to the palace. If she were ever free again, she decided that she would make it a point to once more ride a birdun.

The panoramic view from so high up was nothing short of breathtaking and would certainly have inspired an exhilarating sense of freedom at any other time. Endless cracked and flattened plains, unlikely spires of jutting rock, gorges of jagged depth and unexpected beauty all passed beneath her. But presently, they only served to remind Allegra that she was being transported back to Mist Tier, once again a prisoner.

A cavalry warman sat snugly behind her on the mount, one hand on the reins and the other wrapped securely about her waist. A second warman and birdun flew parallel to them, locked in speed and altitude. The reason for their consistent configuration was a makeshift cage suspended between the two birdun and attached to each. Inside was Everson, still swaddled in the hardened web but, thankfully, minus the device that had smothered his face.

Everson stared sorrowfully at Allegra. He dared not speak in front of the warmen, but oceans of understanding passed between him and the equally silent princess. She had brought this upon him merely by existing.

Allegra had long known and accepted that she was a liability to her father, but this was different. Everson had been doing something selfless. He had been trying to do something good. And now, because of her, because of her desire to be free and lead a normal life, this young man who had awakened unexpected feelings within her was now a captive in this cruel prison that was her life.

This could not be what the universe had in mind. There had to be justice. Fairness. Allegra knew little of the ways of the worlds, but it didn't make sense to her that good deeds would not result in just rewards. There was so much about recent events that she couldn't fathom, but it seemed clear that there was a larger plan, one that she couldn't see at present because she was mired in the immediate details. She could only hope that there was some unseen reason behind this calamity as they continued to wing their way toward the capital city.

I will find a way to get him out of this, she swore to herself. *Maybe that's what my part is meant to be in all of this. Maybe I'm destined to save him. Whatever the cost.*

* * *

Word swirled like a sirocco through the streets of Mist Tier: an Indiran soldier responsible for murdering The Which had been captured and would soon be on display for all to see. The siege was suspended, and the palace gates opened wide. Entire families flocked to the Great Square and its attendant balcony from whence every imperial proclamation was pronounced.

A near festive air filled the regal space, the newly liberated citizens buoyant after being shut in under curfew and marshalled for far too long. Standing room became scarce as the palace guards stood by and watched scores more join the crowd to witness this historic event.

An exultant cheer rippled through the thousand-strong gathered in the square as the royal couple and Chancellor Olaf entered the loge high above them. Queen Nor's eyebrows arched upward, but no one was more surprised and pleased than Xander. With the Aurora Alignment a mere day away, it seemed that the curse had been lifted and that the once-in-a-lifetime event was now cause for celebration rather than a day of national mourning.

Excited shouts erupted near the square's massive gates, and a field of heads turned in unison like flowers in a breeze. The crowd parted and Xander's heart leapt as he caught sight of the entourage entering the square. He nudged Olaf in excitement. When the chancellor didn't respond, Xander turned to look at him, curious as to why his closest advisor wouldn't be equally elated. Olaf seemed stunned, his eyes reaching across the distance, trying to catch first sight of the captured Indiran.

Like so many times before, Xander believed he could read the man. It was covetousness and disappointment that made Olaf's long face seem even longer. The counsel to the king could take no credit for any of this. The glory was not his and Xander knew that the man lived to garner praise. *Too bad*, Xander thought smugly, *it's not your day, Olaf. It's mine.*

Grinning and near giddy, the king leaned on the railing, now determined to be the first to see the prisoner.

Two birdun approached, a cage suspended between them. A contingent of palace guards walked alongside them, controlling the ogling onlookers with menacing pikes. Xander could see the huddled form of a man inside the cage, but was unable to make out any detail.

Xander looked to his queen. He had spent so much time bearing the weight of the Prophecy by himself that he now wanted everyone to share in the exuberance of his reprieve. But Nor wasn't looking at him and she was not likely to do so. She was focused intensely on the upright and proud form of their daughter, who was being held firmly astride the birdun on the left. Xander hadn't even noticed her at first, so intent was he on the cage, but now it was clear that she was being held in place by a warman seated behind her. She was, after all, in essence, under arrest.

He studied Nor's expression. She seemed wounded, and Xander could understand why. Nor had betrayed his trust by defending her, and here was how Allegra repaid her—by throwing in with an Indiran.

A bit of paranoia doesn't seem so crazy now, does it? Xander thought exultantly, remembering the pitying stares, the scoffing glances. He would never let them forget how they had doubted him. Any of them.

As the entourage made its way toward the balcony, the citizens of Mist Tier pointed and stared, but, like Xander, they were disappointed that there was not more to see. Obviously, the prisoner had been wrapped securely for shipping. The casing denied them the pleasure of counting his limbs or commenting on the ghastliness of his skin color. Still, the fact that the alien was here, in their midst, was enough to incite wonder and excitement.

The captors and the captured were much nearer now, and Xander noticed something in the crowd that he had not noticed before. Many of his citizens, mostly women and young girls, were not looking at the prisoner in the cage, they were looking at Allegra.

Xander squinted, studying the upturned faces, trying to make sense of their seemingly enthralled expressions. There was curiosity, to be sure, even wonder. But there was something else. As he watched teenaged girls whisper to each other behind cupped hands, their faces beaming; as mothers and grandmothers held their hands over their hearts and their eyes misted over, Xander realized what they were feeling. It was admiration.

It had never occurred to him until now. No one, not a single Manolith outside the palace, had ever laid eyes on the princess. But they knew of her. Obviously, she had been much discussed, the conditions of her storied life fantasized about and romanticized by starry-eyed girls. The Prophecy had painted her as a figure of near legendary proportion. And now here she was. Close enough to touch. It didn't hurt that she was beautiful, that much Xander had to concede. He smirked ironically. Under any other circumstances, he might have actually felt a modicum of pride.

How could they be so wrong? King Xander wondered. Did they not understand that the princess was a traitor? Had they forgotten that her birth alone had set the Prophecy in motion? He shook his head. He would never understand the populace, what swayed their hearts and minds. He had been remiss, he realized. Moving forward, he would take control of public sentiment and bend it to his will.

I'll give them something to marvel at, Xander thought, a plan, like an ember, beginning to glow in his mind.

The procession finally stopped below the balcony, and Nor and Olaf joined Xander at the railing to get a better view. Allegra sat astride her birdun, seething. The princess met her mother's wounded gaze across the distance, and as expected, her petulant face filled with loathing and disgust. It actually amused Xander that, for once, her youthful indignation was not directed at him. Only when a palace guard reached up to assist her from her beast did she sever her heated stare.

As soon as Allegra had alighted, her handmaiden, Geneva, broke through the crowd and threw herself, sobbing, at the self-possessed princess. Allegra shrugged her off without so much as acknowledging her presence. Geneva appeared stricken, and the palace guards collected her as if she'd been discarded. Before they could do the same to Allegra, she set off through the crowd without allowing them to lay a hand on her. They trailed behind her, trying to look official, even as the crowd parted before Allegra's confident stride.

Rather full of herself for someone in her position, Xander thought. *She's mistaken if she thinks her actions will have no consequence.*

Once this Prophecy was past, he'd have to give some real thought to a punishment that his clever little daughter would appreciate.

* * *

Everson watched Allegra until she was swallowed by the crowd. He had seen her venomous glare at the balcony above them, and he had hoped that she would give him one last look of solidarity before being taken away. When she didn't, Everson could only guess that she blamed herself for his predicament and couldn't bear to look at him.

He regretted not speaking to her, in spite of the presence of the guards. He would have told her that, given the chance to do it over, he wouldn't have changed a thing; that, from the moment he saw her in that vision, his life had taken on a purpose that he had never known before.

Then the two cavalry warmen dismounted and moved to open his cage. The commoners closest to them leaned forward as much as they were allowed, the pikes of the palace guards keeping them back. The cage door swung open with a metallic squeal, and the warmen removed Everson and dropped him roughly to the cobblestones.

Everson expelled an audible *oomph*, eliciting titters from the spectators nearest him.

Looking up, Everson could see three heads peering over the railing of a high balcony. Even at this distance, Everson instantly recognized the haggard face of Xander from his vision. He had a sudden epiphany. If the vision was accurate, then he and the king were destined to meet again.

Somehow, he would be freed.

One of the warmen drew his sword and stepped up to him. Everson's eyes grew wide with confusion and concern. This did not look like the path to freedom. Showing no emotion, the warman placed the tip of his sword below Everson's chin, the sharp point dimpling the skin of his neck.

Everson heard brutal cries of bloodlust from the crowd. But the warman didn't plunge the sword through his neck. Instead, with one swift and smooth flourish, he swiped the weapon down the length of Everson's body.

The hardened shell of webbing around him split open with a resounding crack and fell away. The warman stepped back, keeping his sword at the ready. Everson waited until the hot, tingling flush of adrenaline subsided, and then forced himself stiffly to his feet. An offended murmur rumbled through the crowd.

Children were lifted onto their fathers' shoulders. Elderly women recoiled in disgust. Everson regarded the belligerent crowd sadly before turning to face his captors on the balcony above.

"We're convinced this Indiran murdered The Which in an attempt to enter the Tree," a nobleman who wasn't the king said, staring down at Everson. His glare was hard and hateful, and

Everson sensed that there was something intensely personal about the man's countenance. The nobleman's hostility emanated off him like the shimmering air above a lava flow, and Everson had to wonder if he had done something specific to offend the man, other than being born Indiran.

It was obvious that he was important, some sort of high-ranking government advisor, but Everson didn't recall encountering him in his vision. That did not necessarily mean that the man wouldn't be instrumental to the upcoming chain of events.

"Did he?" King Xander asked, with an undertone of trepidation. "Enter the Tree?"

The advisor continued staring at Everson rather than his king. "Obviously not, or we could not have caught him, sire."

"I caught him, Olaf," the woman Everson assumed to be Queen Nor snapped. "And your logic is faulty. If he is the one foretold—"

"He is," Xander interrupted rudely, his reddened eyes blazing with conviction. "I feel it. And now I have him."

Everson listened intently though the level of the conversation had risen to the point where their words were quite audible and clear. Even the commoners nearest him had ceased their murmuring and were eavesdropping on the royals. He watched the people on the balcony very closely, observing the power dynamic between them.

Everson wondered if this might not be the moment to speak up and appeal to King Xander's humanity. What better time to petition peace than in front of a citizenry who had grown weary of war?

One glance at the intractable king and he dismissed the idea. The two people with him were making no headway. He doubted the words of a prisoner would carry any more weight even if he could raise them above the crowd that would likely shout him down. These three were the players who might pave his way to the throne room for that fortuitous meeting, so he might be better served to just listen and collect information. Besides, the queen was trying to maintain some sense of civility, though Everson couldn't be sure what her agenda might be.

Nor took a beleaguered breath and began again. "If he is the one foretold, then what better way for him to enter the palace than by our own escort?"

"That no longer matters," Xander insisted. "He will never leave. The Prophecy is now under my control."

"What is your command, Your Highness?" Olaf asked.

"Repeal martial law completely. Suspend the curfew. Keep the palace gates open," the king commanded. "Declare tomorrow a day of national celebration."

Queen Nor moved closer to him, and Everson noted that her bejeweled hand stopped just short of grabbing his arm. "Xander, perhaps we shouldn't grow complacent too soon. Let the Aurora Alignment pass."

Xander raised his voice to a level that made his words audible even to the citizens further back in the crowd.

"I want a public spectacle! I want everyone to see that Xander the Firm is still very much in power. I will treat the people to the first public Inflammation of an Indiran. Nothing like a good burning to raise morale."

Everson swallowed hard. *Inflammation.* Xander was going to burn him alive for the entertainment of his people. He could plainly see the shock on the queen's face. The noble named Olaf disappeared behind the king.

Dimly, Everson registered the renewed excitement among the citizens who had heard the king's barbaric pronouncement. He knew that the news would spread to those out of earshot like...well, like a blaze. As the king raised his arms victoriously and the approval of the crowd swelled, Everson realized, beyond any doubt, that there would be no reasoning with this man.

Two of the guards grabbed his arms roughly and started to muscle him away. He strained to throw one last look to the balcony. Everson saw Queen Nor casting about desperately, no doubt looking for the departed noble to enlist his aid against the power-crazed king. Much like the Indiran, she had no ally in sight.

* * *

Chancellor Olaf hastened down the stone steps leading to the dungeon. He arrived just as two palace guards roughly shoved the Indiran soldier into a cell. One look from the chancellor, and the guards stepped back in deference, allowing Olaf to close the heavy, barred door himself. Shielding the electronic keypad next to the door with his body, he quickly changed the locking code to one only he would know.

"Leave us," he barked over his shoulder. The guards departed without question.

As soon as they were alone, the Indiran turned away from him, discouraging conversation. Olaf sighed, not impressed with the soldier's attempt at being cavalier but willing to allow him to examine the severity of his situation. A firm grasp of reality would only bolster Olaf's eventual negotiation.

The walls of the cell were constructed of stone so sturdy as to instantly dissuade any notion of escape. The fourth wall where Olaf waited was comprised of thick and rusted metal bars, spaced close enough together that a normal-sized person could not pass but wide enough that the imprisoned could find no privacy.

A golden ray of late afternoon light streamed through a barred opening near the ceiling, revealing that the cell sat below ground level, and the soldier stared at it rather than Olaf. The aperture was so small that it was really more of a chink in the wall than an actual window, but it allowed some brightness into the otherwise bleak cell. Even if the soldier were somehow able to pry the bars away, his body would never fit through the opening.

Finally, the soldier turned to him, but he didn't look as worried as Olaf hoped he might, given his lack of options. The chancellor studied him, trying to keep his own raging and conflicting emotions from registering on his face. This was the man who had laid low his beloved. He was also, quite possibly, the indispensable key to his success.

The Indiran was surprisingly young. Olaf conceded that he was handsome, but that was a detail he considered relevant only in respect to whatever cooperation he might be able to coerce from the princess. But heroic? Hardly.

Looking down his nose at the soldier, Olaf surmised that he had sent many far more impressive men to their deaths.

"I'm Chancellor Olaf, counsel to the king," he said flatly. "I want what you took from the Tree."

The demand seemed to catch the soldier off guard, not only with its abruptness but, more pointedly, with its accuracy.

"I don't know what you're talking about," the soldier lied.

Olaf had no doubt of it and continued undeterred. "I know that you do. I also know that you don't have it with you, or we would've found it when we searched you. No matter. It's of no use to you now, and I don't believe it's necessary for my purposes."

The Indiran stared at him, and Olaf could practically hear the gears grinding.

"You mean the Tinderbox," the soldier said finally, and Olaf was sure that he was goading him. It took all of his considerable discipline not to react.

"So you must be in collusion with The Which," the soldier continued, and, at this, the chancellor felt the need to look away. "She's the only one who knew what I had. Did she tell you? What purpose might you have, Chancellor, you and The Which, that differs from the king's?"

Olaf slowly raised his eyes to meet the soldier's. If his gaze alone could Inflame him, the young Indiran would have been nothing more than a smoking pile of ash. "You may never mention her again," Olaf hissed. "I'm tempted to scoop your eyes out of your head because you were the last person to see her alive, and that privilege should have been mine."

"She's dead, then," the soldier said. "I didn't know for sure... I'm sorry."

His response gave the chancellor pause. Was he implying that he didn't kill her? That he was not directly responsible for her death? The soldier seemed sincere enough. Still, Chancellor Olaf desperately needed to change the subject. After all, the past could not be undone, and the future needed to be secured.

Olaf gathered himself, moved nearer to the bars, and lowered his voice though there was no one around to hear. It was force of habit since the counsel to the king was also aware that surveillance cameras had never been placed in the seldom-used dungeon.

"Xander has given you a cell with a view of the courtyard so that you can witness your own pyre being built," he said.

He indicated the poor excuse for a window behind the soldier. The man didn't turn to look.

"Your obstinance buys you nothing," Olaf snipped. "You know you're going to look eventually, so don't be coy. I'm trying to help you."

"I find that hard to believe," the soldier replied, but he turned to look anyway.

The view into the Great Square was clear and unimpeded, the crowd having dispersed after the king's pronouncement and the Indiran's disappearance. Four burly Leftists were already hard at work, methodically assembling a large platform. Judging by the amount of building material they had stacked nearby, the soldier's deadly stage would be high enough to provide everyone in the square a pristine view of his burning.

"He wants you to think about how you will burn," Olaf said, hoping to wipe the smug expression from the soldier's face. "He's not a subtle man."

"But you are," the soldier persisted.

The young man regarded him expectantly, no doubt hoping he would blurt out some useful bit of information. The chancellor quickly ascertained that there was nothing more to be gained from being argumentative. This common soldier was far more than meets the eye. Hope began to bubble up in the previously stagnant pit of his aspirations.

"And you seem to be an insightful young man," he said. "I want you to think as well. I want you to consider the alternatives to that pyre. When the time comes, we'll speak again."

Olaf left abruptly. There was precious little time to implement a new strategy, but, perhaps for the first time, the rapid advance of time might actually work in his favor. While Xander had grown complacent, the chancellor had become energized. Now, he was racing to keep up with the stars themselves.

* * *

A ribbon of amber still graced the horizon, but an air of soiree had already descended upon Mist Tier along with the darkening sky. Pedestrians crowded the recently desolate streets, reveling in a rekindled sense of community. Those commoners who had been fortunate enough to have a clear view of the prisoner regaled their neighbors with the sensationalized details of their sighting.

Many reported that the Indiran's silence was certainly an indication of his lack of intelligence. Some interpreted his involuntary grunt at being dropped as an animalistic bark. Still others swore that they had seen a tail.

Queen Nor stood exactly where she had stood not that long ago, outside Allegra's room, looking in at her daughter. Her demeanor, this time, was decidedly less detached, her cunning giving way to compassion. She had been standing there for some time, quietly watching as her daughter moved through waves of grief and anger. She was finally quiet, the sobs having subsided, and she sat at her vanity, face down in her folded arms.

There would be another day after the Prophecy had passed, that was more evident than ever. So while Xander ghoulishly anticipated his public burning, despite her protests, Nor turned her mind to the residue that was sure to follow.

She had left her husband alone with a fresh bottle of terrazka to celebrate by himself. Funny how Xander's delight and despair required the same prescription: liberal application of liquor. She was done with him. But her daughter would still be her daughter, and Nor had given her assurances that she fully intended to honor.

Queen Nor took a bolstering breath and entered Allegra's room. She knew instantly that the rustling of her robes had announced her because her daughter's shoulders tensed and her head came up alertly. Allegra leapt to her feet and spun around.

"Geneva, I told you to leave me alone," Allegra snapped. But when she saw her mother standing in her room, her words trailed off.

"Allegra…" the queen began, the hesitancy in her voice surprising even herself.

Nor had been disconcerted by the depth of empathy she had felt for her daughter upon seeing her returned to the city. All afternoon, she had struggled against her emotional disquiet until finally, in an effort to clear her mind and her conscience, she had decided to confront Allegra with the hope of brokering some semblance of peace or understanding.

The queen realized instantly that it was a naïve undertaking.

Allegra exploded almost immediately. "You used me to trap him!"

Queen Nor sighed. Obviously, reason, logic and even civility were not to be components of this conversation.

"How else do you think I could protect the kingdom?" Nor demanded reflexively. This was not the way she had intended this to go.

"At the moment, I care little for the kingdom," Allegra said furiously, fresh tears filling her eyes.

Queen Nor had a realization that shook the foundation of her long-suppressed maternal instinct. Her brow furrowed.

"You really love him, don't you, Allegra?" she asked softly.

Allegra expelled a short but bitter laugh. "I'm surprised that you can recognize the emotion, Mother." Allegra fixed the queen with an accusatory stare. "Have you ever really been in love?"

Nor was startled to find herself at a terrible loss for words. It was not a question that she'd ever been asked. The queen heard her own voice as if from a distance.

"No, Allegra. I'm afraid I have not."

Nor saw Allegra's face fall, the anger draining out of it. Her daughter's disillusioned expression wounded the queen more deeply than her unintentional insight. Allegra had lashed out in spite, but it was clear that she had been unprepared for the simplicity and finality of the answer.

Queen Nor suddenly felt as if she were on morally inferior ground. The rational and justifiable defense of her actions seemed empty in comparison to the purity of her daughter's love. She stood for a moment, uncharacteristically slack-jawed, until she realized there was nothing more to say. The queen simply turned and left the room.

* * *

Baron Ayers screamed in agony. Rivulets of electric blue flame rippled over his torso and then dissipated like burning alcohol. The proud baron was reduced to whimpers. He hung by his arms, suspended from the ceiling by chains, his chest naked and covered in sweat, which, unfortunately, increased the conductivity of the electrical current to which he was subjected every few minutes. He had endured this torture for some time now without breaking, much to the dissatisfaction of General Bahn.

He stood a short distance away, just beyond the range of the spittle that sprayed involuntarily from the baron's mouth every time he was shocked. He was still near enough to know that the baron had soiled himself. Despite the expected weakness of the man's bowels, the general was impressed. He had never expected the genteel noble to show such fortitude.

He waited for the man to recover sufficiently enough to speak. The baron's head lolled forward limply, his breath coming in shallow, wheezing gulps, his body still erect only through the support of his restraining chains. One of Bahn's officers stood expectantly by the sagging baron, holding the heavy metal cudgel that delivered the debilitating voltage.

The inquisition was convened in the communication room of the ancient ARC deep below the baron's palace. The general had been furious to discover the clandestine chamber. How a secret of such potential military importance had gone undetected for so long was beyond him. As far as Bahn was concerned, the deception and duplicitousness ended here.

"I will ask again," Bahn said. "What did the soldier tell you? What are the Indirans planning?"

With much effort, Baron Ayers raised his head but did not meet the general's eyes. "I told you, I don't know."

The general nodded to his officer. Without hesitation, the senior warman touched the cudgel to the baron's exposed belly. There was an instant spark of contact, a sizzling smell of burned flesh, and blue flame washed over the noble in an undulating wave. The baron's head jerked toward the ceiling, his every muscle standing out in static tension. His scream reverberated off the walls of the cramped communication room.

The process was growing tiresome. It had been such a long time since the general had been forced to personally engage in such a practice that he was feeling admittedly rusty. He wasn't sure how much more of this the baron could take. Killing the man was obviously not desirable, but neither was a fried state of incomprehensibility.

He waited patiently for the baron's twitching to come to a stop. Bahn then approached the noble and was pleased to see signs of life even though the man hung flaccid like meat in an abattoir.

He addressed Ayers in a tone that was nearly sympathetic. "You can stop this, Baron. Simply talk. Do you not care for the welfare of your people?"

At the mention of his "people," the baron gathered what little strength he had left. He eyed the general defiantly.

"Honor to Mano," he rasped. "And I mean that in ways you will never understand."

General Bahn smiled thinly and nodded to yet another warman standing by the door. Baron Ayers watched fearfully as the man departed.

"I'm impressed, Baron," Bahn offered conversationally. "You're quite good at withstanding your own pain."

The second warman returned quickly. Terror gripped Ayers as effectively as an electrical current upon seeing what he had. The warman held his daughter, a striking young woman named Miranda, firmly by the arm.

She threw off her captor's hand with a defiant shrug and faced the general with a proud and impetuous sneer. Bahn nodded appreciatively, but it did not temper his determination.

"How strong will you be when you hear the screams of your daughter?" he asked.

"No! Not that!" gasped the baron, struggling against his restraints with renewed and desperate vigor.

To her credit, the baron's daughter refused to be intimidated. She took a step toward the general as if to attack him, but she was quickly restrained by the warman who had brought her. Bahn was actually disappointed. He was curious to know just how far the fiery young woman might have gone. His interaction with young women was limited, but, if there were more like this one, he might have to reconsider his all-male military. Miranda held her challenging glare for a moment more before turning back to the baron.

"Father, it will be all right," Miranda said.

Bahn did not consider himself to be a cruel man. But neither was he sentimental. He was a realist, who had seen his share of pain and suffering. So it was with cold-eyed certainty that he knew that the young and idealistic Lady Miranda was about to receive an education in how quickly things can become not "all right."

He gestured for the officer with the cudgel to commence. It all happened very quickly. The officer closed the distance to Miranda in a few long, decisive strides. She barely had time to turn toward the approaching warman, her face unafraid, before the cudgel made contact. There was a pop and a flash of spark. Miranda screamed in spite of herself. She crumpled as if the prod had dissolved all the bones in her body.

"Stop!" the baron shrieked. "I'll tell you everything!"

Bahn turned his obsidian gaze expectantly toward the baron. It was an ages-old warrior's creed, but here it was again. Though family could inspire great strength and courage, it could also prove to be a man's greatest weakness.

"Continue, Baron," the general said, "or I will."

"Father, no!" Miranda protested with all the strength she could summon. She was still slumped on the floor, the cudgel-wielding warman looming over her. She looked up at her father through her disheveled hair, remarkably unbroken in spite of the excruciating pain she had just endured. Bahn was impressed with her grit and actually thought twice about torturing her. But it was a fleeting thought. He would do what was needed.

Ayers regarded his child with an expression both sorrowful and resolute.

"I'm so proud of you, my beautiful daughter," he said gently. "And here I thought not a single one of my words had ever pierced that hard head of yours."

"You know better," Miranda replied and actually managed a small smile. But then her eyes grew hard and her gaze shifted between her father and the waiting general. "And you know what we have to do. We have to give him time. Whatever it takes."

"I gain nothing if I lose you," the baron said firmly. But then he nodded and gave his daughter a frail grin. "It's out of our hands now, Miranda. What will be, will be." He turned to Bahn with a calm that bordered on the eerie. "But I can tell you, General, you'll bottle fire faster than you can stop the future."

TWENTY-FOUR

PROPHECIES, BY NATURE, were deceptively straightforward. They were cut and dried. Black and white. They presented a simple proposition and had finite expectations although the ramifications were far more complex. *Similar to marriage vows*, thought Commander Giza—which was probably why he had never married.

Giza was beset with worry. He wasn't by nature a superstitious man, but, here he was, launching a massive campaign whose timing seemed solely dictated by a myth. He found the Prophecy practically laughable, but it did remind him that so much about war was unpredictable. No matter how much one might strategize, the best-laid plans could still go awry, and simple fate seemed to play more of a role than Giza would like to admit. A battle could turn with a shift in the wind. A bullet could find a man after bypassing scores of others. More simply put, you could prepare all you want, but you still can't beat luck.

Such were Giza's thoughts as he stood alone on the observation deck of his transport, the jagged red rock of Mano floating before him in the floor-to-ceiling viewport. The last time he had set foot on the planet, he had been met with unqualified failure, and that could not happen again.

His previous defeat had undoubtedly been due to incomplete and tardy intelligence, among other things. Presently, communication with Baron Ayers had become impossible once they had departed Indira, so Giza was again forced to proceed blindly with only the hope that nothing had changed drastically on the ground.

He led a force that was more than ample to achieve the objective of taking Mist Tier, but the very size of that force would prevent improvisation should unforeseen circumstances arise. It was an all-or-nothing gambit. Commander Giza shook his head and, once again, found himself on the verge of disgust. He had been bested at the Grand Schism because they had been outnumbered. And why was there a massive buildup of Manolithic troops? Because a teenaged girl was not allowed to see a soldier.

Like a bad joke that was impossible to forget, the Prophecy kept repeating in his mind. *If Allegra weds a common soldier, the reign of Xander the Firm will come to an end.* Commander Giza wondered wryly if it wouldn't be easier to stage a wedding rather than a war.

With that in mind, a few choice details from the last communication with Everson had remained with the perceptive commander. The prince had left himself latitude for whatever personal agenda he wasn't discussing, but such an agenda existed nonetheless, of that the commander was certain.

Everson had said that he had "reason to be here" when speaking of Mano. And when informed that the incursion was to target Xander's palace itself, he had shown no surprise but, instead, had urged that the battle be "as surgical as possible." It was not a long walk to arrive at the doorstep of Princess Allegra. Did the young prince suddenly consider himself the protagonist in a fanciful fairy tale? Especially now, since he had been made a soldier, just as the Prophecy required. Giza chuckled darkly. He had been responsible for that, too.

Whatever Everson's intentions, Commander Giza fervently hoped that his efforts would complement rather than complicate the focus of the expeditionary force. They were fast approaching the coordinates where the armada would begin its surreptitious orbit of the planet, waiting for the stars to align.

From their vantage point in space, the Indirans would be able to view the Aurora Constellation the very moment it became complete, long before it would be evident to Xander and the planet-bound Manoliths.

The twin suns were just now creeping around the edge of the planet, bringing hard truth to all the conjecture.

* * *

General Bahn was more frenzied than he had ever been. The horizon behind him appeared to be on fire, the copious clouds of dust raised by his convoy backlit and glowing orange as Femera and Amali ignited the day.

He pushed his TRAUMA to its limits, a long line of other war machines and troop transports in single file formation behind him as they desperately motored for Mist Tier.

The baron had provided information that was both concise and chilling: The enemy was already en route to deliver certain destruction to the seat of Manolithic power. Upon hearing the baron's pained confession, Bahn had called for the immediate mobilization of troops. To his immense frustration, the majority of his men were already sleeping and needed to be roused.

To make matters worse, the hindmost of his battalions had only just arrived from Front Tier, and they had had no rest at all. Bahn had been forced to wait as his officers scrambled to organize the soldiers into their various fighting formations. He had set out the instant the last bootlace had been tied.

The convoy quickly traversed the flat span of desert around Middle Tier, but then came the Tarara Mountains. The general's lead vehicle began the treacherous ascent, and he found reason anew to curse his incompetent king. It had been lunacy enough for Xander's paranoia over archaic and dubious predictions to render the capital bereft of defense, but it was his long-standing mismanagement that would also contribute to the calamity at hand. To Bahn's way of thinking, an amorphous prophecy was merely an excuse.

King Xander had never deigned to improve the roads. What had he cared if commerce, emigration, even information moved at a glacial pace between the tiers? As Bahn navigated the narrow winding road at perilous speeds, he could not help but reflect that bridges, tunnels, decent pavement—all would have shaved precious time.

General Bahn could only grit his teeth in anger, knowing full well that the kingdom might finally pay the price for a king who had no interest in ruling.

* * *

Tobias stood outside and sadly surveyed the rubble that, until recently, had been the beautiful courtyard of his patron's palace. It would take a staggering amount of time to rebuild it, and the manservant sorrowfully acknowledged that much of its grandeur had been derived from its timeless permanence.

That glory would never be reclaimed.

He realized that they had been fortunate until now. This household had been well aware of the war, but they had lived privileged and protected lives within the baron's cloistered keep. They had no doubt been handled harshly now as if in retribution for their former immunity.

The manservant had spent a sleepless night attending to the battered baron. The poor man had writhed in his bed all night long, unable to find comfort or relief, every muscle in his body bruised and tender from the punishing electrical shocks.

Baroness Carlotta and Lady Miranda had never strayed from his bedside. It was they who had applied salve to his many burns and who had tried unsuccessfully to feed him. The women had not slept and neither had they wept. They had ministered to their patriarch in sullen silence, but Tobias could tell that this injustice would never be forgotten and would not go unavenged.

The Leftist now stood in the ruined and slowly brightening courtyard, holding a handful of terranuts. Everson's mysterious little box was still tucked safely in his tunic. He had told no one about it. He had no idea what it was. He only knew that it seemed to be of vital importance to Everson.

Tobias had been there quite a while, shouting a name over and over into the silence and the skies. Patience was finally rewarded when Tobias heard the rush of powerful wings approaching. Taj's hooves clicked crisply in the morning silence as the birdun landed heavily on the flagstones. The Leftist was more convinced than ever that he and the curious creature had a peculiar bond because of the stranger who had brought them together. The beast quickly spied the food in Tobias's hands and eagerly clopped closer.

Tobias smiled and held out a terranut. "Hello, Taj. Want to go see Everson?"

* * *

Everson sat awake as the morning light and the activity increased in the square. He peered through the window at the preparations. He had endured a sleepless night, assaulted by the racket of his pyre's construction. His empty stomach had also kept him restless and alert.

His captors hadn't thought to provide him with dinner or a drop of water. Why waste the food if he was destined to die? Besides, he would probably burn better if dehydrated.

Even before dawn, many vendors had laid claim to the prime locations around the pyre, and their tables and stalls were now near completion. Everson heard a raucous clamor coming from the direction of the palace gates, and he craned his neck to see.

A gaggle of churlish urchins ran through the square, laughing and jeering at irritated shopkeepers. Everson saw palace guards chuckling at their antics, but they did not raise a finger to intervene.

The scalawags surrounded the scaffold, producing handfuls of incendiary rocks. They gleefully threw the rocks at the feet of the Leftist laborers still hard at work on the structure. The rocks exploded in bursts of flaming orange, the percussive reports reverberating harshly in the enclosed square. The hapless Leftists danced as quickly as their cumbersome limbs would allow, protesting with their high-pitched shrieks. The cackling adolescents only stopped when they ran out of ammunition. They scattered, but Everson was certain they would return once they reloaded.

The grumbling Leftists dutifully returned to their task. Everson watched them with dismay. A stout post had been erected in the center of the scaffold, and to this, the laborers attached heavy metal shackles. True to Olaf's observation, Everson could envision all too well how he would burn.

He knew that this blatant display was taking its toll on his psyche. He was tired. He was hungry. And his suffering was apparently reason for rejoicing.

Everson began to doubt that his vision was a certainty, that the throne room, the battle, even Princess Allegra might just be taunting possibilities only to be realized with the perfect execution of a specific chain of events.

His ethics advisor in Agrilon, an overly analytical man named Master Ruben, had once constructed a massive contraption to illustrate to the young prince the delicate balance of cause and effect. The moving parts were so many and so intricate as to be almost indecipherable. It was a long and complicated course comprised of ramps, chutes, levers, levels, springs, arcing arms, spiraling funnels, blind tunnels, weights and counterweights.

The objective was simply to roll a small ball from one end to the other in an uninterrupted journey. The device was so painstakingly articulated that any imbalance or deviation from the design would result in the ball falling from the course without reaching its destination.

Everson suddenly felt like that very small ball.

* * *

Though the morning was growing late, Allegra still had not risen from her bed. She lay motionless, staring numbly out her balcony doors. There was no cloudshine this morning, nor even any clouds. The day promised to be stark and unrelenting, and Allegra dreaded facing it.

Her night had been excruciating. With every fitful billowing of her balcony curtains, she had bolted upright, hoping to see the mysterious black box materialize in her room. It never came. In the dark moments between interludes of restless sleep, she resented herself for still believing it would.

Her mother's pronouncement that she had never known love was devastating. Allegra had long assumed that her parents' love had become a small, hard thing, withered by the calcifying effects of age and responsibility. To be informed that it had never existed in the first place left her feeling hollow and alone.

If there was not love, what was there? Was this the example she was destined to replicate? She would rather die and put an end to the painful pretense of hoping. If Everson were to be Inflamed today, she might find a final use for her accursed balcony.

Allegra heard a sound and grudgingly raised her head to look. Geneva stood in her doorway. The handmaiden's expression was so full of sorrow and sympathy that the princess burst into instant tears. Geneva rushed into Allegra's outstretched arms.

After a moment of much-needed reunion and commiseration, Allegra held her confidante by her shoulders, turning, as she was wont to do, from despair to determination in the blink of an eye.

"There was laughter, Geneva! Laughter, drifting through my balcony doors from the streets below!" she exclaimed. "It's been nothing less than torture. They are celebrating and their gaiety has been purchased with Everson's life!"

"Everson?" Geneva asked, her plaintive face struggling to remain supportive. "He's the Indiran?"

"Yes," Allegra replied, wiping her moist cheek on her sleeve. "But he's so much more than that. This can't happen, Geneva. This is lunacy. We have to find a way to stop this."

"What can we do?"

"How is it in the rest of the palace?" Allegra asked, desperate for any thread of information she could spin into a plan.

Geneva's face fell. "Bleak, I'm afraid. Your father has opened the gates to the citizens, but he's doubled the guard within the palace. Even my own movements are restricted. I'm allowed to your wing and to the kitchen to fetch you food but nowhere else."

Allegra bit down hard on her emotion, tired of being overwhelmed, angry at the years of inaction that had led to this moment. She wondered why she had dared to hope. When it came to her imprisonment, her parents had never been anything less than diligent and unmoving. They had never relaxed their guard or stepped back from the cruel conditions of her incarceration.

She could be pleasant or petulant, it was all the same, her behavior affected their leniency not a whit. Allegra had done her best not to engage in self-pity, but now, when she wanted mercy for someone other than herself, her helplessness wounded her to the core.

"Is there any chance your mother might help?" Geneva suggested hopefully.

"My mother?" Allegra retorted, literally snorting in derision. "Then I suggest you start searching the palace."

"I don't understand." Geneva sat back slightly, obviously suspecting that she was being teased. "Why?"

"If you're going to ask my mother for help, then first you must find her misplaced heart."

* * *

General Bahn cursed himself. In his haste to depart Middle Tier, he'd neglected to alert the capital of his emergency mobilization. When the thought finally occurred to him, they were on a vertiginous mountain road surrounded by a labyrinth of cliff walls that made radio transmission impossible.

It also occurred to the general that he was directly defying an official decree by bringing soldiers to Mist Tier, but for the first time in his military career, he was willing to bypass the chain of command and deal with the repercussions later. He might have forgone contact with the capital entirely, but he felt it imperative to raise the guard and fortify the palace.

Now that he was on a downward slope and the sheer cliffs had given way to rocky outcroppings, he keyed his radio repeatedly in an effort to connect with the palace. Finally, the static cleared, and a reedy voice filled the interior of his TRAUMA.

"General," Chancellor Olaf said, "what is it?"

Bahn grimaced like he had walked into bodine flatulence with an open mouth. He was tempted to turn off his radio, but duty intervened.

"I need to speak with the queen," Bahn reluctantly replied, then quickly added, "or the king, if he is so inclined."

There was a short pause, which the general filled with images of Olaf dancing for all he was worth. Eventually, the chancellor answered, "They are indisposed at the moment. They are making plans now that the Prophecy has been circumvented. Thank you for collecting the Indiran, by the way."

"The Prophecy is the least of my concerns, Olaf," Bahn barked. "The Indirans are on their way to invade Mist Tier."

The general was not sure what sort of response he expected, but what he got was not it. Static filled his TRAUMA again. Olaf was gone.

* * *

Tobias was astounded by the sight of the crowd from the air. Given the devastation and depression he had left in his own tier, he could not easily fathom a reason for celebration here in Mist Tier, the capital city.

He urged Taj down to a clearing adjacent to the palace gates. The Leftist quickly dismounted and joined the flow of commoners streaming into the square.

Once beyond the massive gates, Tobias was even more amazed. The pavilion had become an impromptu bazaar, and he still didn't know the cause for such a convention. He finagled his way through the mob, his bulbous eyes scanning for clues, one large hand protectively pressed to his chest where Everson's box remained tucked safely away in his tunic.

Entire families were hunkered down on blankets, as if awaiting a parade. Tobias loved parades, but, try as he might, he couldn't understand why anyone would be celebrating anything during these dark days.

The air was filled with the cries of vendors standing in slapdash stalls, hawking everything from tunics to roasted terranuts. Smoke swirled about the heads of the revelers, carrying the savory scent of grilling meat. The smell led Tobias to a clutch of carcasses freshly slaughtered and dripping from their hooks.

The manservant heard a grumbling from his considerable gut and remembered that he had not eaten this day. Deciding that he could gather information standing in line for food just as easily as he could anywhere else, Tobias shouldered his way toward the nearest grill.

The manservant took his place at the end of a queue, and a few Manoliths immediately moved away, apparently uncomfortable sharing space with a Leftist and one so well-dressed at that. After a moment, normal conversation resumed.

As he pieced together snippets of chatter, Tobias forgot his hunger. Horrified realization was just setting in as the final piece of evidence revealing the cause of the gathering walked past in the guise of an enterprising salesman.

The man had fabricated a basketful of commemorative curios and, as he passed Tobias, he held up one of the items. Tobias could clearly see the rustic, homemade figurine in his hand. It was basically a doll, grotesquely painted black and clad in Manolith finery not unlike the outfit Everson had last been wearing.

Tobias felt sick as he heard the salesman exhort that the likeness was suitable as a souvenir or could be burned in effigy for the delight of family and friends.

The manservant desperately scanned the square, fortunate that he towered over the heads of normal Manolithic people. He spotted a scaffold rising ominously at the far end of the pavilion, nearer to the royal balcony. He bullied his way through the crowd, expecting to find Everson there.

Instead, he discovered four Leftist laborers seated on the cobblestones, their backs against the scaffold, enjoying a meager meal now that the work was done. As Tobias got closer to them, he realized they were eating roasted verm, and he politely tried to keep the revulsion from his face.

For the life of him, he could not imagine a circumstance where he would dine on the garbage-dwelling creatures by choice. Although, the wings did look crispy. It was a reminder that he had led a privileged life and that social strata existed, even among his own people. He diverted his eyes and examined the structure behind them.

The pyre was complete and ready for use, needing only the human fuel to spark the celebration. Once again, the fine attire of Tobias made a statement before he could open his mouth. The four workers curiously regarded the posh Leftist, their lantern jaws slowly chewing their verm. There were palace guards nearby, but true to form, they paid no more attention to them after their initial smirks at Tobias's clothes. The manservant held his arms out in what he hoped was an appropriate greeting. He had never been to Mist Tier, and he was understandably intimidated, unsure if local custom might be drastically different here in the capital.

"My friends—" Tobias began, but he was quickly cut off.

"I have no friends who dress like that," the eldest Leftist said, and the others chuckled. Tobias quickly ascertained that he must be the leader. He also quickly regretted holding out his arms since the gesture might have been misconstrued as him showing off his clothes.

"Are you sure you're a Leftist?" the elder continued. "Maybe you're just a bloated Manolith."

His coworkers laughed out loud at that, with one of them nearly choking on a verm wing. Tobias chuckled with them, hoping to smooth over the friction of the initial exchange.

"If clothes made the Manolith, I might agree with you," he said, nodding agreeably. "But it's really just my uniform. My job. It might not look it, but I know a little bit about work. My name is Tobias and I'm from Middle Tier."

"My name is Lucius and I'm the head handyman here in the palace, so I know a lot about work," the older Leftist said proudly.

"I can see that," Tobias replied, making it a point to examine their handiwork. "It's a magnificent structure. Well built. Solid. I pity its purpose, though."

"What do you mean?" Lucius asked, taking immediate offense. Tobias sensed the others stiffening as well.

"You're going to burn another person alive," Tobias said. "I've never been to Mist Tier, but I don't know any Leftists who could be that cruel."

The four burly Leftists, led by Lucius, rose to their feet, dropping their unfinished verm onto the dusty cobblestones. Tobias took an involuntary step backward. Perhaps he had overreached.

"It's an Indiran," Lucius snapped, as if that explained every-thing. "And it's not my doing. Maybe you don't know much about King Xander out in Middle Tier, because if you did, you wouldn't be so surprised."

"I may not know much about King Xander..." Tobias hedged. He actually knew quite a bit about Xander thanks to the baron's long-winded diatribes, but that was beside the point right now. "But I do know the Indiran who's supposed to burn on this very scaffold."

Tobias relished their shocked expressions, pausing for a moment to allow his admission to sink in. He threw a wary glance at the still unmindful palace guards and then stepped in conspiratorially.

"I think you may have judged him as quickly and as incorrectly as you judged me," Tobias said, looking into each of their now receptive faces. "May I tell you about him?"

* * *

The scourge of the Leftist workers and vendors alike, that rowdy gang of ruffians had returned to the Great Square. Sadly, for them, they had failed to replenish their supply of incendiary rocks and so could not continue their campaign of terror. Sadly, for Everson, they had discovered the tiny window to his cell and were inspired to devise a new game.

Their dirty faces were crowded side by side in the opening as they took turns trying to spit on him. The competition had been going on for some time, and Everson was forced to the far side of the cell, his back against the bars.

Everson sighed, crossed his arms, and stared at his tormentors, who had a seemingly endless ability to produce saliva.

The eldest of the gang was seized by sudden inspiration, his face lighting up. He elbowed his cronies out of the way and stood, immediately fumbling at his trousers. Everson shook his head in disbelief.

Before the reprobate could unveil his weapon, a pair of very large legs appeared behind him and delivered a resounding kick to his backside. Intrigued, Everson watched as the would-be pisser squawked and scrambled away. His toadies protested, but they gave way before the hulking stranger.

Once the delinquents had departed, the owner of the large legs dropped to his knees, his large face alone able to fill the window.

"Tobias!" Everson shouted joyously. The Leftist wasted no time with niceties and reached into his tunic, extracting the Tinderbox.

"I thought you might need this," the manservant said and slipped the object between the bars.

Everson scrambled over and reached up excitedly to receive it. Tobias beamed at him, looking as proud as Everson had ever seen him.

"You know." Everson grinned, clutching the Tinderbox fiercely with both hands. "Someone once told me that you Leftists have 'decreased mental capacity.' But I'm onto you."

Everson winked. Tobias chuckled for the first time in Everson's recollection, and the sound was oddly musical. The manservant nodded and his face grew strangely wistful.

"My father was forced to be a servant his entire life, and he taught me a very important thing," he said. "It takes a smart person to play dumb."

Everson regarded his unlikely friend. They had much to talk about when this was all over.

"Find us a safe place to meet. I'll be there shortly."

TWENTY-FIVE

OLAF STRODE PURPOSEFULLY down the corridor leading to Allegra's bedchamber, thankfully not encountering any stray staff. He was keeping the general's disturbing report about an Indiran attack to himself for the moment. The less said to anyone, the better.

He slowed as he reached Allegra's door, casting a cursory glance at the surveillance cameras positioned at either end of the hall. He was not overly concerned since he was the one who mostly monitored the movement within the palace. Still, he could ill afford complacency. Lately, if a plan could go awry, it did.

He heard muffled voices within the room and cautioned a peek around the portal.

The princess and her handmaiden sat on Allegra's bed like two little girls. The pair were very close to one another, their heads bent together in conspiratorial communion.

Allegra was relaying the traumatic events of the previous day while Geneva responded with the requisite sympathy and disbelief. The details of the arrest were of little interest to the chancellor, but he waited patiently for more useful information. Finally, Queen Nor was mentioned, and the chancellor held his breath as Allegra's tone grew cold and accusatory.

Apparently, the queen's betrayal of her daughter was the final, unforgivable affront. Allegra's mother was cruel, calculating, conniving, opportunistic, insensitive, heartless and a lot of other negative adjectives that the erudite and articulate princess was able to list in short order.

Olaf's eyes narrowed. The moment was ripe. Allegra would need little or no encouragement to repay the queen in kind. It was time to act.

The chancellor hurried down the stone steps to the dungeon, his mind awhirl with his improvised plan. No doubt his prisoner had spent a cold night contemplating the agony of the pyre and would now be open to any alternative. Olaf also suspected that the soldier was as enamored of the princess as she was of him.

Olaf's proposal, in a manner of speaking, should receive no rebuke.

Transporting the highly conspicuous Indiran prisoner might be his only problem, but the wily chancellor had already settled on a sound solution. If any of his underlings had the temerity to question him, he would claim that the king himself had demanded an audience with the prisoner prior to his Inflammation and that the ever-dutiful chancellor was simply escorting him to the throne room.

Once in the upper corridors, it would only take a quick detour to arrive at Allegra's chambers. Olaf already decided that the airy room was a perfectly suitable site for a wedding, perhaps on the balcony overlooking the ocean with that giddy handmaiden as a witness.

Though he had never been called upon to perform one, Olaf, as counsel to the king, was well aware that his position empowered him to officiate marriage ceremonies.

Presently, he reached the bottom of the stairs and entered the dungeons. He quickly arrived at the appropriate cell and came to a jarring stop. His heart dropped heavily into his handsomely handcrafted footwear.

The cell was empty.

"Oh, blue blazes!" he cursed.

* * *

In a clearing adjacent to the palace gates, Tobias, Taj, and Lucius and his three laborers stood side by side, forming a virtual wall. Now that he was relegated to merely waiting, Tobias was able to appreciate the palace, its rambling size and towering construction. The wall that surrounded the Great Square was easily five times the height of the wall that surrounded the baron's mansion, and the parapet at the top boasted evenly spaced battlements where palace guards stood watch.

A surprising number of people continued to enter through the massive main gate, an arched opening in the palace wall as high as it was wide, but the flow of the foot traffic had slowed, obviously because there was less and less room to be had in the square inside. Before long, admittance would be impossible and the latecomers would have to settle for secondhand news. Tobias regarded them darkly, all of them here to witness his friend being burned.

They had been standing here longer than Tobias had expected, and he began to shift nervously from foot to foot. Lucius gave him a sideways glance of concern. He had been able to give the Mist Tier Leftists a heartfelt and confident appeal to save Everson, hence their presence with him, but now, he had no idea what would happen next. He sincerely hoped no one would ask. Tobias heard Taj huff worriedly, and he turned to see what was rankling the birdun.

Taj's body faced forward, toward the wall like the rest of them, but its supple neck was twisted so that it was looking directly behind them. It wore an expectant expression and the birdun trilled lightly as if sensing something not yet apparent to Tobias. He followed the birdun's gaze, confused because there had been nothing of note behind them when the group had taken up their waiting position.

Before Tobias could fully turn, a sudden whoosh caused him to flinch and blink though there was no attendant gust of wind. The rest of his entourage whipped around at the odd sound just as a large black box materialized out of nowhere. It was like nothing Tobias had ever seen, and the usually unflappable manservant felt an unexpected tremor of fear. He had once called Everson unpredictable, and he now realized what an understatement that had been. The object he'd returned to Everson, that unassuming little tinderbox, had power far beyond the realm of his experience or even understanding. Before the immensity of it all could flummox him even further, two doors opened on the face of the imposing black box and Everson emerged.

Tobias flinched again as Taj warbled loudly upon seeing Everson, throwing its head back and forth in excitement. Tobias didn't know how, perhaps some animal sense that was felt rather than seen, but obviously the birdun had anticipated Everson's appearance and was now overjoyed. As the Indiran approached and the black box disappeared behind him with little fanfare other than the whoosh, which didn't seem as dramatic now, Tobias looked to Lucius and the other Leftists standing with him. Not surprisingly, they were staring at him, eyebrows raised. In lieu of an explanation to his cohorts, which he didn't have anyway, the manservant resorted to good manners.

"Master Everson," Tobias said, indicating the eldest Leftist. "This is Lucius."

Everson stepped forward and extended his hand. Lucius looked at the Indiran's proffered hand as if he'd never seen anything quite like it before, which, in many ways, was true. He turned to Tobias, an expression of wonder on his large face.

"Is it not as I said?" Tobias asked, nodding.

As Lucius took Everson's smaller hand firmly in his, Tobias grinned at the other Leftist laborers, who were already nodding their approval. He had told them all about this soldier who had treated him with respect and kindness, how that equanimity had extended to every Leftist and Manolith he had encountered, even to the poor and downtrodden. Tobias couldn't be more pleased that Everson was proving him right and upending the long-held notion that the Indirans were nothing more than barbaric invaders.

"Have you ever had such a handshake?" Tobias asked, gleefully clapping Lucius on his broad back.

"Never," Lucius marveled, shaking his head. "Not even from a Manolith."

"Lucius has agreed to take you into his home," Tobias added proudly as Everson quickly shook hands with the remaining laborers. "They would never think to look for you there."

"Follow me," Lucius said. But before the group could set out, the air was split by the piercing sound of a siren. Tobias had no idea what it meant, but Everson looked instantly concerned.

"They've discovered I'm gone," he said.

* * *

Xander pushed himself violently away from his table and rushed to a window, the siren wailing in distressed repetition. The king had been enjoying his first hearty meal in ages and was incensed at the interruption.

Queen Nor sat motionless at the table. The food on her plate remained untouched, the wine in her glass, ignored. Before Xander had taken his first bite, he had suggested, almost cheerfully, that they banish their daughter to Back Tier. The stringent conditions of her imprisonment could be lessened, of course, because where was there to go in Back Tier, really? The added benefit, politically speaking, would be that the nobility of Backward Tier—and Xander paused to chuckle at his cleverness—would finally believe that the Crown had given them something special. He had concluded by adding, quite like the doting father, that Allegra had defied them, both of them, and that she had brought retribution upon herself. Quite simply, it was their duty as good parents.

When Nor had not responded to his enthusiasm in kind, the king had smiled at her though his eyes took on a hardened glint.

"Perhaps you're right," he had responded to her silence. "Perhaps banishment is too uninspired a punishment. You've always been the cunning one. I'll give it some more thought."

Now, with the incessant siren literally making the glassware rattle, Olaf erupted into the room.

The king turned on him furiously. "Why has the alarm been sounded?"

The chancellor glanced at the queen as if she had the answer. Xander registered the look, resentful that Olaf would turn to the queen before him. He also noticed a brightening of Nor's demeanor, as if she were finally engaged.

"Olaf!" the king barked.

Olaf stuttered over a response. "Th-the prisoner has escaped."

The blood drained from Xander's face and his knees nearly buckled. He had to lean on the windowsill to stay upright. "How?"

"We don't know," Olaf admitted. "He simply...disappeared."

Xander's hands went to his tangled hair, pulling at it in wretched remonstration. "It's witchery!" he screamed. "Find him. Find him! I want every last palace guard searching this tier!"

Olaf straightened his back and composed himself. "Your Majesty, I'm afraid that is not possible at the moment. We must fortify the palace. I've just received word from General Bahn. The Indiran fleet is even now on their way to attack Mist Tier. The general is bringing warmen here as fast as he can."

Xander could contain himself no longer. He flew into a rage, sweeping food and fine china from the table in one explosive lunge. Then he stood, hunched over, panting like a beast. He glared at his wife.

"For the love of Light, Nor, say something!" he snapped.

"To what end, Xander? You hear what you want to hear," she said to him calmly. "And now that my place has been cleared, I'll take my leave, thank you."

Queen Nor walked out of the room. Chancellor Olaf turned to follow her.

"Olaf!" the king bellowed.

The chancellor cringed but dutifully turned back.

"Is there something more important than me that requires your attention?" Xander sneered.

Olaf simply shook his head, his eyes downcast to the floor, standing forlornly by the exit as if he were nothing more than a doorman.

* * *

Geneva had been gone fetching lunch for a while, and Allegra suspected that she had been detained in the kitchen when the palace siren sounded. The maddening alarm mercifully ceased, but still, Allegra stood on her balcony, desperately trying to glean any information she could from the distant voices and the equally remote figures she saw scurrying far below.

The people of Mist Tier, so soon after finally being released from curfew, were ordered to return to their homes. Exasperated vendors were forced to abandon their stalls and their wares, and soon the palace pavilion was empty save for slabs of meat slowly charring untended on grills.

Amid the exodus, Allegra also noticed clusters of palace guards hustling to take strategic positions around the grounds, many of them disappearing beyond the limited view of her vantage point. Twice, she had been startled by the rapidly pounding footsteps of additional guards running past her room. She could only assume that someone, Olaf or her father, was doubling the watch posted outside her sequestered wing. Allegra felt hope rising along with her heart rate.

She could imagine what it all meant. Something big. Something unexpected. Having experienced so much disillusion of late, she was afraid to wish for a miracle, but Allegra was certain of one thing; whatever had happened, it meant that Everson's immolation was delayed. They had more time. *She* had more time to possibly devise a plan to get them all out of this.

The door to her room flew open, and Allegra spun to see her mother rushing in. The news was written all over Queen Nor's face.

"He's escaped, hasn't he?" Allegra asked, throwing discretion to the wind.

"Yes," Nor admitted.

"I knew it!"

The queen crossed the short distance between them and placed both her hands firmly on her daughter's shoulders. "Allegra, listen to me, please! If he bids you come to him, you must refuse. You must give me time to set this right."

Allegra angrily shrugged her mother off. "Right for whom, Mother?"

Nor's voice grew strident and her hands grasped for her daughter as if trying to force a concept physically into her brain.

"What possible future could you have by siding with the enemy?" Nor asked. "They are coming here to kill us!"

Strangely, Allegra was moved by the queen's uncharacteristic show of vulnerability. Rather than repelling her, the blatant display of emotion drew her in. At last, her mother was acting human. Nor's hastened breathing slowed as her daughter took both of her outstretched hands.

"If only you knew Everson, Mother, then you would understand," Allegra said. "My safety and even yours, even Father's, were his only concern."

Queen Nor's head tilted to the side as if to better hear the words still hanging in the air. Her eyes narrowed and her mouth opened and closed in silent fits and starts until she finally managed, "Everson? Everson, the son of King Raza?"

It was Allegra's turn to be astonished. "He's a prince?"

The queen could only shake her head and mutter in reply, "Of course he is."

If ever Allegra had doubts about the Prophecy, about the existence of destiny or something greater than themselves, they were washed away in a wave of irony that literally made her skin tingle. Her mother was still shaking her head as if she were trying to shake the stunned expression off her face.

"I swear by the Light above, Allegra," Nor said, "if the Prediciders were standing before me right now, I'd box all their ears for being too clever by half."

Allegra stepped forward eagerly. "This changes everything, doesn't it?"

"This changes nothing," Nor corrected her. "But it just might give us some leverage."

TWENTY-SIX

KING RAZA THE Forty-Seventh stood in front of the panoramic observation window of his troop transport, a panoply of twinkling stars before him, but only three points of light merited his attention. A large holographic overlay of the Aurora Constellation glowed before the glass, many of its coordinates already aligned with the stars to which they coincided. The monarch watched with unblinking concentration as the three moons of Indira slowly rotated into their rendezvous with their graphic counterparts, effectively crowning the waiting Aurora. The moment they locked into cohesion, the entire display flashed red and began to pulsate rapidly, announcing the coronation to all present.

"The Aurora Constellation is complete," King Raza said, thinking that the flashing red display looked far too much like a warning.

Nearby, Commander Giza turned to Colonel Canaan and said, "Prepare for amphibious assault."

* * *

What little food Lucius had to offer was unselfishly spread upon his rough-hewn table, and Everson spoke between mouthfuls. He was the only one eating, but he had noticed that Tobias had curiously inspected his food from a discreet distance, and he could only assume that the manservant could not relinquish his duties as a food steward. The meat was unknown to him, but it was delicious.

"It is my hope that the palace can be taken with little bloodshed," he said.

Everson was heartened by the fact that his cadre of five had been joined by several other sympathetic Leftist rebels who had been able to sneak away from their duties during the hectic fortification of the palace. They stood shoulder to shoulder in the humble one-room hovel with a ceiling much too low for its inhabitant, listening intently as Everson strategized.

"How can that be done?" Tobias asked, sitting across from him.

Everson wiped his mouth with a napkin and nodded his thanks to Lucius. "The Indiran troops can easily overwhelm the palace guards." He addressed the resolute circle of faces. "Especially if they can enter the palace without resistance. I need you to ensure that as many entrances as possible are left open."

Everson saw a smattering of agreeable nods, but it was Lucius who spoke for them all.

"It won't be difficult to enlist the help of many of the palace Leftists," he said. "We've been held down and mistreated for far too long. People need more than just food and shelter to live their lives. They need respect. Dignity. A reason to hold up their heads. We just never thought we had the right to ask for it."

"I hope to change that," Everson said, regarding the elder Leftist with conviction. He sensed the solidarity in the room and knew, should he survive this, that he would remember this gathering as the moment when a simple thought became a movement. He stood up from his seat at the table to better address them all.

"Now, we must get moving. The attack will occur near dusk. Prepare the way, and I will secure the princess as soon as the Indirans have entered the palace."

* * *

"I can't see. Damn the Light, I can't see!"

King Xander tore himself away from the observatory's telescope in anguished futility. The amber light of the late afternoon amplified the king's flushed and sweat-soaked face.

"But I know it's happened," he practically frothed. "The stars are aligned, and my time is at hand!"

Olaf stared at him unsympathetically, two palace guards dutifully standing sentry at the entrance behind him. Olaf had stressed his need to oversee the battening down of the palace, but Xander had been adamant that the chancellor remain by his side.

Olaf scrambled to concoct a reasonable diversion that would occupy the king and free himself. "Sire, perhaps it would be best to flee," he offered weakly. "Leave the tier and regroup."

"No!" Xander shrieked, stomping his feet and waving his arms vehemently. "No, I might as well give up the Crown. There's only one thing left to do..."

The king grew suddenly still. Chillingly so. He was still breathing heavily. His eyes were wide and staring, but clearly focused within. His voice took on the subdued tone of near lucidity.

"Kill Allegra."

Chancellor Olaf took an involuntary step back, as if he had suddenly realized that he was teetering at the edge of an abyss. Even the guards gasped in disbelief. The stunned silence was shattered by a ferocious denial coming from the observatory door.

"No!"

Both the king and Olaf spun around to see Queen Nor standing just beyond the entrance, framed by the startled guards. She moved into the observatory like a vengeful wraith, her face a battlefield of horror and hatred.

"Xander, you've gone mad!" she hissed.

The king once again grew strident. "I have no other choice!"

"Yes, you do!" retorted the queen, matching her husband's volume. With considerable effort, Nor seemed to gather her anger. "The soldier is the son of King Raza. Find him and we may be able to negotiate."

Olaf's eyebrows rose, but Xander seemed unmoved, his expression alarmingly aloof in response to such momentous news.

"It's too late," he said. "There is no time. This is the only way to outwit the Prophecy and it must be done!"

Nor could see that the king was beyond reason and so was not surprised when Xander turned to the guards and said, "Confine the queen to our chambers."

Caught between two monarchs, the guards were frozen by indecision. A resigned, but subtle nod from Chancellor Olaf decided them. They nervously approached the queen, but before they could reach her, Nor squared her shoulders and elevated her chin.

"Do not touch me! I am still the queen, and this is treason." She turned her icy gaze on Olaf. "Be mindful, Olaf. Unless he plans on killing me as well, I will seek justice."

Queen Nor looked one last time at Xander. The king stared back at her as if she were nothing more than another prisoner armed only with useless curses. Then the queen stormed out, and the two guards, not knowing what else to do, followed her.

No sooner had she gone than King Xander sneered at Olaf with all the righteousness of a madman and said, "Do it."

* * *

Tobias was realizing how lucky he was to have randomly engaged Lucius. The elder Leftist, as the head handyman for the palace, knew the codes to every locked door.

Lucius opened the rear door to the spacious kitchen, the one reserved for deliveries, and let in the nucleus of rebel Leftists that had gathered in his home. The delegation drew only passing interest from the kitchen staff, primarily Leftists themselves, since the workers were busily engaged in taking inventory and stockpiling supplies for a potential siege.

Lucius left one of his laborers at the rear entrance to disable the keypad, and signaled the others to disperse. Each of them set out for their appointed points of ingress throughout the palace to assure access and to possibly conscript additional support. With his guerrillas deployed, Lucius nodded for Tobias to follow him as he headed for the front of the palace.

The pair emerged into the square through a discreet door beneath the royal balcony and quickly scurried behind the unused scaffold. Tobias nervously eyed the pavilion walls, where scores of guards were manning their posts on the palace battlements. Lucius nudged him and silently indicated the closed palace gates.

Tobias saw a small sentry box that was almost unnoticeable next to the gigantic gates. Inside sat one lone guard. The manservant instantly realized that the control panel for the gates must also reside within.

He glanced back to Lucius, who nodded. Tobias understood and drew a deep breath. When the time was right, they would need to overpower the guard and take command of the controls.

What good is all this size if you don't know how to fight? he thought miserably. It was all well and good for Lucius, who was obviously skilled with his hands, but Tobias realized that the extent of his handiwork was limited to knowing where to properly place tableware. He closed his large eyes for a moment to center himself, and another bit of his father's folksy wisdom came to him. Tobias could see himself as a young Leftist, complaining that this chore or the other was too hard. He heard his father's firm but soothing voice telling him...

"We were made tall to be given tall orders. Measure up."

TWENTY-SEVEN

THE UNRELENTING EVENTS of the day had tumbled one upon the other, and Allegra suddenly found herself on the downslope of the afternoon. Geneva still had not returned. Her mother had departed with her unspoken agenda, but Allegra now had tenuous hope that she was on a mission to inject sanity back into this place. Queen Nor had conceded that Everson being the prince of Indira had given them "leverage," and Allegra chose to interpret that to mean that, even if he were caught again, he would not be executed.

Everson is a prince, she had exulted after her mother had left. It explained so much. She didn't mean to gloat, but perhaps her mother now understood that her judgment might not be so frivolous after all. Allegra found it impossible to remain calm knowing that Everson was free and, more than likely, scrambling to evade recapture. He might even be trying to get to her. Though she had never met with success before, she decided to once again investigate her boundaries and perhaps find a previously undiscovered opening. A quick peek into the throne room, just down the hall from her own quarters, revealed a cadre of guards on duty, defending not only the entrance to her wing but the stairs that led to her parents' royal bedchamber. She went to the far end of the hall and discovered more of the same.

The princess questioned the guards stationed just outside her wing and inquired whether they had been placed there specifically to defend against the fugitive Indiran. Allegra gleaned quickly that the security detail was woefully short on details. They were ordered to stand guard, so they stood. Unfortunately, the one directive of which they were very sure was not letting the princess get past their post.

Presently, she stood on her balcony again, but instead of looking out, she was looking down. Allegra wondered how far down the wall she could get if she tied every one of her bed-sheets together, end to end. The answer left her hanging.

Someone cleared their throat behind her, and she spun around guiltily.

"Princess, you must come with me," Olaf said hoarsely.

Allegra nonchalantly straightened her dress, as if she had been disheveled by the wind. Something was certainly afoot, and Allegra feigned indifference. Chancellor Olaf had never deigned to speak to her before, yet here he was, unannounced and look-ing like his knickers were ablaze.

"Where are my parents?" she asked, moving into her room from the balcony.

"They are needed to make the palace ready for battle. An at-tack is imminent. I've been instructed to see to your safety," Olaf answered without hesitation.

"An attack?" she said, her mind suddenly awhirl. "In response to..." She stopped herself just short of revealing what she knew about Everson.

"To the Indiran we've brought here?" she continued. "And, yes, before you tell me, I know he's escaped. My mother informed me. Still, I'm sure the Indirans aren't aware of that."

The chancellor pursed his lips and looked down his nose at her. Allegra was reminded that just looking at him could often irritate her.

"Princess," Olaf began after a moment. Obviously, he, too, was choosing his words carefully. "Respectfully, I don't believe the Indirans would launch a major attack for the benefit of a common soldier."

He didn't know, Allegra concluded. Everson's identity was safe until the queen decided to use it as a bargaining tool. But her mother's purposes were decidedly different from hers. Al-legra reasoned that the opportunistic Olaf might adopt an idea and present it as his own if it meant saving the Crown and gar-nering some glory. She might get what she wanted yet.

"Perhaps not," she said, stepping toward him. "But, Chancellor, provided we can find him, would it not be advisable to return him to his people and possibly avert bloodshed?"

"Were it that easy," Olaf replied. He smiled and it looked somewhat odd on his face. "Continue to think that strategically and you will make a fine queen one day. But I can assure you, the two are not connected. I have no doubt that the timing of the attack is based upon the Prophecy. We are currently undergoing massive preparation to defend the palace. I have been tasked to make you safe. By the Light, hopefully both the battle and the constellation will pass."

Allegra studied Olaf. He stared back at her without blinking. Everson had indeed told her to seek the safest place in the palace, to take those she cared about with her. Obviously, he had been aware of this impending attack and hadn't told her. She was sure that he had his reasons. Allegra realized that this moment could very well be the test of her trust in him. Regardless, with Olaf's escort, she could finally get passage from her wing. She could improvise after that.

"Where are you taking me?" Allegra asked finally.

The chancellor started down the corridor, obviously expecting her to follow, which she did. Olaf inclined his head toward her, speaking in a quiet voice as he led her down the hall. Allegra noted his intimate tone and wondered whether he was trying to imply complicity or if he was trying not to be heard. Either way, it struck her as curious since they were the only ones present.

"You may find it odd, Princess, but I believe the dungeon to be the safest place for you at the moment, he said. "No one will have reason to seek you there."

She hesitated for a moment. Olaf stopped and waited for her, nonplussed, the mention of a dungeon apt to give anyone pause. But Allegra was not frightened, she was thoughtful. The dungeon was where Everson had been taken, and it was the place from where he'd escaped. She couldn't help but note the odd symmetry. If there was indeed a grand plan at play, then these seemingly random developments might actually make sense.

She nodded to the chancellor and he turned immediately and set off again down the hall.

Not without some misgiving, Allegra glanced back to the safety of her room. In doing so, she caught sight of Geneva peeking out from behind the double doors that led to the throne room. Obviously, she had been making her way back from the kitchen and had taken the shortest path.

Her eyes were wide with concern, and Allegra immediately worried that Geneva was about to rush to her side. She warned her off with her eyes and flicked a wrist at her for good measure. The last thing Allegra wanted was for her handmaiden to also fall under the chancellor's control. Then she hurried after Olaf before he could turn around to check her progress.

Princess Allegra sincerely hoped that Geneva had heard enough and that she would do something useful with the information. They strode purposefully beyond the far end of her wing with no incident other than the guards nodding deferentially to the passing chancellor. Allegra felt a little thrill as the sights of her own home, previously unseen, proved to be new and interesting to her: intricate tapestries hung on the walls, finely wrought furniture filled countless rooms, windows opened onto views that she had never seen—intimate courtyards, the jumbled rooftops of Mist Tier. It was easy to forget, for the moment, that she was quite likely in danger.

Everson had warned her not to raise an alarm, but that seemed to be hindsight now. Evidence of the impending invasion was everywhere. The palace staff bustled about locking doors and shuttering windows. Mere pages armed themselves though very few appeared remotely capable of combat. Palace guards appeared at every intersection within the palace, lending credence to Olaf's claim that he was conveying the princess to safety.

He and Allegra approached the stairwell to the dungeon and discovered a young palace guard standing sentry there.

Olaf immediately commanded, "You're required upstairs to defend the throne. Go now."

The guard departed without question. Allegra was momentarily offended that Olaf could assume her so clueless. Even so, she followed him down the stairs without comment.

They descended the steps quickly and soon arrived in the cell block. Olaf moved directly to a cell at the far end, where he entered a code to open the door.

Once completed, he swung the barred door wide and attempted another one of those ill-fitting smiles. "You'll be safe in here."

"You can't be serious," Allegra said.

"Trust me, Princess, I am. Strange times call for strange solutions."

Allegra pursed her lips at the obvious condescension. "I'm not sure this is necessary. I've grown quite accustomed to staying put."

Olaf stepped closer to her. "Precautions, Princess. I worry more about people getting in than you getting out."

It all became suddenly clear to Allegra. Olaf did not expect battalions, but, rather, he feared a single spy. She eyed the chancellor with a directness she no doubt inherited from her mother.

"He can find me, you know. Bars will not stop him."

This time, Olaf smiled with real sincerity. "I'm counting on it," he said. "However he does it, I want your soldier to find you. Away from prying eyes. And then, as chancellor, I have the power to marry you."

Allegra's mouth fell open and she instantly resented the smirk it brought to Olaf's face.

"Why would you wish to fulfill the Prophecy?" she asked.

Chancellor Olaf's expression hardened. "I am true to Mano, Princess. Your father is no longer fit to rule. However, your mother is shrewd, and I know what she holds dear. I expect just reward for saving your life and this kingdom. Now please." He extended his arm into the cell. "Get in. I've already taken the precaution of changing the code, so you will be quite safe."

"Safe?" Allegra asked, raising a dubious brow. "Your code is obviously inconsequential to an Indiran invasion. So what makes you think that I am 'unsafe' in the immediate sense?"

Olaf sighed and Allegra could tell that this conversation was occupying much more of his time than he had intended. He fixed her with an expression that was both resigned yet righteous.

"I didn't want to be cruel, Allegra. But if you're forcing me to be specific, then so be it," Olaf admitted. "Your mother is currently under guard by your father's order. His instructions for you were much more drastic. I am refusing to carry them out."

Allegra's eyes widened, stunned by what she was hearing. Her mind raced, wondering if she could take the slippery chancellor at his word. Olaf seemed to sense her doubt, so he continued, committed to securing her cooperation.

"Xander's concern is for the Prophecy. Mine is for our people. For each of us individually," Olaf said, his eyes drilling into hers. "I suspect that you know, as well as I do, that the Indiran is no common soldier. He is the son of King Raza."

Allegra gasped in spite of herself. He had allowed her to posture, to believe that she was withholding information about Everson. Her mother must have told him. Why would she do that? And was that the reason the queen was now detained? Once again, she felt outplayed by the wily veterans of the royal court. She did not always feel young, the burden of her imprisonment aging her prematurely, but now, in this moment, the princess felt quite young indeed. She wondered how she could have ever anticipated the maneuvering, the ruthless gamesmanship.

"And so now, I implore you, Princess," Olaf continued. "Give me the time to use that fact to our advantage. It may be the only thing that saves us. Please."

Still stunned, Allegra moved past the chancellor without a word and entered the cell. Olaf quickly closed the door behind her, entered his secret code on the keypad, and locked her in.

"I shall return shortly," he said.

Olaf turned on his heel and left Allegra standing alone at the bars, not knowing what to think, not knowing whom she could trust. This labyrinth of palace intrigue boggled her mind, but Allegra still hoped that her heart had not led her astray. Everyone but Everson had proved to be duplicitous. Even Geneva had un-

dermined her, though the princess acknowledged that her betrayal had been born of sincere concern for her well-being.

Only Everson's actions, thus far, seemed above reproach. She
decided she would hold fast to her faith in him. And, as always,
to her own unerring sense of what was right.

Everson had told her to seek safety during the time of the constellation. That seemed a little imprecise to her, but Allegra assumed that he meant tonight, after dark, when Aurora would be visible. She had lost track of time, but she felt that this over-stuffed day couldn't last much longer. The burnt orange light trickling through the cell's stingy window seemed to confirm her supposition. Allegra left the barred door and started across the cell to see what she could see, when she was shaken by a deafening sound.

She shrieked as a second explosion followed quickly after the first. Dust rapidly filled the air, blinding her, choking her, as the ongoing blasts shook the very foundation of the palace itself. Allegra was suddenly terrified, realizing that now she was trapped in the inescapable cell with the weight of the palace groaning and shuddering above her.

She scrambled to the cell's tiny window, her arms held protectively over her head as larger shards of rock rained down from the ceiling. She threw herself against the hard stone wall and strained to find the source of the explosions.

The tiny window didn't afford a view of the sky, but it didn't really matter. Allegra was instantly arrested by the sight of a large scaffold built in the center of the square. It was yet another example of her father's intentional cruelty, and she could only imagine the anxiety it must have caused Everson, having to witness its construction and anticipate its use. Not that she needed convincing, but it also lent credence to Olaf's claim that her father had planned to do her harm.

Movement near the base of the scaffold caught Allegra's eye. Two Leftists were huddled, as much as their significant bulk would allow, behind the structure, obviously trying to hide but finding little success given the scant cover. As the explosions increased in frequency, rattling her nerves as surely as they rattled the bars in her cell and the stones above her head, she watched as the elder of the Leftists broke away and hurried off to somewhere she could not see. The princess felt badly for the one left behind until she realized that she might actually be witnessing a plan in action.

Allegra shouted to get his attention. There was no response, probably because he was peering intently at something on the other side of the scaffold beyond the periphery of the window's view. She tried again. And again, raising her volume to compete with the explosions that had become as rhythmic as a drumbeat. Finally, the Leftist looked over at her.

Before she could say anything, the Leftist held out both hands to her, palms down, and pressed them repeatedly toward the ground. Frowning, Allegra could only assume that he was either telling her to stay put, which was a pointless suggestion, or to be quiet.

Hardly, the princess thought.

"What is it?" she yelled. "What's happening?"

Inexplicably, the Leftist pointed toward the sky. Not the most helpful of gestures considering she couldn't actually see the sky. There was no further explanation.

It suddenly came to Allegra. She recognized the Leftist. His genteel clothing gave her no doubt; he was the manservant she had encountered in Everson's room, the one who had hidden that odd little box. Hope surged through her fear. If this Leftist was here in the palace, then Everson must not be far away.

"Don't come out, whatever you might hear," Everson had told her.

Allegra exhaled a long, fluttering breath. She had to have faith that there was a plan. Not the easiest of tasks, she knew, as the relentless explosions continued to pound at her resolve.

* * *

From the first percussive report, Everson had known what the explosions were: sonic booms. The Indiran force had arrived. Though he had been cautioned to stay out of sight in Lucius's house, he couldn't bide his time in idle ignorance. He had to see.

He stood in the deserted side street outside the hovel, his eyes trained skyward, conflicting emotions quickening his pulse. Massive circles of smoke materialized high above as the armada perforated the sky. The reverberating blasts, almost constant now, accompanied the opening of each aperture from space. Beyond the jagged skyline, the air above Mist Tier was speckled with the silhouettes of warships.

Everson nervously turned the Tinderbox over and over in his hands, forcing himself to wait. By now, Tobias and Lucius should have secured multiple entrances into the palace. Unless something unforeseen had prevented them from doing so.

By now, Allegra should be sequestered someplace safe within the palace. But he had no assurance that that was the case. And if she had followed his instructions, whom had she taken with her? Had she included Xander? If so, was Everson going to step out of the space cabinet and back into the clutches of the king's guard?

Perhaps worst of all, what if Allegra had simply changed her mind?

So many intangibles to what had seemed such a simple plan. Everson suddenly felt as if he were floating down a fast-moving river on a raft made of twigs. And there was a storm coming.

* * *

Queen Nor's view from the royal bedchamber was bleak. The enemy swarm rapidly saturated the air around Mist Tier. The kingdom's reckoning had come. Even when the initial barrage of sonic booms abated, the ensuing silence remained thick with kinetic inevitability.

Queen Nor glared at the two palace guards still tasked with detaining her. "Do you see? Our kingdom is in peril and here you stand! Are you men? Would you rather fight for Mano or babysit the queen?"

Their manhood sufficiently besmirched, the guards glanced at each other and bolted for the door. They nearly ran headlong into the diminutive Geneva as she rushed into the room. After an awkward dance in the doorway, the flustered guards extricated themselves and dashed away. The harried handmaiden scurried urgently to the queen.

"Your Majesty..." she said, bowing low.

Nor swept down and grasped the handmaiden, pulling her upright. "Where is Allegra? Where is my daughter?"

"I...I saw Olaf going to her room, and I hid. I overheard them talking. I know where he took her."

"Show me," Nor demanded without hesitation. "Quickly. And pray that we're not too late."

The queen and Geneva moved through the bustling corridors, cautiously at first and then with growing confidence and haste. The palace guards, busy with their appointed tasks, occasionally acknowledged the queen's passing, but none attempted to detain her. Nor could only assume that Xander's orders to confine her to her room had not filtered down through the ranks.

These frenzied siege preparations, Nor had no doubt, were the orders of Olaf. She no longer considered Xander capable of such minutia, of the custodial attention to detail that such mobilization required. It occurred to the queen that a crisis like this would provide the perfect opportunity for a power grab. And if she had thought of it, it likely had also occurred to Olaf.

But any potential concern she had for the Crown came in a very distant second to the thought that was foremost in her mind, the thought that motivated her determined pace to become a near run, with Geneva hustling to keep up. Queen Nor heard it over and over in her head; the last directive that the chancellor had received from the king: *Kill Allegra*. For the first time ever, Nor prayed for Olaf to be inefficient.

They rushed to the dungeons and into the lower cell block, Geneva close on Nor's heels. The air here was still thick with dust and debris dislodged by the foundation-shaking arrival of the Indiran armada. The queen waved her hand before her face, the fading light from the meager windows turning the atmosphere the color and opacity of dried blood on a looking glass. Nor strained to see through the murkiness, scanning the empty cells as she moved down the cellblock. She began to fear—or hope—that Geneva had been mistaken and that Olaf had taken Allegra elsewhere.

Queen Nor's heart stopped when she caught sight of a huddled form in the far corner of one of the cells. She slowed her pace, her steps becoming heavy and deliberate. She finally allowed herself to breathe when the shape moved.

Allegra had made herself as comfortable as possible on the cold stone floor, jamming herself into a corner of the cell to avoid the falling rock. At the sight of her mother, she jumped up with a show of relief that Nor found surprising.

"Femera and Amali be praised, you're alive!" Queen Nor cried, converging with Allegra at the door.

"Why wouldn't I be?" Allegra replied flippantly, quickly reverting to her insouciant demeanor.

"Forgive me, Allegra, I thought this is what you wanted," Geneva said to Allegra, her head already bowed as if she expected rebuke. "Your mother was the only person I could think of to help us."

"It's fine, Geneva," Allegra said. "You did well...I've read that poison itself is sometimes the antidote."

Nor briefly regarded her daughter with put-upon patience. There was no time to quibble, and the queen spoke even as she fingered in the code on the keypad.

"The world is falling apart around us, Allegra. Please just accept that I am grateful you are unharmed," Nor said. "Now we must get you out of there."

The lock did not disengage. Nor realized that, in her haste, she might have entered the code incorrectly. The queen again pressed the appropriate numbers in the proper sequence. The lock remained unresponsive. The chagrined queen glanced at the princess. Allegra's eyes betrayed a flicker of concern. She had never seen her mother be less than capable.

"Olaf changed the code," Allegra said.

Nor wiped a hand across her brow, as if to smooth the brittleness of her expression. "You might have told me that before I started pressing buttons. By any chance, did you see what he changed it to?"

Allegra's eyes lowered in a moment of rare contrition. "I'm sorry, I wasn't paying attention."

Queen Nor took a breath and focused. Not only was she custodian of the kingdom, she was its self-appointed historian. Unlike her husband, Nor prided herself on the retention of important dates and events. She cared about their shared legacy and the lessons one could learn from it. Since Olaf had changed the code, the sequence would not only be important to him, it would be a number that was easily retrievable. He had done this in haste with little or no preparation, the queen reasoned, so what event would be top-of-mind for the meticulous but notoriously unsentimental chancellor?

A single date floated like a bubble to the surface of the queen's considerable pool of knowledge.

She quickly entered the number. The lock buzzed agreeably, and the cell door popped open. The queen arched a smug eyebrow at her daughter, and Allegra couldn't help but give her a grudging smirk in return.

"Nicely done," the princess allowed as Nor opened the door wide. "Not that I want to give you the satisfaction, but how did you conjure the code?"

"Handel was Olaf's father, before your time," the queen explained. "He was a page, first to your grandfather and then to Xander. Olaf always thought he was better than him. The day Handel died was the day that Olaf finally surpassed him. That was the code. The chancellor's ambition has always been his most obvious characteristic."

Queen Nor stepped aside to allow Allegra to pass. "Now, please. Enough of ancient history, we must look to our future."

Oddly, the princess did not move. "Mother, I think we should stay here," Allegra said. "Everson instructed me to find somewhere safe, and here seems as good as any. And you two are the very ones I wanted with me."

Joining her daughter in the cell was not a consideration for Nor. She stood her ground, expectantly holding the door ajar.

"Olaf knows you're here," she said. "And, perhaps by extension, so does the king."

"Olaf fancies himself a hero," Allegra observed with a disdainful curl of her lip.

"I don't trust him. If he obeys your father, you're in danger. If he defies Xander, then he is being treacherous. We have only ourselves to rely on."

The princess seemed not to believe her own ears. Her face was frozen for a moment in consternation, like she was working out a complicated equation in her head. Hesitantly, she asked, "Am I to understand that you're taking my side?" Allegra took a tentative step toward Nor. "Why now, Mother?"

Nor's regal demeanor relaxed into an expression of unvarnished sincerity. She stepped into the cell and placed both her hands around her daughter's face. This time, it was not a gesture of admonition or treachery, it was a display of infinite affection and solidarity. The queen stared pointedly into her daughter's eyes.

"You asked me if I have ever been in love," she said. "I realize now that I have. You are my only love. I would rather lose the Crown than lose you."

Allegra threw her arms around her mother and squeezed her more tightly than she ever had. Queen Nor returned the effusive embrace but only for a moment. Before she could be overwhelmed herself, she pulled away and regained her composure.

"Come," the queen said, quickly and discreetly wiping a tear from her own cheek.

Allegra followed her mother out of the cell and toward the steps. Geneva hurriedly pushed the door closed and it shut with a resounding clang. Puffs of dust jarred loose by the closing door powdered the air, swirling as the trio hastened up the stairs.

* * *

Responsibility could be an annoying thing. There was a time when Everson simply could have said "come what may" and often did. But now he actually cared how things might work out. So he couldn't wait. He had to ensure that Allegra was safe because, as surgical as he had asked his father to be, war was war, and bombs didn't discriminate.

He summoned the space cabinet. The ebony doors eased open and Everson eagerly emerged.

"Allegra?" Everson called, but it only took seconds to realize where he was. In the very cell he'd been in before, motes of dust dancing lazily toward the floor as if they'd only just been disturbed. The cell was empty, the door closed and locked, but Everson noticed something on the floor that had not been there before. More footprints in the dust dislodged by the sonic booms. Smaller footprints, inside the cell and out, giving him a fairly clear diagram of what had happened. He might very well have just missed Allegra and, by the looks of it, the two women who released her. Their trail led away from the cell, up the stairs and into the palace.

He had instructed the space cabinet to take him to Allegra, but he suddenly realized that it was an inefficient delivery system if the princess was on the move. Everson threw his hands up in exasperation.

"Oh, for the love of Light!"

He was right back where he had started.

TWENTY-EIGHT

THE INDIRAN TRANSPORTS descended like a meteor shower, splashing heavily into the Ocean of Manorain and sending up towering geysers of water. Despite their immense bulk, they remained submerged for only moments before bobbing buoyantly back to the surface.

In a relatively short amount of time, the Ocean of Manorain was churning with a veritable flotilla. The amphibious fleet maneuvered into formation and made way for the cliffs of Mist Tier.

Through his field glasses, General Bahn observed the entire arrival. He was perched atop his TRAUMA, parked on a bluff overlooking the capital city, his army rumbling and ready in a long line behind him. The birdun cavalry hovered like a cloud over the rear flank. In spite of himself, the general nodded in grudging approval.

The Indirans were concentrating their assault on the unprotected ocean side, away from the fortifications and battlements bolstering the palace's main entrance. Bahn calculated that the enemy would reach the cliffs and begin their ascent before he could deliver defenders to the palace.

General Bahn lowered his field glasses and raised a communicator to his mouth. "Send the birdun warmen ahead. And bring me a mount."

A birdun was quickly brought to the general and he climbed aboard, determined but realistic. Never before had he entered a battle with the odds so severely stacked against him. He had long resented that the Indirans outpaced the Manoliths in technology and military innovation, but he refused to let that be an excuse for failure. As supreme warman he had learned to depend on those weapons in his arsenal that could not be manufactured. Training. Strategy. And most certainly, courage.

Luck never hurt either. The twin suns, Femera and Amali, were descending and unencumbered by clouds and, fortunately, directly behind Bahn's desperately charging birdun cavalry. The general hoped that their glare would sufficiently mask their approach until they got close enough to launch a counterattack. Even then, his expectations were realistic since the cavalry was armed with only close-quarter weapons. With his cluster of birdun warmen close behind him, General Bahn approached the cliffs circling the Ocean of Manorain, and the misty, swirling air began to sting his cheeks. The sight that he looked down upon was equally as bracing.

The Indiran transports floated side by side in a daunting line not far from the base of the surf-soaked cliffs. The palace sat atop the jagged height like a crown, painted golden by the suns. In near synchrony, ramps on the prows of the transports opened to reveal their cavernous interiors.

Out of the darkness came the legion of Indiran Marauders. They rushed forward, launching from the lowered ramps of the transports and splashing into the water like a mob of swimmers.

The Javelins then appeared, buzzing out of the transports in an angry swarm that assaulted the sky. They streaked toward the summit.

The palace guards perched in the battlements were virtually useless against an ocean-side attack. Not true warmen, the hapless guards were armed only with swords and small handguns that couldn't repel aerial assaults. Strafing gunfire from the enemy Javelins raked the palace walls and the guards, and scores of bodies fell from the battlements.

A second flight of javelins circled the palace, their pilots searching for ingress. It did not take them long. A balcony at the rear of the palace overlooked the ocean, and its double doors remained invitingly open. The Indirans banked hard and circled it.

Bahn, still distant but closing, watched as one of them approached the lofty balcony at speed, the Indiran pilot leaping from his machine and landing on the balcony and quickly making his way inside.

Within seconds, a second soldier repeated the acrobatic maneuver. And then another. And another. The general grimaced angrily and urged his mount to greater speed. Given the location of the balcony at the rear of the palace, Bahn knew exactly whose room it was. It belonged to Allegra. He was still not a believer, but General Bahn had to concede that, if the Prophecy did exist, it was irritatingly persistent, even if it had to enter through a back door.

As yet another pilot approached the point of departure, the Indiran's Javelin suddenly exploded beneath him, sending the soldier hurtling to the rocky cliffs below. Bahn allowed himself a moment of grim satisfaction. Apparently, his HEX-throwing arm was still strong and accurate. The birdun cavalry had arrived. Bahn turned to the birdun warman hovering nearest him.

"Secure that flaming door!" he yelled.

The warman complied instantly, expertly maneuvering his birdun to the balcony and nimbly leaping from his mount and over the railing. He raced inside, sword drawn, hopefully to neutralize the enemy soldiers who had entered. The general raised his communicator to his mouth, reining his birdun about to face the cloud of cavalry behind him.

"Warmen, mark me well!" the general boomed in his clear, commanding voice. "There will be no retreat. I repeat, there will be NO RETREAT! We defend or die. Now make me proud, warmen. Honor to Mano!"

With a massive flurry of wings and a ferocious battle cry, the Manolithic cavalry swooped into action. Machine and beast engaged in fierce aerial confrontation. Hurled HEXes filled the air, and many found their mark. Ribbons of greasy smoke from disabled Javelins swirled around wounded birduns as both Manolith and Indiran suffered damage and death.

The battle for Mist Tier had begun.

Far below, the Indiran Marauders continued their advance toward the palace. They looked like immense and insistent insects and had reached the rocky shore. Bahn knew what would happen next. Not only had he faced them in desert battles like the one at the Grand Schism, he had also dealt with these machines in high-altitude skirmishes in the Tarara Mountains. The sheer cliffs wouldn't be a deterrent. Robotic arms extended from the sides of the assault vehicles, the ends of the appendages equipped with metal claws, the tips as sharp and penetrating as pitons.

The arms arced upward alternately, the heavy metal claws smashing into the cliff face and securing a strong grip. The arms then telescoped inward, pulling the marauders up the vertical face as the opposite arm repeated the reach and grab. The cliffs echoed with the relentless pounding as the convoy crawled methodically toward the palace.

Bahn yelled into his communicator, "Cavalry divisions one and two, focus your attack on the Marauders! They are carrying infantry and cannot be allowed to reach the summit. Divisions three and four, continue to provide cover and repel the javelins from any other access."

Bahn was thinking again of Allegra's room and the Indirans who had entered there. Logistically, her wing was adjacent to the throne room, which, in turn, led to the royal bedchambers. In truth, every entrance to the palace could conceivably lead to the inner sanctums. It reminded him that he had no idea where Xander might be at this very moment. Wherever he was, the general worried, he was likely unprotected.

He had no illusions that his outmanned cavalry could stop all of the heavily armored Marauders. There were just too many of them. Inevitably, some of them would reach the top, and then it would only be a matter of time before the Indiran forces overwhelmed the rear entrances. General Bahn knew that the remainder of his infantry and the more lethally equipped TRAUMAs were on their way, but he had no guarantee that they would arrive in time to prevent the Indirans from entering the palace.

He had to find the monarch and create a bulwark around him. He would only have the assistance of the palace guard, who were pitiful fighters in his opinion, but they were better than nothing. If their bodies became only fodder, at least they would buy him time. Reluctantly, the general turned away from the battle at hand and winged toward the front of the palace, his mind rapidly strategizing where to make a final stand.

* * *

Everson crouched in a corner, hands protectively over his head. He was not cowering in fear, he was defending himself from the shower of sparks spraying about the cell.

Rex stood at the cell door, using yet another nifty attachment of her hand to cut through the steel bars.

Even over the shrill whine of her saw, Everson heard gunshots and explosions. He knew now with certainty that the battle had commenced.

The torrent of sparks abruptly stopped, and the dainty circular saw retracted into Rex's hand. With little more than a gentle nudge, she pushed the heavy steel door away from its still-molten hinges. It clattered against the solid stone floor, and Everson scrambled to his feet.

"Thank you, Rex," he said. "Obviously, we're one step behind the princess. We must find her. I need you to protect me, but, please, try not to kill anyone."

She nodded. With Rex close behind and keeping pace, Everson raced up the stairs, the vision of a fateful rendezvous vivid in his brain.

* * *

Olaf found the king exactly where he had left him—in the observatory. Xander stood at the opening by the telescope, watching the aerial battle being fought above the palace, a useless spectator to his own destruction.

He turned when he heard Olaf approaching, then ran to him. "They're upon us, Olaf!" he cried. "The Indirans are upon us! We have little hope without Bahn."

The chancellor walked past him and to the opening, gazing with strange detachment at the fighting. The battle had arrived before he could wed the young lovers. The Prophecy now almost seemed an afterthought to mere survival.

"The birdun warmen have engaged," Olaf said. "The general can't be far behind."

Chancellor Olaf could sense Xander behind him, but he refused to turn. He knew what he would see: hunched shoulders swaying over nervously shifting feet, darting eyes that seemed to focus on nothing in particular, unkempt hair spilling out from underneath an askew crown—the very walking metaphor for the decay of a once glorious kingdom. Just when he thought he could not be more disgusted, Xander asked him a question that made Olaf's shoulders contract.

"Allegra? Is it done?"

Olaf didn't answer. He quietly looked beyond the fray and into the distance. The sky had grown dark above the teal hue of the horizon, and the Aurora Constellation was clearly visible in all her complete glory.

There is no turning back, he thought.

Chancellor Olaf had stopped to retrieve something from his room before seeking out the monarch. He pulled it from his tunic as he turned to face the king.

"She lives," he said, "which is more than I wish for you."

He raised his dagger high and rushed at the king. Xander's expression of shock was near comical. But before the chancellor could reach him, Olaf's body jerked once, something hitting him unexpectedly from behind. His steps faltered and he came to a stop. He lowered his blade, his face suddenly stricken.

Looking down, Olaf saw the long, bloody blade of a warman's sword protruding from his chest. Olaf might have laughed, but his mouth filled with too much blood.

Deliverance had come, only it had come for King Xander and not for him. The ignorant still prospered. Chancellor Olaf collapsed to the floor, surprised at how little dying hurt. Wondering if death had been as merciful for his beloved Which.

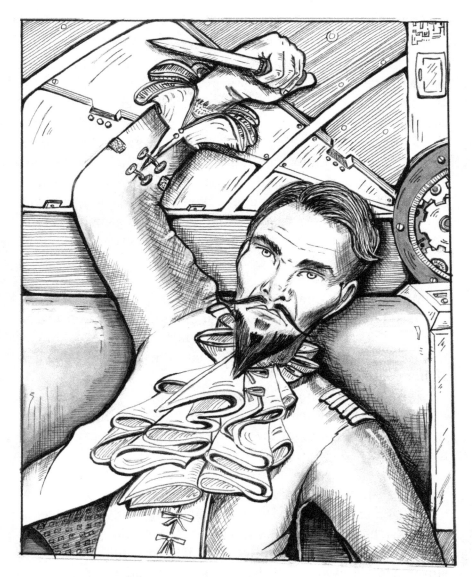

Olaf watched as Xander's confusion turned to relief. He followed the king's grateful stare and discovered General Bahn hovering atop a birdun in the open arch beside the telescope. Obviously, it was his sword protruding so rudely from his chest. The supreme warman leapt into the observatory. He approached the still-trembling king, striding past Olaf, who was struggling to keep his eyes from rolling back in his head.

"Your Majesty, I recommend you stay here," Bahn said. "My cavalry has arrived, and we hope to contain the Indirans on the lower levels. I came to ensure your safety. Apparently, I arrived just in time."

Xander's eyes drifted back to Olaf, the blood pooling around his body. The chancellor's breath was shallow and reedy. He began to shiver as coldness crept up on him. He knew it wouldn't be long. Still, he was not necessarily surprised when the king's face grew red again with rage.

"I gave you one order!" he screamed at Olaf. "One order and you failed!"

Olaf tried to speak, intent on not allowing this madman to have the final word. But before he could find the strength, Xander had already turned his attention back to Bahn.

"Find Allegra," Xander ordered.

"I will, sire." Bahn nodded curtly. "I anticipate the infantry arriving shortly, and when they do, we'll establish a line of defense. Gathering the royal family and sequestering them in safety is my personal priority."

"Good. Find Allegra and kill her."

An expression of utter incomprehension on the general's face prompted Xander to explain.

"If you kill Allegra, all of this will stop," Xander said.

Bahn stared blankly at the king. A wheezing sound brought their attention back to Olaf, and they both realized that the dying man was laughing. The chancellor actually smiled at the general, his words gurgling through his bloodstained teeth.

"Looks like you might have killed the wrong man," Olaf said. The stunned expression on the military man's face suggested to Olaf that he agreed.

"Do it!" Xander roared, severing the moment between Olaf and Bahn.

"Stay here, Your Majesty," Bahn said in reply, but Olaf noticed that he refused to look the king in the face again. The general quickly left the observatory.

Olaf watched him go, the edges of his eyesight blurry, as if he were looking through beveled glass. Movement pulled his tremulous focus back to Xander, and he watched helplessly as the king stalked toward him. He fully expected the man to give him one last kick. Instead, Xander pulled the general's forgotten sword from his back. Finally, it hurt. Excruciatingly.

The pain brought clarity, or so it seemed. Chancellor Olaf could see the face of his beloved, The Which. She gazed at him with an expression of beatific expectation. The amber stone in her forehead, polished and perfect, began to glow, brighter and brighter. Olaf was washed in its warmth until the light consumed them both.

TWENTY-NINE

FEELING UNDENIABLY LIKE a target, Tobias walked bravely and alone down the center of the vacated pavilion. He only had himself to blame since being a target was exactly the duty for which he had volunteered. His eyes nervously fluttered upward from time to time, the battle still raging above his head even as dusk continued to darken toward night.

There was the very real possibility that he could become collateral damage simply by virtue of being in the open.

As he continued to advance on shaking legs, the Leftist kept telling himself that this was important. This was very important and had to be done. He nearly jumped out of his skin as a disabled Javelin smashed into the square, much too close for comfort.

The crash of the vehicle finally alerted someone to Tobias's presence and none too soon as far as the manservant was concerned.

The palace guard assigned to the gates had been looking skyward, standing just outside the sentry box that housed the controls. Tobias saw him make eye contact, which was followed by a perplexed frown, no doubt because seeing a Leftist strolling through the square dressed as if he were on his way to a party was not ordinary here in Mist Tier.

For good measure, Tobias waved.

The guard pointed pointlessly and started to march aggressively toward him. He didn't get far. A hammering blow from a meaty fist struck the guard on the back of the head, sending him sprawling to the cobblestones, unconscious. Lucius nudged the limp guard with his foot to make sure he was out.

Satisfied, the elder Leftist nodded his approval at Tobias and moved quickly into the sentry box to open the gates.

Tobias hustled closer as the massive metal gears groaned to life and the gate began to open. Peering through the ever-widening gap, the manservant became stunned and terrified. He saw not Indiran troops approaching, but a mass of TRAUMAs and Manolith warmen.

Tobias shouted and frantically waved his arms. "Close the gate! Close the gate!"

Lucius looked at him, incredulous. The warmen on foot raced ahead of the TRAUMAs and began to pour through the still-opening gate. The elder Leftist desperately tried to reverse the mechanism. The horde of warmen rushed by Tobias, ignoring him, as usual, on their way into the palace. The massive gears squealed their protest, but they complied nonetheless, and the gates started to close back up.

Tobias watched anxiously, unable to calculate whether the opening would be sealed before the TRAUMAs could arrive. His heart pounded in his ears. He stared as the war machines rumbled toward him and, for reasons he himself couldn't fathom, Tobias raised both hands, palms out, as if this simple gesture would encourage the vehicles to stop. The manservant thought of his father and willed himself to stand his ground.

Then, with a comforting thud, the gates came together. Tobias could hear the TRAUMAs skidding to a stop outside it. He could smell the closeness of their noxious exhaust.

Lucius scrambled from the sentry box, checked the security of the massive gates, and offered Tobias an ecstatic thumbs-up. Tobias was just about to return the gesture when he heard the muffled whump of numerous grenades being launched.

Almost before he could register the sound, the massive gates and the adjacent wall exploded inward from the force of multiple blasts. Tobias was blown backward.

He could hear nothing. He writhed on the ground, not sure whether his haziness was due to damage to his eyes or the thick cloud of dust that now filled the pavilion. Somehow, Tobias pulled himself to his feet. Unsteadily, he faced the immense gap-

ing hole that, just moments before, had been the palace gates. The TRAUMAs were moving again, accelerating, materializing through the still-swirling smoke of their incendiary grenades as if they had been conjured from a cauldron.

Whether he was still stunned from the blast or merely hypnotized by his oncoming death, Tobias did not move. He stood, rooted to the spot, staring at the fast-approaching vehicles. It was clear that the foremost war machine was going to run him over. The impact alone would probably kill him, but the heavily studded tires were sure to crush whatever life was left.

A sudden whirlwind gusted about Tobias's head, buffeting his hair and making him blink. Something grabbed him firmly by the collar, and the Leftist felt himself being pulled off his feet as if he were a small child. The wind continued to gust rhythmically as he was dragged, his arms flailing for balance, his boots bouncing and tripping over the cobblestones. Whatever it was released him and dumped him unceremoniously on the hard ground, a yelp forced from the manservant's surprised mouth.

Tobias looked back as the lead TRAUMA rumbled past, not slowing in the least, so close to him that his face was peppered with dirt and pebbles. The other vehicles roared close behind, all screeching to a stop near the palace entrance, instantly disgorging their loads of warmen.

The Leftist wiped his face, heaved a sigh of relief, and looked up and saw his savior. Taj was standing over him protectively. The birdun looked down at him in concern, its head swaying on its undulating neck, its powerful wings still twitching from the rescue. Satisfied that he was fine, the beast turned its attention to the swarming troops, and Tobias had no doubt that Taj would bite anyone who came near.

With the debris still flaming in the pavilion and sending up plumes of acrid black smoke, Tobias watched as the Manolithic warmen poured into the palace. The battle was inevitable, but Tobias hoped that he had made a difference. The manservant's eyes then fell upon his friend. Lucius lay in a bloody heap, nearly buried by debris from the decimated sentry box. Tobias could not tell whether he was alive or dead.

* * *

Everson had no idea where he was going, but he was going there in a hurry. He and Rex turned a corner into a wide corridor, and he saw an intersection ahead that led deeper into the palace. One that, perhaps, provided access to the upper levels.

Unfortunately, he also saw two palace guards between him and his destination. They rushed at him, brandishing their swords. Everson was about to turn and run in the opposite direction when Rex stepped forward and pushed him aside.

The descending sword of the first guard impacted Rex's arm with a ringing metallic clang and a flash of sparks. Before the guard could blink, Rex backhanded his face with a metal fist, and he crumpled like a marionette relieved of his strings. Rex then ducked a horizontal swipe from the second guard's blade. With the sweep of a silver leg, she kicked the guard's feet out from under him, and he flopped heavily to the floor. Before he could recover, Rex stepped forward and neutralized him in much the same manner as she had the first, with a single blow to the face that rendered him instantly unconscious.

Everson could only marvel. "Well done, Rex."

Rex politely gestured for him to continue on his way down the now secure corridor. As Everson ran, he strained to hear the sounds of conflict, hoping they'd lead him to the throne room.

* * *

Commander Giza was beside himself with worry. Rather, he was directly beside King Raza and that was precisely the reason for his worry. Their Marauder had finally reached the summit, directly behind the palace, and they had emerged into a virtual hailstorm of HEXes. The Marauder nearest them was just cresting the cliff when multiple explosions flipped it away from the edge. It tumbled end over end back toward the ocean, impacting yet another Marauder halfway up the cliff face. Together, they landed in a screeching, tangled mass of flaming metal on the jagged rocks below.

Giza drew his handgun and reached out with his other hand and placed it on Raza's shoulder, determined not to let the king get more than an arm's length away from him. He looked up into a frenzy of motion, indistinct and nightmarish against the darkening sky. The staccato flashes of light from explosions and gunfire illuminated the Javelins and birdun warmen as they battled above his head, simultaneously attacking each other and the scrambling swarm of Indiran soldiers below.

Giza could tell that a contingent of the cavalry was exclusively dedicated to repelling the Marauders still climbing toward the summit, desperately trying to prevent more Indiran infantry from joining the fray. Fortunately, the Javelins were seriously impeding their ability to attack with impunity, and Giza was counting on the reinforcements once they breached the palace.

Manolithic ground forces had not yet arrived, so Raza and Giza led the charge toward the rear of the palace unchallenged from the front. The threat seemed to come exclusively from above, and Giza quickly realized that gunfire and exploding HEXes were not the only cause for concern. Bodies rained down from the sky. The dead and dying from both sides fell from their mounts and onto the heads of hapless soldiers on the ground. Worse still, wounded birduns and riderless Javelins crashed down on the troops, claiming even more lives.

Breathing hard from the mad dash, King Raza burst through the rear entrance of the palace with Commander Giza protectively flanking him. It was not lost on Giza that the ease of their entrance was made possible by a disabled lock. He credited Everson. They moved quickly into the kitchen to make room for the flood of soldiers following them. The tight knot of Indirans immediately fanned out, poised for contact and scanning the spacious room. For a moment, they encountered nothing but the kitchen staff, mostly Leftists, who fearfully backed away, holding their hands up in surrender. The lull did not last long.

A mob of palace guards entered the kitchen from the interior door. The guards in front stopped abruptly, shocked by the sheer number of Indirans present and with many more obviously crowded just outside the door awaiting room to enter. Almost in unison, Giza and Raza drew their swords, the former using it along with his handgun. Within seconds, however, both Giza and the palace guards were dealt an even bigger surprise.

Many of the Leftists caught between the two factions suddenly turned on the guards. They attacked the Manoliths with pots, pans, kitchen knives and utensils, anything within their immediate reach. The foremost guards fell quickly, but the remainder of the palace defenders surged into the room and repelled the ambush. They were not so successful with the Indiran forces.

King Raza took advantage of the distraction and closed quarters, forcing the commander to keep pace with him. They battled shoulder to shoulder, and it occurred to Giza that they had not done so since the early days of their training, when the only thing at risk had been their pride. There was so much more at stake now. It was an odd and inconvenient thought to have in the middle of a swordfight, but Giza realized that King Raza, Queen Patra and the son that he had almost cost them were the closest thing to family that he had ever had.

The outnumbered guards were easily overrun as the Indirans methodically and mercilessly hacked their way to the interior door. It was readily evident to Commander Giza that the king had maintained his skill with a sword over the years.

With the door secured in short order, the king turned, his face splattered with blood, but, it seemed to Giza, strangely invigorated. He surveyed his troops, some by the back door who had not even been able to engage in the limited space within the kitchen. All looked eagerly to their monarch, ready to follow wherever he would lead.

Raza also had the attention of the kitchen Leftists, none of them having suffered serious injury during the brawl. It was obvious to Giza that, beyond the initial insurrection, they had no idea what the plan might be or what their part would be in it. King Raza eyed them curiously, their hulking forms, their bulbous faces staring back at him.

"Who are these...people," he asked quietly, "and why have they chosen to fight for us? Should their allegiance not be with the Manoliths?"

Giza replied, "I believe your son has paved the way for us, sire."

"I believe you might be right, Commander," Raza agreed and put a comradely hand on Giza's shoulder. Commander Giza knew this would be his last chance.

"Your Majesty, I beseech you," he began, fully expecting Raza to cut him off. "You have gotten us this far. You have inspired the men. Please do not risk your life needlessly."

The king started to protest, but Giza stubbornly continued.

"Do not let this little skirmish fool you, sire. These were palace guards that we just defeated. They weren't soldiers. The warmen that we are sure to encounter will be better trained. Better equipped. So I beg you, stay here and secure our flank. Allow me to lead the force into the teeth of the fight."

The king looked down momentarily to collect his thoughts. Giza knew, whatever he said, he would say it once and only once, and it would be the final word. Raza stepped even closer and met his eye.

"My friend, I appreciate your concern. Truly...but make no mistake, Giza. One way or the other, this ends today." Oddly, the king seemed wistful as he continued. "My wife, your queen, is right about many things, but one thing in particular has vexed my conscience. She called me a 'warring king.' There is no arguing the point. I have made war for my entire life. Today, I will confront King Xander, man to man, face to face. And we will broker peace. Or one of us will fall. Either way, this war will end. This is my decree."

King Raza looked briefly back at his men, all of them poised for action, patiently awaiting his command. He tilted his head even more intimately toward Giza.

"If I do not survive, Giza, I need you to ensure that Everson takes the throne in my stead."

The commander felt the king's hand squeeze his shoulder. He saw the certainty in his oldest friend's eyes, but he also saw the pride.

"He's ready," King Raza said and nodded once.

Though it was the friendliest moment the two had shared in Giza's recent memory, his face remained unsentimental as he said, "I know he is. I know that I will. But I also know that I will not let you die on Mano."

King Raza smiled for both of them. He turned to his troops and raised his bloody blade aloft.

"Indira in Dignity! Indira in Death!" the king bellowed.

The Indirans echoed the mantra, full-throated and ferocious. Without another moment's pause, King Raza led his troops into the palace proper.

* * *

Queen Nor knew they were losing. The aerial battle over the pavilion had migrated to the rear of the palace, but from what she had already seen, they were outnumbered and outgunned. The palace guard had put up a pitiful defense, but they had been picked off the parapets by the score, easy targets for the fast-moving enemy aircraft. The birdun cavalry fought valiantly but with limited success, and Nor felt personally responsible that their weapons were not better. It was not their heart but their hardware that was lacking.

The war had always seemed so distant, but now, when it was here on their doorstep, the queen regretted that Xander's immediate concerns had taken precedence over any real preparations for defense. They had seen the storm coming but had refused to shut the windows. She had heard the massive explosion at the front gates and had hoped that it meant that the infantry had arrived, but without the ensuing sounds of battle, Nor could only assume that the fighting had moved inside.

They were improvising. Scrambling without a strategy. It was only a matter of time now.

She had begun to consider what conditions of surrender might be acceptable when General Bahn entered the royal bedchamber.

"Your Highness..." he said, offering a perfunctory bow of his head.

Nor faced him as Allegra and Geneva rose from the chaise where they had been sitting. "General, how is it?" she asked.

Bahn's gaze flitted to Allegra, and Nor had the sudden misgiving that the general was there to carry out Xander's insane wish to kill Allegra. She stepped forward, ready to throw herself on the imposing man if necessary, but Bahn returned his attention to her and allayed her fears.

"I'm glad to see you're all here, together and safe. But the rest of it...not good, Your Highness," Bahn said. "The Indirans have breached the palace. I fear I may have arrived too late."

As the queen absorbed the report, Bahn glanced again at Allegra, his expression troubled.

"There is something else, General?" Queen Nor asked.

"Chancellor Olaf is dead," Bahn said abruptly.

All three women in the room gasped involuntarily.

"How?" the queen demanded, her mind rapidly trying to assess the ramifications of such a shocking development. "Was it by Xander's hand?"

"I'm afraid I don't have time to explain," the general said and moved quickly to the balcony. Nor suspected there was conscious avoidance in the general's sudden busyness.

"Is there any sign of Everson?" Allegra asked, and the queen understood her daughter's concern. Allegra had put all of her hope in the young prince, but he had yet to appear. That couldn't be easy for her. Olaf's sudden and unexplained death suggested that absolutely nothing was going to plan. For anyone.

"I don't know who that is," the general responded as he raised his communicator to his mouth and issued a brief command.

"He is the son of King Raza," Allegra declared, obviously offended by the general's ignorance. "You arrested him, remember?"

"Allegra," the queen interjected, still sorting out her own complicated feelings concerning the chancellor's demise, "one calamity at a time, please."

Nor looked past the general, who stood in the open doorway to the balcony, and she could see the Aurora Constellation fully formed and rising into the night sky above the still-glowing banner of evening. She had approached this night with logic. With calculated intelligence. Yet the sight of this harbinger of the Prophecy filled her with dread.

Allegra's information had captured the general's attention, and an opportunistic glint came to his eyes. The queen could tell that he was far from surrender, and his intrepidity strengthened her. He spoke to Nor while Princess Allegra stood by, bristling and barely contained. "I have reports that Raza has accompanied his troops. If we could capture either of them, then we might be able to cut this battle short and save the kingdom yet."

Before Nor could respond, Allegra commanded, "He must not be harmed."

"That I cannot guarantee," Bahn said, barely acknowledging her. He turned and began waving his arms at a cluster of approaching birdun cavalrymen.

Allegra seemed aghast at the casual affront to her authority. Queen Nor had been pricked by guilt so many times this day that she had lost count, but the expression on her daughter's face made the sting fresh. Of course it was her fault. Allegra had been locked away for her entire life. Unseen. Unheard. How could the princess carry any weight when she was little more than a ghost? It was yet another thing for Nor to rectify if tomorrow ever came.

Birdun warmen arrived at the balcony, and one by one, they abandoned their mounts and entered the royal bedchamber. Bahn waved them through and down to the throne room. After expediting the last warman, General Bahn addressed the queen.

"Your Highness, I urge you to retreat to the observatory. It's the only place left defensible. I've left Xander there."

"Cowering and impotent, I'm sure," Nor scoffed.

The queen's obvious disgust seemed to embolden Bahn to risk reprimand. His response surprised her. "I take it you know that the king has lost all reason?"

"He would kill us all to save himself," Nor said.

In an uncharacteristic display of intimacy, Bahn placed a hand on the queen's shoulder. Nor accepted it gratefully as a gesture of allegiance, and an optimistic sign that there might very well be a new day to follow this accursed night. She would need allies, she knew that. And not just to protect her but to protect whatever legacy the Manoliths might hope to retain. In that moment, Queen Nor realized she was sad at Olaf's passing.

"Then, please, keep him where he is," Bahn advised, interrupting her reverie. "We'll deal with him later."

The general took his leave and hastened toward the battle. Queen Nor watched him hurry through the door and immediately noticed someone missing.

"Where is Allegra?"

Geneva glanced about in confusion. Her cheeks flushed crimson as panic flooded her face.

"By the stars! I'm so sorry, Your Majesty. I...I don't know. I was listening and then there were all those warmen coming through. I didn't see her leave." Flustered, she started for the door. "I'll find her!"

"No. You stay here!" the queen snapped, stopping Geneva in her tracks. "And if she returns, I expect you to keep her here, even if you have to sit on her!"

The young handmaiden nodded at her shoes as Queen Nor marched for the door, angrily muttering under her breath, "Now is not the time for this, Allegra."

* * *

Everson was able to find Allegra's room by taking every staircase that led upward and following the view of the ocean through the windows, though many were shuttered and he had to peek through the cracks. She wasn't there.

He stood for a moment, Rex by his side, awash with every-thing that had happened since he first stepped out of the space cabinet and into this very room. It seemed like such a long time ago now, but Everson knew that it wasn't really, understanding more than ever that time and experience could travel at drasti-cally different rates of speed. He became captivated by the view, Allegra's view, and the timeless yet restless quality of the ocean at night. But then, above the rumble of the surf, Everson sud-denly became aware that the distant sounds of battle no longer seemed so distant.

He dashed from the room and turned toward a pair of mas-sive doors, currently closed, that stood at the near end of the hall. He covered the distance to them quickly, grasped the door handles with both hands, and threw them open wide. The pan-demonium that greeted him forced him to step back reflexively, his every nerve now on edge. The battle that raged in the cavern-ous room was so ferocious, so frenzied, that Everson could not distinguish between the two sides.

He instantly flashed back to the battle at the Grand Schism, and like before, he felt overwhelmed, as if the swirling, uncon-trolled violence would simply swallow him and he would cease to exist. His heart suddenly pounding in his chest, Everson stood fast in the doorway, his fists clenched in defiance against the fear that threatened to spiral into inaction. But there was one mas-sive difference between the previous battle and this one. He had chosen to be here. And someone was waiting for him on the oth-er side of this fight.

Somehow, movement above the fight captured his attention, and Everson looked to the corner of the room where a grand, sweeping staircase descended from a second story. A lone figure barreled down the stairs, taking two at a time, and Everson rec-ognized the brawny man as the general who had apprehended him at the baron's home.

Bahn, he recalled was the man's name.

General Bahn drew his handgun and began firing repeatedly into the fray, as if he didn't care about running out of ammuni-tion. Briefly, Everson wondered why he didn't have his sword.

When he had been incapacitated on the baron's guest room floor, he remembered having a very impressive view of it.

Bahn had barely reached the bottom of the staircase when he was immediately set upon by an Indiran soldier. The general pointed his weapon at the charging Indiran, but, even at this distance, Everson could hear the hammer click on an empty chamber. He ducked, surprisingly nimble for a large man, and the initial swipe of the Indiran's sword passed harmlessly over his head.

General Bahn rose with a powerful uppercut and clocked the soldier solidly in the jaw with his empty gun. Before the Indiran could crumple, the general discarded his now useless weapon and caught the soldier in his arms. He flipped the smaller man around like a ragdoll, and with a move that was as crisp and efficient as a dancer's flourish, he broke the man's neck.

Everson could believe that the military man had risen to the highest rank possible through his sheer physical prowess alone. Bahn dropped the dead man and claimed his sword. Now armed, he waded into the brawl.

As General Bahn disappeared into the kaleidoscope of combat, Everson was struck with a thunderous epiphany. *He* was standing in the exact same vantage point from whence he had seen his vision in the Tree. A shudder swept through his body as he realized that, from this moment forward, he had seen all of the events that were about to transpire. To a point. What before had seemed dreamlike was now visceral and horrific. It was a melee, with Indiran, Manolith and Leftist swirling in blurred and frenetic combat.

It was not clear who had the upper hand as more Indirans flooded the room from the doors opposite him, only to be met by Manolithic warmen, who seemed to be successfully blockading the advance. Regardless, Everson knew that the battle was destined to last until the last man standing unless something unforeseen could stop the fighting.

He looked to the top of the distant stairs, where he knew Allegra was supposed to appear. She wasn't there. Not yet. What he did see was the flash of a flying sword flipping end over end and heading directly for him.

Before he could react, a silver hand lunged in front of him and caught the sword a whisper away from his face. Rex stepped forward and offered him the weapon. He had completely forgotten that she was with him.

"No, thank you," Everson said. "I don't think that's how it's supposed to happen."

Rex nodded without question and dropped the sword clattering to the floor. Everson swallowed hard, his eyes fixed on the empty space at the top of the stairs. On the far side of this vicious battle. He pointed and his silver helpmate turned to look.

"I'm supposed to be up there," he continued. "I need you to get me there. After that...we'll see what happens."

THIRTY

THE TERRIFYING SOUNDS of the fighting carried even into the observatory. Xander slashed at the air with Bahn's bloody blade, trying desperately to familiarize himself with its heft. The king executed an awkward backhand parry, spun around and discovered Queen Nor quietly watching, mocking him with her very expression.

"King Raza is risking his own life to fight alongside his men," the queen observed as she sauntered toward Xander. "I see that you're not cut from the same cloth."

Xander wiped sweat from his face and refused to be distracted by the petty insult. "Where is Allegra?"

"I wouldn't tell you if I knew," said the queen, stopping a short distance from him. Her gaze went to the lifeless body of Chancellor Olaf sprawled in its darkening pool of blood. She shook her head, almost imperceptibly, and her expression of pity and regret only infuriated Xander more.

The king squeezed the hilt of the sword so tightly that it began to shake. As if it were electrified. As if his anger had a palpable energy. "How can you abandon me now?!" Xander exploded. "Remember your duty as queen!"

Nor seemed neither impressed nor intimidated by his volume. She spoke to him evenly, though her words dripped with venom. "I know my duty well, Xander. But you are a weakling. You could be king as long as the power of the Crown was behind you, but I see now, you have never had the strength to be a father." She glanced again at Olaf. "Or even a friend."

Her composure melted into a sneer, and Xander could not recall having ever seen that expression on her face. It was ugly.

Hateful. Now that the mask had been taken off, it could never be put back on again.

"The Prophecy was an excuse," she continued. "An excuse to be the victim. An excuse for you to indulge your worst qualities. Your selfishness. Your cruelty. And I allowed it. We all did. Our concern was only for you, and because of that, we may have lost everything. Congratulations. You are now king of nothing."

Xander approached the queen, his legs stiff, fury emanating from his every pore. Still, the queen did not back down.

"I made you. I made you queen. I made you a mother. Without me, you are the one who is nothing," King Xander hissed through clenched teeth. And when her defiant expression gave him no satisfaction, he hit his wife in the face with his closed fist as hard as he could.

Queen Nor went limp and fell to the floor, unconscious. With one last vindictive look at his disloyal wife, Xander stalked out of the room, sword in hand.

He would show her. He would show them all.

* * *

Commander Giza had been right, but King Raza didn't have the time to tell him so. He no doubt already knew. The king would not have done a single thing differently, but he liked to give due credit to good advice. He sincerely hoped that they would have the opportunity to needle each other good-naturedly about it at some future, more peaceful date.

The Indiran force had surged through the corridors like a flash flood, rolling over the isolated pockets of palace guards until they had arrived at the throne room doors on a wave of confidence and bloodlust. Together, Raza and Giza had burst through the double doors only to stop in surprise and sudden concern.

Manolith warmen, a mass of them in the cathedral-like room, were waiting, swords and handguns drawn, already organized into an aggressive wedge formation. This was obviously meant to be their final stand. The Indiran leadership barely had time to register them before they charged.

Raza rushed forward to meet them, intent on making room for his incoming troops and determined not to be pushed back from the Manoliths' highly defensible position. He saw Commander Giza in his peripheral, matching him step for step as if tethered to him. Their advance was quickly rebuffed, but the king sensed his men fanning out all around him, engaging without hesitation. The clamor of battle erupted with the force and volume of an explosion, the cacophony achieving a madhouse intensity that would only subside when most of them were dead.

The king could not have pinpointed the shift, but he realized that the Indirans were suddenly in a position of defending rather than attacking. His sword was in constant motion, deflecting mortal blows and delivering thrusts that met with matching dexterity. Giza and the soldiers fighting alongside him were faring no better.

No, the king acknowledged ruefully, these were not palace guards practiced in the art of pomp and presentation or the securing of doorways. These were fighting men. Men of war. In hand-to-hand combat, and without the benefit of their superior outdoor firepower, the Manoliths were undoubtedly their equal. Moreover, they fought with the courage of the cornered, well aware that the throne behind them was in literal danger of being toppled.

Raza redoubled his efforts, every step forward a hard-won victory slick with blood. With a feral bellow, the king pulled his sword from the heart of a Manolith warman. The enemy attacker fell away, giving Raza a clear view of the chaotic throne room.

Raza then saw something that froze him. His sword lowered to his side, momentarily forgotten. If not for Commander Giza leaping in front of him to defend him, he might have been killed.

"Everson!" Raza called.

Either his son couldn't hear him over the din, or he was blatantly ignoring everything around him. It certainly appeared as if Everson were strolling nonchalantly through the war like he didn't have a care in the worlds. He even gazed upward as if contemplating stars not visible to anyone else.

And then Raza spotted a strange silver humanoid that appeared to be shadowing his son.

The king watched, dumbfounded, as the shining figure moved so fast as to be everywhere at once, defending the prince from the rear, clearing a path for him ahead.

The mechanical being was unlike anything Raza had ever seen. Perhaps it was some pre-Schism technology that the Manoliths had kept in store, but what struck the king as even more odd was that, for some inexplicable reason, the thing was partnered with his son. It seemed that Commander Giza had been right on more than one count; Everson had paved the way in ways as yet undiscovered.

It didn't matter how. It was working.

Everson progressed unimpeded through the fray faster than any of Raza's own men, heading for the grand staircase that curved upward from behind the thrones.

* * *

Rex moved around Everson in an impenetrable dance of defense. Her silver arms blocked every thrust of a sword or blow from a mace, knocking the attackers senseless if they persisted. She heaved warmen physically aside, and many of them sensibly declined a second assault. Her metallic torso sparked and pinged as she deflected bullets intended for Everson.

Perhaps most impressive of all, Rex adhered to his command and didn't kill anyone.

As Everson approached the foot of the grand stairs, Allegra appeared at the top of them.

Strangely, he was not filled with elation upon seeing her. What he did feel, however, was an overwhelming sense of the inevitable.

This was destiny distilled, and Everson knew what would come next.

He began to ascend the stairs as he had before, his eyes never leaving Allegra's. The princess returned his gaze with unwavering intensity. There was emotion and expectation in her expression, but Everson thought he could see more. Traces of sorrow. A hint of the cost.

It was the knowing, Everson decided as he climbed. It was the cumulative and hard-won wisdom of their experiences, their separate paths through the painful and profound lessons along the way that had brought them to this moment.

"Everson!" he heard a familiar voice call.

Everson was more than halfway up the staircase and was loath to tear his attention away from Allegra. She stood, a point of stillness in the chaos, and he feared that if he severed their tenuous connection, the world would come crashing in and everything, *absolutely everything*, would change. But that voice that he knew so well called again to him, more insistent this time.

"Everson, I'm here!"

He turned, almost reflexively. King Raza stood at the bottom of the stairs, Commander Giza behind him, guarding his flank. The king held his free hand out to him, his bloody sword gripped in the other, and Everson understood that his father intended to protect him. The prince was suddenly beset with conflicting emotions. Gratitude, most certainly, that he and his father at last seemed aligned, but also a greater sense of duty to his mission, which lay completely in the opposite direction.

It occurred to Everson that this was the first deviation from his vision, and he wondered briefly what it meant. Was this a temptation? The opportunity to turn away from a possibly dire fate? Was he capable of simply returning to his life as it was? Did he even want to? The answer was a resounding no. He had found his heart on Mano, and he was bound to follow it now.

Sensing his hesitation, King Raza stepped onto the staircase, and Everson thought that he meant to physically retrieve him, as if he were ten again and lost in the palace gardens. But Raza didn't have the opportunity to take a second step. The mighty swipe of a broadsword sliced the air before him, and the king recoiled from the threat. General Bahn leapt onto the staircase in front of Raza and Giza, determined not to allow them passage to the royal bedchamber. King Raza and his commander set upon him.

Everson turned back to the climb. If he was going to die at the top of the stairs, at least his father would see him die bravely. He neared Allegra and, again, his skin rippled from the sense of eerie familiarity. His moves became predetermined. He had the bizarre sense of watching himself, as if he were outside his own body even as he felt his feet moving mindlessly from one stairstep to the next.

Allegra's actions as well seemed predicated by the script. Her alabaster hand floated toward him and he took it, that same electric touch arresting his breath. Then he leaned forward for the kiss that he knew would not be fulfilled.

"Never!"

Everson pushed Allegra aside and saw the mad king hurtling at him, the bloody blade poised to strike. It would fall, Everson knew. It would be the last thing he would ever know.

He braced himself for the lethal blow as the sword descended with fury. And in that split second, Everson seized upon another inconsistency in his vision; in addition to the added presence of his father and Giza, there was *Rex*.

In a flash of silver as bright and unexpected as lightning, Rex's arm appeared before Everson's face. Xander's blade struck the solid metal with a resounding clang and bounced harmlessly away. Using her other hand, Rex gave the surprised monarch a forceful shove, and he stumbled backward.

Xander kept his feet and flailed with his sword at the advancing automaton. He only succeeded in spraying sparks. Another two-handed shove from Rex, and the king was thrown to the floor.

She was on him in a flash, crouched over his prostrate form, a silver fist poised to deliver a finishing blow. Ever the obedient DOG, Rex turned expectantly toward Everson.

King Xander looked to him as well. His eyes were wide in fearful anticipation, as if judgment and punishment, for him, would have been a foregone conclusion.

"No," Everson said, stepping toward the fallen king. Rex relented and stood, dutifully awaiting further instruction.

"King Xander, understand, I have not come here to destroy you," Everson continued. "We can bring peace to our people."

The king hesitated, his mouth twisting into something scornful. Princess Allegra moved decisively to Everson's side.

"Father, please," she said, and Everson felt it was more of a prompt than a request.

Everson had seen animals caught in traps before. Always defiant to the end, their teeth bared in denial of their fate. That was how the king appeared.

Everson turned to Rex. As further proof of his sincerity, he said, "Rex, you may stand down."

She evaporated into thin air. Everson then extended his hand to Xander. "King Xander, please," he said. "Let's end this."

The monarch glowered at him and then, to Everson's deep concern, gave his own daughter an equally hateful glare. It was obvious that, by standing next to him, she had declared herself the enemy. Or, recalling his previous conversations with Allegra, perhaps Xander had always viewed Allegra as the enemy. Seeing it for himself, the prince began to understand how completely futile his own entreaties must be.

With some difficulty, Xander pulled himself into a seated position, and for a brief, hopeful moment, Everson thought he might actually take his hand. But then…

"You've taken my family," he said in a voice barely louder than a whisper. "You will not take my planet!"

Xander gathered himself and lunged. In that moment, Everson realized that the madman had not relinquished his sword. And now Rex was gone. He instinctively stepped in front of Allegra to shield her with his body.

A brown hand pushed the prince aside. Commander Giza took the full force of Xander's thrust into his own chest. With a cry of pain, he fell away from the blade, his own sword falling from his hand to land at Xander's feet.

He collapsed backward into Everson, and together, they crumpled to the floor.

With a cheated snarl, Xander gripped his sword in both hands and raised it high above his head. He stepped forward, intent on finishing Everson. Before he could bring down his blade, Xander's face registered painful disbelief.

Giza's dropped sword had been thrust upward, its point penetrating just below Xander's rib cage. Allegra kneeled protectively over Everson, holding it. She and Everson locked eyes, her expression equal parts concern for him and shock over what she had just done. Everson was stunned as well, his mind reeling as he tried to make sense of this blur of events.

"I'm fine." He nodded at her, even as he realized that Commander Giza was mortally wounded. Before he could turn his full attention to his commanding officer, a rasping cough from Xander drew his attention. The stricken king was trying to speak. Allegra tightened her grip on the sword that impaled him, using both hands, as if she were afraid that he could miraculously extricate himself and wreak vengeance upon them.

"Finally, you bend a knee to me..." King Xander declared, his rheumy eyes gleaming. He smiled, but the effect was more macabre than it was ironic.

"I didn't want this, Father. I never wanted this!" Allegra said, and Everson could hear the plaintiveness in her voice. "You forced my hand. I only ever wished to be free!"

"And so you are..." Xander replied. He blinked and it was clear that his focus was slipping away, the upturned face of his daughter sure to be the last thing he would ever see. His head drooped slowly to his chest. Allegra released the sword, and King Xander the Firm fell back, no doubt dead before he hit the floor.

Everson had no time to rejoice. He could feel Giza fading fast in his arms. He placed both hands over the wound, but blood seeped through his fingers in an unabated flow. Giza reached up, grabbed a handful of Everson's tunic, and pulled him closer.

"Tell your mother that I kept my promise," Giza said, his eyes drilling into Everson's.

"Tell her yourself, Commander," the prince retorted before the emotion could choke his words.

Allegra looked on sympathetically. Abruptly, she laid her hands over Everson's, not flinching as Giza's blood began to stain her hands as well. Everson was deeply touched by her selflessness, though he suspected there was nothing that either of them could do to save the man's life. Giza released Everson's tunic and placed his own hand over theirs, patting them reassuringly like he was a kindly uncle blessing their union. Helplessly, Everson glanced at Allegra, but she was looking over his shoulder.

Despite the numbing abundance of emotion he'd endured, Everson still felt a jolt of fear when he turned and looked behind him. The hulking form of General Bahn stood on a step very near the top of the stairs. His blood-splattered face was impassive, but it was clear that he had witnessed everything that had transpired. His sword was held low, presently nonthreatening, but the blood dripping from it made Everson immediately fearful that he had lost his father as well.

He looked to the bottom of the stairs where he had last seen Raza. He found him halfway up the staircase, struggling to climb the steps, determined to save his son from the looming threat of General Bahn. He was bloodied and wounded, but still very much alive. Father's and son's eyes met across the distance, and a hard-won moment of understanding passed between them: Everson's gratitude, Raza's paternal devotion.

Behind the king's desperate climb, the battle still raged throughout the opulent throne room, those weary combatants still left standing fighting on with grim determination.

General Bahn sensed Raza's approach and he raised his sword, the bloody blade horizontal to the ground. It seemed an odd posture, and Everson couldn't tell whether he was signaling the Indiran king to stop or if he was cocking his sword to decapitate him. Fortunately, he didn't have to wait long for an answer.

With his free hand, General Bahn raised his communicator to his mouth. In a strong voice loud enough to be heard in the room as well as over his device, the general said, "Our king has fallen! Warmen, cease fighting! Xander has fallen."

Relief flooded King Raza's face. He slumped against the railing, took a moment to gather his breath, then raised his voice to join the general's. "Indirans, desist! Take no more lives."

As every eye below turned to the landing, all that could be heard were the sounds of many of the warriors dropping their weapons and the moans of the wounded.

"Manoliths, lay down your weapons," the general bellowed, turning to face his troops in the throne room, his authoritative glare finding those who had not yet relinquished their swords. "The king is dead."

Everson looked down into the face of his commander. Giza met his gaze with an expression that he could only interpret as satisfaction.

Everson understood, but he felt the need to give the military man one last assurance.

"The queen will receive a detailed report, Commander. You have my word," Everson vowed.

Giza smiled, and with the last of his strength, he raised his own communicator to his face.

"Cease fighting," he rasped. "Cease fighting. The battle is won."

Everson watched with blurred vision as the fight left Giza's eyes. Allegra squeezed his hand, and he leaned against her. Her hair stuck to the tears on his cheeks until she pulled away to look into his eyes. The sheer number and complexity of the emotions they both were feeling was too much to articulate or process in the moment. They settled for acceptance.

Queen Nor appeared on the landing, and both Allegra and Everson turned to her. The two women regarded each other for a long moment, the still form of the fallen king between them but no longer a barrier. Everson knew many words would come, but for now, all of them seemed content not to disturb the peace there was in silence. The silence there was in peace.

EPILOGUE

ONE YEAR LATER...

"Just pick one, Jonas, for the love of Light," Mare said, nearly exasperated.

Jonas slowly raised his good hand, index finger extended, painfully aware of the derision he might be calling down on himself.

"One each," Mare amended. Their daughters were standing beside her, their expressions just as expectant.

Jonas dropped his hand and sighed heavily, not for the first time. The farmer knew many things, but the ability to differentiate and judge between party dresses was not in his skill set. He stood in front of their simple table, Mare and his three girls assembled on the other side, staring at him as if they were a panel of magistrates. The evidence was laid out as neatly as possible on the table between them, but, to Jonas, it was still an intimidating and perilous pile the likes of which he had never seen. There were so many choices of garments that the farmer's eyes grew blurry with color, cut, and design.

The normally patient Mare put her hands on her hips and arched an eyebrow at her flustered husband. "Are you telling me that a man who can pull miracles out of the ground can't manage a decision out of the depths of his brain? Don't be daft, Jonas. Certainly you have an opinion?"

"I have an opinion, Mare," Jonas grumbled. "It's my opinion you're trying to trap me and make me look foolish."

Mare pursed her lips. "Don't tempt my sarcasm, Jonas. I'd rather not disrespect you in front of the girls."

She plucked a dress from the top of the pile, a frilly frock of deep green, and held it against her eldest daughter.

"We're entrepreneurs now," she continued, casting a critical eye at the fussiness of the dress. It was evident that her daughter didn't mind it. "It's time we stopped acting like a motley clan of simple farmers."

"Entrée manure? Wherever did you learn such a word?" Jonas asked, frowning.

"*Entrepreneurs* and never you mind," Mare snipped. "It's what we are and how we'll behave."

"Well, if it means I know how to pick a proper dress, then you've got the wrong word. One seems as good as the other as far as I'm concerned."

Mare clucked and sighed. "Then go, Jonas. Just go. You're more of a hindrance than a help, anyway. No fashion sense whatsoever."

"Fashion nonsense, you mean," Jonas muttered as he headed for the door.

"I heard that," Mare snapped, and Jonas's good shoulder cringed toward his ear as if he expected something to be thrown at him. He escaped to the yard without further incident.

There were times when he was acutely aware that he was outnumbered and outmatched, and this was one of them. And he often thought that the fairer sex frequently forgot to be fair. So Jonas was perfectly happy in his exile, basking in the warmth of the suns and his own accomplishments. He would rather contemplate botany over bodices any day.

"*The stupidest farmers have the biggest terranuts.*" It was an old Manolith saying, and one that Jonas hated even though it seemed to apply more often than not. It discounted hard work, sacrifice, and even inherent ability. All the attributes that governed Jonas's life and the life of his father before him.

Still, Jonas could not deny that the suns continued to shine upon the simple. So it was with supreme satisfaction that his own terranuts had been renowned and that his new crop would only further his reputation. He wandered to the back of his house and gazed in contentment at the lush and sturdy plants laden with hydreeds.

He resolved to make harvesting them his first order of business when his family returned from Mist Tier. He had promised the first cutting to his patron, Baron Ayers, but Jonas figured he had time. After all, the Family Ayers would be attending the very same event to which his own royally anointed family had been invited.

Jonas swelled with pride, remembering that he would be regally announced as Jonas the Cultivator.

* * *

Tobias was running terribly late and he knew it, but feeding Taj was a chore that he truly loved.

The Leftist was not so presumptuous as to believe that he now owned the creature, as close as the two had become, but Everson, who claimed not to be fond of heights, had happily ceded proprietorship to him. Tobias took full advantage of the privilege.

The odd couple frequently flew back to Tobias's former home in Middle Tier, sometimes merely for the joy of taking to the air. On one such trip, with the great expanse of Mano's unforgiving but beautiful terrain far below him, Tobias concluded that no Leftist had ever soared so high.

He shared his love of flying with Allegra, who also became a cherished friend. Tobias remembered well that her introduction to birduns had been less than optimum, coming courtesy of Everson's capture. But to Tobias, it was evidence that something good could come from something very bad.

As a result, Allegra was equally as likely as he to be seized by a random fancy of flight and give Taj a chance to exercise its prodigious wings. Tobias would watch them soar over the Ocean of Manorain from his room in the palace, standing on his very own balcony. So much had changed for Tobias since his days at the baron's mansion and not just an upgrade in his accommodations. As the manservant in the House of Ayers, Tobias had always been quite proud of his clothes and had been fastidious about their care. Which was why, presently, he still found it very odd to have his clothes laid out for him, even if it was for the celebration to be held later in the day. As one who had served for so long, the Leftist was doubtful that he would ever get used to being served himself. Though, as he slipped a ceremonial sash over his head, Tobias did concede that it was a time saver.

It allowed him to concentrate on the one line he was meant to recite in his official capacity. He had been practicing it repeatedly in his head for some time now, but he was unconvinced that he had it just right, and that uncertainty made him, admittedly, a little nervous. A lot nervous. Though Tobias had officiated over smaller affairs, today's ceremony promised to be the most spectacular and well-attended event thus far in his short career as chancellor and counsel to the king of Mano.

Not much later, a supremely content Tobias watched as Lucius stretched expansively, sighing and folding his rough hands atop his prodigious belly. The front row of the grandstand was so spacious that the massive Leftist was able to stretch his legs out as well.

"I'll tell you, lads, I never imagined I would have the satisfaction," he proclaimed to the gaggle of Leftist laborers sitting around him. "Never in my wildest dreams did I ever think that I could build something with my own hands and then be able to make use of it myself, like I was a flaming noble or something."

"With your own hands, Lucius?" Tobias teased. The two had grown close over the course of the year, so much so that Tobias felt comfortable enough to needle the elder Leftist. Lucius's recuperation following the devastating blast that had destroyed the palace gates had been long and painful, and Tobias had spent much of it right by his bedside.

"Well, yes!" Lucius responded to Tobias's cheeky question, his eyebrows raised in wounded indignation. "I'm the one who did all the pointing!"

He unfolded his hands and pantomimed giving orders. "Put this here. Put that there. Pick that up! That's a flaming full-time job!"

Lucius broke out in raucous laughter, as did the burly co-horts surrounding him. Tobias, leaning on the railing before them, grinned in good-natured agreement. He looked up at the massive grandstand as it continued to fill with revelers, Indiran and Manolith alike, with the lower rows, the best seats, really, reserved for dignitaries.

Tobias swelled with pride. It was true, Lucius and his team had built these impressive bleachers, but, in times past, it would not have been a foregone conclusion to include the Leftists in this celebration. Once again, Everson had confirmed and justified Tobias's belief in him. When Chancellor Tobias had made the request, King Everson had not hesitated to approve it. And now, here they were. In the front row.

That was precisely the reason he had not been able to resist the temptation to stroll through the pavilion before the ceremony, greeting those attendees whom he knew and making the acquaintance of those he did not. He would be on the balcony soon enough, above the throng and the focus of so many eyes, but Tobias knew, as chancellor, that he never wanted to lose contact with the people. Another lesson that had stayed with him from his walk through the marketplace in Middle Tier with his strange Indiran friend, Everson. Besides, Tobias had to concede to himself, his outfit was so fabulous that the citizens deserved to see it up close.

Lucius sighed heavily after his boisterous laugh and he flexed his meaty hands in front of his face. "No, these won't ever be the same, but that's fine by me, I reckon."

The elder Leftist looked around the pavilion, his large eyes growing nostalgic, a memory lurking everywhere from corner to cobblestoned corner. It occurred to Tobias, seeing his expression, that they were not far from the very place where they had met, at the foot of the scaffold where Everson might have died.

"There's not a spot in this palace that isn't soaked with my sweat," Lucius continued. "I believe I've given enough. As you well know, I could've given a lot more."

He winked at Tobias and nodded, happily reconciled to his new reality.

"No, I'm perfectly happy being a head handyman who uses his head more than his hands," Lucius concluded.

"Hear, hear," Tobias said, thinking it sounded sufficiently official and chancellor-like. The gaggle of Leftists seemed to agree with him because they broke out in hearty applause. Lucius doffed an imaginary cap, but despite the cavalier gesture, Tobias could tell that the moment was more meaningful to his friend than words could express. He reached across the railing, patted Lucius on his outstretched leg, and took his leave.

Tobias strolled before the growing crowd, his ceremonial sash proudly proclaiming his new position. He basked in the goodwill he felt from many in the stands although he was well aware that not all of the attention he received was friendly. There were those whose minds would never change and who viewed his ascension as nothing less than an abomination and a sign of societal decay. Still, he kept a smile plastered to his large face even when he encountered an upturned nose or judgmental glare. As sensitive and self-conscious as he was, he knew that he would always be inwardly wounded by such slights, but he refused to apologize for what he was and, even more so, for what he had become. Chancellor Tobias realized that change could literally be a battle and, like with any conflict, the first warrior into the breach was sure to catch the most arrows.

Before he could become too discouraged by the lack of complete and enthusiastic support for him, he saw something that made him ecstatic and eclipsed any self-doubt he might have had. Baron Ayers and his family occupied the best seats in the grandstand, front row center and directly in line with the royal balcony. Tobias approached them, beaming, only to realize that the baron was crying.

"He's been leaking all day," Baroness Carlotta said as she passed her husband a handkerchief. "But it's lovely to see you, Chancellor Tobias."

Before Tobias could respond, the baron interjected even as he was dabbing at his eyes, "And I don't have a bit of shame about it, my dearest Carlotta. This is the most monumental day in the history of Mano since the Great Schism itself! But I will say that I am so flaming proud of you, Tobias, I'm surprised I'm not sitting here a cinder."

Tobias bowed his head humbly. The baron's approval meant more to him than just about anyone else's.

"Thank you," he said, grinning bashfully. "And congratulations to you, too, Baron. Or should I say, Minister of the Interior?"

"Oh, yes, that. More like the Minister of the Inferior, if you ask me." Baron Ayers smiled and shrugged dismissively, waving his damp handkerchief for further emphasis.

Everson had obviously been so impressed by the baron's pontificating that he had put him in a position to do something about it, going so far as to create a post that had not previously existed on Mano. The baron deflected the attention from himself and gestured behind him where a large contingent of Indirans were sitting. The foreign dignitaries' clothing was so colorful that the Family Ayers looked as if they were posing for a portrait before a bright and vibrant backdrop.

The baron continued, "I'm sure you remember our Indiran delegation?"

A long row of dark faces smiled at him, and Tobias clasped his hands and bowed deeply in return, hoping the polite gesture would suffice since there was no way he would remember all of their names. He had met them on one of his previous visits to Middle Tier, but that was before he had realized that details such as names, positions and titles should be important to a public official.

The visiting men and women were experts in agriculture, industry, economics, science, technology, education and the like, all of whom had been housed for some time in the baron's manor in an ongoing summit to remediate Mano's substandard infrastructure. There were so many of them that Tobias could not help but think that Manfred, the head chef in the baron's home, must be cooking constantly from morning to night, which automatically made him secretly grateful that he was no longer responsible for each and every place setting.

"Believe me when I tell you I'm not being facetious when I say they have brought a whole new world of ideas to our humble reconstruction," the baron said, beaming at his new friends. "I envy you, Tobias, the Mano that you will see in your lifetime."

"Chancellor Tobias," Baroness Carlotta murmured to her husband as she stood to better survey the grandstands. Tobias instantly intuited why.

"Are we thinking of a painting, Baroness?" Tobias asked.

"We most certainly are," Carlotta replied without looking away from the crowd. "And I am in agreement with my sentimental husband, this day has been eons in the making. I intend it to be a companion piece to my Great Schism painting. Full circle, as it were. A balm to the divide."

"I look forward to seeing it," Tobias said and meant it.

"But you'll have to visit us long before then," Miranda chimed in. "We miss you terribly."

"Of course, Lady Miranda. I miss you very much as well."

Now that she had his attention, a gleam came into Miranda's eye, and Tobias braced himself for the inevitable interrogation.

"Good. So now that you've spent so much time in the palace, I've been wondering..." she began, leaning forward with a mischievous smile. "Our new queen can't possibly be as perfect as she seems. Does she snore? Chew with her mouth open? A tidbit. A morsel. Please, Tobias, tell me something. I'll take anything!"

"Chancellor Tobias," her mother corrected her as she sat back down.

Tobias hemmed and hawed for a moment, unable to come up with a diplomatic response. Fortunately, a change of subject approached him along the front row of the bleachers.

"Oh, look!" Tobias exclaimed. "It's Jonas and his family!"

The Family Ayers turned to look, Miranda's attention mercifully diverted. Tobias did not doubt that the focus would remain there because the farmer and his wife and daughters were a sight both unexpected and impressive. Jonas himself looked a little ill at ease in his new clothes, but Tobias conceded that his misshapen shoulder must make him hard to fit. But the women in his family were stunning, each with a dress of a different color, the style and cut perfectly suited to their individual ages and temperaments. His wife must have done the choosing, Tobias thought with amusement. They greeted the baron and his family and proudly took their places in the preferential seating.

Chancellor Tobias realized it was time for him to take his place on the royal balcony. His one line began to repeat and re- verberate in his mind like an echo.

* * *

Everson stood on Allegra's balcony, wondering what it must have been like for her to be imprisoned here yet taunted by this glorious view. It wasn't the first time he'd contemplated this, but the result was always the same; he loved and respected Allegra even more. And with its tidal temperament and barometric tan- trums, the Ocean of Manorain had also grown on him though he stopped just short of loving it. He came to think of it as a symbol of the constant but ever-changing nature of life.

Still, to him, it would always be exotic. Fortunately, with in- terplanetary travel now permitted, he could visit Indira when- ever the strangeness of Mano provoked the occasional bout of homesickness.

Everson felt a friendly hand on his shoulder and turned to see the smiling face of his father, King Raza.

"It's nearly time...Your Majesty," he said.

Queen Patra, sitting with Queen Nor, looked up as the regal pair entered Allegra's former bedchamber. Since the massive upheaval of the Unifying Battle of Mist Tier, as it would forev- er remain memorialized in the history books, the two female monarchs had found much common ground and had developed a respectful and diplomatic relationship, bordering on the affec- tionate.

They were, after all, now family.

Queen Nor had been designated, or relegated, depending on her cynical mood, to the position of queen mother. Nor seemed content with the honor, for the most part. Everson and Allegra were admitted neophytes to ruling and often consulted her on all matters Manolithic. In truth, Everson had never desired the throne of Indira, so he had no ego about the crown that he wore now. He was happy to give her the respect she deserved, accept her guidance with equanimity, and view the title as a relative thing.

The newly crowned Queen Allegra, with a beaming Geneva attending nearby, tilted her chin at her husband's mysterious smile. "May I ask, King Everson, what amuses you so?"

"My own stupidity," he said. "Even when I was shown the future, I didn't know what I was looking at," he said, happily certain of what he was looking at now. "The DOGs showed me two DNA strands. I always assumed they represented you and me. I never imagined that they foretold this."

King Everson gazed blissfully into a large bassinet occupied by his newborn babies, fraternal twins, one male, one female. One light, one dark.

"Well, if you had known that—" Allegra laughed "—all the stars in heaven might not have dragged you into my arms."

The young king smiled. "On the contrary, I'd have faced a thousand armies."

* * *

The royal entourage had all soon dispersed for the final preparations. The time for the ceremony was nigh, but what good was it to be queen if you couldn't be late every once in a while? Geneva, who was busily refreshing her curls, seemed to read her mind, and Allegra wondered if she had inadvertently sighed or shifted impatiently.

"I know, I know," Geneva murmured. "But, believe me, they will happily wait. We must ensure that everything is absolutely perfect for your adoring citizens."

Allegra chuckled in agreement. "One must never forget the 'present' in 'presentation,' as my mother would say."

Queen Allegra smiled to herself. It was not uncommon now for her and her mother to exchange these little nothings, these inconsequential intimacies that defined real friendship. Especially now that their relationship didn't hinge on cosmic events or matters of life and death. To say that they had both relaxed was like saying the ocean was sometimes wet.

She sat on a cushioned stool before her vanity, where she could see Geneva in the looking glass, happily attending to her hair. Behind them both, the remainder of her bedroom suite was visible, impressively spacious and tastefully appointed, the furnishings and art reflective of both the Manolithic and Indiran cultures. When she and Everson had decided to convert her old room into the new nursery, they had taken two rooms just down the hall, removed the walls, and constructed a private space that eclipsed even her parents' royal bedchamber in its elegance. Every single day, Allegra thanked the stars for her fresh start.

Almost subconsciously, Allegra's gaze found the Tinderbox. It was sitting on Everson's bedside table like a book or a pillbox filled with medication. They would not have arrived here without it. Looking at it, she was reminded of another one of Nor's favorite sayings, one that she used to tease her with when she was a little girl. "Big things come in small packages."

"Maybe I could go out after the ceremony?" Geneva suggested lightly, interrupting Allegra's thoughts. She was near completion on Allegra's hair and, not surprisingly, her thoughts were racing ahead. "With all of the visitors to Mist Tier, I'm sure there are many interesting things to be found at market."

"Of course you may, Geneva. I'll be fine," Allegra replied, barely containing her amusement. She knew exactly what her handmaiden might find interesting. It had long been obvious that Geneva's first encounter with warmen, in her mother's bedchamber on that fateful night, had left a lasting impression.

More than once, Geneva had come home empty-handed from market because she had gotten caught up chatting with warmen. They were now allowed to guard the capital city, even though there was less reason for them to do so, and they were as commonplace as the streetlamps Everson had ordered installed.

Even so, Queen Allegra knew that she would never take the commonplace or the mundane for granted. She had fought too hard just to be normal. She also knew that she and Geneva had both grown bolder, if that was possible.

A bigger world had made them braver. To experience was to know, and Allegra hungered for knowledge more than she ever had. In her solitude, she had read every book available to her, but she truly felt that she had learned more in the last year than an entire library could have taught her. It came down to a very simple thing for her—she would never have truly understood the word *green* if she hadn't seen the jungles of Indira.

In addition to traveling to Everson's home planet, she had made state visits to each of the other tiers, the trips made incredibly convenient courtesy of the space cabinet. She would have used the same conveyance to travel to Indira, but she and Everson had discovered that the space cabinet's reach was limited to terrestrial Mano. It was just as well. Boarding a transport with King Raza and Queen Patra always proved to be a highly valuable bonding experience.

Allegra was startled when Geneva clapped her hands together as if dusting them off.

"Done and done," she proclaimed. "Not a hair out of place! Now for the finishing touch."

Both Allegra and Geneva turned expectantly as a figure rose from a hassock in the corner of the room. Allegra's ceremonial crown was larger and more ornate than the one she wore every day, and Rex had been dutifully polishing it until it gleamed like the gold of the setting suns. She carried it to the waiting women, her own silver body sending shards of light bouncing about the room.

"Thank you, Rex," Allegra said as the android placed the opulent crown gently on her head. Rex curtsied politely, a gesture that never failed to tickle Allegra. Together, Geneva and Rex, who had become quite the team, began to fasten the headpiece in place.

Allegra appraised herself in her looking glass and she was pleased. She was nervous, yes, but she was also clear-eyed and composed. She knew that her experiences had not only expanded her mind, they had expanded her heart as well. She was no longer consumed with only her own needs and concerns. She cared deeply for the well-being of her people, the welfare of their children. That included the citizens of both planets. That sense of protectiveness came with being a mother, she knew, but it also came with the role she was now proud to inherit.

As queen, Allegra felt more blessed than her mother had ever been. Because she had learned the many ways it was possible to love.

* * *

Another balcony, a different view.

Everson looked out over the pavilion, heartened to see the diverse and enthusiastic throng that extended far beyond the packed grandstand. The one advantage of the ruined palace gates, which were still under construction, was that it provided a gaping opening through which the overflow crowd could easily see.

However, *overflow* was a massive understatement. It seemed to King Everson that every single citizen of Mist Tier had been joined by the richest representatives of every other tier along with a substantial showing of ambassadors from Indira. It was almost overwhelming, the upturned faces little more than tiles in a panoramic mosaic, the details growing soft and indistinct with distance.

He stood just inside the balcony doors, not yet having emerged, Queen Allegra close by his side. The ceremony was beginning, and the entourage was settling into place on the balcony in clear view of the spectators. The Wisened of Indira stood with the three remaining Tellers of Mano to his left.

On the opposite side, General Bahn respectfully made room as Raza, Patra, and Nor took their positions ahead of the royal couple. The anticipation of the crowd grew electric, and Everson shared a nervous glance with Allegra. Her expression of disbelief matched his. Even after a year on the throne, moments like these made them feel like they were playing dress up.

A murmuring surge like the surf of Manorain rippled through the crowd as Chancellor Tobias approached the railing and held out his arms exultantly. As grand and confident a gesture as it was, Everson could see that his friend's large hands were trembling.

Still, in a voice that was high and musical but also strong and clear, Chancellor Tobias loudly proclaimed, "All rise for King Everson and Queen Allegra."

His one line had been delivered with aplomb.

He then stepped aside, and Everson and Allegra stepped onto the balcony, hand in hand. As they waited for the thunderous applause to subside, Everson almost laughed at the expression of immense relief on his chancellor's face, coupled with the visible sheen of sweat on his expansive forehead. The two grinned at each other like schoolboys with a secret until Everson caught sight of General Bahn's humorless face as he stood at attention just behind Tobias. Bahn wasn't looking at him, so he didn't sense any judgment in the military man's demeanor, but Everson had long ago decided to never test the general's patience. With a gentlemanly tilt of his head, Everson encouraged his wife forward.

Allegra stepped to the railing and raised a hand to quiet the still-clamoring crowd. Everson knew what she was going to say and could probably recite it along with her. Allegra had done most of the writing and had even helped him with his own speech. They had practiced together, snuggled in bed after the babies had been put down. Everson was happy, anticipating that this was how they would rule, in unison and with thoughts that might as well be interchangeable. He glanced at his parents and was pleased to see they were looking on with complete approval. Everson faced forward again as Allegra began to speak.

"Citizens, until recently, you lived in fear. A fear imposed upon you by the irrational beliefs of another. King Xander, my father, Femera and Amali be merciful, lived in fear that his reign would come to an untimely end. It was his undoing. He became the architect of his own demise. He could not imagine that an ending could also give way to a new beginning, a transition as natural and as welcome as the rising of our two suns. I tell you today, joined citizens of Indira and Mano, that we will no longer live in fear and that we will move from the darkness and into the light. Together."

Queen Allegra turned to King Everson as the crowd once again exploded in cheers and applause. He saw the flush in her cheeks and knew it wasn't simply from the pressure of public speaking. This was the first time she had publicly aired any grievance with her late father, and Everson understood the strength it had taken to arrive at this resolution. This closure.

Everson stepped to Allegra's side and began to speak. "This enlightenment will be defined by the good in all of us. By our compassion. By our reason."

The king and queen glanced at each other and turned, as they had during the numerous rehearsals they had endured in the throne room, attended by the entire royal entourage and directed by the exacting hand of Queen Nor, who had vowed to never again leave anything to chance. Waiting expectantly were the two respective grandmothers, each with a baby in her arms. Queen Patra passed the fair-skinned daughter to her son while Queen Nor relinquished the boy to his mother. The royal couple turned back to their subjects, and King Everson continued.

"Dear citizens, I can think of no better symbol for a new beginning than the birth of our children, a twin boy and girl who truly represent the Harmonious Equal. I present to you Manolo and Indigo, named for the planets of their parents. Their arrival heralds a New Age of prosperity and peace for all. From this day forward, IndiraMano shall once again be as One."

THE END

CPSIA information can be obtained
at www.ICGtesting.com
Printed in the USA
LVHW091508291020
670184LV00005B/52